ARIA:

LEFT LUGGAGE

Geoff Nelder

ARIA: Left Luggage

ISBN: 978-1-905091-95-9
Paperback version
© 2011 by Geoff Nelder

Published in the United Kingdom by LL-Publications 2012
www.ll-publications.com
57 Blair Avenue
Hurlford
Scotland
KA1 5AZ

Edited by Billye Johnson
Proofread by Janet Schelke
Book layout and typesetting by jimandzetta.com
Cover art ©2012 by Andy Bigwood (http://topaz172.deviantart.com)
Cover design by Helen E. H. Madden (www.pixelarcana.com)

Printed in the UK and USA

ARIA: Left Luggage

"Geoff Nelder inhabits Science Fiction the way other people inhabit their clothes."

—Jon Courtenay Grimwood

"ARIA has an intriguing premise, and is written in a very accessible style."

—Mike Resnick

Robert J. Sawyer calls ARIA a "fascinating project."

"Geoff Nelder's ARIA has the right stuff. He makes us ask the most important question in science fiction—the one about the true limits of personal responsibility."

—Brad Linaweaver

Other Books by Geoff Nelder

Escaping Reality

Exit, Pursued by a Bee

Hot Air

ACKNOWLEDGEMENTS

This novel would not have been possible without a Dawes Super Galaxy allowing me to cycle up the Welsh slope of Horseshoe Pass, North Wales, making my heart thump so fast my brain – freshly oxygenated – buzzed with the original idea in *ARIA*.

Each chapter cranked their way through the critique group of the British Science Fiction Association's Orbiters. Encouragement came from *Battlestar Galactica* co-novelist Brad Linaweaver, award-winning SF writer Jon Courtenay Grimwood, and *Stargate* novel writer, Sonny Whitelaw. Urging me on were publisher Neil Marr of BeWrite Books, friend and guru Les Floyd, M. Kenyon Charboneaux, and literary agent and friend, Rebecca Pratt. Bec Zugor, advised me on the mad Doctor Antonio's Italian language.

I am the first person I know who has received an email from space when Leroy Chiao gave me technical help and a wish of good luck – *while* he orbited Earth on the International Space Station!

In addition to the above, my friend, Robert Blevins of Adventure Books of Seattle, gave me moral support as did Gladys Hobson, a fine British writer from Cumbria. The world expert on pleonasms and tight narrative, crime writer and agent Allan Guthrie gave me valuable advice and support.

During this time other novels and over fifty short stories had fled my fingers into the world, so my style evolved, and is still developing. Perhaps it is in the bronze age now. In the last minutes Zetta Brown and Billye Johnson tweaked and poked *ARIA* further. Thanks to them and everyone.

DEDICATION

None of this would have been possible if my wife had insisted I went out and found a proper job after I left teaching, so ultimate thanks to Gaynor and to my ever-tolerant grown-up kids, Eleanor, Rob, and their exuberant kids. Above all, they understand that when I am staring out of the window, I am really working.

PROLOGUE

Wednesday 15 April 2015:
Outside Dryden Space Laboratories, Edwards Air Force Base,
California.

THE DESERT HEAT PENETRATED Jack's shirt, giving him a familiar, unpleasant wet trickle down his back. Sunlight lasered through holes in the bus shelter's roof, making him shuffle.

Climbing into the homeward-bound bus, he helloed Greta, the driver and then winked at familiar travellers.

An unseasonable heat wave made the PVC seat sticky. At least the journey was short. The bus's climate-control system had failed, so he had to share lungfuls of sweaty air.

Jack thought of his secret. None of the other passengers had handled an alien artefact today. The first in the world, and yet, darn it, he wasn't allowed to holler "It was me!" at anyone.

Gazing out of the vibrating window at the passing ochre desert, he caught a childhood aroma, one that he'd thought he'd forgotten—butterscotch.

Jack massaged his forehead. Strange, he only grew fuzzy heads like this with hangovers, but he'd not swallowed beer for days. It had to be dehydration.

The desert town of Rosamund slid into view, so Jack queued, strap-hanging, in the swaying aisle.

A few seats back, he caught Ken's eye. "Hey, Jack, did something special happen at work to you today?"

A few passengers nearby looked up at Jack.

He distracted himself by looking through the windows at the white-walled tract houses decelerating by. He and his colleagues were not allowed to speak of work at the space lab, but that wasn't it. He gazed up at the rectangle of blue sky in the roof. He couldn't remember what he'd had for breakfast let alone the morning's work schedule.

Ken persisted. "You okay, Jack?"

Hot though he was, Jack's face heated more. A special day. He'd done something unique—a first, but darn it, he couldn't remember what it was. His knees gave way, and he flopped into a seat. His head buzzed so loudly, it must have annoyed the other passengers. He remembered catching the bus to Edwards, but was that yesterday?

He muttered to himself. "Don't be stupid. Come on, man, what was in today's newspaper?" Damn, he was losing his memory...or his mind.

Then he caught a whiff of talcum powder and gardenia. His grandma used to reek of it. Smells alluded him these days. Something was messing with his brain.

Through wet eyes, he noticed Greta looking back down the aisle at him. "Jack, your stop, buddy."

He hadn't noticed the usual lurched halt. He staggered up and patted Greta's arm. Then he looked back at her as she rubbed her head. Other passengers rubbed theirs.

As he dismounted, he spotted a newspaper billboard announcing Wednesday's lottery results. Hey, he thought it was Tuesday. Was amnesia his problem? Maybe it could explain why he couldn't remember the morning's events.

The heat from the sidewalk baked his feet through cheap shoes as the bus grumbled away. He gazed after the bus disappearing in its own dust cloud, and he thought of the bus driver, what's-her-name.

Her face had looked sallow, green. Maybe he'd picked up a bug and infected her too. If her, then maybe all her passengers would get it and new passengers and their kinfolk. That's one hell of a messed up world.

CHAPTER 1

The previous day, Tuesday 14 April 2015:
The shuttle, Marimar, *in orbit, is approaching the International Space Station docking port.*

Peering over Vlad's shoulder at the porthole, Jena could see the International Space Station rotating. Damn, it shouldn't have been. Along with the other four crewmembers, she couldn't speak, holding her breath as she thought through possibilities. She'd worked darned hard to get a seat on this mission, and it looked screwed already. Several long seconds later, she touched the Ukrainian's arm.

"Vlad, let me see."

"In a moment. Ah..."

She gave him the full force of a glare at the back of his head as if telepathy worked. She wouldn't use feminine wiles in spite of unjust accusations to the contrary. She knew her success was based on skill and cunning, but in this charged atmosphere, nothing worked on Vlad. Tall, slim, and wearing his dark hair longer than the American male astronauts wanted to, he was selected for this mission because of his phlegmatic coolness, which could be annoying when Jena was in a hurry.

"Vlad, can you tell why it's spinning?"

"I think so, but I need another angle. Ah, found something."

Jena tried a push at his elbow to gain a better view. All she could see was her own reflection: jet-black hair and a scowling face—she smiled at herself.

Dan's worry lines pulled his black eyebrows too high. "You know why the station is tumbling?"

"There, Commander," Vlad said, "in the solar panel supports: a metal box. It must have given the station a nudge when it jammed there. Looks like a silvery suitcase."

Jena prodded Vlad's shoulder. "It's not that I don't believe you, but I like to see things for myself, move the hell over."

A hand warmed the back of her neck, followed by Antonio's breath. "Let me see too. It doesn't look as if it belongs there, does it? *Una bomba?*"

"Come away now, Doc," Dan said. "Of course it's not a bomb. Everyone strap in for final manoeuvring."

IT TOOK TWO HOURS for the five-man crew to match the spin, dock, and transfer to the ISS. Anxious to investigate the aberrant object, Jena rushed to the new control module. It smelt of plastic and fruit juice spilt by the installation crew. She focussed on a view screen, her nose twitching at the blackcurrant aroma. Her annoyance with sloppy work was mollified by the prospect of an intriguing problem to solve.

Surprised at seeing her breath condense, she realized how much cooler the station was compared to the shuttle. She made a mental note to check then cancelled it— health and environment was Antonio's remit. Their occupation with the enigmatic led to the danger of procedure slippage. She glanced around, noting scuffmarks on the grey plastic and aluminium curved walls. Her frown deepened at the sight of scribbled numbers on a locker. Anyone would think the place was a building site. Then she smiled— that's exactly what it was.

Dan disrupted her inspection. "Jena, snag that suitcase with the remote-control grabber."

The metallic case was just big enough for a weekend away. An apparent seam existed where a holiday suitcase would have been squashed shut but no padlock. The aluminium struts on the space station were not magnetic, and yet...

Jena frowned. "Damn, it won't shift. Someone might have to go EVA."

Vlad headed for the suit locker. "I'll go. I've nothing much else to do until my observations start."

"Hang on," Dan said. "Vlad, you set up the remote radiometer. Let's see if the case is emitting nasties. If anyone is going out, Abdul has more experience."

Jena knew Vlad would be disappointed not going for the EVA. "I know I said an EVA might be needed, but I can't see how Abdul's going to move it from out there if this robotic arm and its four tons of prodding power can't."

Vlad winked at Jena. "He might see what's holding it down."

Jena gave up on the remote grab. "Any ideas on what it is before you go for a walk, Abdul?"

Abdul twitched his thin moustache. "Could the case have come adrift from another part of the station? Part of the antenna housing, yes?"

"No." Vlad looked at Jena for confirmation. "I worked on that last year. It looks nothing like the antenna components. The case out there has a raised mark on its side."

Jena looked again at the camera image. "I agree there's a mark. A chevron."

She looked at Dan for the EVA go-ahead.

"We really ought to await compliance from Houston. Okay, I appreciate they might take so long that whatever it is out there becomes a danger if it shifts. So, Abdul...I don't have to tell you..."

"Take no chances? Of course."

Jena put her hand on her hip. "What's the protocol for handling possible alien artefacts?"

"It's never happened, so there is none. Or..." Dan's eyes darted between them.

The after-thought that the case might be alien hit Jena. Dan's high blink rate told her his mind and emotions must be in turmoil too. But Jena knew the crew must occupy a scientific detachment. What was she, a machine? Even so, she bottled up her growing exuberance.

"Protocols were possibly drawn up fifty years ago, *penso di si,*" Antonio said. Nothing ever fazed him.

Jena loved his Turin accent but there was something unsettling about him. She said, "We'll make up a protocol as we go along. No, that wasn't a joke. I mean we didn't have any training on handling alien artefacts." She thumbed up at Abdul as he headed towards the suit lockers.

Dan muttered as he sat at a console. Keyword searches on the procedure for handling alien artefacts came up blank. "I don't know... Maybe I'm being over-cautious, but we should wait clearance from Houston, even if they have to convene meetings with the President—it could be that important—"

Jena interrupted Dan, noting his thinning hair as if he'd lost more with this worry. "I don't think we should wait for Caroline Diazem to make up her presidential mind."

Antonio smiled, his almond complexion a result of Italian breeding and Mediterranean sunshine. "Commander, this is an international mission. President Diazem is delusional. Thinks she rules the planet, *si*? If we wait for the United Nations to decide on what to do with the case, the end of Time might arrive first."

"Commander," Jena said. "Abdul's suited up and already on his way out." She paused, noting that Antonio was studying Dan with interest. Dan had been chosen to command two other shuttle and International Space Station missions, not just for his intelligence and resourcefulness, but for his unflappability. She'd observed that serenity didn't always achieve respect from eager astronauts like Abdul and wondered how Dan would handle such blatant insubordination.

"I suppose I kinda gave him a go-ahead," Dan said. "But we mustn't let our excitement over this case get in the way of procedures. We must consider all the options."

Jena concealed a smile and yet knew Dan had little choice.

After deploying the sensors, Vlad activated the cameras to record Abdul's EVA. Jena knew that Vlad wanted to be the one out there. She put an arm round his shoulders.

"I love the beautiful silence," Vlad said. "To the purist, it isn't infinite, but it is to me."

"Me too. You Ukrainians don't possess a monopoly on the awesomeness out there, although you sure have a unique way of expressing it."

Dan called over to Vlad, "Anything from the remote sensors?"

"Nothing detectable emanating from the case, sir."

On screen, Abdul swam into view. After he clipped his boots into a strut, he opened the jaws of a light titanium grapple and touched the case. It moved.

Antonio said, "I see it's been programmed to be helpful in the presence of humans."

"Or in the presence of Arabs, praise be to Allah," Abdul said, as he prepared to take the case to a small holding dock on the station.

Jena waved a hand at the screen. "Maybe Abdul's disrupted some kind of field."

Vlad, touching Jena's hand, looked at Dan. "I don't suppose—"

"No way. We're not going to try and open it until Houston orders us to."

Jena hoped to change his mind. "Wonder what's inside though."

"It would make more sense for it to be opened up here than Earthside," Antonio said.

Vlad pulled a long face. "Thank you, Doctor. That presupposes we can open it and that it's really a bomb."

"Not a *bomba*. We have to be prepared for it to represent a hazard. It's my profession." Antonio tapped a folder bearing a silver caduceus.

A full minute of silence passed as they contemplated what could be a stupendous decision.

"Look at it from another point of view," Jena said. "It might be easier to figure out what it might be if we knew who'd left it here."

"And why," Dan said. "Let's list the options, no matter how crazy. One is that it's a breakaway component from this station. There are thousands, many already redundant."

"Two," Vlad said, his eyes bright, "is that friendly aliens from Proxima Centauri have sent us a greeting."

"Three," Antonio said, "the greeting is a mix of viruses we have no immunity against."

"Or blueprints to cure all diseases," Vlad said, batting back. "Oh, that's still number two."

Dan said, "Four, it's not a breakaway but a piece of equipment left behind by some clumsy engineer. I've been worrying about just this sort of incident now that we have up to five different consortiums and nations sending people here."

"It is an *International* Space Station," Jena said. "In theory, we could have two hundred countries sending suitcases up here. Oh, and five, it could be debris caught in the struts from any of the hundreds of orbiting artificial satellites. They could be ruptured by meteoroid impacts and—"

Vlad interrupted her. "The constant orbital surveillance team at NASA would know—"

"Not necessarily," Jena said. "I did a duty with them last year."

"So what? They always have at least one operative looking for aberrant satellite behaviour," insisted Vlad. He waved at Abdul making his way back to the hatch.

Jena waved too. "Sorry, Vlad, there are often bursts of overkill of data. They still haven't got the threshold for alerts to a reasonable trigger level. For example, when the Chinese destroyed their own satellite in 2007 there were tens of thousands of parts scattered in that polar orbit. Okay, so the large pieces were tracked, but there were ricochet effects off other satellites. It took a big effort to track everything from that one event. Some satellites rupture with micrometeorite hits, and—"

"So, a satellite could be knocked off course and no one notice?" asked Vlad.

"If the satellite was switched off or dead, it could be weeks."

Abdul joined them after his EVA.

"Move along, my friends." He grabbed an iced lemon tea from a wall dispenser and drew through the straw before letting out a long breath. "It's not from another satellite."

Jena stared at him and then noticed the others were too.

"Well, I have never seen anything like it." He relished centre stage.

"Isn't it metal?" Jena said.

He danced his hands. "Probably, but the symbol on it—"

"I thought it was a simple chevron," Vlad said.

"Yes, but it's holographic."

Dan objected. "That's nothing new."

"Properly holographic; it had several centimetres depth of solid matt black."

Vlad whistled.

Jena said, "But it'd need a continuous power source, and it would be difficult to make it opaque."

"And, who would want to? Just to decorate a box?" Dan said.

"Maybe it's not decoration but communication," Vlad said.

Abdul smirked. "Then there is the little fact that it's soft."

"What?" Jena said.

Abdul waved his hands as he explained. "The grapple went into it as if it was made of rubber, then when the point of contact moved, the indentation levelled again. And there's something solid inside."

Dan looked shocked. "You didn't shake it, did you?"

"It shook itself," Abdul said.

Leaning forward with his brown eyes opening wider, Antonio said, "You mean it's alive? *Interessante...*"

"Oh, come on," Dan said. "Is this station alive? Yet there are all sorts of equipment that come alive, so to speak, triggered by sensors and time."

Antonio persisted. "So, the case reacted because a human was near it? Or?"

"Yes, yes," admitted Abdul. "I shook it, but it was more than just a box rattling around inside."

Jena rested her chin on steepled fingers. "So we have an alien artefact—the world's first. And it's been placed on our space station where only human presence can move it. And we're the lucky ones to find it. Guys, we are history in the making."

Vlad rubbed his hands. "So, when are we going to open it?"

Staccato beeps drew Dan to the comms console. He took a few light leaps in the artificial low gravity. "Hold it, we've new mission orders."

Vlad grinned at Jena. "They've seen sense and told us to crack the case up here out of Earth's atmosphere and—"

"They want us to examine it remotely with all the instruments we have."

"Done," Vlad said.

"—then send it to Edwards, because it's a remote Air Force base with research facilities."

"What?" said Jena. "On its own?"

"It makes sense," Antonio said. "Handling the case could be hazardous. Although as far as I know, the isolation lab has not been tested with any real hazards."

"What lab has?" Jena said, reaching for her cell phone-sized NoteCom. "Look at the frenetic worries about the dangers of moon rocks, but nothing came of them."

"Wouldn't exposure to direct solar radiation have sterilised it?" Vlad said.

"I hope you're not all angling to bring the case in here to take a peek," Dan said.

Abdul said to Vlad, "I don't suppose the fact that you're Ukrainian and I'm an Arab has anything to do with the CIA not wanting us to see what's in it?"

Vlad gripped Abdul's shoulder. "Wouldn't it be *fantasticheskii*? The first to see what's inside?"

"Forget it," Dan said. "Abdul and Jena, remotely manoeuvre the case, in its holding dock, into the AutoLander—and I mean so remote, you can hardly see the damn thing."

CHAPTER 2

Wednesday 15 April 2015:
Edwards Air Force Base in the Mojave Desert, California.

RYDER NAPE KNEW HIS SHOCK OF BLACK HAIR GRABBED ATTENTION. He didn't want aberrant hair but didn't trust American hairdressers. Apart from that, he enjoyed being in America. When he graduated, it wasn't in astrophysics or higher mathematics; it was in media studies—a butt of jokes. He had the last laugh. As an expert in New-Concept electronic presentations, he had been snapped up by a high-profile TV company at IMAX, London, and had leapt on exchange jollies like this one to Edwards Air Base in California.

When the *Marimar* blasted off for the Space Station, Ryder watched it with his friend, the Dryden Lab Education Officer, Manuel Gomez. Two days later, the news came in about the case.

Manuel was the largest man on the base. The engineers told him if he visited the Space Station, he'd have to go up as two separate payloads. Ryder was with him in his plush, pale green office when Manuel had just read a message on his phone and wore a mock morose face.

"Sorry, Ryder, buddy, all non-essential personnel are to leave the base."

"So, where are you going, Manny?" Ryder said, hiding his disappointment.

"*You* have to leave, you jerk." Manuel laughed a bear-sized guffaw. "Although you're right, my department has to leave the site."

"But you'll find a way to hide, won't you? Stay here, take a glimpse at the case. How could you not resist it?"

"I know what you're doing, Ryder. But you can't stop, even though you'd be easier to hide than me."

TWENTY MINUTES INTO HIS FLIGHT back to London, Ryder watched a patched-in monitor on his NoteCom. With Manuel's connivance, he was able to monitor the case. His pulse, no doubt in tune with everyone else's at Edwards, galloped as the crewless AutoLander, no bigger than a minibus, banked left to make a perfect touchdown.

The Dryden labs at Edwards Air Force Base in the Californian desert were designed for research, not to protect the planet from back-contamination by putative alien organisms. Ryder remembered a lecturer at Houston who had concluded that it was impossible to bring rock samples from Mars without microbes leaking into the Earth's atmosphere within a month.

A buzz irritating his ear made Ryder realize that Manuel was talking. "There's a stew going on here. The retrieval system to get the object is fucked up. So they've sent suited guys in with a big metal case to put the little case in—"

"But, Manny, I thought they were going to isolate the whole aircraft."

"It's in a hangar with the usual plastic dust screen—nothing special."

"No negative air pressure in the hangar to stop back-contamination?"

"Actually positive, if anything, to stop the desert getting in. I know, buddy, but they…I don't know."

Ryder wiped sweaty hands on his trousers. Perhaps he should ask the flight attendant for a brandy. "So, they've opened up the AutoLander's cargo bay and retrieved the case in the hangar, then put it in another case."

"I'll patch you in. They're walking it to the lab."

"Yes, thanks, but Manuel, why bother with taking precautions against back-contamination? They've already exposed the case when they opened up the cargo bay?"

"Yeah. At least they haven't opened the case to see if the *Marimar* crew put sandwiches in. Do you have a view of the lab now?"

"Got it, cheers, but presumably they're going to test it unopened for days."

"I'm not privy to their plans. Reckon most tests were done in space on the ISS. You're probably in the safest place on that airplane." Manuel's voice raised a notch from his usual deep resonance. "All they're doing at the Dryden lab, Ryder, buddy, is decontaminating it. Usual stuff: fumigation dry chems followed by prolonged spraying with antiseptic and ending with pure water and clean-air drying. Don't worry. They'll send it to Goddard for its grand opening."

Ryder was too excited to sleep while the other passengers enjoyed their zeds. His state-of-the-art NoteCom wasted its talents, giving him a static scene. Added thrills came from a moving camera viewing the holographic chevron but even that lost its novelty after the first hour.

He could call his fiancée, Teresa, but she should be asleep. She hated him leaving her in London slaving away at her lecturing career while he jetted to wherever an exciting space mission beckoned. He'd thought she'd be used to it after a year or so, but...

Instead, Ryder called Derek O'Connor, his boss and producer of cutting-edge TV, but was astonished that instead of snapping up this event, he sent back derisory quips about chasing UFOs. Ryder uploaded an illustrated report to him anyway.

WHEN RYDER REACHED HIS LONDON APARTMENT at breakfast time, he noticed Teresa, languishing in bed. No doubt her difficult temperament seeking another excuse to get at him.

"Ryder. Don't think about getting in bed with me." Her sharp tongue matched her short, spiked, blond hair. "Ugh, look at you. Didn't sleep on your flight, did you?"

"Just wait till you know why."

Insisting on going straight to his den instead of to Teresa's bed was the easy bit. Getting useful information from NASA was not.

"I'm ringing Karen. She might have been on shift last night at the Goddard Space Centre. Remember the party when she snagged that job there?"

Teresa had risen from bed and stretched her arms wide while peering over Ryder's shoulder. "Your sister spends so much time optimising the diets for astronauts, yet she's a balloon herself."

"That's a bit harsh. Anyway, you wouldn't be so slender if you'd had a couple of kids."

"It's to do with having the appetite of a rugby team."

"Good, she's online. Hi, Karen. You're looking well." He glanced at Teresa's sneer and then back at Karen's image. "How're Eric and the children?"

Karen's mass of milk-chocolate hair matched her tan. "They're all fine, thanks, Brother. Isobel takes a crucial seventh grade test next week, and Glen has a final audition for the Pre-Teen e-Musician 2015 on the same day."

"But isn't that cheating?" called Teresa. She stood, arms folded, to glare at Ryder's sister on screen.

"Well, he's thirteen now, but not when we filled in the forms."

Teresa walked out of the webcam's view shaking her head, releasing a blond hair glistening, twisting in the light.

Ryder tried to pump his sister for information on the case. "And, Karen, they're still enjoying their grub up there?"

"Why shouldn't they be? I planned the carb bits myself."

"And they're still alive?"

"Cheeky sod. You did want favours?"

"You know I'm kidding, Sis. I'll catch you tomorrow. Give my regards to your Eric and the kids."

Her responses, in an indirect way, told him the astronauts had no significant ill effects from their proximity to the case.

He couldn't raise Manuel, but then it was just after midnight in California, so he'd have to contain his information thirst. He wondered how long the odds were of being welcome in Teresa's bed.

CHAPTER 3

Thursday 16 April 2015:
London.

IT HAD BEEN A FRUSTRATING THIRTY HOURS FOR RYDER. An official news blackout from the Dryden Labs at Edwards. He sat on his apartment's wood-block floor surrounded by newspapers but found only the occasional puzzled reports, no startling revelations, not even the expected scaremongering. His thumb ached, thanks to a sticky button on his TV remote control, in his vain attempt to find news of the case. If he hadn't had inside information via Karen and Manuel, it would've been any normal day where the most important world news consisted of celebrities scoring points off each other.

He couldn't understand why Derek and Teresa weren't excited about a probable alien artefact. Maybe it was his overactive imagination, fuelled by his early-years' indulgence in Sci-Fi. It could be that NASA had deliberately played down the discovery so as not to be alarmist, or they might have believed it originated on Earth, left behind by a negligent astronaut.

He had to wait for Manuel to finish his breakfast before pumping him, again.

"It's going to be opened today, Ryder, so—"

"Patch me into it, Manny."

"The security's hellish tight, but I'll see. You'd better keep this channel open in case I can only feed you intermittently. Gotta go, buddy. Ciao."

It was just as well that communications were ultra-broadband and multi-channel, even so, Ryder thought he'd better let Teresa know, in case she shut off the link. He was writing her a Post-It note when she arrived home.

"Look at this place. It's filthy," she said, trawling a finger along a sideboard.

"Really? Look, Teresa, I'm waiting for a call—"

"We're going to have to sack Elsie. It's no good."

"—only they're opening the case today."

"I suppose she told you that she had to leave early to sort out her daughter's marital problems again. I hope we don't produce offspring like Loopy Lisa." She draped herself over his shoulders as he sat at the computer.

"'Course not...What?"

"You're not listening to me, are you? Ryder?"

"What was it? Something more important than mankind discovering we're not alone in the universe? Sorry, I shouldn't be sarcastic."

"Oh, were you? Even if little green men burst out of the case, we would still need our flat cleaned."

"Elsie did ring," said Ryder. "Lisa is having problems, again. I would've mentioned it as soon as you came in, only—"

"You were watching out for E.T."

"You're a biologist, Teresa. Aren't you enthralled by the idea of extra-terrestrial life, which must exist if that case isn't from Earth? And there might be microbes, bacteria, even small life forms in the case."

"My uni teaching job is complicated enough. Stuffing the heads of hung-over students with a fraction of what there is to know about life on Earth."

Ryder didn't want to take his eyes off the screen in case he missed something. "Good point. But how would you like to be head of a new department? You could call it—"

"Faculty of Little Green Men and Other Mental Disorders. Hey, is that your computer?" said Teresa.

"Great. It's the patch into the Dryden Lab at Edwards. Look, there's the case."

"There are some like it on special offer in Lo-Cost."

"Funny girl. But can you see that logo?"

"No. You see, Ryder, there's a known condition where the part of your brain that interprets signals from the optic nerve is overridden by wishful thinking. Oh...I see it now. It's holographic yet looks solid. I assume you're referring to the chevron symbol that appears to hover just above the lid—if that's a lid." She raised an eyebrow at him.

He was relieved she was interested at last. Apart from needing a fellow human to share ideas and wonderment, Teresa's biological expertise could be useful.

"I assume that the lab's glove-box will prevent back-contamination in the event of putative organisms getting into the atmosphere?" she asked.

"Manuel says they're using sterile nitrogen."

"Not a vacuum?"

"Back in the late sixties, when they built the first NASA lab to handle moon rocks, the technicians found a vacuum glove-box unworkable. And the gloves leaked. In fact, no one's been able to make a completely leak-proof containment lab. They concentrate on attempting to prevent the escape of infectious diseases."

"Yes, Ryder, the best place for doing this opening-the-case stuff is out in space."

"Can you guess why they didn't?"

"It has to be politics."

"No flies on you, kid. The US government doesn't want anyone else to know what's in it."

"That begs two questions, Ryder. Aren't they going to be a bit peeved at us, in London, being able to watch it being opened?"

"What they don't know...and the second?" he asked.

"Are they so naïve as to think aliens have put blueprints in the case? Maybe to end all diseases, a perfect weapon and a mass hypnosis machine so that mad woman, Caroline Diazem, can stay president forever."

"You're right, Teresa. Look, they're using a robotic probe to open it."

"Looks like they're trying the knock-three-times method."

"I think they've already tried sending it *please open* messages, using all the frequencies in the electromagnetic spectrum. Usual codes. Prime numbers, pi, Fibonacci series, our DNA sequence—everything."

"Have they tried human speech with open sesame?"

"As if the residents of Alpha Centauri or wherever would be conversant in English and—"

"D'oh! Listen up, Homer. If an intelligent alien species left a package for us to find on our doorstep, deliberately, on one of our most sophisticated pieces of technology, they must have researched us. They'd know our languages, history, and legends. What would be the point of using non-human means of opening it?"

Ryder threw apart his hands. "As a test?"

"Haven't you been listening? They already know how dumb we are. So it should be easy to open the case." When Teresa used logic, it was always impeccable.

They watched the futile attempts to use the robotic arm until boredom won. Even so, long after Teresa called it a night, he stayed up.

In spite of the swallowed double espressos and Pro-Plus intake, Ryder drifted in and out of sleep in the lounge while a static screen washed his face in fluorescent pale blue.

He sat bolt upright. A technician must have gone into the

containment lab beyond the gloves. He wore a protective suit, complete with helmet and air supply. He placed his gloved hand on the case.

"No vibrations," the technician's voice came through.

Ryder grabbed both sides of the screen, desperate not to miss a single pixel. It would've been eleven p.m. at the American lab. Maybe they chose this time because management would not be around. Such political complications flitted through Ryder's head as he concentrated on the technician.

"My hand passes through the chevron logo with no effect. I'm going to lift the case...It's about ten kilograms. There doesn't appear to be a seam or a handle. I can't feel any lumps."

Ryder was surprised at the speed the technician was handling and manipulating the case. It struck him that the idiot was either an exasperated maverick or being paid by an outside agency to get a quick result. He had to wake Teresa. If anything was going to happen, it would happen soon.

"This had better be worth it," she said.

They both returned in time to see the technician remove his gloves.

"No. The idiot," Teresa said.

"It had to happen sooner or later," said Ryder, excited and defensive at the same time.

Teresa banged the table. "But there could be contaminants."

"All the tests have been done. Anyway, there might have been a time limit of some sort. What's he saying?"

"There is a vibration when I stroke my finger on the case. It feels warmer yet we know the temperature is the same as the air in here."

Teresa's hand covered her mouth. "My God, he's handling it with no gloves."

"I'm curious about the vibration, so I'm putting the movement sensor back on the case. No...Like before, it's not picking up anything even though I can sense it with my hand. What does that mean, guys?"

"Who's he talking to, Ryder?"

"Other techies, I suppose. Do you think the vibration is generated somehow in his hand because he's organic unlike the movement sensor?"

"What? Ryder, he's going to pass his hand through the logo. Ah, that did it. A seam has appeared in a red colour."

"Shush."

"The vibrations have increased and a dark orange medial line has appeared around the sides of the case. I'm going to lift my hand. Yes, the line disappears. I'm putting it back. Yes, the line has reappeared. I'm putting my fingers on either side of the case to see if it will lift— hey!"

And so, at last, the case split. It appeared to be animated, opening as if triggered and now under its own volition.

The mouths of Teresa and Ryder opened in time with the case.

The technician had taken his hand away and stepped back, but the case continued to open. The screen opened another window displaying digital readouts, but none of them indicated any emissions from the case.

The technician manoeuvred. "There are solid blocks...green-lilac colour...Trying to remember where I've seen a colour like it. I know, it's like the supernumerary rainbow colours you sometimes get inside a primary bow. I'm going to pass the mobile sensor array over them."

"At least the idiot's not going to grab them with his bare hands," said Teresa, clenching her fist.

"Give him another minute and he will," said Ryder, alarmed but pleased that the quarantine period had been circumvented.

"No reaction," reported the technician. It wasn't quite accurate: a suited security man appeared on-screen and manhandled him away.

Teresa slumped back in a chair. "Well, that's that."

"The case is still open. Ah."

The security man reappeared then closed the case.

After another hour, the screen went blank.

CHAPTER 4

Saturday 18 April 2015:
London.

MANUEL'S ID SHOWED ON RYDER'S SCREEN."Are we connected again, buddy?"

"So relieved to be in touch, Manny. What happened?" Ryder tweaked to transmute the screen snow to a meaningful image.

"You weren't the only one watching our renegade techie unwrapping the present."

"Stop teasing. I guessed he wasn't doing it just out of scientific curiosity."

"The man, Second Engineer Tipless, had a supplementary income from *The New Fortean Times*, and he's still being debriefed."

"I bet he is. I'm not getting a picture, Manuel."

"Well, this Tipless guy infringed a billion procedural regs—"

"I mean I'm getting voice—no images."

"—so, no info is supposed to get out at all, Ryder, buddy. I'm doing a spot of infringing with this audio uplink."

"I get it, Manny. No visuals for fear of getting your neck stretched. Tipless opened the case and breached containment forty-eight hours ago. Where's the case now?"

"The incident sent shivers down NASA's straight backs, so it's been shifted, by jet, to Goddard. It's in a more secure lab. Say, Ryder, isn't your sister big at Goddard."

"You know how to pick your words. I blame your damn American donuts."

"Ha. What I meant was that the pressure's off me to sneak these feeds to you."

"And I'm hellish grateful. Before you go, Manny, what's going to happen to Tipless? Besides interrogation?"

"Went with the case to Goddard."

"Changing tack, are you and Sheila back on an even keel?"

"Sheila ran off to her mother's. Two witches in one cauldron. Signing off, Ryder, before I change my mind and let her back in."

"Sorry to hear you've split up, Manny. Take care."

Eager to see what Goddard Space Flight Centre was doing with the case, Ryder buzzed his sister, even though she'd deny knowing anything, except what the space crew was eating.

"I'm really busy, Ryder."

"Custard gone lumpy?"

"It's the best way in space or as a gel. Is that it?"

"I wondered if you could get me patched through to the alien-case investigation, Karen, dear sister."

"On your bike, Ryder. You're always trying to get me sacked."

"It's about time you had a holiday."

"The directorate is remarkably relaxed about that case. Tipless is still in detention. One of my staff has seen him to fill out a diet-need e-form."

Ryder smiled. "Do you mean a menu?"

"He was bewildered."

"As in couldn't decide between mash and fries or didn't know his name?"

"He knew his name, job, history all right, but he had no idea why he's in custody. He even thought he was still at the Dryden labs in Edwards and expected to return to his own lab-bench routine this morning."

"Shock does strange things," Ryder said.

"True. Maybe he's blocked the recent truth to keep his sanity."

"Or, if I was a cynical copper, Karen, I'd suggest he's playing dumb to protect someone else."

"His entire motive was greed; his bank account overflows with newspaper money. But he might've flipped. Gotta go, bro. Love to Teresa."

"Yep, and to yours, Karen."

RYDER FLICKED THROUGH recent NASA photographs while he waited for the web-cam window to leap into life. Teresa had wanted them to go for a pub dinner but, because Ryder wouldn't leave, had to cook instead. He'd hoped she'd have been understanding, but the cacophony from the kitchen denied it.

He never doubted that Karen would try to get him patched in. But as time drifted, he worried that the pre-emptive activity of Tipless, instead of precipitating the investigation, would fudge it. Politicians might get involved. He groaned. He'd met Caroline Diazem, the President, at a rally. Her arrogance was such that nothing about the case would be released to the public unless the aliens gave her a glorious endorsement.

The waiting reminded him of his childhood weekends. Ryder's

father was a teacher in order to spend long holidays trekking. Friends were impressed knowing that Ryder had been the world over, peering over the planet from mountain tops every weekend. But the reality was a distant mother, who preferred her Surbiton wine circle to base camp. Rock scrambling over the Peak District scarp slopes was brilliant, but waiting your turn in the cold drizzle at the bottom of a near-vertical cliff drained all Ryder's enthusiasm for the sport. On the other hand, it gave him time to listen to his digi-media player; music and *Hitch Hikers' Guide to the Galaxy*.

Ryder's childhood recollections disorientated his concentration; his shoulders drooped, then jolted back when the web-cam window burst into bright light.

"Teresa, we're in." But she'd gone to bed, leaving him a plate of sausage sandwiches for dinner.

He called Derek O'Connor at his Imax TV studio again and got the answering machine. "Derek, even if you're not interested in this piece of history taking place, I'd like the studio to record my link, so don't erase it, yeah?" This would give Ryder a back-up beyond his own equipment at home. He could put it on the web, but he might find himself incarcerated in the public interest.

A sudden movement on screen caught Ryder's eye. A technician had ambled in front of the case. He wore a white lab coat but no biohazard suit.

Ryder's pulse raced when he realized the sound was off. Oops, too loud. The speaker filled his room with laughter. Not just an embarrassed, I-shouldn't-be-here giggle, but raucous belly busting.

Another voice joined in. "What about the one I want to die like my grandfather, happy and in my sleep, not in terror and screaming like his passengers." Both technicians fell about in derision as if there was no mystery case in there with them. To Ryder's amazement, the off-screen joker walked in, straight up to the case and waved his hand over the logo. His eyes widened when it opened.

For the first time, Ryder had a clear view of the strange-coloured blocks inside.

Ryder was hoarse shouting to Teresa, who strolled in rubbing her eyes.

"Bloody hell."

"Exactly."

Teresa slumped in an armchair. "Security's bound to charge in at any moment."

Ryder stood with excitement. "He's trying to lift one of the blocks."

"They've already tested for toxic emissions, yes?"

"Not finished. There's no radiation or gases, though their temperature is a degree above ambient."

"So something's happening in there."

"Producing laughing-gas, apparently." Ryder turned his head toward the faint buzzing from the next room. "Is that my mobile?"

Teresa couldn't take her eyes off the screen. "You left it in the bedroom."

Ryder ran before it rang off. "Hey, Manuel, exciting stuff."

"Yeah, we're about to test a prototype data-gatherer into the sun's corona."

"Why's that, Manuel? Did the one last week fail?"

"Sorry, Ryder, what are you talking about? I can never tell when you're teasing. Anyway I assume you want a pass?"

"Manny, I was there for the Corona Discovery launch, but NASA sent me back to the UK when the case arrived. Remember?"

"What case, Ryder? Oh, never mind, everything's going nuts around here. Head's killing me. I'm desperate for some sleep. Sheila kept me up all night—you can guess, eh? See ya, Ryder."

Mystified, Ryder sat hard on a chair. It was unlike Manuel Gomez to get so confused. It was his extraordinary organisational abilities that kept him in his job at Edwards. Perhaps he'd had a few too many. But then what was that about his fiancée, Sheila? He'd split up with her last time they talked.

Teresa's excited voice broke through. "Ryder, come and see this."

There were so many technicians and security people milling around in the lab, the case couldn't be seen.

Ryder contacted Karen at her home in Washington.

"Hi, Ryder. Hurry up, Brother, dear. I've to get some mince for our tea."

"Good God, Karen, never mind the shopping, what's happening in the lab?"

"Which lab, Ryder?"

"The one with the case from Dryden—there's unprotected people all over it."

"Really? What case? How's Teresa?"

"I'll get back to you, Karen. Bye, and take care."

He wished he could've seen her, but she must have been using her wristwatch-phone.

"I wish I'd talked to her instead," Teresa said.

"Why? She's obviously been infected with something relating to the case. Just because you talk about kids and clothes..."

"Idiot. It could be her confusion is just tiredness."

"There's the ultra-rational biologist coming out in you, Teresa. Been on any psycho courses lately?"

"Don't need to. I live with a real, live nutter, don't I?"

"I suppose the crowd of people in the room was a mass-hysteria effect?"

"You don't know what decisions had been made higher up, do you? They might've determined there's no back-contamination issues, no putative organisms floating around and so withdrew the access restrictions."

"How likely is that?" Ryder raked his fingers through his hair as if it helped nearby brain cells.

"Fair enough. I would keep it secure for a month. So would you, but we're not there. Perhaps you'd better try Derek again to see if his contacts can be alerted to the situation." Her hand went to the plate. "Hey, you ate my sandwiches. Right, I'm throwing together a spag-bol."

RYDER RANG DEREK. "It's about the situation at Goddard and maybe at Dryden."

"That's where you and Manuel Gomez had a freebie trip wasn't it?"

"Yes, Derek, but there's a developing problem."

"In what way, Ryder?"

"The case that the astronauts sent back from the ISS appears to be affecting technicians who have been up close to it."

"Who exactly?"

"Manuel, Tipless—the technician who opened the case–"

"That's two, who else?"

"My sister Karen. She works at Goddard, and the worrying thing is that she's not been near the case but mixed with staff who have."

"And what's the developing problem with these three individuals, Ryder?"

Ryder paused, tapped his fingers on his desk as if it was a miniature piano. Distraction therapy to calm himself down in case Derek thinks he's losing it. "They're acting strange and forgetful."

"Like someone not a million miles from here. Ryder, you'd be worried about your sister. Maybe your creative imagination is getting the better of you."

"Derek, just allow the possibility of something going awry because of the artefact found on the space station."

"Go on."

Ryder knew he could appeal to Derek's self-importance. "You've met NASA's chief administrator, Robert Keefo."

"So?"

"Could you get on to him? Let him know there appear to be problems with staff conn—"

"No way, Ryder; three reasons. One: don't you think he would know already if there were problems with his staff? Two: he wouldn't thank us for interfering in what's just your warped mind. Three: you're not supposed to be spying for us. Brief me with an update tomorrow."

Ryder had to leave the call empty-handed. At least he wasn't told to abandon what he considered to be the biggest news item ever— even if he was the only one to think so. It could be that Manuel, Karen, and the techies were just overtired, confused, or intoxicated with excitement. If it was more than that, then it would be more developed at Edwards, maybe with the technicians who handled the case. Ryder banged his fist on his desk, making his cup rattle as he realized it was too late to ask Manuel for their phone numbers.

CHAPTER 5

Wednesday 15 April 2015:
The day of the arrival of the case at Dryden Laboratories, Edwards Air Force Base.

IT WASN'T EVERY DAY Jack Balin was told to put an alien suitcase onto the lab-specimen table. Even though he wore the anonymity of a biohazard suit, he beamed at the privilege. He couldn't wait to tell his wife, Irene. Payback after all her carping on about his low technician's pay. It would be sweeter still when he gathered his stepchildren to tell them. Eddie, who at thirteen, absorbed and magnified any snippet of space news. Debbie, a hardnosed cynic at nine years old would say, "boring," but her eyes would deny it. Of course, he shouldn't tell them anything, but it was too hard not enriching their evening mealtimes with sneaked information when the fireman next door filled his kids with incinerating awe every day.

He couldn't leave the lab area until reporting the slight leak in his biohazard suit to his shift super. Nothing unusual, and it would be patched for the next time, again. He nattered to the evening cleaning crew as he jotted perfunctory answers on a clipboard. In his outside clothes, he sauntered down the corridor where the smell of fresh coffee drew him into the staff room.

"Hey, Jack," called Ken Hardman, from a corner table. "Bring your coffee over here."

"Can't stop, Ben, bus leaves for Rosamond in ten."

"Well, between slurps, Jack, how heavy was that case? Tony here reckons it must be full of Russian stash."

Jack joined in the laughter. "Too heavy for any of you guys." They knew he mustn't talk about it, even though he was going to at home. Maybe it was a tinge of guilt making his head buzz.

He drained the coffee and nodded at the dozen colleagues before heading on down the corridor. Hurried footsteps made him turn to see his supervisor.

"Jack, glad I've caught you. Come in two hours earlier tomorrow, can you? Overtime rate?"

"Sure."

Jack reached the exit and he chatted to a guard for a minute as he signed out.

With his shirt sticking to his back in the Mojave Desert heat, Jack caught the bus to his hometown of Rosamund. By the time he disembarked, his head hurt real bad, and he'd no idea what he'd done that morning. He kinda knew he should have been celebrating something. Heck, it was damned hot.

Shaking his head and stirring his legs into action, he convinced himself he'd be all right with a drink and a lie down at home.

Just in time he remembered it was his turn to provide the family meal, obliging him to call in at a KFC. The queue shuffled amiably enough. The wallpaper music masked the fuzziness in his head.

He was dizzy by the time he tumbled the paper bucket full of battered chicken and fries onto his kitchen table. He grabbed a glass and wouldn't talk until he'd filled it with water and swallowed it. Through the distorted bottom of the glass, he saw his wife Irene holding a salad ladle up.

"Jack, you brought home dinner yesterday. I've started a salad for tonight."

"I have to be in by six tomorrow," he told her, pleased he remembered something and blurting it out in case it left him later.

Sitting at the table, he splattered ketchup over all the food.

"Aw, Jack. No."

"It'll be overtime rate."

"You know I don't eat ketchup."

"Sorry, Reenie. You won't forget to get me up for the bus, will you?"

"I'll have to scrape it all off now. Eddie, don't stuff it in your mouth like that."

He realized his step-daughter was talking to him. "You all right, Jack?"

"He's tired. Leave him be, Debbie."

"I'm okay, kid. I'll get the bread and cola." He stood, then staggered to the sink.

Irene followed him and gave him a comforting hug. "Are you okay, honey?"

"Sure—it's been a funny kinda day."

"Damn hot, that's for certain."

"I mean at work. Can't you get nothing right?"

"Oh, get you. Don't take your work stress out on us, you pig."

Eddie ran in, disrupting the developing fight. "Jack, you promised to tell me..." It broke the spell.

"What promise, Ed?"

"You know—about astronauts and stuff."

"Well, Eddie, something different did happen today...what was it.

Something to do with aliens."

All the family shrieked with laughter. He stomped to the ugly white fridge and grabbed a beer to gulp and sulk till bedtime.

THURSDAY 16 APRIL 2015

Jack pushed soggy cereal around his breakfast bowl.

"You'll be late for your bus, Jack. It's half past seven."

He knuckled his forehead. Something was missing. He pushed back his chair and strolled to the door. He looked back, still miffed he couldn't think what was wrong.

As he paused, Eddie called from watching TV.

"Hey, Jack, you messing with this case-thing on the news?"

"Don't know what you're talking about. And you better not be talking about my work to nobody—do you hear?" Eddie shrank from his stepfather's outburst.

"Leave the boy alone, Jack. Just because you've got a sore head, you don't—"

"Shut the fuck up."

"Wha..." She didn't finish. Damn. He knew she was too stunned. He never swore.

He had to run for the bus—and made it, but the driver was being shouted at by his passengers for departing too early, leaving not-so-fast runners on the sidewalk. Jack heard the driver insist he was right on the current schedule and not the old one. When the fuss died down, Jack settled in his shiny green seat and tried to think about what he did yesterday. His brain didn't work too well: maybe he'd had an excess of beer after supper. The Activity Log in the lab would tell him, if it still bothered him.

But he was bothered. He remembered snippets about yesterday, but—last week... What happened last week? It hurt his head trying to work it out.

He wasn't alone. He'd never experienced such chaos since that sponsored poker and drinks night when the staff dragged themselves into work the following day, drinking strong coffee and lousing up so much work, it took hours to get back on schedule. He warmed at the memory of how he and his colleagues covered up their misdoings. Maybe that was it. And why could he remember that incident from last year but not what happened last week?

Off the bus, he wandered down the corridor, heading for some clearing-head air-conditioning but was stopped by a whistle.

Bret, one of the supervisors caught up with him. "Jack, you're not one of these damn zombies, are you? Came back from a damn expensive holiday in Vegas last night to see this shift in chaos. What's going on?"

"Wish I knew, Bret. Like having a real bad head after a binge night."

"And did you? Along with the rest of the shift?"

"No. I dunno. To be honest, I don't remember nothing about last night." Jack didn't want to confess to his supervisor that he was muddled about all last week, maybe more. His head buzzed again. He had to find a chair.

"You okay, Jack? Just a quick question, then. I've arranged transport to fly that weird suitcase-thing to Goddard. Do you have anything to add to the handling notes? Just stuff you'd noticed. Unusually heavy for the look of it, vibrations, lopsided weight inside, anything?"

Jack realized he must have looked as if Bret had asked him what sort of cheese the moon was made of.

"Hell, Jack, I'd give you the day off, but it looks as if the whole shift is the same."

Looking down at his shoes, Jack had a gut feeling that they might as well have all been sent home although some wouldn't be sure where their homes were.

He loaded the crated suitcase onto the NASA LearJet used for small, urgent transports. Its pilots and crew laughed at Jack's bewilderment. At least the case was on its way. Just as well. Bret told Jack he was getting a headache too.

JACK FOUND THE BUS QUEUE was more of a mob than usual. Yet quieter. The confused home-goers were introspective rather than talkative, drooped shoulders not caring that they were in scorching sunshine. The only chattering was between a handful of worn-out cooks from a new burger-bar across the wide dusty road. Jack looked at them, wondering if they were going to have buzzing heads any minute and whether in the morning they'd remember where they worked.

The driver was new. A rarity for Kern County Buses and his cheerfulness contrasted with, and pained, the passengers. Jack overpaid for his fare because, although he kinda guessed it had gone up, he couldn't remember by how much. He stood for a while waiting for change then when the driver grinned but offered no money, Jack knew why the driver was so cheerful. Jack shuffled down the aisle to find a seat on the shady side.

At least it wasn't his turn to make the dinner, or was it? Just in case, he bought a bag of donuts on the way from the bus stop.

By seven in the evening, Jack was still alone. He checked the phone then the calendar in case he'd overlooked meeting up with the family at the bowling alley.

The problem remained over where his folks were, but thank God, the buzz in his head had switched off. He exhaled with relief.

His face cracked with a smile all the way to the fridge, and clutching an ice-cold Bud, back to a TV chair. Maybe his memory problems had left with the headache, but he resisted testing it out.

A calendar rested on the coffee table. Jack grimaced at the scribbled birthdays and appointments in front of him—a small comfort in the written word. He looked at the can—ready to drink in celebration—then at the calendar and worked at what happened the day before.

Damn his head. He couldn't remember the assignments from work yesterday or the day before and even from last week. He grabbed the calendar, ripped it to shreds, ignored the lager, and went for the whiskey. It didn't improve any recollections, but it meant he didn't care.

FRIDAY 17 APRIL 2015, 10 P.M.

A thought surfaced later. He was alone in his house, and it should've been boisterous. Where were they? What had he forgotten today? He struggled to focus on the conversations that must have taken place at the morning's breakfast table, but his brain blurred. He fell asleep in the shimmer of TV chat shows.

He couldn't believe the time when he woke with a groggy head. Two in the morning. Suppose Irene had taken her kids to her mom's and he'd forgotten, or she hadn't wanted to tell him? He'd had enough.

THE POLICE PRECINCT WAS PACKED with a mob of confused people spilling outside, so Jack drove on by. Rosamond wasn't a large town, but half of it congregated in one of two places. Jack went first to the Church of Saint Theresa, but it was worse there. Someone told Jack that Father Blah was new to the district, but Jack couldn't remember his name. In which case, maybe it was true. He remembered stuff from two months back, no problem, but damn it, he couldn't recall what he'd had for breakfast or whether he'd had any. With no leader at his church, he turned the Ford around and went to join the crowd at Rosamond Police precinct.

It didn't take long to find them. A huddle of three bewildered people were glad to see him.

Irene beat her children to finding a voice. "Jack." They enjoyed a group hug. "But where were you, Jack?"

"I was going to ask that. I was at home, our home."

Irene broke down, recovering enough after a few minutes to speak through the tears. "I collected the kids from school to take them for a Big Mac, then we couldn't remember where the new house was."

"Figures. It's new to you, but I've been there three years. Just a minute—what's with all the rest of these people? They can't all have new homes they've forgotten about."

"There's been a power cut on the east side. They came to find out what's going on. Come on, let's go home."

Jack's wife and stepchildren had headaches like he kinda recalled experiencing. As he drove, he tried to think what would happen if the night shift didn't turn up at the power plant or they forgot new procedures. Maybe it was just one ‘engineer lousing up. It'd happened at the Dryden Labs. One man forgets to pull a switch or set a relay. An overnight burn trial of a prototype engine blew the roof off when the coolant stopped flowing because a since-fired techie threw a Coke can that connected with and then disconnected a switch. It didn't hit the papers. Suppose it couldn't—the reporters bought off. But if that could happen then, what the hell could happen now?

CHAPTER 6

Sunday 19 April 2015:
London.

TURNING HIS BACK ON THE MONITOR didn't make the crisis go away, though Ryder could focus on Teresa instead.

"You're wrong about this, Ryder."

"If only. I'm worried about my sister, Manny and, damn, it will reach London."

"Once again, you overreact."

Ryder bristled with her dismissals. "Not just us. *Everyone* on the planet is in danger."

"Ryder, you need to chill."

"Is that what Charles the Second said to his physician warning him to leave London when immigrant rats ran ashore with plague-ridden fleas? 'No, you're overreacting, go splash vinegar on them.'"

"Is that what you think is going on over there, Ryder? A memory disease?"

"Yes."

Teresa laughed. "How do you investigate an infectious disease without getting close to a patient?"

Ryder pointed back at the screen. "Already doing it, aren't we? Remotely on the web. But we need compelling evidence to persuade people here that we're not barking."

Teresa pointed her coffee at him. "Too late, dear. And your line-manager, Derek, doesn't want to make waves. Go over his head. Do something bold, Ryder, for Pete's sake."

"Who? Robert Keefo, head of NASA?"

"Oh yes, he's going to say thanks for bringing attention to NASA bringing a plague back to Earth. Assuming mere mortals like us can't talk directly to our Prime Minister, Ryder, who do we know?"

"Your faculty dean, Maurice Dover. Doesn't he have friends in high places?"

"I'll try him. Hey, Ryder, your sister's back on."

The screen showed Karen's lab, but the freckled face and shock of red hair belonged to her senior techie, Julia.

"No, Karen's not here. Hell, I shouldn't be here either, Ryder. It's Sunday, you know."

"You working on the case, Julia?"

"What case? Oh that. I will be later. I've been on leave but came in to be presented to some VIPs this afternoon."

Ryder's heart raced now he was talking to someone either not infected or at least remembered her present-day schedule. He briefed her on his fears, expecting her to laugh at him.

"Funny you should say that, Ryder."

"Looks more scary to me."

"My colleagues are crazier than usual. Now you've given me a reason why. Umm, maybe I should go home. I don't suppose you've any idea how it's transmitted?"

"That's just it, Julia. I don't, except it's fast, and I'm afraid it's quite possible you've already..."

"Gee, thanks for the warning. I'll—"

"Hang on, Julia, I have a favour to ask. I'd like you to chat to my fiancée. She's a biologist and she wants you to do something very important. Wait there...Teresa."

Teresa, with a sucking-a-lemon-face, came in to the study, papers in both hands. She hated being disturbed when planning lectures.

"I've got Julia, Karen's senior techie, on line, just arrived so she's clean—so far."

"Out of the way," Teresa demanded, pulling Ryder's arm.

"Julia, can you get a blood sample from one of your infected colleagues?"

Ryder clenched his fists. "Oh great, just scare the woman to death."

"Haven't time for niceties, you moron. Either she's going to help or she isn't. End of."

"Hi, Teresa. I think I can, but I don't want to hang around here for analysis. Shall I post it you in an airmail bio-sample container?"

"Good idea."

"No, it isn't," Ryder said. "It could spread the contamination over here too quickly and—"

"Idiot, have you any idea how many infected people would have flown to the UK and Europe today?"

"Even so, it'd be safer to be analysed in the States and the results sent to us. And a postal package might not reach the airport."

"I heard all that, you two." Julia frowned, and yet she stayed cool enough to plan. "I'll take a sample with me. Jeez, it means I'm infected already. I'll drive upstate to the isolation lab and set up the auto Mass Spectrometer."

"That mightn't be enough, Julia."

"I know, Teresa, but are we going to have time to grow cultures?

We have a speed culture setup there. We can also do auto GC, electrophoresis, biochemical, microbiological, and protein characterization. I'll link it to your PC."

"When can you have it set up by? Can I suggest you make a quick reminder note about it now?" asked Ryder, worried she might have forgotten by the time she drove to the isolation lab.

"You think it's that quick?" She looked paler. "I'm fucked, aren't I? It'll be a couple of hours or so for the linkup. Signing out. And thanks, guys. I think. I'm going then. Catch you both later."

Ryder looked at the now-blank screen. He heated with worry but tried to be positive. "Useful."

Teresa waved a dismissive hand. "Don't count on it."

"Your glass half-empty again? Hello, Karen's monitor's on again. No, it's the reception at Goddard. A load of people. Didn't Julia say something about VIPs paying the lab a visit?"

"Good timing to pick up nasties. Do you recognise any of them? You're the lucky one who gets to go on all those trips."

Teresa brought coffees to help wakefulness while watching the screen.

Ryder fidgeted in his seat. "Hey, look that's Doug Reeman, chairman of the Senate's NASA Acquisition Committee. More cronies...senators, CEOs. My God, they'll take it back to the White House and—"

"Isn't that Manuel?"

"Looks out of it, poor chap. I've got to get on to Faculty Dean Maurice Dover. Get the British Government to take notice."

"Not listening, Ryder, were you?"

"What? You mean about infected people from the States already here? Can't be that many and we have to do *something*."

"Loads of people must have left the States, mostly by air, some by road to Mexico or Canada."

"What? How did they all know?"

"You're an imbecile. Why do I stick with you? None of them would've heard about infectious amnesia. Just normal trips, but they're carrying the infection anyway."

"So, what are we waiting for? Let's tell family and friends and get out of here. At least we should leave London and head for isolation. Just a minute. This needs careful consideration. We should inform the government. They might be able to activate some contingency plans. You know, isolation bunkers."

Teresa threw her hands in the air. "Ryder, the nuclear-war bunkers set up in the 1960s were dismantled years ago. Get real, for God's sake."

"We should make sure somebody other than us knows what's going down."

Teresa threw him a tired look. "I know."

"Do you? I'm talking end-of-the-world stuff."

"Let's not get carried away. It's most likely a case of *temporary* amnesia for *some* people."

"I wish I had your optimism, Teresa. I'm telling Maurice. Put the onus on him to enlighten people higher up." He looked straight at her but instead of another defiant, hand-waving gesture, she had a far-away look and walked off. Ryder knew the look. It meant he'd find out about it when she'd accomplished her mission. She loved her little secrets.

He dismissed the idea of e-mailing Maurice, her boss; better to talk to him face-to-face. As he stood, he glanced at the monitor displaying the US lab. Meandering lost people.

CHAPTER 7

Monday 20 April 2015:
Edwards Air Base, Dryden Labs.

JACK BALIN, ALONG WITH HIS COLLEAGUE, KEN, stood facing the Dryden lab entrance. The morning sun was thwarted by a corrugated metal awning.

"What's going on, Jack? Why are there only a few of us coming into work?"

"Beats me. Your people at home up the creek as well?"

"I've come here to get away from flying crockery." He rubbed a bruise on his forehead. They were pulling a few more times on their cigarettes before going into the building.

"Thought I'd lost my whole family last night. Stupid critters forgot where we lived. Wondering if the same will happen tonight," Jack said, pleased he'd recalled something of the previous night's chaos though Irene hadn't slept and had reminded him. He'd forgotten but wasn't letting on. Maybe he should try going without sleep.

"Jack, we going mad?"

"I've promised Irene I'll keep off the booze, but—all right, stop laughing—it can't be the alcohol, can it? Kids are just as confused."

"You're right, unless you've been knocking back Ankers. Hey, you do."

"So?"

"Local brew, Ankers. Artesian well at Bakersfield. Man, it's used for all local drinks. Maybe we're all being poisoned."

"Could explain a lot, Ken. Can't think what else it could be. Let's go in and get some work done. I'll buy bottled water on the way home."

On automatic, the two waved at the security guard and signed in. They plodded the corridor to the locker room, changed into overalls, adopted their another-day-another-dollar attitudes and strolled to the schedule office. Except there was no list of work to do. All the relevant supervisors were new to Dryden and hadn't turned up.

"Does that mean we go home, Jack?"

"Do you want to?"

"Hell, no."

"Let's grab a coffee until a super comes along."

Ken led the way to the canteen.

"Yeah, maybe Bret's there."

"Sure, Jack. What the hell?" Ken's mouth dropped at the sight of a dozen colleagues in the canteen. A Road Runner cartoon kept some occupied while others clustered round their coffees.

"Hey, Jack," Gibson called at the drinks machine. "Wanna white sweetened, as usual? Welcome to the Dryden Retirement Club."

Jack considered that observation. There was no one there who had started employment during the last few months.

"It's as if no one new knows where to go, man. Is that how you see it?" Jack asked.

"What? You think there's a case of mass Alzheimer's? Nah, Jack, it'll be one of them flu virus things. Mary and the kids have headaches with it, and me."

"So did I. Doesn't explain why we're losing our memory though. You remember what you did last week?"

"Hell, after a few drinks, I don't know what I did yesterday. You're messing with my head, Jack. Watch TV."

Jack accepted a coffee from Gibson and made an effort not to think. He saw that his friends were not as relaxed as their language. Several were holding heads and looking at watches. A few made a huge effort to be absorbed in Wile E. Coyote's not-so-cunning plan to dynamite the Road Runner. Jack glanced at an ACME ambush device about to be detonated when the large screen switched to an image of NASA's reception at the Goddard labs.

"What the fuck," shouted Dwight Pulaski, a beefy engineer who grabbed the remote off his neighbour and jabbed at the plastic.

Jack, although slim-built, came up behind Pulaski and, without saying a word, took the remote to reselect the Goddard visit.

"Give that here, Jack."

"No, Dwight, it's important."

Shouts of encouragement to both men should have filled the canteen with onlookers, but silence shoved everyone back into their seats.

Pulaski puffed up, towered over Jack, shrugged, and sat down. All stared at the screen.

ROBERT KEEFO, NASA'S CHIEF ADMINISTER, couldn't believe his eyes. The NASA reception should have been the pinnacle celebration of the year's progress. Astronauts on their best behaviour should have been toadying up to senators and congressmen. Instead, VIPs wandered around as if in a daze. Many NASA staff hadn't turned up, and those that did were either overworked or confused.

"Keefo, what the hell's going on?" Congressman Philips' demand bounced around the room.

"Sir, I have no idea but, ah, there's Michael Evans."

The Flight Center Director looked confused. "Robert? I mean Mr Keefo? What are you and all these people doing here?"

"This, Michael, is a very important pre-arranged visit. You're all behaving like zombies looking for very early retirement—damn it!"

"Director, what the hell...?" The congressman's red face looked overheated.

Keefo had the congressman's elbow, steering him to the VIP suite where there were nibbles and copious alcoholic drinks.

The congressman threw a parting shot at Evans. "Damn lucky for you the President is on a plane away from this charade. She wouldn't be impressed."

BACK AT EDWARDS, Jack guessed the link was on a pre-arranged auto setup or they wouldn't have seen the debacle. He gasped as he realized the highest government offices would be infected in just a few hours. His head hurt again like a bad dose of influenza. He wanted to believe that's all it was but knew it was much more. Something else nagged at him, but although he knuckled his head real hard, he wasn't able to figure it out. A bear roared behind him and Pulaski's elbow crashed down on his head.

The flimsy table and chairs collapsed under the two grunting men. Jack jerked back an elbow into Pulaski's face and heard his cheek crack. Blood and spittle splattered the floor before friends of both yanked them apart.

Crashing the canteen door open, supervisor Bret Cornfield shouted over their heads. "Jack, I want you in the comms office now!"

Shocked from being attacked, Jack shook his head then raked his fingers through his thick hair. They came away greasy. Could the new buzzing in his head seep into his hair? Cracking up.

"What the fuck does he want? Hey, Gibson, I thought none of the supers got in today."

"Bret's the only one who made it in. He's all right, Jack."

"I'm in no mood to be sociable to no one. Even you, Gibbo."

"Like I care. Don't see him then. Go home, stay home."

"All right, don't go on about it."

"Huh?"

"I'm going. See?" Jack found co-ordinating his thought processes difficult, but the need to hang on to his job was ingrained, so he followed supervisor Cornfield to the comms room where links to other labs, including the orbital ISS, fluoresced the room.

Bret grinned and waved Jack into a chair. "Now, Jack, I need your help."

"What? Oh, that's all right then."

"I've been forgetting stuff, just like everyone else round here, but there's a difference between me and you morons. Isn't there, Jack?"

"You're a bigger prick?"

"I've noticed abuse is replacing intellect. I'm just hoping that it happens to me later because I've got more brains."

"Naw, you're just a bigger prick." Jack laughed at his own joke, and by the look on Bret's face, humour was infectious.

"There you go. Anyway, Jack, I've been making notes on my NoteCom so I can catch up each day. Clever, huh?"

Jack fumbled in his pocket for his own NoteCom wondering if he'd remember to use it.

"Look at this screen, Jack. It shows you suited up and handling a case found on the outside of the space station."

"Yeah, so?" Jack struggled to remember being that responsible; squeezed brain cells half-recalling his son admiring him being in touch with aliens. It was too much.

"So the case went to Goddard, opened, and then what?"

"No idea."

"Well, look at them. Chaos. Also at JPL, Pasadena they're not normal—my friends, Jack. They're loopy. I tried to grab a drinking pal at Tucson...you listening, Jack? Good. Hank recognised me and he was at work. I thought he was normal for a few minutes until he got irritated at strangers in his office. Obviously he'd forgotten they were colleagues."

"Anybody *normal* out there?"

"The guys on the space station are okay."

A light switched on in Jack's head. "Hey, the space station. Will they get—"

"Supplied? God knows. Doesn't look like it, but they can return under their own steam."

"Can we link to Goddard? That VIP visit—"

Bret pointed at a blank screen then played with some buttons until a picture flickered up.

"This is bad, Jack. We're looking in the VIP lounge, can't hear jack shit, but the body language shouts enough. And those bodies decide budgets. Hell, what am I jabbering on about, this thing is bigger than NASA's survival.

"Jack, *why* have you and others here lost their memory? Yesterday's a bit foggy for me but you guys have lost weeks."

Jack stood to examine the screen closer. "Your turn will come."

"Suppose I'm immune? Hey, don't go telling anybody or they'll be cutting me up to find out why. Ha."

"You don't understand. Tomorrow I won't remember this chat. Who's going to work on you? All the medics are sure as hell like me too." He slumped onto a chair. "Why is it happening, Bret?"

"Must be that case from the ISS. You got contaminated then everyone else. Big question is how's it going to stop?"

"Maybe if I was exposed to the case a second time. You know, two negatives make a positive."

"Yeah, but two positives stay positive. Anyway, Goddard's a goddamn long way to walk. Last I heard, most flights out of Bakersfield and some from Edwards, here, have been cancelled. Staff not turning up."

"There must be pilots coming in who haven't been contaminated, for want of a better word."

"Hey, my head's buzzing. Oh, fuck."

"Bret, my headache's gotten better, but we should warn people who are clear—tell management."

"Jack, today we are the most senior here. It'll take hours trying all the other labs."

"There's Goddard on the screen. And Keefo. If we can see him through this, we can talk to him, and we can't get higher than NASA's chief administrator."

"Go for it, Jack."

CHAPTER 8

Monday p.m. 20 April 2015:
NASA Goddard Labs, Maryland.

ROBERT KEEFO, CHIEF ADMINISTRATOR OF NASA, juggled scenarios. A budget meeting scheduled for next week needed more cunning than keeping apart a foxy lady friend and a smart wife. Add to that a lost-contact Mars mission and a bucketful of failed communications from all over the place; he was having the worst goddamn headache. He'd met with and conquered bureaucratic fuck-ups before, but the bungling of this VIP visit to their flagship lab was a nightmare. Keefo's blood surged, pulsing and pushing against arterial walls. The increased blood pressure forced him to loosen his top shirt button. Damn the incompetents here. Just when he had to focus to manipulate the anti-NASA congress members.

Making his way through the partygoers, he grabbed the elbow of Michael Evans, the director of Goddard, and tugged him to a corner.

"Michael, what the hell's going on?"

"Don't worry, Robert, I've already drawn up layoff notices for these idiots."

"Did you include yours?"

"If you insist. But I was in Darmstadt till yesterday. Anyway, I've an ace."

"You might need two."

"Doug Reeman. As acquisition chairman, he's the most influential critical bastard in there."

"And making the most noise—at least I double charged his whiskey," Robert said.

"Done better than that. You know Isobel from R&I?"

"Do I want to know this?"

"Let's just say Reeman's squeaky-clean marriage is a liability for him, especially with his eye for sultry women."

Robert Keefo knew he had to keep aloof from such activity, so he welcomed the interruption by an official bringing his attention to a communication from the Dryden Lab at Edwards.

Evans pulled at Keefo's sleeve. "We don't need this, Robert. We've the VIPs to pacify."

"On the contrary, Mike, I need to get away from those attention-seeking creeps. Engineers want to talk aeronautics and space. Real things—no contest."

The most senior NASA man wasn't so sure he'd got it right when at the screen he scrutinised the image of the two men. They looked awful, in particular the older, thin one with JACK BALIN on his badge.

"Mr Keefo, am I glad to talk to you," Bret said, closing on the camera.

"Mr Keefo is too busy," Evans said, moving to stand between the screen and Keefo.

"Just a moment, Mike, I'll choose who I'll talk to, thank you. Is everything all right, Mr...?"

"Cornfield, Bret Cornfield, sir. No, sir, things are going very weird, aren't they, Jack?"

"Sure, Bret."

"Come on, guys," Keefo said.

"People are losing their memory, sir."

The chief administrator laughed. "Been having a party, Bret?"

"No, sir, begging your pardon. It's much more serious. People have been forgetting where they work, where they live, who they're married to—"

"I've had days like that." Keefo grinned at Mike Evans.

"Sir, there have been power blackouts where engineers forgot procedures, buses ran out of drivers, the local TV isn't on air and—"

"Bret, I'm sure there's been a local festival, Mardi Gras, Democrat Convention, or whatever. It'll be all right, I'm sure."

"No work is being done here, sir."

"Now that's serious. Can you put your director on? Matt Ewloe?"

"Appointed last month, wasn't he, sir? The only workforce turning up are those who've been here at least a year."

Evans turned the connection off. "We don't need to listen to cranks. They've had too many beers. I'll see they're finished."

"Hold your water, Mike." Keefo turned the connection back on. "Like I said, I'll decide who I listen to. I'm gonna be angry as hell if I find you've covered up a major event."

Evans shrugged as if he didn't know what the problem was.

The screen flickered to reveal Jack's retreating back and a pore-revealing close-up of Bret tapping at the screen.

"Bret."

"Ah, you're still there, sir. It's that case from the ISS, sir, it must have had something odd inside."

Evans butted in. "Take no notice, Robert. I'll sort it."

"What's wrong with your man Evans, Mr Keefo?"

"Classic case of denial, Bret. Either that or he's in league with the aliens or whoever left their case out in space." Keefo stopped himself. After all, Michael Evans was the head of Goddard and was just attempting to protect NASA from allegations of negligence. Nevertheless, he had to decide if action needed to be taken or whether the problem, like so many others, would blow over.

"Bret, I want you to find the most senior—no, let's say experienced—personnel in Edwards, who have not been affected by this amnesia problem and get them to communicate to me in an hour. Can you do that?"

"Sure thing, Mr Keefo, if I can. It won't be easy. I'll try and keep this link open. Over."

Evans had a self-satisfied grin. "Just what I'd have done. But what have you in mind?"

"I wish I knew, Michael. But I know what my family is going to do."

"I expect my wife and kids will be on the same flight to London."

Robert flipped open his cell phone. "I have a feeling London is not far enough, Mike, not nearly far enough."

CHAPTER 9

Tuesday 21 April 2015:
Baltimore, five days after amnesia started spreading; many people
have lost thirty-seven weeks of their memory.

MANUEL GOMEZ SUFFERED. The bright sunshine helped cheer him. He never tired of blue skies, never longed for those growing cumulus clouds and their cooling showers of New England. It must have been instinct for him to lift his otherwise saddening face to the sunbeams for some childhood memory. He remembered like yesterday, better than yesterday, eating an ice cream while sitting on an iron bench at the Moorish Alhambra Gardens in his home Spanish city of Granada. His sister, Maria, having finished her cornet, pointed behind them and the distraction allowed her a surreptitious lick of his ice cream. Another twenty seconds and the unrelenting sun melted several licks-worth of ice cream, necessitating his mother to rush over with a handkerchief but too late as he had licked the dribbles.

His smile broadened at the recollection but twisted once more as he attempted to recall where his workplace hid today. Had he worked the day before? If so, where? He knew his job as Education Officer for NASA took him all over the States and sometimes abroad. He could picture some establishments, such as Edwards and Goddard, but not where he was supposed to be today. That was it. His diary should tell him. He fumbled his NoteCom out of his inside jacket pocket and switched it on.

Tuesday 21 April 2015
10:20 meeting with Michael Evans at Goddard.
14:00 video link update with Ryder Nape.

So helpful. It even told him he'd missed a VIP reception at Goddard the previous day and a doctor's appointment. Why did he need to see the doctor? He didn't feel ill. Maybe the failure to attend explained the reason. The one certainty he knew hammered at him: he could only remember the odd damn thing from recent days. Other things niggled at him: half-forgotten comments from someone like Ryder about just this problem. At least he remembered Ryder, one of few genuine guys in the media business. A good friend.

He struck a deal with himself. He used his electronic calendar to call the doctor and bullied his way into an immediate appointment. Not that difficult when patients forget to turn up. The deal? To keep the NoteCom as a more detailed diary, at least until the doctor gave him a panacea.

A shadow blotted the sun as a cloud threatened Baltimore's aridity. He stood for a moment outside the doctor's street door, admiring the brass plate. The door was ajar. Not trusting the lift, Manuel took exercise by walking up three flights of stairs.

MANUEL THOUGHT HE'D WALKED INTO A MEDICAL MUSEUM. The doc was walled in by dark oak panels, walnut desk, and with the sunlight so enfeebled by wooden window slats, he had to walk real slow until his eyes adjusted. A comfort these days.

"So, Mr Gomez, you miss other appointments but expect just to waltz in whenever you like," said the elderly doctor whose crotchety words argued with the twinkle in his eyes.

"I only missed one appointment for the very reason I am here."

"Don't tell me. You're losing your mind."

Manuel sat in an ancient red-leather chair. "Is that what it is, Doc?"

"What?"

"You tell me. I assume if I'm losing my mind, you must still have your doctoring one intact."

The doctor walked around his huge desk and perched on a corner. "Mr Gomez. Let's start again."

"Okay, Doc. My memory is going fast. I assume it's an early onset of Alzheimer's."

"I doubt it. You can't remember what you did yesterday, can you?"

"Nor the last couple of weeks."

"And your lapses of memory are going backward in time?"

"That's right, Doc. What is it?"

"Damned if I know. It isn't Alzheimer's or any other amnesia symptom I know of, especially with the other feature." The doctor wiped his nose with the largest tissue Manuel had ever seen.

"Go on, Doc."

"It's infectious. My notes tell me you're the tenth I've seen in the last couple of days with the same problem."

"Hell, it's good of you to see me, then. Aren't you worried you might catch whatever the bug is? Shouldn't you be hightailing it for that remote cabin you rich doctors always have?"

"No point is there? By the time us medics realized it might be communicable, we were already infected. I should have retired this week, Gomez, but my replacement hasn't turned up. Guess why not?

"I haven't got anyone to forget everything with, and since I started this business thirty years ago, it'll be a while before I forget where it is."

"Is there anything I can do to slow or reverse the memory loss?"

"You could try eating more oily fish for its omega-3. Maybe apocryphal, but some reckon it helps with brain function. And Huperzine-A, if you can find a drugstore with some left. Look, Gomez, you're already ahead of most folk. God. You turned up here, which means you had something to remind you."

Manuel showed him his NoteCom calendar. "But what happens when the utility people become whacko and there's no food in the stores? Maybe your idea of getting to the back of beyond with a well-stocked cabin isn't such a bad idea. You might be an old wrinkly, Doc, but you have an analytical mind."

"So what's left of my mind must have been working on what happened to the rest of it? Sure I have, and consulted colleagues. Never seen infectious amnesia before."

"You've done CT scans and blood tests?"

"Not me." The doctor waved his hand at his old PC. "Does it look like I have the latest wizardry?"

"I thought I only had to spurt a drop of pee and bleed a little for your nurse to reel off a stack of symptoms."

"Oh, that's just to confirm what the patient tells me they've got anyway. Alzheimer's, Huntington's, Creutzfeldt-Jakob disease, and a load of other dementia-type stuff are still damned difficult to diagnose without heavy-duty equipment. But I called colleagues who reckon we have something new here. The trouble is, Manuel, we don't know how this retrograde infectious amnesia is communicable. It might be contagious and infectious. I can't see it not being viral. We're keeping notes in case we forget all about it tomorrow. Of course, most of the doctors have the lurgy themselves."

"That an official name? Lurgy."

"No, we're calling it RIA, after Retrograde Infectious Amnesia. I suppose it's the fault of you NASA guys?"

"Oh, sure," said Manuel, recalling his NoteCom reminding him about the case today. "So add Alien to the beginning, and we have ARIA."

"Good one. Making a note, see. I'll put it on the web while I still know how. A-R-I-A. One of my more intellectual colleagues made a comment that might interest you, Gomez. He is writing down the most crucial chunks of information we need to get by."

"Whoa, Doc, that's a really tall one. Once you've got your personal ID stuff down like family, phone numbers, address, car and work info, what comes next? You can't note down everything you've learnt."

"Depends on the job, Gomez. A lot of what we do is instinct tempered with adaptive behaviour. I doubt anyone hungry will wave a sandwich around, not knowing which hole to put it in. We have a huge amount of redundant memory in our brains."

Manuel rose for a stretch and then sat again. "Yeah, Doc, most of which were locked away before ARIA arrived."

"But it was all there. Everything your senses pick up in life is recorded. Okay, so only those memory scenes revisited often come to us easily and much of the rest deteriorates as the synapses linking them weaken."

"I know, Doc. Everything we see gets into our brain box, but we're too dumb to recall it all."

"Not too dumb, Gomez. Just suppose you could have instant recall of everything you've seen and heard."

"It would do my head in. I get you. The brain filters out the inconsequential. It's like the difference between data and information. Most people treat them the same, but I remember our lecturer writing 36-24-36 on the board. A woman shrieked sexist accusations at him until he said it was a car registration. Then she got the point. Information is meaningful data."

"I like that one, Gomez, I'll write it down. We should concentrate on what's really important."

"But how is that related to this ARIA thing? Everything is going, isn't it?"

"Apparently, but since not everything is important, maybe by relearning essentials we can at least cope. Maybe even be better for it."

Manuel shook his head. "Nuts. Like I said, you can't jot down everything you need to do your job when it took years at uni then more in training. This damn ARIA is stealing our memories at the rate of maybe a year per week. It's like having a breakdown. Imagine a father whose child is lost, thinking, oh I must scribble down the combination to my office door or which colour button not to press to flood Sacramento Valley."

The doctor opened his hands. "Damn it, Gomez, you're right. I'm better off sticking to skin and bones. It'll be all I'm good for in a month or two. Hey, if you're right about the speed of this thing, I'll just know the medical ways of the 1950s."

"I'll only remember how to break into the women's dorms at CalTech by then."

The doctor smiled back—tired, resigned. "Gomez, it's a real bummer. Take care."

WHEN MANUEL LEFT THE DOCTOR, he found the sidewalk was no different. Rectangular slabs glistened from an impetuous rain shower throwing back fractured reflections of the five-storey cream and grey blocks that characterised this off-central Baltimore. He had no idea where he'd left his car yesterday or the day before. But the dregs of his memory from the last few years allowed him to recognise the Baltimore-Washington Parkway Route 295 signs. He could have taken a taxi; if he could find one, stop one, and the driver remembered the way. Same for buses and trains. Best if he rented another car. Maybe he already had.

Bugger his meeting with Michael Evans, the arrogant sod. But he liked Ryder and would try to remember to call him. Funny. He could remember things he'd looked up during the day even if he lost it by the next.

In the meantime, he had a hankering to go home. Granada. Family and old school friends. A glow of nostalgia and security conjured themselves up when he thought of old comrades and cousins.

He rushed as fast as an overweight pedestrian could to his Baltimore apartment, had another scout around for his car, failed, and poured himself a Scotch.

An hour later, after lunch in his apartment, for which he thanked his stars he'd lived there for years so still remembered it, Manuel called his friend, Ryder.

"Hello, Manuel. It's good to see you. You look done in. How are you coping with the memory loss?"

"I'm learning, Ryder. Weird shit, eh?"

"Yeah. Look, Manny, last time we saw you, you were at a shambles of a VIP reception at Goddard."

"Really? I was there? I thought I'd missed it. Hey, maybe that's where my car is parked. I must have had a lift back home." He rubbed his forehead as if stimulation of the frontal lobes restored lost memories.

"You certain you're okay, Manny?"

Manuel rubbed the back of his neck while straining upwards to see outside at the heavy clouds dribbling. "Ryder, I believe I'm a wheel short of a bicycle. I'm real scared."

"Hell, Manny. I'm not surprised. What are the doctors over there calling it?"

"A fucking nuisance. But apparently the ones who remember politeness are calling it ARIA."

"As in singing for your lost memory?"

"Yeah, or as in—just a minute, I jotted in my NoteCom—Alien Retrograde Infectious Amnesia. Will that do you?"

"A melodic euphemism for something so dreadful, but I suppose it helps to have a handle. Have you got somewhere in the country to go?"

"That's what my doc said. What's so good about the frigging country?"

"I'm afraid you are likely to witness a severe breakdown in services, followed by—"

"Okay, I get the picture. I was going to Spain where a lot of my folks live. Granada. Great, I can still remember."

"That's fine, Manny, but aren't you afraid of infecting your family?"

Silence. Then, "Bugger."

RYDER'S FACE TWISTED WITH THE GUILT of gifting Manuel with the concept of communicating ARIA to his relatives. Teresa came in and caught his contorted expression.

"What have you done?"

"Upset Manuel. Teresa, you know these things. How many people travel in and out of the USA every day?"

"I know as well as you how to know these things, lazy lump." She tapped on her communicator for a few seconds. "A hundred thousand, give or take an airplane."

"Oh my God. This ARIA broke out on 15 April and it's the 21st today. So that's..."

"Ryder, only a few would have it now. It's an exponential growth, but no one leaving the US likely had it on the first day or two."

"You are forgetting, Teresa dear, that it started at an air base so infected travellers might well have left the first day. Then every time one infected person arrives at an airplane, everyone on board gets it. What am I talking about? Everybody in the airport gets it. And on the bus or taxi there. Subsequent bus and taxi journeys."

Teresa dropped her communicator on the desk and collapsed onto the swivel office chair. The action sent it back a few inches until it collided with a table. She tossed her blond hair back and with a maniacal laugh said, "That's it then. Why were we trying to get our bosses to persuade the government to stop people leaving America when it was already too late after day one?"

"Well, it would have slowed the diffusion a little. Giving the rest of the world time to have a plan."

"Yeah right. The plan of action is?"

"Hey, come on, Teresa. Anyone would think it's all my fault the way you're getting at me. Maybe I can get in touch with Karen again."

Teresa dipped a celery stick in a hummus pot, brought it to her mouth, but hesitated. "So, your plan is while an alien virus is creeping towards us, let's video conference as many people as possible, especially those in America, where the situation is much worse, then fall about like zombies when we catch it."

"Putting it like that, we need to do something more positive," said Ryder, grabbing a celery stick.

"Try running like bloody hell."

"At last we agree. But where to?"

CHAPTER 10

Tuesday 21 April 2015:
Chester Zoo, UK, five days after amnesia started spreading; many
people in the USA have lost thirty-seven weeks of their memory, but
local people in Chester, UK are uninfected, so far.

LESTER GODWIN PUSHED THE SECURITY BUTTONS gleaming at him from the staff entrance of Chester Zoo. Sandstone blocks formed the gate, their rosy hue harbouring tiny red mites and ants in gravity-defying scurrying. They darted around shiny, green-leaved stonecrop plants with their shocking-pink flowers. A miniature zoo for those who couldn't afford the entrance fee of the real one. He once led a puzzled school biology class out of the zoo and made the students count the species of fauna in this old wall. Although the kids were gob-smacked at the micro ecosystem, they still preferred to see elephants.

Laughter lines evidenced Lester's reputation as the zoo's chief prankster. He attributed his madcap humour to playing with chimpanzees all day. Five chimps knew Lester as their main human contact, but his glow that morning had nothing to do with monkeying around. Not in the zoo sense.

The previous night, a gorgeous black-haired woman had appeared on his doorstep.

She'd hauled luggage after her. "Well, let me in."

"Katherina, how's your sister in Bakersfield? Oh right, come in why don't you?"

"Look, I'm tired. You could've met me at the airport. I'm famished."

"How about your favourite, Chicken Tiropita in white wine?"

"Hey, Lester, you're improving."

"Right, I'll get it out of the freezer. Shall I put these bags in the lounge for now?"

"Whatever, I'm too knackered to unpack and I suppose you want me knickerless while the dinner cooks. Give me ten."

Lester froze while halfway to the freezer. He wondered if his ears had malfunctioned. He'd not encountered Kat in such a good mood for all their married years. He threw the frozen dinner in the oven, scattered cutlery on the table, took a second longer to light candles, had a quick wash, and galloped up the stairs.

A pass of his hand over a sensor softened the wall colours of the bedroom from neutral ivory to erotic sunset pink. He wished he'd changed the sheets, but at least they were dry.

He heard the shower, and while wrenching off his clothes, he couldn't resist admiring Kat through the frosted-glass. Any reservations he might have had dissolved with the sight of peachy curves, shimmering to the delicate off-key singing. Remembering just in time, he sprayed his hairy bits with a bay rum deodorant, rushed round the bedroom to hide any incriminating letdowns, and dived into bed. He glanced under the sheet at himself. He worked hard at the zoo playing with chimps and so had no flab to speak of. He threw off the sheet.

Kat came in wearing a small blue towel.

"Where's my dressing gown and Black Night perfume spray? Have you been tidying, lover?"

"That's right, sugar, don't bother drying, come here."

His eyes followed the soft edge of the towel falling as if in one-tenth gravity. The same physics, or the beer he'd been drinking, appeared to make her breasts more fulsome yet buoyant and her waist slimmer. He'd heard that, at forty, women either go to pieces or just get going. They shared the same birthday week, and he hoped premature excitement didn't spoil the occasion. Liquid gold from a new bedroom plasma light reflected off her glistening curves.

"My God, Kat, I'd forgotten how lovely you are."

"Yeah, right. Just make sure you last."

Slower now, they relaxed into their favourite sixty-nine with mutual moaning. Minutes passed in controlled gratification until Lester's tongue became too fatigued to continue.

He used it to utter, "On your back, sugar, you must be tired."

"Sod off. I may be tired and my head keeps buzzing, but I know what I like. You lie on your back. That's a good boy."

Bouncing breasts brushed his face as his hands groped moist, round buttocks. Bliss.

The bed helped. Not a waterbed but it had sensuous characteristics. Clever sensors made the necessary predicted adjustments. All the undulating and counterpoint enhanced lovemaking. All the slurping and gurgling came from them, along with gasps, sighs, and escaped squeals.

He drew up his knees to affect bounce assist, working through mental gymnastics to both relish the experience, yet think of a game of cricket to prolong it. The cricket lost, but in their own chorus of gasps, they both climaxed together.

AN IRRITATING BELL DREW HIM BACK FROM SLEEP. He could have ignored it but then the smoke alarm would have kicked in.

"I'd better finish preparing the dinner. You look more gorgeous than when we were married, Kat."

"What are you on about?" Her eyes remained closed.

"I like the new flamenco dancer look."

"No, I mean you said when we *were* married."

"Well?"

"Lester, I'm tired and just done a turn. My head's been playing up for days even before jet-lagging. Stop pissing about and tell me what you mean."

"You do remember we got a fast-track divorce last week?"

"What? I know I was going to get rid of you. I lost my airline tickets, all sorts of stuff and so have other people over there. Chaos. Just a minute—you just had me!"

"We're both free agents, love. Maybe you should move back in while you get better."

LESTER PASSED THROUGH THE SECURITY SCREEN at the zoo's staff entrance. It hurt his head but then it often did. He stifled another snigger as he recalled rogering his divorced wife the previous night. She even made him breakfast. Maybe he should be more bothered, but he had to monkey around.

The staff canteen was louder than usual. Working with the world's more exotic creatures compelled humans to be more garrulous when together: compensating for the lack of human contact during the day. As with pet owners, the keepers tended to acquire certain characteristics of the animals for which they were responsible. A small price for mutual dedication.

By lunchtime, Lester's head resumed normal service and he relaxed into his work. Brian, the oldest chimpanzee and father of several others, pulled at Lester's hair, even though it didn't host lice, until leaving the enclosure. Although sociable, chimpanzees distrusted most humans, even keepers, but Lester knew familiarity made him a chimpanzee Number Two. They fed and cuddled him. Charles, the head keeper, quipped that Lester and the chimps had a meeting of minds.

Lunchtime bananas for the chimps reminded him to feed himself, so he laughed his I'll-be-back to Brian then strolled to the staff canteen. He bought pie and chips and sat with Charles. Lester munched while staring through one-way Plexiglas at the well-kept gardens, watching the overhead monorail treating visitors to a cage-free environment for the elephants and giraffes. He didn't take his eyes off the scene when Charles spoke.

"Luke says he saw your Katherina at the airport yesterday. Is she all right?"

Lester struggled to answer. A thought linked to his ex-wife raced along a neuron. The impulse fired a synapse triggering other neurons that when linked allowed Lester to remember incidents, odours, names, and a myriad of life's history. Every day, some impulses faltered and reached a dead end where the myelin sheaths around the neurons were eroded by alcohol, disease, or genetic wiring faults. The electrical currents in his brain, carrying memory, suffered shortcuts, travelled the wrong way, making him forget a can of sardines on a think-only shopping list. So the knot of neurons responsible for knowing about his divorce and last night's frolics remained in his brain but had been cut off. The virus had erected no-go signs in his head.

"She's okay."

Tommy, the catering manager, brought his own burger and sat with them. "You've seen Katherina, then?" He looked puzzled.

"Why shouldn't I?"

"Hey, Lester, don't get mad. It's just you said you were relieved to have divorced her."

Coloured lights sparked in his head. Divorce? Hadn't he said something similar?

WEDNESDAY 22 APRIL 2015

The code didn't open the staff door at the zoo. It buzzed back at him making Lester grit his already gnashing teeth until a voice-activated intercom asked him for his identity.

"You know who I am, Eddie. Just open the fucking gate."

"It looks like you, Lester, but where's the funny one-liner?"

"I'll give you one when I see you. Have you changed the code?"

"Not since last week. What did you punch in?"

"Four nine three six."

"Bloody hell, Lester, that's last month. Try six two two three, and smile or it won't open."

He wrote it on an envelope he found in his pocket. Lester's vision blurred as he changed into his work clothes. He shook his head but that brought on a dull headache. He'd boasted about his excellent health. A one-hundred percent attendance record. Wow, but today, he crashed into a chair in the staff canteen, sending a coffee across the table into Charles' lap.

"Hey, Lester, watch my paternal potential with that hot drink!"

"I'm doing society a favour to stop more clones of you running around." Others shut up in shock. Charles was easy going but had the respect of his staff.

"You're due some holiday leave, Lester. Take a break. Those chimps are getting to you."

Lester, elbows on the table, rubbed his head. He needed to do something for one of the chimpanzees in his care. The more he tried to remember, the sharper the pain stabbed his brain. He shouted bugger off to everyone, hung his head, and left.

He walked an hour into Chester's city centre. Alongside the River Dee, he rented a boat, rowed upstream into the Cheshire countryside way beyond his hour's hire period and idled the day away in a fuzz.

THURSDAY 23 APRIL 2015

A quieter man, Lester arrived back at the staff entrance the next day. He found the envelope in his pocket and punched in the code.

He recognised old Brian and stroked his black and grey hairs, sharing affection. He looked at Isabella, another chimp, sat in the corner of the same enclosure, and an emotion tugged at him but in vain. Lester read her information board, which told him she'd come from London Zoo. He assumed some other keeper was responsible for her welfare, medication and emotional needs.

ISABELLA WATCHED LESTER WITH BRIAN and waited for some personal attention but didn't get it. Every day, he cuddled her. Every day, he gave her extra titbits. Every day, he inserted something sharp in her arm. Every day, he made his utterances. He had stopped. Tears rolled down her cheeks.

TWENTY MILES AWAY a large articulated truck stood idle next to a refrigerated warehouse. A loader should have driven his forklift, whistling while filling the truck each week with green bananas, apples, and bags of ground nuts. He hadn't turned up. Neither had the office girl, whose job was to oblige the orders to be fulfilled and relief loaders to be ordered. The driver hadn't arrived. The ingredients of the hungry animals' a la carte menu started to rot.

CHAPTER 11

Wednesday 22 April 2015:
London. Six days after the amnesia infection started. Many US inhabitants have lost forty-five weeks of memory and many in other countries have started to lose theirs.

RYDER RAISED HIS VOICE TO EMPHASISE THE URGENCY. "We shouldn't be going to work, Teresa."

"I'm going to my biology lab. You've used your media-edutainment imagination on the amnesia problem in the States. I've experiments running and my lab techs need guidance. If you're right and we should head for the hills, I have to wind things down and collect essentials."

"Make this the last time. It's always possible someone there is infected, even the dean, who I need to see."

RYDER DROVE THEM BOTH TO THE UNIVERSITY and was relieved to see only a handful of students and staff. His stomach tensed when he saw the dean in Teresa's lab.

"Hello, Teresa, and this must be your young man." Maurice Dover smiled. Ryder flashed teeth at him. It would have been the clever thing to do since Maurice tugged Teresa's department's purse strings. Ryder's extra inches allowed the lab's neon lights to reflect off Maurice's bald head and polished cheeks.

"Hi, Maurice, sacked anyone today?" Teresa said, to Ryder's surprise.

"You'd be the first to know," he said, picking up a ten-inch alloy thermistor off a trolley and twiddling it in his fingers. He probably didn't know it was an anal thermometer. "Ryder, you left me an odd message, yesterday. 'Be here at eleven.'"

Ryder, red-faced from knowing he was to tell this influential man about a difficult-to-believe scenario, had his hand shaken as if it was an old village pump.

"Maurice, I—*we*—need a huge favour of you."

"I'm not withdrawing your invitation to the May Garden Party. What, bigger than that?"

"We need to speak to your close friend, Brendon Stone. It's so urgent."

"Of national importance?"

"Global."

"Then why stop at Brendon, he's merely the prime minister? I'm on nodding terms with Altrecht Finkner, the UNO General Secretary."

"Brendon is here in town, Finkner is in Malawi, and what we need to ask of the PM affects the UK, Europe first. Oh, I don't know. It's likely to be too late anyway."

"Try me, Ryder. But you know I can't get Brendon to push open a window in his schedule without good reason, even for me."

Teresa spoke up at last. "Ryder thinks the Americans have brought an alien virus from space, and it's spreading fast. We thought the government should know and possibly shut down travel out of the States."

Maurice took a step back. "Whoa. I need evidence. You both have integrity, so I'll contact him. Set something up. Have you contacted the NIPB?"

Teresa threw up her hands in a show of exasperation. "I tried to but all I got was their answer-phone saying, 'National Immunology Protection Board—if we're not answering, we might be dead, but leave a message anyway.'"

"Well, their joking aside, they'll need to be involved with any isolation procedures."

Ryder raised a finger. "I sent them a scrambled-code query about it with some footage from NASA a couple of days ago. No response."

"You didn't tell me." Teresa frowned then reddened.

Maurice rubbed the thermometer like Aladdin's lamp. "Perhaps their loony answer-phone message is a cover. They could be onto it already and Brendon already knows." Ryder had now met a fly-in-the-face-of-danger optimist.

Maurice walked over to a corner of the lab, nattering into his mobile phone. Teresa glowered at Ryder who shrugged back. He was in trouble, again.

Maurice turned from his phone. "Three p.m. with the PM. At the Foreign Office, not Number 10."

"Did he say he already knew about it?" Ryder asked.

"Not as such, but Brendon didn't sound shocked. He was in a meeting with the US Ambassador who'd flown in from the States this morning. What?...Why are you looking at each other like that?"

"I AM NOT GOING YET." Ryder responded to Teresa's tearful pleas for them to run from all the problems and not go to see the government now that ARIA was in the city. "Let's try the NIPB once more."

Teresa used a computer in the lab and discovered that a request had gone to the NIPB counterpart in the US for a twenty-four-hour hold on external travel.

"That'll help," she said, brightening.

Ryder smiled at the limited progress. He picked up the temperature probe Maurice had then remembered what it was for and put it down. He coughed then said, "Okay, so diffusion of ARIA by air can be slowed down, but how can it be policed? Even if all the major ports and airports were closed, thousands travel to Mexico and Canada—small boats, you name it. And we're assuming the people doing the enforcing remember their orders."

Teresa placed a hand on Ryder's arm. "I know where we can go."

CHAPTER 12

Thursday 23 April 2015:
Transatlantic flight New York (LaGuardia) to London.

THE DREAMLINER 7E7 cruised so sweetly, co-pilot Linus Bingham had to keep reminding himself they were travelling at 600 miles per hour, six miles above the Atlantic and that he and Captain Gilmore Drayton held the lives of 250 passengers at his fingertips hovering over touch-sensitive controls. The airplane didn't need pilots at all. The damn thing preferred to use its own computers and navigation system from take off to landing. Even to taking emergency re-routing around violent weather systems. Engineering didn't need the human touch. Even the cabin crew had less to do since health and safety regulations and price wars ruled out hot meals and drinks.

Linus admired the sky and sipped illicit hot coffee. The sun, setting behind the plane, sent illuminated ripples under the highest of the ice crystals making up the cirrostratus in front. He'd find no birds at this height, but he saw another airplane spew out its condensation trail, a long, elegant river of ice, pink with the low sun, and the crystals already drifting down like lace curtains.

"Isn't this the cushiest of jobs, Gilmore? We take over from auto when we feel the need to practice, but otherwise, we're here only to make passengers feel safe."

"I'm not worried, Linus. If they want to retire me, let them, as long as the pension lets me go to the Hawaiian beachside homestead I've invested in."

Linus glanced at the captain's neat-but-grey beard. "Cap'n, I've not heard you look forward to ending your flying career before. You ill?"

"Hell, you're right. I don't know what came over me. I've had a funny head all day. Got a feeling that LaGuardia Airport has sick-building syndrome."

"I know what you mean. Do you want to have a lie down for ten? I'll let you know if any gremlins try to take over."

"I'm not tired. Just can't wait to get to...Paris."

"Paris? When's that then, Gilmore? I thought you were booked to fly the return trip tomorrow."

The captain, confused, tapped the flight schedule.

"Of course, Heathrow. You know, Linus, maybe I will take a nap. I should wake up as sharp as this Dreamliner's nose."

LINUS LOOKED CONCERNED for the pilot but also for himself. Joking aside, he'd never been affected by the constant drone and vibration of jet engines. At thirty-three, twenty years the junior of the captain, the stresses in the job didn't get to him in the same way. Maybe his blood pressure and pulse rate leapt when taking off and landing, but not as much as the worry of his wife finding out about Hazel Draper. How could any red-blooded man resist her? She wouldn't win beauty contests, but she'd win any contest for Miss Lust-After. Her sleek, long, black hair, full, sensuous airline-pink lips, and deep, come-to-bed eyes drew out Linus's primitive urges. And she knew it.

He pressed the buzzer, calling for her.

Closing the cockpit door behind her, she looked around.

"Hey, this is a bit much; throwing the captain overboard just to grab some nooky with me."

"Yeah, I gagged and tied him up in the officers' rest room. Now come and sit on the co-pilot's lap and loosen some clothing, you minx."

"I don't think your wife would approve. In any case, we have a problem with some of the passengers."

"Not again. Another riot over wrong cheese in the sandwiches?"

"If only. Several of them acted confused when they boarded then one, a Mr Cowley, insisted we take him off because he had a funeral to go to upstate."

"You've dealt with weirder situations..."

"But his business partner with him said he went to the funeral last week. Others are missing a lot more of their memories and don't remember booking this flight. I wish I hadn't come on it now."

"Well, you are allowed to give difficult passengers sedatives. Get the other cabin crew to help you; the sedative in the sweets should help them sleep off the rest of the flight."

"Okay. Linus, what's going on? The crew aren't so hot either. No jokes."

"I suppose I'd better put my smart hat on and do a captain-like reassurance tour then."

"Excuse me, you are not supposed to leave the cockpit unattended even if you don't do anything useful all flight."

"It'll be all right for a few minutes. We are on autopilot and Gilmore's only having a brief nap behind the curtain there."

LINUS HADN'T ANTICIPATED the ugliness of passengers when they were confused. One red-faced bully of a woman insisted they continue their flight to Chicago even after he'd explained their schedule. In desperation, Hazel sought his help to stop an old man from repeat-swallowing beta-blockers. Linus took the old man's tablets off him and told Hazel to lock them up until they landed. The old chap's wife just muttered away in Russian.

A distraught mother hit him with a rolled up in-flight magazine because it must be his fault that her two-year-old son had forgotten how to talk sense. He didn't help the situation by pointing out her boy had teenaged before his time. Linus hadn't welcomed the sanctuary element of the cockpit so much.

He should wake the captain and let him placate the passengers. Gilmore had that mature ship's captain air of comfort and experience that quelled any brewing unrest. First, he'd like to check on their progress, see what near misses they might have had. Now, where were they going?

He decided to fly the Dreamliner on manual for a few minutes. He leant forward to flip off the autopilot. It wasn't there. He sat back, reddening, feeling his face heat from his neck upwards. There on the control panel, a green-lit LED shone at him. Of course some were proximity-sensor operated these days. He shook his head. Fancy thinking he was back in the older 747s.

The aircraft belonged to him as he took control. She handled beautifully. Even on manual, most of the adjustments depended on computerised actuators and relays. He couldn't crash this bird into another aircraft, mountain, or office block. A lot of failsafe engineering would have to be disabled for a pilot to have complete control these days.

A few more slow deviations to port and starboard, not so much to spill the ever-higher-percent alcohol drinks no doubt being served behind him but enough to satisfy Linus he could fly. As long as he stayed in the air.

IT WAS CLEAR GILMORE DID NOT WANT TO WAKE UP even though Linus shook his shoulder.

"Ah, you've caught me red-handed. Just a few hops in a crop sprayer near Sacramento."

"Captain, I need you awake."

Gilmore continued talking in his sleep. "What, me?" followed by a soft laugh.

"I envy your bliss of ignorance, Cap'n, but please wake up." Linus, stood for another moment before resorting to using a cup of iced water. Through his fuzzy headache, he listened to the drone of the aircraft, some muffled shouting, and the secondary cabin door slamming. He'd locked the security door to the cockpit. He wished it would all go away.

"Captain...Captain...Gilmore, I need you awake now. Ah, there you are. Do you feel better now? Only I could use another brain to deal with some pesky passengers."

"I'm all right, er, Lin...Linton. Give me a few moments to clear my head." His half-open eyes betrayed his confused state.

"Captain, we have a problem."

"Go on then, L—er, I'm sorry, what's your name?"

"Linus Bingham, your co-pilot. What's your surname, sir, if you don't mind me asking?"

"What? Don't you know who I am?"

"Yes, of course, Captain, but weird things are happening and—"

"I am Gilmore Drayton. Get it?"

"Relieved to hear it. You have no idea the madness going on, Captain Drayton. Can I ask another question?"

"Hurry up then, man, we have a plane to fly."

"Okay. Where are we flying to?"

The captain evil-eyed the co-pilot long enough for another ten miles of the Atlantic to pass beneath them.

"Damn you."

"You are not on your own, Gilmore. That's why I woke you. At least half the passengers don't understand why they're flying at all. I'm your co-pilot Linus. We are on schedule to Heathrow. I had to check to remind myself."

"Linus, I have no memory of you. Nor coming on board."

The co-pilot put a hand to his head. "You aren't the only crazy bastard on board, sir, if you excuse me."

The captain found a cup of cold coffee and drained it. "Have we any Pro-Plus?"

A knock and the cabin door admitted Hazel, after Linus tapped a key. Some strands of hair loosened from their earlier tight creation, Hazel's eyes fear-widened.

"Captain, they want you to turn back."

Gilmore staggered from such a shocking revelation, and the plane chose that moment to skid over some turbulence. "I've never heard of such a thing."

Hazel modified her news. "Not all of them, sir. But most have their homes back in the States rather than Europe. I know it sounds far-fetched but hardly anyone remembers why they're flying at all.

They assume they are on holiday or visiting old family, a few might be on business, but only a handful are sure why and where they are going."

"That's interesting," Linus said. "In these situations, it is the anomalies that give clues to the big picture."

Hazel looked at him with surprise. "You've met this situation before then?"

"Ah, not that I remember."

Hazel and Gilmore looked at each other before she said, "I was referring to those who have diaries, NoteComs. Having said that, I suppose it might be worthwhile asking if any of the 250 passengers are definitely not affected. Are we turning back?"

"Certainly not," said Captain Drayton. "To break from a logged flight plan needs all kinds of permissions from air traffic control."

Linus, hands gripped on the control stick, spoke up. "Gilmore, I have a feeling this computerised aluminium tube won't let us do a one-eighty on its pre-programmed course. Not that I'm in agreement with turning round."

"This whole situation is terrible," the captain said, collapsing into his plush pilot's chair.

"Hey, Gilmore, keep it together."

"We should inform the authorities we have a medical emergency," Gilmore said.

"Maybe and maybe not." But before Linus could explain, the cockpit door received a battering.

Hazel opened it before the two men could stop her.

A group of irate passengers shouldered each other and shouted.

The captain attempted wild-animal control.

"We want to go back home," bawled a beefy, grey-suited passenger, as if he led the rest.

"Home is in Europe for some passengers," Captain Drayton said, keeping calm. Linus was impressed.

"They want to go back to New York too." The lumberjack in a suit looked beyond reason. "I'll make sure of that."

"Shall we sit down in the premier suite so I can lay out the options?" said the captain.

"No. Just fucking turn this crate around or I will," said the huge man.

"Reassuring though it is that a passenger can fly this complex Dreamliner, Mr...?"

"Rogers, not that my name is important."

"Mr Rogers, if we don't get clearance for altered flight plans and landing rights, we could—"

"They're not going to shoot us down."

"I am glad you have had personal assurance of that, Mr Rogers. You've not heard of the Home Defence Anti-Hijack Strategy then? Since 9-11, if we attempt to enter US air space without permission, we certainly will be shot out of the sky."

With that, the crowd hushed but not for long. A more articulate, pushy passenger with a shock of red hair tried again.

"Then get your frigging permission." A chorus of yeses followed.

"You tell them, Julia," said another passenger.

"Or we'll force you to turn and we'll land in the Caribbean," said Rogers, regaining dominance. But a small voice dissented behind the baying crowd.

"Some of us want to go to London." The woman then stood, but a large man rose from the seat behind and brought both hands clenched together on her head. She crumpled.

Gilmore tried to step forward "Hey, that's enough of—"

"You saw a glimpse of the future, Captain," sneered Rogers. Hazel pulled at him to edge back to the cockpit door.

"I'm worried about the cabin staff, sir."

"Rogers, where are the flight attendants?"

"You look after us, Captain, and we'll look after them."

"Who the hell do you think you are?" Gilmore's voice belied the weakness in his position. Linus could see him shaking, but he continued, "What's the point, Rogers, in landing anywhere in the world...as a criminal? And the rest of you would be accomplices." His speech slowed them. He turned and whispered to Linus, "How far are we out?"

Linus checked the console. "Point of no return coming up in five, Captain."

He thought he'd said it too hushed for Rogers to hear.

Rogers roared, angry with the assumption that the Captain had played them for suckers with delaying tactics. To the shouts of "No!" from Gilmore, the mob surged forward. Gilmore didn't have a chance to get out of the way before Rogers used a fire-extinguisher to dent his head. Linus was pushed into the pilot's seat, too shocked to speak, and then he passed out.

CHAPTER 13

Thursday 23 April 2015:
Flying over the Atlantic.

ROGERS STOOD LOOKING AT THE CONSOLE, puzzled at the relative lack of buttons and instruments. He'd always seen the airplane movies where the number of dials rose in direct proportion to years passing.

"Now what?" Julia said to Rogers, having pushed Hazel back out into the main cabin.

"This is going to be easier than I thought," he answered as he pointed to the digital compass and the autopilot sensor. They pulled the limp Linus out of the pilot's seat and dumped him in the co-pilot's chair. Rogers glanced at the captain, alive or dead on the floor. Rogers settled in the chair and flexed his large hands.

"Are you sure about this?" Julia asked, at last demonstrating worry.

"You kidding? It's sure now or never."

He jabbed at the autopilot's green-lit rectangle, not knowing it only needed the heat from his finger rather than be broken by a hard poke. The light turned red and the plane lurched four degrees to the left.

Rogers grabbed the half-moon joystick and turned it clockwise 45 degrees. The Dreamliner yawed right and dipped its nose. Panicking, he yanked the stick-wheel back, but too much. The plane dipped its nose more and started a roll. The engines screamed, matched by the passengers who fell forward into the cockpit, which was crowded when it contained four well-behaved crew.

"Get the fuck back, you morons," Rogers yelled, but they were now at such a steep angle, they couldn't. Anything not strapped down—and little was—joined him at the console. Crockery, clipboards, comatose co-pilot, and frantic, struggling people.

"Look what you've done," screamed Julia, her red hair flying.

"It's not me, it's you guys piling too far in front." He knew the error lay with him, but no one heard above the cacophony of engine and human howling.

Clever programming decided the time had come to rescue the stupid humans and overrode the manual operation by kicking in the autopilot. The plane pulled out of its gyrating dive and levelled off, found the original flight plan instructions, and by degrees, resumed the predestined altitude and direction.

Rogers, discovering he must have lost a litre of perspiration and urine to add to that of the others, grunted. "There, told you I could fly this bird."

After a prolonged silence, Julia, small but assertive to the point of aggression, said, "You nearly killed us, you fucking ass." Rogers swiped his large arm round and knocked her to the floor.

Another passenger pushed his way forward. Blood dripped from a gash on his forehead. "I'm going to sue this airline for so many bucks, my bank manager will have a heart attack. Hey, Rogers, look at the compass, we're still heading the wrong way."

"You think I don't know that? It's the damn autopilot. Something must have knocked it back. I'm thinking of pulling its wires but can't see how to get this panel off."

Julia sat up from the floor, rubbing her head. "I don't think we should be ripping the innards out of this plane, or we'll be taking the shortcut down again."

"What the fuck do you suggest then? The co-pilot is out of it and the captain's a gibbering wreck, though we might pull him round if we sit on one of his flight attendants."

Julia struggled to her feet. "Let's ask around. There's bound to be a flyer among the passengers. If I'd have known, I would have signed up for a flying module instead of learning to be a biology technician."

One of Rogers' acquaintances brought forward a scared, tall man. Navy blue suit trousers, white open-collared shirt, and shiny black brogues—the apparel of confidence misrepresenting the truth.

"I hear you're a pilot. Name?" Rogers said, scrutinising the man.

"Findley. I'm not exp—"

Rogers had stopped listening, because he'd switched to wondering at how easy it was for him to have slipped into this masterful role. He ran a large business in the Bronx importing shirts. Something had gone wrong. It must have, because his electronic diary told him he had a meeting tomorrow with his backers in London. He couldn't remember what the problem was. Better to go back and sort it. His head hurt, and he had to get this damn plane turned around.

"Right, Findley, you really a pilot?"

"I've not flown one of these Dreamliners."

"Boeings, though?"

"Sure, but this bird is totally different."

"Listen, Findley, I managed to fly it a bit—"

"We all noticed."

"Yeah, well. We need an experienced pilot who won't plunge us into the Atlantic when turning it round."

"I don't want to turn round. My fam—I, want to go on to London."

"I don't give a shit about what a few Brits like you think. We're heading back to America where we need to be with our families."

"Or else what? Crash-land in the sea? Without authority, we might get shot out of the sky as suspected terrorists."

"Naw, the captain tried us on that one, but it won't wash."

"Well, put him back in the driving seat, because I am not helping."

Rogers' assistant smacked Findley across his head from behind. His fingers caught the pilot's nose, which bled profusely.

"Nice one, Gav, now find out where his family are seated and sit on them." The big man turned to the cries of Findley.

"Okay, okay, just leave my family alone."

"Come over here." Rogers took the conscript to the captain's seat and pushed him into it. Linus was dragged out of the co-pilot's chair and dumped on the floor next to the captain. Rogers sat in the co-pilot's chair while fellow mutineers crowded round behind them, not being too careful about trampling the two on the floor.

Findley volunteered his observations. "I've seen this console on a training mock-up. Altitude ten thousand metres; speed point eight five mach; we have eighty-seven tons of fuel; autopilot engaged. What's this? Ah, the transponder indicator is on."

"Just a minute. That means we can be tracked," Rogers said. "Turn it off."

"All right. Oh, that's neat, proximity sensors. There's the HHS."

"Just hang on there," Julia said. "He was too quick to agree to turning off the transponder. Do you think that its being off would set some air-traffic control buzzer going?"

Findley wriggled. "They would definitely see us doing a U-turn if I left it on."

Rogers struggled to work out if Findley was pulling a fast one. "Could be a bluff, turn it back on."

"Okay."

"Or a double-bluff." Rogers' head upped its internal buzzing volume. "Off."

Findley shrugged and touched it off again.

Julia pointed at a display indicator. "What's that HHS you mentioned?"

"Nothing. Just the Heading Hold Selector."

Rogers nodded too fast for his headache. "It's lit green, so it was on when I turned the plane and it made it come back."

"Could be. Shall I turn it off?"

"Yes, or should it be no? Damn you, Findley. Listen, if you want your folks to come through this, you'd better behave yourself."

"All right. Let us suppose I successfully turn us round, and then things go wrong again. If I have to make adjustments and we are not going in the right direction, you have to understand, yes?"

Rogers knuckled his own head. "I believe you can fly this plane back to America, so no tricks, Findley. Now the autopilot is off and that switch keeping the heading on hold is off, so make the turn."

"I see we are heading eighty-three," said Findley, keeping as calm as a pilot could be with his family held hostage.

Rogers said, "That's eighty-three east so we need eighty-three west."

"Stupid," Julia said. "It's...seventeen west, no, it's..."

"You are thinking of two-six-three if you want to head in the exact opposite direction of where we are going now. But not necessarily if you want to head for LaGuardia."

"I get it, wind direction differences?" said Rogers. "It doesn't matter which airport as long as it's American."

"Well that's no help, dummy," Julia said. "The plane can't just head west for America, it needs to know exactly which airport."

"She's right," added Findley, glancing up at both. "Boston's Logan Airport is probably the closest US airport that can handle this plane."

"Go there then. How do we find out the direction?" Rogers hated having to rely on others.

"This button activates the enATIS HUD."

"Whoa, what the hell is all that about? I don't trust–"

"It is the enhanced Automatic Terminal Information Service, and we'll see it on the head-up display, see? Now, if I punch in BOS, which is Logan Airport's international call sign, the Dreamliner will not only head for it but will make all the necessary adjustments and even land the plane for us."

"Well, do it," Rogers said.

"Hang on." Julia said. Rogers noticed her forehead freckles disappearing into creases. "He's done this all too easy. I bet although the plane could land us there, we would be shot out the sky before we reached the coastline. They've already done it twice to planes they weren't sure of."

"May I make another suggestion?" Findley said.

Rogers gritted his teeth. "What now?"

"How about I ask permission to turn. That way it raises no suspicion."

"Surely they'd need a damn good reason."

Julia joined in, "How about mechanical failure?"

Findley stayed quiet but Rogers noticed.

"Why wouldn't that work, Findley?"

"Well...we are nearer airfields in front than behind us. We could declare a medical emergency for a passenger for whom his only hope is a US specialist."

"Oh yes." Rogers was relieved to hear the perfect solution.

Julia cuffed Findley over the back of the head. "They'd never fall for that. Too far-fetched, and you know they'd interpret it as evidence of something else wrong up here."

"Yeah," said Rogers, "let's forget about telling them anything. Make the fucking turn."

"All right, here we go."

Findley punched in BOS on the enATIS. The plane made a gentle clockwise turn, compensating with extra throttle and semi-assist flap control to maintain altitude. Even Rogers was impressed.

980 MILES AWAY, Johnson, a bored USAF administrative clerk, peeved at having to do compulsory overtime, sat bolt upright. All Atlantic air-traffic had their transponders and other transmitting devices intercepted at Lajes Communications Centre in the Azores air base run together by the US and Portugal. Closer to Europe than America but as central to mid-Atlantic as you can find dry land. Time to scramble interceptors, if something nasty travelled in any direction over sea. Most aircraft had their several "black boxes" transmit data in real time; computers in Lajes picked it up, analysed it, and then either archived, acted, or slipped into watch-this-space. A few engineers and a select pilot-group were privy to the installation of covert cams with microphones dotted through new international planes. One such cam hid in the console panel above the windshield. The image of the Dreamliner's captain being battered and the mutinous melee zipped to Lajes and brought Johnson to his feet.

Three events occurred simultaneously: the circus on the Dreamliner; a message from a European Immune Protection Group relaying information from the UK Government disallowing landing rights to any aircraft or shipping from North America unless they've passed their point of no return; and a radio message he could see being received on the plane.

"Heathrow to Dreamliner, flight VGE 223, your transponder is faulty. Over."

Johnson called his commander.

"What is it?" The burly man finished off a croissant.

"This Dreamliner from the States, sir. Originally a sensor alerted me to the cockpit door being open for over twenty minutes. As you know, they have to keep it locked between every movement in and out, so it meant a problem. Then the cam showed fighting and a change of control. The passengers have taken over the cockpit and are turning the plane round. Heathrow are asking for details. Oh, and we've had a communiqué banning in-bound to the UK. sir."

"Succinctly put, Johnson. I'll buzz security at Heathrow."

Johnson continued looking at the screen where Rogers, Julia, and Findley were locked in argument. Rogers in particular had the reddest complexion Johnson had seen on a monitor.

"SEE? NOW CAN THEY STOP US, FINDLEY? What can they do?" said Rogers to his conscripted pilot.

"There's a lot of clever stuff on aircraft like this, Rogers. Even decades ago, planes didn't really need anyone in the cockpit: it could all happen by computer, even remotely. I suppose, in extreme situations, they could take control of this plane and fly it wherever they want."

"Even with us in the cockpit, trying to stop them?"

"Oh, I expect so. They can probably isolate the entire console in here. We'd just be passengers with a front-window view."

Julia spoke up. "They haven't though, have they? Look, we are still heading for Boston."

"Yeah," said Rogers. "With the transponder turned off, can they still locate us? Surely radar is too far away."

"From the UK and North America, we are out of normal radar range. But they can find us with other methods if they've a mind to. Black boxes transmit data up to satellite relays; they don't wait for a crash. Come to think about it, there was little point in turning off the transponder, they probably know we've turned. What do you want me to do?"

"Shut up for a fucking minute while I think," Rogers said.

"I think, in the light of what Findley has at last decided to tell us, we should ask permission to return. Pretend we have some emergency—play it by ear," Julia said while she rubbed her temple as if trying to make a hole to let a demon out.

"Okay, do it."

JOHNSON SUCKED A PENCIL while watching the screens in front of him, knowing the outcome of the forthcoming radio call. The Dreamliner passengers and crew were under strain, but what was the precise problem? The original captain had a struggle remembering details of the flight, and the flight attendant reported passengers having similar problems. Okay, he was no medic, but he'd never heard of a group of people losing memory like that. Maybe it was one of those mass-hysteria events. And what was London talking about? They've had refusals for landing permissions before but always on terrorist alerts not medical. Maybe they knew what was happening on the plane. Maybe it was more than the plane.

With that thought, he punched a single button to call his parents in Idaho.

"Hi, Pop, how ya doing?"

"That you, Billy? Can't see so well these days. Bren, get my glasses, I can't see this view screen proper."

"Pop, it's me, Billy. You folks okay?"

"Talk to your mother. I can't understand these contraptions. Bren, it might be Billy, Lord knows."

"That you, Billy-boy?"

"Yes, Mom. Turn your head so yous can see the view screen, unless you've grown eyes through your ears. Heh heh."

"What's that? You our Billy-boy?"

"Yes, Mom. I rang to check on yous two?"

"Where are you, Billy-boy? Your supper from last night's still on the table. You've been out all night again with Bernie?"

"Christ, Mom, Bernie left for New Mexico last year and I'm in the Air Force, remember?"

"What's that, Billy-boy, the Air Force? Hey, Pop, our Billy-boy's a pilot. Did you know that?"

"No, Mom, I'm a clerk. Say, has Aunt Chrissie's problem gotten to you folks?"

"I dunno, son. Your mom and pop aren't feeling too good. When you come home, bring some fresh milk from the store."

"Jeez, Mom, I'm not due home for another month."

"A month? Stop fooling, Billy-boy. You're not too old to get walloped."

"I am, Mom, I really am. I'll get home as soon as. Promise. Bye, Pop, bye, Mom."

He waited, but they didn't return his farewells, just wandered off out of camera sight. He sought his commander.

"Sir, I need compassionate leave. My folks aren't well."

"Johnson, much that I have the utmost respect for your folks, you are the fifth one in the last two days to make such a request. That's why you, and me, are on double shift. There's a bug sweeping the States, but consider this: it isn't here, is it?"

"That might be a good point, sir, but I think my folks have got Alzheimer's or something like it and need urgent help."

"Yup, that's what the others said, but Alzheimer's ain't infectious, so rule it out. Anyway, Johnson, I can't let you go until next week when replacements arrive. Assuming they do."

"Haven't you got any folks stateside, sir?" Johnson fidgeted, on edge with the double whammy of having his parents ill and not being able to leave the base. Even if he ran off, where was he? On a small island in the Azores, miles from anywhere. The only airplanes were under USAF and Portuguese control. He had no choice but to go along with his commander and hope for the best.

"Sure I have, Johnson. A mother and sister in Vermont. They chatted normally yesterday. What's happening to that Dreamliner?"

"Given the clearance to go to Boston, but..."

"I know. If Europe is worried they're bringing an infectious disease, then why does the US want them, and what about the other twenty-odd flights on their way?"

"I guess the flights already closer to their European destinations will have to land and be quarantined, but are there facilities at Boston?"

"I doubt they'll be allowed to land. Isolation airfields dot the East coast for quarantine purposes. Keep monitoring them and any other alerts from the US."

ROGERS AND JULIA JIGGED A RIDICULOUS DANCE in the too-tiny cockpit as Findley looked glum. His conviction that air traffic would never have allowed them to turn without good cause had given him false hope. Yesterday—he thought—he'd been scared stiff for his family after seeing colleagues in the airline he worked for at Kennedy lose their memory. Local radio ran jokes about it, but his father died last year with complications including Alzheimer's. A cold worm slithered down his back as he recalled the day his father died in utter confusion. Findley hadn't lost his memory. No more than everyone else forgets the odd bunch of keys.

"Can I go back to my family now?"

"I suppose so," Rogers said, but Julia disagreed.

"There might be trouble, yet. Let one of his brats come up for a few seconds so he can see they're still kicking."

"Yeah. Anyway, Findley, you're driving, aren't you?"

"Not really. Like I said, air traffic could fly this plane from the other side of the world."

Julia frowned. "Any changes you can tell?"

Findley gave her a wry laugh, glanced at the console and then joined her in frowning, "It isn't going to Boston anymore."

Rogers went apoplectic. "The frigging liars. They said we could return to the States."

"We are," said Findley. "But not Boston. The enATIS indicates CYAW, but I've no idea what or where that is."

"You've thirty seconds to find out," shouted Rogers, baring yellow teeth. Findley reeled back at the stench of his beery breath.

"Will five seconds do?" he said as he tapped CYAW into the console. It returned HALIFAX SHEARWATER.

"But that's not even America," shouted Rogers.

"Canada is counted as being in North America," said Findley, whose sarcasm was rewarded by Rogers hitting him on the head.

"I know about Shearwater," said another passenger looking aghast at Findley picking himself off the floor. "It's not used, except by coastguards, because it's always fogged in. The main Halifax International Airport is fifteen miles up the road."

"Did you know this, Findley?" Rogers said.

"No. Look, Rogers, I didn't know we were being diverted until you did. Do you think I've done it? God, man, I want to go to London."

"I don't trust you, Findley. Why would they want us to go to the back of beyond instead of Boston?"

"It's obvious," said Findley, hoping his frankness wasn't going to get him into more trouble. "They want to quarantine the plane and all of us."

"But if it is foggy there..."

"Doesn't matter anymore," Findley said. "They can land this plane in fog in the middle of the night with no lights. The only weather problem would be high wind."

"You're a smart ass, Findley. I want you to stay there in the hot seat, and when we're twenty miles out, turn us back to Boston."

"What! You're kidding. They've certainly taken over all the controls. Look, Rogers, let me lower the landing gear. If I press that button we should hear the nose wheel go down and a green light on the panel there. It has nothing to do with the autopilot unless they've taken everything over. Shall I?"

Everyone who could squeeze in tried to watch. Findley pressed the gear-down button. Nothing happened. He tried turning off the autopilot first, but still nothing.

Rogers pushed past and brought his fist down on the inactive panel.

Findley couldn't help himself. "If you'd let us carry on to London, we would have landed and you could've caught the next flight back."

He had another smack in the face for his audacity. As he shook his head, he realized he talked nonsense if other flights were being turned back to other isolated airfields. Would there be enough medical personnel for all the returning flights, considering some would forget to turn up for work? No. So, it would be remnants of confused National Guards looking after them, if anyone. So there would be a chance to slip over to the other airport and get another flight. Maybe he should write it down in case he forgot in the next four hours.

CHAPTER 14

Friday 24 April 2015:
Earth Orbit.

JENA KOCHI, ASTRO-ENGINEER, enjoying her third spaceflight, tried to focus on the specks of light in the black velvet through the porthole while listening to Wagner's thundering music, *The Ride of the Valkyries*. She imagined herself in the role of the heroine, Brunhilde, riding war horses to the blood-thumping chorus. Losing herself in the harmony made it easier to forget their problems. Staring harder, she decided the motes of light in the blackness belonged to her own optic nerve.

A sudden knock brought her rest period to an abrupt end and she switched on the dorm light.

"Good, it's you, Antonio, come in. We have much to discuss about our situation up here."

The doctor shook his head. "I know what you are going to say, Jena. You want us to depart immediately for Earth, but I think we stay a little longer, *per favore*?"

"Antonio, yesterday's supply ship didn't arrive, and we get no sense out of Houston."

"We are not going to run out of air, food, or water for weeks, Jena. You are panicking without cause."

Jena looked at Antonio's Mediterranean-tanned face. He could have been a film star at a snap of his elegant fingers, not that she went for pretty men.

She tried again. "Fine. You've been able to talk to your people with no trouble. They're in Milan and there's no trouble there, but you, as a doctor, must be petrified at what's happening in the States. Our uplink is spasmodic, none of the Mission Control communicators know us. I'm worried, Antonio. We've got to convince Dan to let us take the *Marimar* back down." She grabbed the doctor's arms.

"I can give you a sedative, Jena. Oops, *scusi, signorina*, wrong thing to suggest. I share your worries, really I do. It's only a matter of time, maybe days, before my family suffer too. Let's consider the situation as objectively as we can.

"As far we can tell, the memory loss happened after the case was handled at Edwards and again at Goddard when it was sent there.

From those two centres, the amnesia infection diffused rapidly. Everyone becomes infected when they are in the same breathable space as an infected person. It must be extraordinarily virulent, maybe over ninety per cent of contacts picking it up. That's way more than AIDS, SARS, and even the common cold. *Di conseguenza,* we shouldn't rush down there."

She hated losing a debate but brightened with another point. "Isn't it like the way the common cold infected almost every Native American when the white settlers breathed on them? But many developed a similar immunity to the settlers. Antonio, we should return, while we can, to a remote spot and wait for resistance to the infection to develop."

He pointed at the console. "We only know what we can pick up from TV broadcasts and the medical staff at Houston who took the trouble to answer us last week with all they knew about ARIA, the memory-eating virus. You are not thinking straight, Jena. We didn't open the case so we are not immune, just not infected. How could we be of use down there when, after landing, we get infected?"

"You assume we'll catch it. I don't, and even if we did, we'll have our records. This infection affects memory not intelligence. So we use intelligent strategies to cope."

"First, *signorina,* we can't separate intelligence from memory. Forget reasoning techniques and your brain won't solve problems as well as it did. Secondly, if you don't keep a diary as habit for years, you could wake up in the morning and forget you started one. Another reason to stay up here is that this ARIA thing will burn itself out. Viruses become less virulent after peaking, before everyone has been touched."

Jena had always found discussions with Antonio more like a game of chess. She sat heavily on her bunk but realized it gave him a height advantage and stood again. "I thought public-health medics are equipped to look for that and produce antidotes."

"Ah, Jena. Consider a public-health laboratory down in Houston. Someone is brought in who is not ill except they're losing their memory. What do you do? Scans, take blood, urine, and biopsy samples. If they find a virus, then what? Every doctor who examines an infected person becomes infected."

She wagged a finger. "Not in an isolation chamber, but I suppose they wouldn't consider that unless someone from up here, Doctor, suggests it and quick."

"I did, Jena, last week. But the medic I spoke to didn't turn up to work the next day, like most of them. All of them. *Bastardi.*"

"Well, I'd like to make sure my folks are okay, but I suppose if I can't raise them, they must be infected by now. I expect our commander will agree with you anyway."

"He does, Jena. Talk to him yourself. He'll call us together to review the situation this afternoon. I hope your family have taken themselves somewhere safe. They might be out of cell-phone range."

"Antonio, what did you disturb my rest period for?"

He walked to her family photo at the farm she'd stuck on the bulkhead wall. He turned and smiled. "Dan and I thought it would do no harm to give ourselves some vitamin and antioxidant boosters as a prophylactic for when we do go back."

"I suppose this is a ten-day course; another diabolical reason why we can't return yet. You related to Machiavelli?"

Dr Menzies produced his best bedside-manner wry grimace.

CHAPTER 15

Friday 24 April 2015, evening:
UK motorway, eight days since amnesia started spreading in the
US. Most US citizens and some UK citizens have lost up to a year's
worth of memory.

RYDER ALWAYS HAD THE URGE to be a van driver, so he was elated to be driving the latest super-transit, courtesy of his boss, Derek. Paying to use the toll motorway sections of the M1 out of London and M6 towards Wales helped to avoid the worst of the traffic congestion. Teresa's biology department maintained a field study centre in North Wales. Dubious because of the high tourism factor on the North Wales coast, Ryder spent hours poring over maps and aerial photographs, which helped him change his mind. There was just one road, built by the Romans, more a track skirting a ridge close to the centre. The centre nestled in a mountain-fringed armchair hollow with a track ending at a small lake, Llyn Anafon. He would have preferred more trees for the centre to hide in, but they went centuries ago and kept away by sheep, feral ponies, and rabbits, who all loved tree saplings for breakfast. Since the vast majority of tourists stay within a few minutes of their cars, they'd only have to fend off the few dedicated ramblers.

"Are you sure it has electricity and water?" he asked Teresa, as he slowed behind a Perrier transporter.

"It has its own wind and solar power with a diesel back-up generator, local stream water supply with filters, a large store complete with sheep and bilberries on the hills. What more do you want? Oh, I get it. Yes, it has a great entertainment room and communications centre."

Ryder looked at her in disbelief. "I was thinking of security arrangements."

"There's a burglar alarm. Not linked to the police, but I believe a red light might blink at the university maintenance office in London."

"Great. Has it ever gone off?"

"I set it off when I forgot the code. I know it now, 1828."

Ryder laughed. "Don't tell me. The year London University started a biology department. It's amazing how many institutes have the year of their inauguration for their door codes. Is there an alarmed security fence?"

"You having a laugh? The only fences around there are around trial seed patches to keep the rabbits and sheep out. But we do have Brian."

"Ah, anagram of Brain, a robotic defence system?"

Teresa braced as Ryder had to abort an overtake. "Sort of. He's Brian Wagstaff, the centre manager. Lives on site with his wife, Bronwyn, who does catering and repairs. She'd run rings round you on electrics and engines. In fact, although Brian is bloody strong though short, if I was an intruder, I'd be more scared of Bronwyn. She's a fiery one."

"Like someone sitting next to me, you mean. Oh my God, two feisty women under one roof."

"Don't forget Laurette in the pickup behind us with Gustav. She's an impenetrable, French, post-grad chief techie for our department and Gustav Schmidt, from Leipzig, her assistant."

Ryder swerved to avoid a rabbit then said, "Didn't Gustav tell you Laurette was impenetrable?" He grinned; she laughed.

"It means she has someone to play with when we're up there for months."

Ryder heard buzzing. "That yours?"

She checked. "Gustav says they need to stop for fuel and provisions."

"Hope they remember to use the self-serve fuel and shop. Hey, Derek, wake up. We're making a pit stop."

"Why have you brought him along?" she whispered. "You said you couldn't stand him."

"He's a prat as my line manager; most media consultants are. But he's a bloody marvel at communications. This super-transit came out of his budget and is full of his comms gear as well as provisions."

"Right, here goes for the motorway services," Teresa said. "I'll remind Gustav and Laurette to put in their nose filters."

"I still think we should wear our full protection gear but for the attention it would get."

A swiped card let them in and the scanned goods debited prices from their bank account as they left. They refuelled, toileted, and shopped without approaching within five metres of anyone.

Derek O'Conner received pulled faces from the others as he piled boxes of cigarettes and whiskey into his trolley. Laurette and Gustav grimaced at the awful selection of cheeses and chocolates on the shelves. Teresa made sure the women had enough toiletries, and Ryder added concentrated fruit juices, biscuits, black beers, torches, batteries, music memory cards, and extra first aid stuff.

"That came to over four hundred pounds," Teresa said.

"And mine," Laurette replied, "but I bet Ryder and Derek's even more."

Derek avoided a response.

"All essentials for body and soul," Ryder said. "Now let's get going before anybody thinks we're good for a hijack."

Keeping to legal speed limits, Ryder followed the old M42 across the border into Wales then Thomas Telford's route along the A5.

"This could be fun if it wasn't so serious," Derek said.

"Speaking of serious, Derek," Ryder said, taking care to stay several seconds behind a meandering Volvo estate packed with whooping teenagers. "You are on a touchy-feely level with our PM, Brendon Stone, aren't you? We've been trying to get to him to stop Atlantic flights, which I believe has happened, but what else?"

Derek finished a chocolate bar. "I know the government have had top level meetings, including a full cabinet meeting two nights ago. But though I coordinate much of the national Internet TV news coverage relating to Downing Street, I can't find out anything that happened in the last two days. The absence of releases becomes news in itself but worrying nonetheless. I know that four days ago, one of the top M15 security policy makers happened to be in Washington."

Teresa and Ryder "ahhed" together.

She said, "Just as well you do most of your conferences online, Derek. It has slowed down the spread of ARIA just a little."

The mini-convoy motored through the spooky deep shadows of wooded limestone gorges, meeting little traffic until turning north on the A470 leading to Conwy on the North Wales coast. With mountains climbing up to their right and a valley falling away to their left, Ryder worried it made a perfect ambush opportunity. He looked to voice his fears, but both his passengers snoozed as if they'd come for a rest. He wondered if he'd packed his walking boots. Then he hoped he'd remembered his prismatic compass in case the batteries ran out on his watch-GPS and he'd bought the wrong sort at the supermarket. Had they brought the large-scale maps and had Teresa transferred enough funds to their instant-access current account? Would that matter in another week or so?

His eyes cried out for sleep too. He should have agreed to his passengers' offers to share the driving. He knew he shouldn't have been so arrogant as to assume only he would be cunning enough to drive without attracting attention. He'd been trained in the US by the FBI while on a documentary assignment and now trusted no one else to drive.

White and amber lights beckoned him from the coastal tourist town of Conwy. Even from five miles, he could see the castle ramparts and the suspension bridge, lit up as if a normal holiday weekend was about to begin. It was possible no ARIA-infected person had sat in one of the quaint cafés or pulled up a deckchair on nearby Llandudno's beach. Getting closer, he could see the silhouette of Great Orme, an outlying hill where, 2,000 years ago, the Romans took over ancient copper mines. What would they have thought of ARIA? Would it have made much difference to them? 'Course it would. Imagine Proximus Septimus, or whoever, waking up not knowing the beauty next to him was his new wife, swapped for rights to graze cattle in a luscious meadow. Or a legion setting off on a three-day march then forgetting what their mission entailed when they arrived and their route back to base camp. Bummer.

He turned left onto the coastal dual carriageway. Accompanied by the occasional Irish articulated lorry travelling empty back to the ferry at Holyhead, he had a short drive to Penmaenmawr where he had orders to wake Teresa for detailed navigation.

The signpost said "Aber Falls" but an overgrown elderberry prevented anyone reading it. Ryder took satisfaction at the covert entrance, even though a scattering of homes meant less-than-perfect isolation. The lane wound its way through hills and past a couple of sheep farms until a gate barred the way.

"Excellent," he said to Teresa as she jumped out. But qualified that with a "Not so good" when he saw that all she did was lift a rope to open the gate. "We'll need to add more obstacles than that."

"Unless you intend to install a three-metre electric fence around the whole valley and the mountain behind the centre, the determined intruder will get in."

"Certainly, but let's cut down the odds by having a solid padlock on this and a second gate around the bend."

"We'll do a reconnaissance with Brian and Bronwyn in daylight. They have local knowledge—hey, watch out, Ryder. The track meanders with a drop to the stream on the right. Go slow. It's only another mile or so."

"I assume Brian and Bronwyn have been briefed?"

"They've been getting our bunks ready as well as extra provisions."

"I mean about ARIA."

"They didn't believe me. Especially Brian, but Bronwyn thought some of the TV presenters had acted oddly, especially on the satellite programmes from the States. And yes, they've been diligent when they've gone shopping. Luckily, although they're Welsh, they're not originally from round here, so we don't have to take in two hundred family members."

Ryder fretted as he drove. "How about locals or tourists in the valley?"

"No one in the past week. Occasionally at weekends, the odd fisherman will drive up this lane to the small lake a quarter mile from the centre, but if we block the lane, I'm sure they'd look elsewhere for somewhere easier."

The transit rocked sideways as Ryder struggled to steer it in pitch blackness over the rubble making up the uneven track. The two pale yellow headlights did more to put rabbits into a catatonic state than illuminate the way ahead.

"Where the bloody hell is it, Teresa? I wish they'd switch on an outside light."

"You told them not to."

"Oh, yes. Wartime blackout rules. Ah, I see it. That must be Brian in the doorway with a torch. Must have heard the van."

"I expect Laurette phoned him when we reached the gate."

"You are all old friends here, aren't you, except Derek and me?"

"We've known each other for five years. Not sure I know *you* at all." She gave him a dig in the ribs.

CHAPTER 16

Saturday 25 April 2015:
Anafon Centre.

Before breakfast, Ryder walked out of the door and strolled around the centre, long, cool grass tugged at his ankles. Swirls of grey mist trailed around the hills, allowing the morning sun to take its time burning it away. At a hundred metres, he turned to take in the centre. It lay beside a small stream trickling from a nearby lake. The steep, rocky Llwytmor mountain on the south side belied the northern, gentle, green-vegetated slope. He appreciated the way the centre blended into the environment. It might be modern brick and pastel shades inside but was constructed of local slate and gritstone outside. One floor but as large as a school in area, half hidden behind large grey boulders.

Still loaded with morning dew diamonds, the shrubs and scattered boulders wore aprons of bright green bilberry, ferns, and grasses. He warmed in appreciation of the isolation and tranquillity. Turning again, he followed a track to the lake in the basin of the vertical mountain walls. In the still water, fish gulping at flies disrupted the reflection of an old jetty.

Studying the idyllic scene, Ryder shook his head to think not as a media man, weighing up a tourist twenty-minute shoot, but as if he intended to raid the place. Why would anyone want to break into the field centre? It wouldn't be long before significant sections of local and national services would fail. Computer-led financial services would take longer to break down than labour-intensive industries such as health, transport, food, and security. People might have months of money left in their bank accounts, but shops would shut for lack of staff. Looting would follow. When the shelves were empty, where would people get their food? Other people's homes and buildings with refectories. The dwindling police force and army, assuming martial law would be declared, might patrol cities, but desperate people would try for more isolated dwellings. Rather like they were doing. In a crisis, houses lose their emotional attachment with generations of families and become mere shelters or places where the starving might find a food cache. Everything becomes justified.

He shivered from the early-morning chill and from the creepy scenario he kept painting in his head.

"Oi!"

Startled, he crouched and looked around.

"I'm not cooking breakfast for you to have it go cold."

Feeling as sheepish as their four-legged neighbours, he tramped towards a short woman with spiky red hair and brandishing a frying pan.

"You must be Bronwyn. Pleased to meet you."

"Cut the crap and sit down. You're late for a meeting."

He rushed to the common room that doubled as a refectory. Tables had been pushed together at which the others breakfasted and chatted.

"There are toilets here, Ryder," said Teresa. "You don't need to fertilise North Wales."

Ryder joined in the group derision.

Teresa added, "We thought it critical to assess our situation."

"Weapons?" Ryder kicked off.

Derek laughed, then said, "Yes, let's not start with introductions and niceties."

"That's my job," Brian said, with a soft Welsh lilt in his voice. "Just to clarify for those unaware of our situation here, I'll give my usual spiel.

"Welcome to Anafon Field Study Centre. One of four run by the Biological Studies Department of London University. My name is Brian Wagstaff. I am the manager of this centre. My wife, Bronwyn, has shouted at all of you already. She does the jobs I don't know how to do, along with the catering. Teresa is a bio lecturer and one of the main reasons for our existence. Ryder is her bit of fluff—sorry, I only do jokes in bad taste. As far as I know, Ryder is an expert on making docs on space-related stuff and Derek is his boss. A dab hand at communications and computers, I hear, so I hope you can take charge of that lot, Derek? Good. Our beautiful French lass is Laurette who is in charge of the techies at the uni, including our Kraut, no offence meant, friend, Gustav. Will that do?"

"Have we any firearms?" Ryder said. "Or are we going to have a role-playing game now?"

Gustav looked worried and speaking in a Bavarian accent asked, "Why would it be necessary to have guns, Ryder?"

Laurette turned on him. "How can you be so stupid? We are here to keep those morons away from us. They'll be coming when they run out of food."

"Yes," Ryder said. "And to shoot the rabbits, sheep, and ponies."

Audible gasps escaped from his listeners.

"We have to assume all mammals may carry the ARIA virus," Ryder said. "It's them or us, which do you want?"

Ryder saw the shock on their faces.

Brian said, "I agree with your suggestions, Ryder, that we should keep this place as inconspicuous as possible. You know, blackout at night, trips to town as few as possible—"

"None at all," interrupted Ryder. "It just takes one of us to catch it in a shop and we've all got it."

Teresa said, "Is there anything we absolutely would need to go into Conwy for? Isn't the storeroom here fully stocked?"

Bronwyn sat upright to assert her quartermaster status in her strong Welsh accent. "It depends on what you call needs. We have enough basic foods to sustain seven people for at least a year, maybe more. You know: flour, pulses, dried foods of all descriptions, three walk-in freezers chocka; then we have a storeroom laden with tinned and bottled preserves and so on. But fresh fruit and vegetables, fresh meat, fish and other short-life foods?"

"We'll have to get along without fresh produce except what we can glean from the valley here," Ryder said.

Brian laughed. "The fish in the lake are not the tasty sort, the sheep are there until you shoot them, but some farmer might decide to investigate if his flock started disappearing. Anyone for wild horsemeat? There's plenty of frozen meat and vegetarian alternatives. In fact, the veggie proteins such as the soya, Quorn, and tofu proteins will last years."

"Brian," asked Derek. "Is this place usually as well stocked as a ship on a world cruise?"

"We often stock up when expecting field trips. This valley is awash with brightly coloured tents when the first-year biology trips descend on us, aren't they, Teresa? Then we usually get summer bookings from London schools—"

"Hey, there aren't any booked in for the foreseeable future, are there?" Ryder asked.

"No. There were a few pencilled in and we cancelled. What I'm saying is that we are equipped for mass catering, and because of our remoteness, storage was built in as a priority. But as for your persistent firearm question, the answer is no."

"Thank God," Gustav said.

"We'll need to acquire some," Ryder said.

"How? We don't have a gun licence."

"Actually, we do," Brian said. "Again, because of our isolation, the university rifle club have weekend practice shoots here. They make a range out in the valley. Come to think of it, there might be a rifle in their locked store. I don't have a key for it."

"Good, let's see," Ryder said. "Otherwise a couple of us will go on a raid."

"*Mes amis*, I'm not happy with lethal weapons," Laurette said, her short black hair glistened from being recently washed.

"We have to be realistic. All the local farmers will have shotguns and their sons will have air rifles, crossbows, stun-dart projectiles, and more diabolical weapons. I wouldn't want to go against them with just a butterfly net. Let's have a look at the rifle club's lockup, Brian."

Brian led the entire group through empty dormitories with their own kitchenettes until, to Ryder's surprise, sunlight hit him as they marched across a small quadrangle with a pond, seats, and slate-floor patio. Into the next building they passed a couple of lecture rooms and labs until they reached the outside again. Embedded in the mountainside, a small building barred their entry with a hefty padlock. Brian held up a crowbar and grinned at his audience.

"No telling, mind."

"Tell that to the cameras," Bronwyn said, reminding everyone of the security cameras dotted around.

"As if anyone's watching," muttered Brian as he levered off the padlock. The small store within wouldn't allow in seven but Brian soon re-emerged. "Three rifles and two competition handguns. Night scopes and plenty of ammo."

"I thought possessing handguns was illegal," Derek said. "Not that I'm complaining."

His query triggered a blank look from Brian, who asked, "Should we leave them here with a new padlock?"

"No," Ryder said. "Anyone could go over the roof and crowbar in like Brian just did. And if attacked, we'd be foolish not to be able to get at them quickly. We'll hide them in the kitchen and lounge. Let's get back, we still have other security issues to sort out."

AFTER A COFFEE BREAK, they assembled in the refectory over a large-scale map of the valley. It showed the lane leading the handful of miles to the nearby coastal hamlet and Aber Falls, a waterfall, which in happier days attracted weekend ramblers.

Brian pointed at a couple of hillside bluffs jutting into the lane. "A gate here would make it difficult for intruders to get their vehicles to us. Mountain on one side and a steep, boggy slope to the stream on the other. We have enough timber and wire fencing for the job. I need a hand though."

Ryder watched a spider crawl up the wall. "I'm sure Gustav will help, and me too. But, Brian, do we have enough fencing for a perimeter fence?"

"Not to surround the centre, say, on the ridge a mile away in three directions. I'd say it was unnecessary. No one is stupid enough to risk breaking their necks coming down the near-vertical mountainside to the centre. We rarely get any visitors, especially from the old Roman road on the eastern ridge."

Gustav chipped in, "I've walked up there, there is a track all the way to Llanfairfechan but, as Brian says, remote. We could put a couple of hundred metres or so of fencing where people might wander down here, just to put them off and an official no-trespassing notice."

"Hey," Derek said. "Don't put 'No Trespass,' they'll come over in droves."

"Yes, I would," Laurette said, to laughter. "A notice saying 'Minefield' would annoy me but keep me off."

"But unbelievable," Brian said. "How about 'Active Firing Range?'"

"I'll rig up some cameras to keep an eye on the lane and the ridges," Derek said. "I'll fit them with movement sensors."

"Don't forget to tell the sheep then," Bronwyn said, making Derek scratch his head to look for an amended plan.

Ryder looked up from his notes. "What happens if someone gets through while we are asleep?"

Derek huffed up. "By the time I set up our alarm sensors and cameras, no one will reach here without us knowing about it."

Ryder noted the spider disappearing into a crack. "I'm sure, but then what? Suppose in a month or so, when we can be pretty sure ARIA will be everywhere, a villager wanders over the hill looking for food? We need to shoot them, don't we?"

Derek banged a fist on the table. "We have to shoot them. For our own survival. If ARIA continues in a person so that they end up with no memory at all—no speech, no knowledge of how to look after themselves, they'll die anyway."

Brian, fidgeting, said, "That's a bit drastic. Not just killing intruders but because they're losing memory. They won't forget to eat."

"Brian," said Teresa, "as we get older, gain intellect and experience, instinctive behaviour is subsumed. Some Alzheimer's patients forget to eat and drink in advanced stages when factors adding to their confusion kick in. I've been struggling to postulate how ARIA might affect someone if it continued to rob them of memory backwards until they were born. It is incredible. Imagine no speech. I expect for a while some cleverer people might cope somehow."

"Not really," butted in Laurette. "They merely employ clever strategies; postpone the worst effects until they forget how to read."

"Grim," said Ryder. "We can't take the chance of an ARIA-infected person reaching us. I'm afraid we'd have to kill them. It's drastic but necessary."

"Afraid so," Derek said. "I don't want to kill anybody, but if it's them or us..."

Ryder knew there was no compromise that made sense. But it might help the group come to terms with the awful decision if they painted it with a veneer of democracy. "We'll put it to a vote, agreed?"

Everyone nodded so Ryder said, "Right, raise your hand if you think we need to shoot to kill intruders."

Long faces looked at each other, each knowing the turmoil and anguish that comes with making life-and-death decisions. Derek put his hand up, followed by Teresa and Laurette. Ryder knew that Brian and Bronwyn had friends and relatives in the locality and would have great difficulties with this decision. They remained holding each other's hands.

Teresa had told Ryder that Gustav would squirm at the thought of any kind of violent action against people, no matter how justified. Gustav stared at his hands, clasped between his knees.

"Bugger," said Ryder, with the casting vote. "Let it be so then, though Captain Picard I'm not."

Some rose to get on with their jobs.

"Hang on," Ryder said.

"Yes, Captain?" said Brian, though his face didn't show humour.

"We have another decision and action plan to implement."

Brian and Bronwyn groaned but sat to participate again; their comfortable lives changed.

"Just suppose one of us makes an inadvertent contact with an outside person. Should we kill each other?"

They sat in a stupor. They hadn't thought it through like Ryder. His job had not the academic depth of Teresa or the technical skill of Gustav and Laurette. What he had, besides the skills of strict target setting and documentary-making, was the ability of spotting one component that could spell a million-dollar loss with a scrapped programme.

"I suppose so," said Laurette, the first to recover and developing a reputation as the one who'd pull the trigger first.

"There is another way," said Bronwyn. "Solomon."

"Did you have to tell them?" Brian said.

"That's his daft name for a mine not far from here. Tell them, Brian, you've been in it plenty of times."

"Eh? How do you know?"

"See, Boyo. You think I don't know where you slope off to with your pipe and bottles."

"Well, there is an old adit mine, they used to get copper and lead, fluorspar—"

"Never mind the geology lesson," Bronwyn said.

"Brian," said Ryder with renewed light in his eyes. "Could Solomon's mine—and I like the name—be an isolation habitation? Is that what you were thinking, Bronwyn?"

"Exactly. If one of us became contaminated, or thought we were, we could radio in and say we were staying in the mine until we knew we were all right."

"Excellent," said Teresa. Ryder looked at her, aware that she knew they were putting off a decision about what to do if the one in isolation had ARIA.

"Also," said Derek, "it could be used as a fall-back position in the event some blighters broke into our centre here while we were out and about."

They agreed to make a start after lunch. Derek loaded a rucksack with electronics and the other three men prioritised the securing of the one existing gate and construction of a second. Teresa and Laurette looked for any news on the web before setting off on a reconnaissance over familiar territory as biologists but now looking at the landscape as an assailant might.

CHAPTER 17

Saturday 25 April 2015, evening:
Anafon valley.

RYDER SAT IN A DECKCHAIR next to Derek, on a patch of gravel outside the centre. "To think we could have been living here in peace for years instead of up to our noses in pollution with our ears full of traffic noise in London." Long shadows of rugged mountains crept up and over them, but the relaxed men faced the golden-sunlit slopes opposite. A few cumulus clouds changed shape as if they tried to emulate the sheep below seeking greener grass.

"The novelty would have worn off, Ryder, and you'd be gasping for the sight of a London bus. I must say, the clean air and serene landscape helps to take the edge off this amnesia infection. How long do you think it'll last?"

"I'm no expert, I don't suppose anyone is, except maybe some alien watching us right now." They both looked up. The sky darkened but was too light for any stars to show, although Venus just peeped over the mountain to the east. "I suppose we hope this ARIA behaves like other viruses that lose their potency. Several months, with luck, and we can sneak back out there."

"And what will we find, Ryder? Will there be any jobs to go to? How much memory is lost per week?"

"My sister Karen guestimated it at around a year lost per week. She was hoping to verify it with some neurological studies in Houston before she was infected. Supposed to be sending us a communication tonight. In fact, I ought to set it up if Teresa hasn't already."

"Yes, she told me. I've put an icon on the screen for her; just click and play."

RYDER AND DEREK GRABBED A COFFEE and found Teresa in the computer lab, trying to raise Karen. The satellite link showed Karen's home with other images of her lab and another of Julia's home, the technician who'd promised to send them results of a blood test. Polished wooden benches housed banks of computers. The lab was built to accommodate a fieldwork class and most of the computers had connections to laboratory equipment. Piles of redundant student files mounded on benches in-between upside stools. A few screens flickered as Gustav worked alongside Teresa.

"Just a minute, Ryder," said Derek. "You said you linked up last Sunday. They've probably lost all memory for the last year."

"Possibly," Teresa agreed, "but they both had the advantage of anticipating it. They'd set up their electronic diaries, both in their personal web pages and synchronised with their NoteComs. Hopefully, they'll keep track and recall re-learnt stuff. We set up this communication to automatically remind them."

The connection burst into life, giving images of labs and a study. Within moments, Julia's face appeared on screen. Her red hair in disarray, her cheeks showed splotchy mascara decorating her red eyes.

"Julia, are you okay?" called Teresa into the mike, but Julia didn't appear to react as she fiddled with the keyboard.

"Maybe she's too upset to speak," Ryder said.

"No," said Derek. "This is a recording; she isn't live, so to speak."

"How can you tell?" Teresa said.

"Data on the task bar." He pointed at a movie symbol. "Just a sec, ah, voice input."

"...awful. I don't know where Karen is. My diary says we met up a couple of days ago when she collected the blood test results on the ARIA patients. She doesn't respond to her phone or e-mail. She might have gone with some others out to the Schenectady lab complex. They specialised in Alzheimer's research there. I have travel plans too. Sorry this is a recording but at least it allows you to know."

"Know what? Dammit," Ryder said.

"Listen, you idiot," Teresa said, batting him with a free hand.

"... inconclusive I'm afraid. We took blood samples from people definitely infected and looked for the same sort of indicators for Alzheimer's. These are variants of the P97 molecules and amyloid precursor protein. Slightly higher than in non-Alzheimer's patients. We used the electron microscope and found the usual assorted pathogens but the image of one I'm sending you with a package of data is a spiked sphere about 30 nanometres across. Looks like an adenovirus, but who knows? Teresa and Ryder, there are so many human viral pathogens to be found in saliva that haven't been identified, so it's damn hard trying to find one or a group of alien ones. There's nothing showing fluorescent green anyway. The one we suspect looks similar to one of the common cold adenovirus pathogens, so maybe that's why it spreads so easily—saliva of those infected is full of them and so would the air they breathe out. There is hope, then, since some people are immune to the common cold, so maybe they're immune to ARIA—I gather from a medic web page that's what it's called. I wish I was immune. Like Alzheimer's, it's probably slower in people who had high intake of vitamin E and ginkgo biloba. We should all be eating vitamin sandwiches.

"It's chaos outside. I don't think many are going to work even if they know where to go. They are too worried to leave home, looking after relatives and friends, defending their homes against mobs of looters. Pathetic really. I came across a hoody teenager carrying a huge holoscreen, crying his eyes out. When I asked, he said he couldn't remember where his apartment was.

"There have been fatalities caused by ARIA. Patients forgetting, or their nurses forgetting, to administer medication. Fresh blood and plasma supplies have dried up—oh, badly put, but you know what I mean. So the transplant and by-pass ops aren't happening. I've heard of long-haul plane crashes but that could be rumour. I'm going to risk it anyway. The TV news is spasmodic—but you must know that from Internet TV. Hope it dies out soon before we all return to Neanderthal behaviour, if we survive that long. I've set this on a timer to run on batteries for this uplink in case the mains power is off as it often is.

"When I can, I'll link up to your website, Ryder, and keep my mobile phone charged—but that depends on the service provider still operating. I'm flying to some of my family in Europe. I have the tickets and written flight numbers on my arm.

"Look after yourselves. Oh, get some Huperzine-A patches, although you might need a hospital pharmacy for that. I love you all. Ciao."

Her tearful face faded out, leaving the group watching an empty lab.

"Momentous and yet she didn't realize it," Ryder said.

Teresa said, "She's identified the virus, quasi-virus, whatever anyone wants to call it." Ryder saw tears in her eyes, but she waved him away.

"It should be called the Julia Tynwald Virus," Ryder said.

"Tynwald's ARIA," Derek said. "Sounds like a Wagner opera."

Ryder looked at his mobile phone for the hundredth time as he sent and checked for messages from Karen.

"There's been the occasional message," he said. "But apart from a couple of 'Hi' and 'Okay,' they've just been spurious characters as though she's lost her mobile and using something from another network with compatibility problems. She said she's coming to Europe. One of thousands trying to escape their situation but only to spread it."

Derek pointed at the screen. "Anybody know what Hyper-whatsit is?"

Teresa wiped her eyes with a tissue. "Huperzine-A is an enzyme inhibitor. Our brain needs acetylcholine for thoughts and memory. But there is an enzyme whose job is to make sure we don't produce too much. One theory is that Alzheimer's is the result of that enzyme attacking too much acetylcholine and so affecting memory. Patients taking Huperzine-A usually find their memory and thinking improves."

Derek's face brightened. "I've been taking gingko biloba for years. I should have been dosing up on Hup-A."

"Gingko is good for memory too, although the jury is out on whether it improves brain function."

"Do we need to raid a chemist?" asked Ryder, worrying about contacting people again.

"I don't know. Hup-A is available over the counter in some places. It's an herbal extract, not a commercially processed substance. We might even have some here, we do get visiting students and lecturers who are really into naturopathic remedies."

Ryder shook his head. "In these weird circumstances, we don't know how ARIA is affecting the brain. Maybe it's enhancing this bad enzyme so it's depleting the acetylcholine, causing short circuits in the brain, leading to memory loss. I would think taking anything that might help inhibit ARIA is a good thing."

"It might make it worse," said Teresa, reading through the text that came with Julia's message. "All we know from Julia is that people infected with the virus lose memory function in such a way it spreads, taking out memory in a retrograde fashion. And this is so odd because we don't consider memories to be well organised. We remember odd events and every time you think about them, the acetylcholine for those neurons increases, making it easier to recall them. This illness takes out memory going steadily back in time. Of course, some chunks of memory link to others but not usually for what happened the previous day or week. The loss of memory with Alzheimer's is more random and slow. Some people forget childhood things one week then vocabulary learned more recently the next."

"At least it's comforting some people are working on it," said Laurette. "Hopefully, they can transmit results and ideas before they become too disorganised."

"Good point," Gustav said. "Can we set up a link to the labs at Schenectady?"

"I can try," Derek said, settling to the task.

TERESA AND LAURETTE HUDDLED IN A CORNER with Gustav to summarise the biological aspects of the communication. Ryder tried to follow Derek's expert fingers dancing over the keyboard when the speaker shouted, "Intruder!"

Everyone stared at Derek.

"It might be a glitch," he said. "I've only set up a few sensors and haven't tested it all yet."

"Can't you tell which beam has been broken?" Ryder said.

"It's the farthest gate on the lane, but it should be padlocked. Brian?"

"Ah, it will be tomorrow. I forgot to take it with me when I took the fencing and spike-wired the top rail. Er, sorry, but shouldn't the camera show us—oops, it's dark, isn't it?"

"It'll be doubled up with an infrared cam tomorrow."

"So, the gate is open now?" asked Teresa.

"Not according to the sensor, and sheep don't usually shut gates after them," said Derek. "Either there's a glitch or someone opened then shut the gate."

Laurette ran to a drawer, brought out two of the competition handguns and offered one to Ryder.

"Ammo," Ryder said.

"They're kept loaded," Laurette said. "Not much use in an emergency otherwise."

"Good point," he said.

Brian took a rifle, checked it and strode to the door leading to the refectory.

Ryder liked the solid metallic feel of the Colt 1911, admired the perfect balance yet hated the need for handling it. They all gathered behind the door.

Five minutes later, Bronwyn spoke. "Just a frigging minute. I'm in the Territorial Army, and it's as clear as jelly none of you have had any training. Gustav, take a rifle and aim it at the door from behind that easy chair. Laurette and Derek, take your weapons out the back way and do a cautious reconnaissance. Brian and I know the layout best, so I'll open the door to the refectory but stay against the wall on this side while Brian goes in at a crouch. Ryder and Teresa, also aim at the door but stay behind furniture like Gustav. On the count of three—counting down from three. Right?"

Everybody said yes—even Brian.

Bronwyn said, "Three, two, one, go."

Standing back against the wall to the right of the swing door, Bronwyn eased it open with her right hand allowing Brian, with rifle levelled, to crouch and enter.

"Bloody hell."

"Hi, Uncle Brian," said a young woman.

Brian returned and closed the door behind him.

"It's my brother's daughter. Should I just tell her to go away? Only, suppose she's infected?"

Teresa, with hands on hips, "Which would mean you are probably infected, which means…"

"Ah."

Bronwyn rushed into the refectory. "Megan. My God, girl, what are you doing here?"

Apart from Derek and Gustav on patrol, they all gathered around the young teenager sitting at a table.

"I'd like a jam butty. And how are you, Auntie Bronwyn?"

"I'm having kittens but never mind me. Why aren't you at home?"

"Mum and Dad went Wednesday to the rugby in London and haven't come back. They use any excuse to have a few days in a nice hotel."

"You should've gone to one of your friends, love."

"But you said I was always welcome here, especially when you didn't have a load of students in."

Bronwyn turned to Ryder. "She's right."

A burst of noise entered the front door followed by Derek shouting. "We've found a bike leaning against the wa—oh. Hello?"

CHAPTER 18

Sunday 3 May 2015:
The Rocky Mountains. Seventeen days since amnesia started
spreading. Most people have lost two years and three weeks'
memory.

MANUEL DRAGGED HIMSELF OUT OF A DEEP SLEEP. He'd have to get a
new alarm clock, because he couldn't stand the racket this one made.
His eyes blinked open to stare at a varnished pinewood ceiling. He
had a plain white ceiling at home so maybe he'd got lucky, at last. His
hand reached out but found empty sheets. So, not that lucky. He
levered himself up on his elbows, but his head hurt so he lay back
down. The unfamiliar log cabin troubled him even though whispers
of déjà vu flitted around his foggy head.

He worked hard to focus through the window at a magnificent
snow-capped mountain across a lake. Two mountains, if he counted
the perfect reflection. Re-focussing, he admired the huge white pine
tree outside his window. It wore a pale grey bark, almost silver,
oozing strength and fortitude, and it soared above the eaves of the
cabin.

"I'm not at home in Baltimore, then," he sighed.

The alarm restarted. He realized the perpetrator liked beetles for
its breakfast, and Manuel drew significant pleasure, when he raised
himself again, to watch the vermillion-crested black woodpecker
send vibrations through the tree.

After a few minutes, reality nagged at him.

"Where the hell am I?"

He staggered to the bathroom, then found the kitchen and
prepared coffee and toast. A NoteCom lay on the table. Feeling the
coffee wake up parts the shower couldn't, he tapped at the key to
reveal a message:

> *You are Manuel Gomez, employed by NASA as their*
> *Education Officer for flight missions with responsibility*
> *to liaise with the media.*
>
> *Except you are on leave along with most of the*
> *population because you have ARIA, an infectious*
> *amnesia deleting your memories at the rate of 50 days'*

worth each day. This probably started for you on the 15th April 2015. It is now Sunday 3rd May 2015 so you have lost 900 days or two years five months and twenty days of memory.

Hit the ARCHIVE button for your potted bio and relevant addresses and details.

Hit the WHO button for names, addresses, and numbers of friends and colleagues.

Hit the CALL button within WHO to contact people in the list.

Hit the NOTES button for information you have added.

Hit the HELP button for details about this NoteCom and how to make it online to the web.

Warning: some of the information may be out of date.

Don't lose this NoteCom.

Have a good day. <joke>

Although the information was new to him, and shocking, he realized that every day for months he must have sat somewhere and read the same message. Maybe in this cabin.

Did he recall his father bringing him camping here? No, not his father—his parents lived in Spain. That was it, he'd won a Young Space Journalist fortnight and part of the prize meant a weekend camp in the wilds of Lake Moraine, Banff National Park in Canada. Before he lost all his wherewithal, he must have brought himself back here. Remembered how remote this area was. No smooth-surfaced promenade walks around tarted-up holiday homes like around Lake Louise. Good to get somewhere far from people. Not too long though, he might have a lot of provisions, but they wouldn't be infinite, and backwoodsman skills were not his strong point.

He decided to check on his stores, wondering if he'd done the old trappers' trick of burying some outside in case the cabin suffered a raid by a bear.

He could survive for months on the basic foods he found, though he already had a yearning to find a damn good restaurant. Suppose he made his way down the track to the road? He must have had a vehicle there and could drive to the nearest town. Maybe he shouldn't. How many times had he debated that?

Midday came, and after a crisp-bread and soup lunch, Manuel decided he needed to find more interesting food. He also had a strong urge to find out how ARIA was affecting folk around here. Maybe it had gone away. What information he gleaned off the web didn't say so.

Grid power didn't work, but electricity flowed from solar cells on the south-facing roof and fed to batteries when not drawn. Even so, he should only use electrical gadgets in the daytime. The news sites carried little information. He had logged on to the web, using the impressive mini-satellite receiver and transmitter on a small pylon he found at the back of the cabin, along with mountains of chopped wood. He must have been bored the last few weeks. There had been general looting and mayhem throughout the country, but he wanted to see for himself how secure his hinterland refuge was.

Manuel threw a rucksack on his back and staggered, knocking over a kitchen chair. He re-packed a waterproof coat, NoteCom, camera—since old habits die hard—dried fruit and nuts, and a flask of coffee. He left the axe and the two-litres bottle of water. He set off down the hill.

Forget-me-nots and bluebells greeted him though he had to watch out for poison ivy scraping his feet at the edges of the track. Here in the forest, life continued as normal. He entertained the wild thought that only sentient beings would know they were losing memory. But then only humans had sufficient conscious thought to notice their failing memory. Dogs would forget where they lived, but many did anyway. Looking up at a lodgepole pine, he wondered if trees had memory. He knew they had DNA and everyone knew about tree rings that enabled a tree to remember the wet and dry, cold and hot years. But that lodgepole pine didn't depend on tapping into its tree rings to know where to go home at night. He peered into the darkness beyond the first few trees, looking for bears watching him. National park areas up in bear country were closed in winter. That should include his cabin, yet according to the NoteCom, he'd been there since April.

He heard a coyote off up through the trees to his left. No worries there unless it was warning its family of a black bear. He didn't fancy the idea of running hard. On the other hand, he was fitter than he remembered. Still stocky, but he'd been pulling up his forty-inch trousers. Maybe all that chopping wood and unexciting staple foods turned some flab into babe-magnet material. As if.

After half an hour of steady downhill stepping around muddy quagmires, he came to a hard-surfaced road. A Dodge 4x4 pickup waited there. Dark brown and tan, it had the registration plate the NoteCom told him it should. There, under the rear nearside mudguard hung the keys. He walked around the vehicle looking for any history: deep scratches, dents, or body parts in the front grill, but all he found was a rock wedging a wheel. The rear of the pickup held a chain, rope, tool bag, and tarpaulin, nothing out of the ordinary.

Careful not to set off an alarm, he bleeped the key-fob and climbed into the black leather driver's seat. More comfortable than in any of the chairs in the cabin, Manuel explored the glove compartment. Maps and gloves. No weapon. Fair enough, but maybe he should have looked for one at the cabin. A cell phone and charge unit via the cigar-lighter stared at him. He wondered if he should charge his NoteCom and decided he would. He popped a discovered mint sweet into his mouth and appreciated the instant sugar boost.

Fuel showed half a tank. Plenty for a twenty-mile return trip to the town of Louise Lake. Manuel switched on. Then again. A third time for it to catch and he revved. After a few moments, it purred like a contented mountain lion. He didn't want to attract the attention of any rangers or wild men of the forest. It would be possible for loners to be uncontaminated out here and assume his transgression into their domain needed sorting. Then he didn't want to attract the real wild life either. He moved off, concentrating so as to keep his speed beneath the 80 kph speed limit, but he couldn't help smiling at the "Grizzly Crossing" signs.

The snow lay on the road like icing on a Christmas cake. A few soft blue indentations gave away the night-time trespass of foxes or coyotes but nothing larger.

Manuel's driving would have attracted the attention of traffic police with his meanderings. He couldn't take his eyes off the mountains reaching skywards on the other side of the lake. He allowed his trashed recent memory to remain forgotten to encourage his soul to soar upwards to the summits. Then there was the glow he acquired from driving over virgin snow and the crunching noise from the tyres. Yet another sweep around a bend and he had to brake hard. The wheels stopped rotating but the pickup travelled another ten metres, the hood colliding with the wooden barrier across the road. The impact shattered the padlock. The gate swung outwards to allow Manuel to pass through and right onto the Lake Louise turning.

This road had compressed dirtier snow but no vehicles to cause him panic. He slowed as he crossed the bridge over the ice-blue waters of the Bow River and across the Canadian Pacific Railway line. He glanced up and down the snow-covered tracks.

Manuel turned into the near-empty parking lot of a shopping mall. He stayed in the Dodge surveying the scene, waiting to see if anyone showed up. One minute passed then five. A dark figure emerged from the entrance of the mall. Male, dressed in a long, hooded coat, he staggered to an old Ford truck. With a wry smile, Manuel watched the drunk climb into his vehicle, which coughed away down the road. Had the drunk bought his goods the old-fashioned way, with money in the shops?

A minute later, a transit van drove by him and on to the mall entrance. Three youths and a girl in an oversized white quilted coat tumbled out and into the mall. Happy enough, they behaved like normal idiot teenagers. Manuel guessed he ought to hang on a while. He couldn't imagine the shopping mall would be open and carrying on its retail and entertainment services as normal. No doubt those youths were looting the pharmacy and grocery store. If he showed, they'd either run away, or at him. He wondered if they had their memory intact. Suppose they'd been at a residential college or camp. It must happen. But then it would have only taken one infected cook to arrive and bingo.

Another few minutes and he parked away from the transit, twenty metres from the entrance with no one in front. His intention was to minimise attention by not parking too close yet making it possible for him to make a quick getaway. Pity he had no firearm. Manuel tightened his rucksack to make stealing it difficult and to protect his back. He crept into the mall, keeping to the right edge made of a large smoked-glass, curved wall. It looked as dark as a cave in there. No electricity. The power in the region came from hydroelectric dams in the mountains but still needed people to control it. It reminded him to look for batteries as well as vitamins and food.

Manuel's nervousness began a debate. Did he need luxury foods like chocolate, biscuits, and English tea when he had the basics to survive in the cabin? He could be jumped or chased. He might be slimmer but would only be able to run as fast as a table. The marble-effect floor, carpeted with discarded boxes, clothes, and drinks bottles, led him past looted clothes shops and cafeterias. He ventured down into the gloom. He shivered, out of fear but also, the retail-cave coldness got to him.

An unrolled bandage led him to the remains of a drugstore. Tablets, sweet-yet-pungent goo, and packaging littered the floor. A small seating area had cola drinks with straws on some tables and mouldy sandwiches. The lights had gone out, ending normality in this place in an instant. Most of the shelves had been cleared, but he salvaged some multi-vitamins and diabetic confectionary. The ordinary sugar-laden stuff had gone. Good, he found a torch and spare batteries. On his way out, he passed a full cabinet of natural remedies. None of the looters valued them, but Manuel helped himself to an assortment and a booklet or two. Now, he could find out how to keep his bowels active, his skin clear and he discovered an apt one on Alzheimer's. Another cabinet had held frozen foods. The ice-creams were a collage of swirls and pretty colours. He heard a scratching noise that sent him into a nervous crouch. More scratching and scuffling came from behind an open door leading to the rear of the store. Maybe the shopkeeper had been tied up, came to, and now tried to get away. Still crouching, he used the torch to open the door wider. A mad scramble of scratching and squeals accompanied two rats running through his legs to the main corridor. Manuel laughed and then stopped.

He heard other noises from deeper in the complex. He switched off the torch and concentrated. He couldn't make out the words, but shouting and fighting sounds reached him. Should he hide in the storeroom of the shop until the looters passed? Suppose they lived there and were defending their territory? There'd be plenty of provisions in the supermarket deeper inside. He waited, but the cacophony of the altercation rose and fell in greater frequency. He decided he ought to be satisfied with his minor haul and escape. Creeping to where the drugstore intersected with the main mall corridor, he waited to hear if the voices increased or diminished.

A woman screamed out of sight, deep in the gloom. The primeval sound made hairs prickle on the back of Manuel's neck. Then he heard heavy running coming his way accompanied by the woman shouting, "I'll die, you bastard. Give it back."

The running steps closed in to where Manuel crouched. He stuck out his foot and the runner fell. Jumping, Manuel landed on top of a dirty tweed coat that had held together a bony, bearded man with long, greasy hair. The man gasped as he fought for air and tried to push Manuel off him. It must have been all that chopping wood he couldn't remember doing, but Manuel overcame the odious heap with ease.

"Thanks, I just want my bag back, mister," said the woman wearing the white quilt he saw earlier. She'd caught up during the fracas.

The noxious man grunted, threw away a holdall, and struggled away on all fours. Manuel let him go while the woman grabbed her bag. He turned to talk to the woman, but she had gone after the still-crawling man.

"I wouldn't if I were you," Manuel called, but the woman took no notice and gave the man a vicious kick in the ribs, making him roll over. He grunted, grabbing at his side while she kicked him again in the balls. Manuel pulled her away, but she shook him off. More shouts could be heard from inside the mall.

"You got transport?" she asked. He studied her white, young face for the first time. She looked fourteen.

"Yes."

She started running towards the exit.

"Shall we go, then?" he called after her. The shouts behind grew louder, giving energy to his acceleration.

He caught up and ran to the pickup, bleeping as he approached. They drove off just as three men emerged, shouting.

"Stop!" she shouted when Manuel passed the transit. She leapt out, making him think she had changed her mind, but she'd left her bag. She jumped back in, throwing the transit's keys on the floor.

"That'll slow them down."

"It won't take them long to steal another vehicle. Is there somewhere you want me to take you?"

"Vancouver. I have family there."

"Excuse me? That's—"

"Just over three hundred miles, that way." She pointed west.

"Sorry, miss. I could take you to the train station. But a round trip of six hundred miles isn't on my agenda today."

"Train? You gotta be kidding. You might as well give me back to those goons."

Manuel didn't want to take a stranger back to his cabin and yet couldn't just let her go. He started up and headed out of the mall car park.

"Why were you with them anyway?" He asked, not sure he wanted the answer.

"Why do you think? I am female. They are male. Do I have to draw you a picture?"

"Why didn't you run away as soon as they got out of the van and went into the mall?"

"I didn't want to go with them. They grabbed me this morning while I was still asleep in my hotel in Banff."

"And I suppose the hotel staff let them?"

"No staff. The place was full of travellers like me. Too far from our own homes and no means of getting there." She hugged her bag. "And they took my bag."

"What's so precious about your bag?"

"You have one. Would you fight for it?"

"Actually, yes, I would. Anyway, we have to make a decision about you. If we just keep driving around this small town, we stand a good chance of meeting them again." He argued with himself for a few moments. "Okay, I'll take a risk and take you to my hideout."

"What makes you think I want to go with you?"

Again, Manuel experienced shock. He'd assumed her priority would be to get to a place of safety. She'd already been the plaything of a gang, so she couldn't be scared of him.

"What is your name anyway? I'm Manuel."

"Jat Qappik and before you ask, it's an Inuit name."

"Jat, I went to school with a Mamit Qappik. Was she your mother?"

"I see through your game. You're old enough to be my father and you might even be him."

They both laughed. "All right, I'll go to your house, Daddy."

"Shouldn't you have been home with your real mom and dad?"

"How old do you think I am, Manuel?"

"Fourteen, fifteen?"

"Ha ha. I'm at university."

"Yeah, sure you are. Which one, Vancouver State High School?"

"UBC Okanagan. Right, old man. To you that's—"

"University of British Columbia. I know. I've given lectures there on media technologies. Yeah, probably to your mum." They laughed again.

He grinned at her, taking in her Inuit face and long, jet-black hair.

"Where did you stay yesterday?" he asked as a test question.

"I guess I was in Vancouver or with those men around here. When I woke this morning, I was scared. Not because of the men. But because I thought I had my last semester exam to do, and I could hardly remember crucial research information for it."

Manuel swerved around an upturned waste bin in the road. "So, what year did you graduate?"

Without hesitation she said, "Twenty-fourteen."

"You've lost a year. You caught the amnesia bug, ARIA, around a week ago, probably in Vancouver."

"ARIA? I didn't know it was called that and probably won't know it tomorrow. Hey, Manuel, how come you know so much? Don't you have the forgetting bug?" Jat put her feet up on the dash as Manuel accelerated to get away from a small group of men on the sidewalk.

"Afraid so, but I keep updating myself with notes. You haven't told me what's so crucial in your bag."

"Okay. A month's supply of Neo-Humulin patches, some syringes in case I use liquid Humulin, needles, and a sugar-level test kit. Satisfied?"

"Right, no need to be annoyed. That's important information," he said, cursing the fact that he was committed to helping out someone who would doubtless be dead of untreated diabetes in a month.

Jat burst into a shout: "Hey, there's a sign saying we can't go up here, and there's a broken barrier."

He grinned, guessing he would score Brownie points from the youngster for breaking laws. "You going to help me put the barrier back to deter others?"

"It didn't deter you."

With some rope from the pickup, they re-erected the barrier, but unless it snowed or rained, any passer-by would see they'd driven up the lane. Any attempt to disguise their tracks would fail and it would be dark by the time they reached the cabin, assuming he could find it again. He'd already lost much of the morning even though he had tried to recall it whenever he had a spare moment.

"Aren't you afraid of bears up here?" Jat asked.

"Nah, they're all hibernating."

"Excuse me. You are talking to an Inuit. Okay, I haven't actually lived as an Inuit, but even I know not all bears hibernate, and those that don't are awake and looking for food."

"I am so glad to be sharing my lodge with someone of more intelligence than the mice I've shared it with so far."

"You can't scare me, Manuel, I've slept with rats." From both, that statement merited only silence.

CHAPTER 19

Saturday 2 May 2015:
Anafon.

A SHAFT OF SUNLIGHT ESCAPED THROUGH A BREAK IN THE CLOUDS. It hit Bronwyn full in the face as she drew the blinds in the kitchen. It made a welcome glow to her developing morose outlook.

Megan banged around, making a scrambled egg breakfast.

Bronwyn could feel the tension running high at Anafon. After years of working there, the evenings were too exciting for her: pillow fights, spilt drinks and food, loud music and raucous behaviour—and that was just the adults. But now, couples would huddle in corners and not for romance. Introspective worrying became the main spare-time activity. Since her niece appeared a week ago, the exuberance of youth added to the small community. Maybe a more wayward dimension than Ryder would have preferred, but teenage angst brought to Bronwyn a sense of normality.

"You know why you can't go to Anne's party," Bronwyn said.

"It's not fair."

"Of course it isn't. Megan, life's taken on a new twist for all of us."

"Here, here," Teresa said. She'd strolled in and sniffed at Megan's scrambled eggs. Megan snatched them out of reach.

"What if I go over the hill and avoid the road completely? I know a gap in the fence."

"Bloody hell, Megan, why haven't you said before? Brian, come here."

"It's only a small one, where one of the horses scratched itself near Two Rocks."

Brian remained cool. "We have to expect some breaches, and we haven't blocked off the mountain. We'd have to go shopping for more fencing."

"No, you wouldn't," Megan said, her mischievous eyes sparkling. "There's plenty of fencing out there. Brand new electric and green plastic ones the other side of Roman Road."

Gustav came in, stretching his sleep away. "You mean steal it?"

"Excellent idea," Teresa said. "Well done, Megan." Teresa knew how to please teens.

"But that's stealing from our friends," Brian said with a long face.

Derek stole a forkful of eggs. "We'd be more secure, and we're less likely to encounter people out on the hills than at a farmers' store."

Bronwyn knew it would help Megan get over not going to her friend's party, which had been cancelled or forgotten. "Megan, you go and burgle with Brian and Gustav and we'll have a party of our own tonight."

"Wicked." Megan leapt, clapping her hands, making Bronwyn laugh and yet feel old.

IN THE COMPUTER LAB, Ryder mined the web, looking for new information about ARIA. Missing people were listed on abandoned websites, but because the Internet servers still chugged away, they could be viewed by anyone with a connection. The most up-to-date medical sites beamed in from Asia and Europe, not North America. He worried about Karen, Manuel, and other friends in the States and hoped they too escaped to rural retreats and that ARIA would soon fizzle out.

An incoming message alert blinked. Three messages and none for him. He had no idea his line-manager Derek knew such high-powered officials. Not that Ryder opened Derek's e-mails, and anyone could make up avatars on the web, including the names of senior government officials. Ryder fought the temptation to peek at Derek's post. His neck heated up because of a nagging fear that their whereabouts had been compromised. He pushed the office chair back from the screen and paced the floor, went for a coffee, and returned no better. He glanced at the clock, estimating when Derek should return after working on more security cameras.

He risked Derek's wrath and opened up his e-mail. Suspicious because it came from the government. Ryder worried about official and contaminated fingers working their way towards Anafon. Ian Riddick he knew as a minister. Strong minded and prepared to stamp his feet over his opponents to get his own way. It worried Ryder that Riddick should be writing to Derek.

> To: derekoconnor@mediagold.com
> From: i.riddick@homeoffice.gov.uk
> Subject: Alternative venue
>
> *Derek,*
>
> *Imperative to get my family to you, even if you are Mull or similar.*

Maybe me and a couple of colleagues.

Can bring money and provisions, etc.

Please reply within an hour as alternative decisions would be needed.

Regards

Ian

So, the Government didn't know about Anafon. At least that gave Ryder a sliver of satisfaction.

"We should be all right now," Derek called, as he came in. "Anyone else for a glass of juice?"

Ryder panicked. He could fiddle with the system so Derek couldn't tell his e-mail had already been opened, but not in seconds. He closed the program down and looked at the webcams Derek had set up just as he walked up to the desk.

"There, we have ten cams set up overlooking gates, passes, the building, and Solomon's mine. I even thought of putting a mobile unit onto one of the horses as a random eye but they wouldn't let me get close."

"Just as well. How do you know they don't have ARIA?"

"It didn't occur to me. But you are right. SARS and AIDS transfer between mammals."

"Yeah, well, nothing's certain. Teresa tells me that although humans can catch up to two hundred infections and viruses from animals, it isn't known how many we give them. Shouldn't be surprising, considering how much DNA we have in common."

The computer sang with another e-mail alert.

Derek sat at the keyboard. He clicked for a while.

"I see you've been busy, Ryder."

"Yes, sorry, Derek."

"You expected me to jump up and down, didn't you? That's because a month ago I would have. Let's see. Yes, I've known Ian from Cambridge. He's been useful to our network, and I've been to his dinner parties. I'd like to help, but we agreed we couldn't accommodate more, didn't we?"

"This Ian is a government minister, isn't he?"

"So?"

"He's been in meetings with other ministers."

"He's almost certainly infected."

"As are his family," said Ryder, wondering if anyone in authority was left unscathed.

"Just suppose, Ryder, that he isn't infected. Now, don't look at me like that. Teresa and Laurette said there are always people who are immune to particular viruses. It would be a waste and a tragedy to not help them."

Ryder shook his head. "We can't bring them here, Derek."

"But if we don't do something for them, some genius out there is going to figure out the likely hideaways. You used logic and Teresa's employment to find this place. Others could do the same."

"What do you have in mind?"

"I know of two nuclear bunkers near London that have been maintained. They have their own provisions, energy, and water; like Anafon, but underground."

"Excellent, tell your mate, Ian, to wrestle the keys off someone."

"I will, but you know what it's like dealing with arrogant bastards. You have to make a suggestion so they think it was their idea. By the way, Megan and the other two were on their way back in too."

"If they organise a safe refuge, Derek, make sure they have web links with us. Other countries will have the same, won't they?"

"I'll mention it to Ian."

"Don't forget our house rule not to use the phone or mobiles. The Internet can't back-track to here with our scrambled IP addresses."

Ryder left Derek to reply to his e-mails while he collected some drinks for the fence thieves. He was worrying about them being seen. He found Teresa in the refectory and told her about Derek's e-mails.

"I'll talk to him. There are sperm and cell banks that need to be made secure. I know, people will have forgotten about them and leave them alone, but that's not enough. They need to be monitored. If their power supply fails then zap, we have no unadulterated humans for the future."

"Barring us, you mean?"

"Hey, don't get that look in your eye, buddy. I don't intend to be a mass baby producer. In any case, if I wanted to look for a virulent and strong gene stock, it might not be you," she said, looking with admiration at Gustav as he beamed at her from the doorway.

BOTH IN EAGER ANTICIPATION AND FEAR OF FAILURE, Ryder attempted to use a secure weblink to the International Space Station. The crew might have abandoned the station or were infected with ARIA when they found the case even though they hadn't opened it.

All the space missions had public websites where anyone could browse through photos and interviews, and peer at live webcams. However, you could post a message and not have anyone read it for weeks. The protocols Ryder possessed, allowed him into a members-only area of the website. On seeing Ryder's ID, they might reject his intrusion. He tweaked the virtual gate on the website.

A green light signalled his entry.

"Hello, ISS crew. I'm just knocking on your door to see who's in."

The data back showed that Ryder's protocol entry ID had been checked, so they know who had just logged in.

"Let me activate the webcam, Ryder Nape? There, now do you know who I am?"

"I confirm I am Ryder and you are either Vlad Pochenko or Dan has had a face job and learnt to speak with a Russian accent." They both laughed, relieved to share their humour.

"How are you all up there?"

"In some dismay watching you all down there. But you're okay?"

"You know about ARIA?"

"Of course," Vlad said in his rich Kiev accent. "We are able to monitor TV and the Internet."

"Obviously, none of you were infected by the case."

"We didn't lay a finger on it, let alone open it, Ryder. But we might as well have, don't you think?"

"So you have a vision of doom, Vlad?"

"Don't you? Just how long before someone breathes on you?"

Ryder tapped the side of his nose. "A small group of us are in an isolated centre."

"Not as isolated as us, I bet. I suppose you have provisions, but do you have medical facilities and protection?"

"Why, are you thinking of joining us?" Ryder hadn't considered that option. Anafon would have plenty of room.

"We decided to sit it out for a while, but there is a limit."

"True, I presume you're not getting any fresh provisions. How long can you last up there before coming down?"

"We're on rations, but with recycling and holding our breath, we could last a few more months before finding a new home."

"Not that you wouldn't be welcome, but I'd have to put it to everyone here. So far, we've not told anyone at all—you understand why. I'm sending you a data file with our website details to pass on to anyone else you think might benefit from sharing ideas."

"I'd have to confer with Dan and the crew. There should be a number of groups like yours. I worried that the number was zero."

Ryder laughed at the Ukrainian's joke but would have kept

smiling anyway. He warmed to have given them hope. "I don't suppose you're getting anything from Mission Control?"

"We expect to from the backups in Hawaii and Australia. We're trying tomorrow. I have to go now, Ryder. Keep in touch."

"Have a sip of recycled water on me, Vlad."

"Bastard." They both laughed as they switched off.

TERESA RAN INTO THE CENTRE, EYEBROWS RAISED. "Ryder, come outside. Brian and Bronwyn are leaving."

Ryder rushed out to find the couple had loaded up food and belongings in their estate car. Brian glared at Ryder.

"You can't stop us, Ryder."

"Come in and talk about this." Ryder looked in their vehicle windows for Megan.

"No way," Brian called out. "You've always had the better of us, giving all the orders. We've had enough."

Gustav came round on Ryder's right and stopped to take in the situation. Ryder nudged his foot at a rock and looked at Gustav with a slight head turn. He knew Brian wouldn't have seen his feet.

Ryder tried again. "I know it's tough here, Brian. We're all going stir crazy. Bronwyn, you wouldn't leave Megan, would you?" Ryder hoped to use Bronwyn's maternal instincts even though she had no children of her own.

"She's out there somewh–"

"Shut up, Bron," Brian said.

"She's inside the centre," said Ryder, bluffing. "Come in, have a cuppa and talk."

"No," Brian said. "We knew you'd try and talk us out of it. We won't tell anyone about this place. You'll get no visitors coming back. We'd rather take our chances. Maybe ARIA's died off anyway."

Ryder noticed Gustav on his belly. He'd placed rocks against both rear tyres and was edging away again. Brian's car was not going anywhere.

"I can't let you leave, Brian. What we have is too precious. We might be the only uninfected community left on the planet. We have a duty to liaise with the ISS crew to see what we can do for mankind."

Brian laughed. "You're mad. It's too late to save mankind. We're going to take our own chances."

Ryder noticed Gustav going back into the centre. He hoped he wasn't going to escalate matters.

"A few more weeks, Brian. Or, I'll tell you what, you and a couple of us will take our binoculars up on the hill and carefully move towards Llanfairfechan to see what's going on. Only without putting ourselves at risk. How about that, Bronwyn? Take things in small steps, safely?"

Bronwyn nodded then looked at her husband who was furious.

"I knew you'd be doing this," Brian said, and started the engine. Gustav came out of the centre carrying two rifles, he gave one to Ryder, who levelled it at Brian, while walking round to the front of the car.

"I'll run you down, you sheep dip."

Bronwyn cried as Brian released the brake. With the rear wheels not being able to move, the engine stalled.

Brian's face purpled as he beat the steering wheel with his hands. He reached behind him and drew out a revolver.

"It's useless, Brian," shouted Ryder. "We can't let you go. We could shoot out your tyres. Give it up, man."

Shaking with rage, Brian aimed his revolver at Teresa. "Let us go, or she'll be the first."

Ryder faced a dilemma. He wanted Teresa to hit the floor so Brian couldn't see her, but she looked transfixed. He couldn't let them go, because they were sure to run into people. The locals knew they worked in the centre and might decide to pay a scavenging visit. All three guns wavered.

Bronwyn stopped crying just long enough to grab at Brian, who struggled with her. Ryder lowered his weapon and looked at Gustav, who had put his down and pointed at the door on Bronwyn's side. Ryder went for Brian's door but just as he reached it, Brian's revolver went off. Bronwyn screamed.

Ryder opened Brian's door. A growing red patch showed through Bronwyn's blue jeans above her right knee. Gustav beat him to shouting to Teresa to help him get Bronwyn out and into the first-aid room.

Ryder found the revolver under the clutch pedal and threw it out into the heather.

"Come on, Brian. We've all been under a strain. Let's get inside and see to Bronwyn." Brian didn't move. Ryder assumed he was too shocked but then thought maybe the bullet went through him too. No. He was withdrawn. Ryder stayed with him since almost everyone inside had medical training except himself. After Derek brought out two welcomed mugs of tea, laced with whiskey, and delivered the good news that Bronwyn's wound was minor, Brian agreed to climb out. A fraught episode that Ryder knew made his own resolution all the stronger.

CHAPTER 20

Sunday 3 May 2015:
Evening in Manuel's cabin, Banff National Park, Canada.

AFTER A SUPPER OF SAUCEPAN-WARMED TINNED MEAT and veg, made possible after Manuel re-discovered the bottle-gas store, they luxuriated with a coffee in front of a log fire.

Jat released a squeal of delight at discovering Manuel's working Internet, but he had to caution against a young surfer's addiction.

"We only get enough juice in the daytime from the solar cells on the roof."

Her bottom lip stuck out. "How are we going to remember that tomorrow?"

"Write yourself a note. Here, have a notepad, keep a diary so you won't have to ask me my name in the morning. I have a NoteCom but I'm not sharing it."

"Fair enough, Manuel. Tell me, do you remember arriving here?"

"No. And tomorrow I'll remember even less. However, I think fragments of today might be recalled if we stick together. I read that memories get reinforced if constantly triggered."

"It is weird, isn't it? Every morning I wake up thinking it's a year ago but also not remembering if I passed my degree exams or who I had sex with over the last year—or yesterday. Look, I have a wedding ring." She showed him a plain gold band on her left ring finger.

Manuel took her hand. His mouth opened at the shock of how bony and white her fingers were. Bruises, scuffed knuckles, and dirty, broken fingernails all testified to her tough survival. He thought maybe it was as well she had amnesia. A paradox that ARIA allowed evil to be created and yet forgotten. He concentrated on the ring. "It's old and you have no engagement ring. I'd say it belongs to your mother or grandmother and it doesn't necessarily mean you are married."

"I've thought that, but I don't know, do I?"

"I don't suppose you know if you're er—"

"Pregnant? I don't know. It doesn't feel like it, and for all I know I've been peeing on test kits every other day for months."

"Drugs?"

"Oh, sure." Jat pulled up her sleeves, revealing needle marks, some recent.

"Well, I got some of those too," Manuel said. "Recreational. I guess some of yours are from your diabetes jabs when you run out of patches or need a quick fix. AIDS? Don't tell me. Neither of us knows much, do we?"

"You know a hell of a lot more than I do, Manuel. You and your NoteCom."

"At what point will the NoteCom not be helpful, Jat?"

"Apart from the obvious, like when you lose it so one morning you have no knowledge of it, there would come a time when you wouldn't recognise it for what it is."

"You mean I won't know how to switch it on? No problem, I'll write a few instructions now to leave with it each night."

"I meant if you forget the concept of gadgets as information providers."

"No, Jat, you'd have to go way, way back. I had hand-held Personal Information Management systems back in the twentieth century. With the rate of forgetfulness, it would take—oh my God— just four months."

"Four months from catching it, which was a month ago?" she said, getting up to make more coffee.

"Jat, let us suppose we survive for a year. My memories would relate to the life I had fifty-two years ago. I am fifty-four. By next April, I will have the knowledge and language of a two-year-old."

"Lucky you. I'll have the memory of a newborn in only twenty weeks. Five months, Manuel. I won't know how to speak, clean, or feed myself. In fourteen weeks I won't be able to write or read the notes I should be leaving to give me basic information. I'll be completely dependent on you if we are still together. I'll have the body with all the hormones and urges of a healthy woman but with the mind of a baby." She shuddered at the prognosis.

"I don't know, Jat. Just because your memory disappears, your body has had two decades of actions embedded in your muscles and nervous systems. I wonder how much of the memory loss is more related to events as opposed to learned or adaptive behaviour. Newborn babies have an instinct to grasp and suckle."

"We won't know for another five months unless we go out and find a child."

"All the more reason to be vigilant about keeping notes to keep relearning what we know," Manuel said.

"Yes, but not so much that five hours of each day has to be spent learning how to survive, who we are, where things are blah, blah."

"Agreed, Jat, we need to know what is important." He grabbed a piece of paper as well as opening a new page on his NoteCom. "We'll always know our own names."

"But not each others'; write them down. What do we say about who we are? You know, with respect to our relationship."

"Umm, you mean when we wake up in the morning, you might think you married me in a fit of desperation?"

"Get lost, Daddy. Are you that desperate? All right, don't answer. Leaving sex out of it, maybe it might be clever to pretend we're married."

Manuel laughed. "How does that work? I thought you'd prefer us to be father and daughter."

"I'm a realist, Manuel. We'll know for months that we are not pop and daughter, but we might believe we got married recently. I must have been smashed out of my mind, but there you go."

"Thanks, Jat."

"My pleasure. Hey, you never know, we might even enjoy fooling around. But, before you get excited, you know what this means to our list?"

He pulled a long face. "Yeah, we start it with a lie. That's awful."

"It shows we are thinking positively about survival. I'm Mrs Manuel? Is there another Mrs Manuel who's going to come after me?"

"Mrs Gomez. I remember getting married in my twenties but it didn't last long. Don't worry, I'll pass on the conjugal rights, for now."

"Whatever. Write on your NoteCom details like birthday, qualifications, last known job..."

"Hang on. Is qualifications and job relevant once you forget all your occupational skills?"

"They are in that they show what our personality and intelligence enabled us to achieve."

"True, but say I was a doctor just qualified, within six weeks, I wouldn't know hyperthermia from a nosebleed. Let's concentrate on real survival data. So date of birth is a must."

"Last known address of parents—especially in my young circumstances."

"Whereas not in mine," Manuel said.

"Do we have a gun?"

"I haven't found one. Frankly, I doubt it. This cabin would have been an empty tourist lodge before I arrived a month ago with provisions. I have no recollection of ever having a firearm, but we could search for one before turning in."

"I've been thinking about that. Going to bed I mean, and no, Manuel, not that either. Maybe tomorrow when I read this note and find we're married. What I mean is: why will everything today be wiped out by dawn? Is the amnesia effect accelerated by sleep or is it merely because eight hours is a long time not to keep going over things and keeping our brains working?"

Manuel rubbed his hands as if he'd thought this through before. "If it's true that we lose about fifty days' memory per day, then that amounts to two days' loss per hour. But that's for retrograde amnesia: forgetting stuff in the past going backwards. Maybe things of today are, like you say, so frequently reinforced with stimulation from having all our senses working, especially with each other to talk to. But when our brains shut down for sleep, it's as if today's thoughts were in a temporary memory then deleted."

"So if we didn't go to sleep, we'd remember more tomorrow?" Jat said.

"Probably, at least of today's events, but then what state would we be in by the end of tomorrow?"

"Yeah, and today's memory isn't that perfect, Manuel. What did you have for breakfast?"

He looked at Jat and then over to the kitchen area as if that would be an *aide-mémoire*. Standing up and then wandering over, he tried to recall whether he'd found cereals or did he have spread on crackers, dried toast? Then again, had he already tried this exercise today?

She shook her head. "I don't remember either. Of course, that might be normal for a lot of people, so let's have a more rigorous test."

"Let's not, Jat. We still have a lot to do before sleep overtakes us."

"Fair enough. Look, Manuel, we didn't get round to using the web today, so let's make sure we leave a note. I'd really like to check e-mails, social sites while I remember how. In fact, I'm writing my webmail address and password and other details. I presume you have all that for you on your NoteCom?"

Manuel shuffled his feet in embarrassment, then sat next to Jat. "I've avoided using the web in fear of what I might find. But you're right. Add 'Ryder.'"

"Your son?"

"A close colleague from the UK. In fact, because of that, he might still be clear. I wonder if I've contacted him already? Nevertheless, put it down. Look. I've found his details on the NoteCom, so copy this bit. What else is crucial?"

They sat there with the list wondering how it was that the most vital information needed to survive occupied only half of a piece of paper.

"We've been through a lot today," she said.

Manuel's tiredness made him drop his cup of coffee on the table making them both jump to avoid the cascade. He said, "Let's get to bed. How do you know to give yourself insulin?"

She showed him a blue pendant round her neck and a medic-bracelet.

"Let's make sure with a note—paper and on the NoteCom."

Both bedrooms had en suite facilities, and smiling at each other, they parted. Manuel hadn't explored the other room but assumed, like his, it housed an assortment of mixed-gender clothes and necessities. But now, he had company. Someone with intellect to bounce ideas off, keep his brain working, and jog memories. But would he have a clue who she was or remember anything of today when he woke up?

CHAPTER 21

Sunday 3 May 2015, 22:50:
In orbit onboard the International Space Station.

ALL ABDUL KHAN COULD HEAR WAS THE CRACKLING HISS OF THE RADIO. For all his communication skills, he could not raise Houston Mission Control. The core-design of the comms depended on permanent integration between the ISS and several grey boxes at Johnson in Houston. Failsafe circuits and switches kicked in when inevitable glitches occurred, but no one planned for a total blackout from the uplink.

Backup control centres existed. They didn't get the fame or have the acres of goggle-eyed wonder-people being entertained at Houston. Abdul had flicked through their frequencies many times. The Challenger Center, Hawaii; Vandenberg Air Force Base, California; and Carnarvon, Australia. They ringed the planet. An altitude-zero orbit. In the main, their tasks involved radio relay, but they underwent control sessions so they knew what to do in emergencies.

Abdul considered a total communications blackout from Houston as an emergency. It had been a week since they received more than a garbled voice message, though they received data transfers until yesterday. Dan told him to switch to one of the other mission-control centres. Vandenberg might as well have been swallowed by the desert, though Hawaii sent *message received* and *please hold* returns. Abdul stopped getting excited by those auto-response messages from Hawaii and gave up expecting a real person to grab the mike at the other end. He had hopes for the more isolated Carnarvon space communications station. Based at the most western edge of Australia and surrounded on three sides by desert it had the best chance of housing healthy people manning the radio.

He set the switch for Carnarvon's frequency and set the call on auto before sitting back with his hands cradling the back of his short black hair. The acknowledge-return call caught him off guard such that he would have fallen off the fixed swivel chair if it didn't have arms.

Maybe their system auto-responded, but hey, there was a blond, blue-eyed young Australian woman, and she talked to him.

"That looks like Abdul. How's it going up there?"

"Never mind us, how are you doing down in Carnarvon? Oh, sorry, can you give your name, call sign, and all that?"

"Ooh, listen to you, Abdul. Go on, guess my name—and it isn't Sheila."

Dan, as commander, came rushing to the console.

Abdul switched off the mike. "Commander, the lack of protocol points to big problems in Carnarvon too."

Dan took over from Abdul, but instead of using his usual strict and aggressive approach, he smiled, "Hi, Australia. I'm Dan, who are you?"

"Dan, you are the famous commander. Wow."

"No, it is me who should say wow. And you are—?"

"Charlotte."

"Hi there, Charlotte, is your controller there at Carnarvon?"

"What's that, Dan, aren't I pretty enough for you? Just joking. Sorry, mate, this station is one of only a handful of buildings left standing in Carnarvon after a flash flood a couple of years back. When a new bar-manager arrived last week and had what we thought might be ARIA symptoms, everybody evacuated on the same plane she arrived on."

Jena pulled a pained face at Abdul, but Charlotte pre-empted their response. "I guess that might have been a mistake, guys? I haven't heard from them since."

"You might be right, Charlotte. But how about you?"

"My parents are in Sydney and told me to stay out here until it all blows over. I volunteered to man the station. Did I do right, d'you reckon?"

"You've done right by us, Charlotte. Just a moment, our physician wants a word."

"Hi, Antonio, is everybody fit and healthy up there?" she said, surprising the crew with her obvious knowledge of who they all were and their function.

"We're doing fine, Charlotte. Would you mind if I asked you a few questions?"

"Shoot, Doc. But before you do, today is Monday May 4, 2015. Don't forget I'm a little ahead of you in time. I had eggs for breakfast and cheese and crackers for last night's supper. What d'you want to ask me?"

"*Molto buon*," Antonio said. "You have no symptoms of memory loss, headaches, tinnitus, or anything else with your head?"

"Sure I do, Doc. I've always been scatty. I get headaches every time I drink red wine, and I'm always forgetting things on the shopping list I left at home."

Dan interrupted Antonio's interrogation. "Yeah, Charlotte, don't we all, but you remember enough to pass your exams to be employed at Carnarvon. Yes?"

"I could tell you I slept with the prof, but kidding aside, I don't have this ARIA thing yet. Any idea what the incubation time is?"

"Stand by to be amazed, Charlotte," said the doctor giving a thumbs up to the others. "You should have been experiencing a dull headache and tinnitus accompanied by increasing loss of memory within twenty-four hours of breathing in the same place as your new bar-manager neighbour. So you know what that means?"

"Well, Doc, I was always a bugger for not getting everyone else's colds and flu, so I guess I get away with it as usual. No big deal."

"No big deal?" His excitement took his accent and language into overdrive. "*Enorme, magnifico, molto importante. Mamma mia.*"

Abdul took over. "Charlotte, our usually calm and collected doctor is trying to say that you are the first person we know of who might be immune to ARIA. Though it's possible your newcomer didn't have it."

"Wow, guys. Hey...creepy...Does that mean sooner or later I'll be the only one who knows anything?"

Antonio calmed down, but Abdul realized he was preparing to tell her that, barring enclaves of isolation, and if she met no one else, then with certainty she would be the only person on the planet in two years' time who would be able to write, read, and speak.

Abdul switched off the mike. "I hope you are not going to give her a straight answer to that one, Antonio. It might freak her out. Let's concentrate on positive aspects of her situation such as getting in touch with Ryder Nape's group." Everyone agreed, including Antonio.

"Charlotte, it is great you are free of ARIA. There are just a few others we know of who are similarly free. We would like to put you in touch with a British group. They have isolated themselves and have medical expertise."

"Yeah, sure. It's boring out here stuck between a desert and the ocean. Maybe I should go to Perth?"

"No, Charlotte," burst in Dan. "Stay where you are. Much safer. Abdul will give you a web address for Ryder's group. Log into it and use the e-mail link to introduce yourself. We'll let him know too, so he'll know you are not some freak who hit on his website randomly."

"Okay, guys. It's comforting to know I have friends on Earth as well as in space. I'll chat to you again on your next orbit. Ciao."

CHAPTER 22

Monday 4 May 2015:
Moraine Lake, eighteen days since ARIA started. Most people have
lost up to two years, four weeks of memory.

MANUEL STRUGGLED THROUGH TO CONSCIOUSNESS. What must have
been a new alarm clock hammered away, making him pull the pillow
over his head. Throwing an unseeing arm at where his bedside
cabinet should've been hadn't silenced the percussion. One eye
opened and found a varnished pinewood ceiling. He could smell
coffee but the unfamiliar log cabin tugged at his worry bone. It
looked like a vacation cabin in the forest but that didn't figure. He
remembered going to bed in his own room: pale-green walls, white
ceiling, cobwebs.

Once he could stand it, he admired the brilliant dawn light hitting
the carpet. Pine trees with a busy resident woodpecker met his eyes.
The alarm clock had feathers.

He scratched an armpit. "So, I'm definitely not in Baltimore."

After finding and using the bathroom, his nose detected toast
along with the coffee. Fearing who he might find, he ventured into
the kitchen.

"Oh, you're up, are you, Manuel?" said a scowling young woman
sitting at a rustic table.

Manuel stood searching his shot memory but failed to locate a
white-faced girl with long jet-black hair among his acquaintances.

"Before you throw a wobbler, read that." She pointed at a
NoteCom placed at the opposite end of the table.

A milky coffee, just as he liked it, waited for him. He pointed at it,
she pointed in return at the NoteCom. He looked up again. Yellow T-
shirt and jeans; he looked at his own clothes—black trousers, white
shirt, and a NASA tie. Good God, he'd dressed for work.

> *You are Manual Gomez, employed by NASA as their*
> *Education Officer for flight missions with responsibility*
> *to liaise with the media.*
>
> *Except you are on leave along with most of the*
> *population because you have ARIA. An infectious*
> *amnesia throwing out your memories at the rate of 50*

days' worth each day. This probably started for you on 15ᵗʰ April 2015. It is now Monday 4ᵗʰ May 2015 so you have lost 950 days or two years, seven months, and two days of memory.

You have remarried to Jat Qappik, who also has ARIA and is probably sitting at the table with you. She is diabetic but cut down her Humilin dose (usually neo-Humulin patches)—see notes.

See the instructions below to access more information...

"You're Jat? My wife?"

"I am Jat, but I have no recollection of marrying you. Don't get any ideas."

"Hang on. My head is spinning coping with waking up in Canada with a disease instead of my home in Baltimore. Look at us, Jat. I'm mid-fifties, you're what, eighteen?"

"Twenty—that's not the big deal."

"No? Well, what is?"

"Look at you. You obviously don't look after yourself, you've deserted your other wife because of this memory business and—no, don't interrupt me—how do I know you don't have any vile STDs?"

Manuel, glad he received the broadside while sitting down, shook his head. "Jat, as far as I know, I have no diseases except one that's robbed me of what must have been a helluva courtship and a cracking wedding night. Me wife left me for an insurance salesman. And though I grant you I'm hiding a six-pack stomach under a keg, I have more muscles than I used to." He did a strongman impression. She turned to face the window so he couldn't see if she was smiling.

"There's a load of chopped wood out back, so I guess you might have been working out," Jat said. He saw her reflection fighting a grin.

Manuel looked at the rough calluses on his palms. "Yep, that's right. Extraordinary, for a desk man."

Jat examined her own hands, showing Manuel her wedding ring. "It's all whacky though, isn't it? I mean, who brought us here, and why?"

"I suppose we brought us here. I have memories of being up here in Moraine Lake as a kid."

"I've virtually no belongings here. A shoulder bag with some clothes and ID. There's my insulin in the fridge. Enough for a month, I reckon. Then I need to go find some more."

"You saw the note about not going into town," he said, looking worried.

"Sure I did. Lawless gangs. In Lake Louise and probably my home city, Vancouver. But where am I going to get my insulin?"

"I don't know, Jat. I guess we'll be risking some forays out there to hospitals and city drugstores, but I have a feeling they'll be trashed pretty soon if not already. I'm surprised more insulin isn't here."

"Which tells us it was a spur-of-the-moment decision, yeah?"

"Like our marriage, you mean?"

"Whatever. Maybe it was for my protection—as if I needed it."

"Or mine. Don't look surprised. Two are better than one in a crisis, even if one is a girl." He had to duck to avoid the plate projectile.

They both sat facing each other across the rustic, long table to savour toast and maple syrup along with the strong coffee for breakfast.

"This syrup would've been better on pancakes," she said.

"Guess so. Found any?"

"I haven't gone through that huge freezer yet."

"Can you freeze pancakes?"

"Don't you know anything about cooking? I suppose that's another reason you chained me to you."

"Hey. There's the door, Jat. And I'll have you know I was the legend of culinary achievement in my place of work."

"Which was a den in your house?"

"Sometimes." He joined in the laugher. "But mostly at NASA's Washington Media Centre."

They finished their breakfast, alternating between sitting and walking around the cabin. Outside on a trestle lay wood begging to be chopped. Without a second thought, Manuel levered the axe out of an old stump, and after spitting on his hands, making Jat recoil with a screwed-up face, he swung the axe, neatly starting a V incision.

"Well, you clearly have your future mapped out," she said. "More therapy than the need for firewood already."

"I've no doubt you're right. It sure feels good to use muscle in the cause of survival. You could always stack up the pieces against the cabin where I've started."

"I could always not."

"Whatever." He could tell that he had an uphill struggle with Jat, and yet, there must have been some endearing quality for them to decide to stay together. He went on a course of reverse-psychological motivation still in his memory. Leaning the axe against the door jamb, he followed her back into the kitchen. He sniffed again at his coffee. "This brew, interesting flavour."

"Spit it out if you don't like it." She'd folded her arms so tight he could see her fingers whitening.

"I'd rather not, thank you. It's just that it's rare to find someone who can burn coffee." He sat, ready to duck again, but she just stood with her back to the window, arms still folded, giving him the evil-eye. After a few seconds he winked at her. She turned to the window again.

"I'm going to leave and get to my folks in Vancouver," she said, maintaining her stare out of the window, watching a red-headed woodpecker annoy beetles.

Manuel drummed fingers on the pine table. He wondered why she voiced her desire to go home right now. He was sure after the warnings on the NoteCom, she wouldn't want to risk travelling.

"Jat, maybe we can buy some insulin on the web. DHL could fly it in."

"My God, I've married a comedian. It's not just about insulin. I can probably live a while without it if I'm careful. But Vancouver's my home. I want to know what's happening."

"I'm not sure it helps to know too much at the moment," Manuel said, but regretted letting his pessimism out to play.

"Yeah, cheers. You have no family, do you, Gomez?"

"Only one around here, Mrs Gomez." They gave each other wry smiles. "And a bunch more in Spain."

"I'm pretty sure you're not going to like me when I go stir-crazy in this wooden box." She slammed down the jar of instant coffee she'd just picked up.

"Yeah, well. Shall we go for a stroll and take in our estate?"

"Are we tooled up?"

"I hadn't thought about it. Who are you expecting to attack us?"

"I dunno. Maybe I have an ex out there objecting to me having a geriatric for a husband."

"More likely one of my friends trying to protect me from a gold-digging floozy."

"Touché, but have we a sub-machine gun?"

"I've no idea. It would be a good idea."

"I was thinking in order to get my insulin by force if I have to."

"Would you kill someone in order to get some, even if you've none left?"

Jat let out an exasperated sigh. "I should have two doses of insulin a day now. If it looks like I'm about to kiss you, Manuel, it's to let you close enough to smell my breath. If you smell pear-drops, and I'm irritable—all right, *more* irritable than usual—and if I'm eating all your stores, drinking all the water, peeing all the time while being out of breath, then I'm probably—"

"About to go into a coma and within a few days I'll need to find the shovel. Point taken. But I might have a plan."

"So have I. Get home."

Manuel had a turn at exhaling a long sigh. "Why do you think there is no answer when you ring your home in Vancouver or the mobile phones of your folks and friends there? You've had the breakfast TV on. No news since I've been in here, just repeats, probably on a loop."

"Not much to go on, is it? Repeats on TV and phones going wrong is hardly news these days."

"And what are these days, 'cos we don't remember them, do we? And that is news, Jat. Too many coincidences. Let's call the police in Vancouver. Hell, anywhere. Call 9-1-1."

Though reluctant to prove him right, Jat tapped 9-1-1. "Nothing. Not even the usual hold message. All the more reason to find out what's happened." She wiped a tear.

Manual gave her a teacloth. "Normally, I'd agree, but what's the most probable outcome? We're told we have a vehicle down the lane. We'd need to drive three hundred miles, which means finding a gas station to get all the way there and to get back—all right, don't look at me as if that's not an option. Maybe we'd run into trouble on the way, let alone when we reach the outskirts and centre of Vancouver. A city full of bewildered and hungry people. I'm painting an ugly picture, I know, and I'm sorry, but that's how I see it."

"All the more reason to find my folks and get them out of there."

He stood and wandered to the window. The woodpecker had rested its beak, but a spring shower threw raindrops against the glass so percussion prevailed.

"I understand that, Jat. Suppose we find them. How many are we talking? Half dozen? More? We'd need more vehicles and maybe get followed back here. My bet is that we wouldn't find them. They might've found their own refuge in the valleys, lost their phones or couldn't keep recharging them. They'd be upset at the thought of you being in danger looking for them when they're safe."

"Or dead."

"We can't keep on like this. How about e-mail? They might've left you a message."

"Now you're talking. Hey, Manuel, do you think we'll have this debate tomorrow?"

"We probably had it yesterday." He switched on the computer, after reading the instructions on powering up the satellite receiver and checking the battery, whose solar recharging had just taken a dive with the rainy weather. "I knew a Brit, Ryder, he might have information for us."

They heard a thud at the back door, which sent both into crouch mode to hide beneath window height. Jat, on her way from the kitchen, grabbed a steak knife while Manuel shuffled around to his bedroom to collect a baseball bat he'd noticed under the bed.

"Maybe it was just the wind throwing some firewood at us," whispered Manuel. "Either way, we'll nip out the front door. You get behind a big tree while I sneak around the back."

"No fucking way. Stop treating me like a little girl. You're so patronising. I've probably been in more scrapes than you have."

"All right, stop going on about me trying to protect my wife. We'll do a pincer movement, if that's okay with you."

She set off before he finished locking the door. He'd already checked the bolt on the back door. Damn the woman. He could hear her running round, just so she could get another score on him, as if all of this was just a game. He had more trouble: holly grew right up to the side of the cabin forcing a time-consuming detour. His right foot disappeared mid-calf in a cold, muddy, leaf-hidden puddle, making him bite his lip to stop swearing out loud. He heard a cry, accelerating his movement.

He rounded the last corner to find Jat on her knees with her back to him. Still a gentle rain falling, she must have wet knees, at the least. Maybe a hole in her chest. Manuel stayed crouched and looked around while moving in on Jat.

"Isn't he gorgeous?" she said, turning to show him the scraggiest mongrel he'd ever seen.

"Is that our intruder?"

"Say hello to Disco. Don't you think that's appropriate for a discovery?"

"I don't think you should be so close to it. Probably got rabies; looks ill, and judging by its mangy coat, it's a wolf-cross."

"He's just starving and cold. Come on, Disco."

"You're not bringing him in the cabin."

"Disco is wet too. Anyway, he might be our lost mutt. Poor thing having owners who forget about him every day."

"There's no mention of a dog in the NoteCom."

"There isn't time to read everything. Better make a highlighted note about Disco so we know for sure tomorrow."

Manuel followed them into the kitchen where Jat wrapped a towel around the animal. He said, "I suppose he could be a guard dog."

"There, Disco, Manuel is a nice man. Forget what I told you earlier."

"Nevertheless, I don't want him in the cabin. Once you've dried him and, no doubt, given him a better breakfast than I had, he can stay on the sheltered porch out front. I'm going to have a look around, try and familiarise. Find the vehicle. Check how much fuel it has. Hey, are you listening?"

"What? Oh, go then. Make sure our mobile phones have both numbers in and take yours with you."

Into his shoulder bag he placed his NoteCom, mobile phone, food, and water. It wasn't that he didn't expect to be back but he had to be prepared for anything. One thing was certain, if and when he returned to the cabin: that perishing dog would be on his bed.

CHAPTER 23

Sunday 14 June 2015:
Rosamond, California, two months after the case was opened.
Many would have lost eight years of their memory. The wife of Jack
Balin, the first to catch ARIA, is in church.

IRENE'S TEARS SPLUTTERED ON THE CANDLE SHE HELD. A dozen other candles held back pitch-blackness in the New Family Community Church. The late evensong service was not listed on the blackboard outside the white-painted stone building, built as a replica of the old Spanish mission churches. Word of down-turned mouths in huddled groups brought Irene and the other women after sundown. Like most downtown buildings these days, no one barred entry through the broken doors. It wasn't only criminals who seized opportunities to break and enter. Irene knew of decent folk, besides herself, whose jobs didn't exist anymore—if they remembered what and where their jobs were. They woke up confused, desperate, and hungry. They had little choice but to scavenge and raid. The church had been looted the least. Understandable, since people desperate for food soon left though a few prayer books might find they've become soul food.

Irene lifted her head. All she could see through misty eyes was blackness, except for a fluttering moth and motes of dust lit by the candles. She knew all the others in there with her: friends, some of whom had much bigger problems. At least Jack came home most days and her children played with others then came home. Not that all was well. Jack didn't go to work; no one did. They had quite a lot of money left in their bank accounts. They couldn't get any of it because the cash machines were empty. It didn't matter. She had money in her bag but there was nothing to buy. Once the shop shelves echoed empty, local farms became popular.

A glimmer of a smile as she recalled Jack's account of his involvement with the farm raid.

"We didn't know. We were all either Edwards men or public service, not farmers."

"Didn't know what, Jack? And where's the food?" Irene asked, arms folded.

"Did you want to eat palm trees or Pampas grass?"

She didn't know whether to laugh or cry. "So, the farm only grew trees and ornamental grasses?"

"There was more money in them than in fruit and vegetables. But we found out where a cattle ranch is only twenty miles away. So we should have steak by tomorrow night." He started to smile but it faltered as if some of the muscles had forgotten how.

"Which cattle ranch is it?" She said, worried because her uncle worked and lived on The Sage Bush Ranch.

"The Six—er—God, I hope Charlie wrote it down."

"Charlie? That goon. He'll have lost the paper and so none of you will know which farm. Anyway, you'll forget all about it by morning."

"Maybe, till our stomachs growl. I'll write another note." He fumbled in his greasy hair above his right ear and pulled out a pencil stub.

"Jack, have you seen all the notes we have in the house? Our kitchen door is covered."

"Yeah, I've not written so much since I forged my tax forms....A joke! Give us a hug." She opened her arms to him, tears of relief for a touch of marital warmth amidst the desperation.

"Don't be so soft, woman," he said, turning to his left, away from her.

"Oh, Jack. Here, just a minute, what's that on your shirt?"

"Leave it, woman. Best you didn't know what us men have to do these days."

"Blood. Come on, out with it. Whose blood?" Tears of anger now.

"We had some trouble with the landowner when we searched his outbuildings."

"And?"

"I didn't know Charlie had a gun. He panicked."

"Oh, the poor man. You damn fool, Jack. And Charlie."

"I did what I could—that's why I'm so bloody."

"Who else was there? Oh, don't tell me. As if we haven't enough to worry about."

"At least we don't need to worry about the police calling. We saw the precinct burning on the way back. That'll keep Duffy busy."

"Is Duffy the only police left on duty? Jack, he's been a friend of your family for years."

"Exactly. He's been doing the sergeant's job for so long, it'll take years for him to forget what to do and where go. Though, with no fire service and no water to speak of, he'll have to work from home from now on."

"Jack, farms use a lot of water, don't they?"

"Sure, so?"

"If there's no water in our taps, Jack, how can there be water at the farms? Won't the crops and cattle die?"

"Jeez, I dunno, Irene. You always think the worst. I expect some farms have those wind-pumps or diesel that brings up water, though it's a hell of a long way deep round here. All the more reason for Charlie and me to go and relieve them before all the stock's spoiled."

"Careful then. Another thing, *we* could do with more water, Jack. Not just for drinking."

"Yeah, the bathroom is disgusting even for me. Those flies are huge. We should use our washing and dirty water for flushing. I'm going to get changed. You going out? See you later."

GUNSHOTS COULD BE HEARD BY THE CONGREGATION.

"Did you hear that, Irene?" whispered her young neighbour, Melantha.

"Yes, Mel. Maybe it's Duffy warning off some looters."

More shots echoed through the lofty church.

A quivering, old-woman's voice travelled through the dark to join the conversation. "Don't think so, Irene. I saw him climb into his Chevy after piling it up with his stuff."

"That you, Senita? Any word from yours?" asked Irene and then regretted asking.

Sobbing told her the answer.

"Sorry, Senita. Damn this memory loss. I can't even remember what's happening to my friends, or my family, for that matter."

The three conversationalists rose out of their pews and in the candlelight found each other for a group hug. In the quiet, they heard a lone voice singing.

"We never get any peace even in here," moaned Mel.

"Better than hearing gunshots," Irene said.

"I thought Liz was coming," Senita said, still sniffing.

"I fucking have," said a voice beyond the candlelight. They heard a walking frame clump on the floor towards them. "Fuck this thing."

"You all right, Liz?" asked Irene. "Did I see your Jacob this morning? Oh God, or was it yesterday?"

"How should I know when you saw him, Irene? But tell you what, when you see him again, any of you, tell him don't bother coming home. That's if the fucker would know where home is."

Senita gasped. "Liz, you and Jacob are so much together. What's gone wrong? Besides this memory thing."

"He can't handle losing his memory."

"Yeah," said Senita, "My Pat's taken off. Dunno when though. I found a few sheets of paper this morning full of numbers. So, I says to meself, I bet he forgot his PIN number and it freaked him out."

"Well, money isn't any use," Mel said.

"It might have been when he forgot his PIN number," Senita said. "Don't suppose you know when Jacob left then, Liz?"

"Probably yesterday judging by the black eye I'm sporting." A rush of candles closing in on her face sent her reeling. "Hey, it's all right, I can do without you setting my hair on fire as well." They all relief-laughed.

A soft singing of "Amazing Grace" reached them but stopped as the sound of an empty plastic bottle dropped on the stone floor made them all look to the back of the church.

"Do you think Father Fielder's here?" Irene asked.

"His car's not in the parking lot," Senita said.

"He might have gone to his family back East," Liz said. "Either way, we've done our praying, ladies, so let's go for what else we've come for. If that fucking warbler's left us any."

Irene's candle, like the others, flickered as they neared extinction so the women walked with purpose to a rear office. An oil-lamp added an amber glow and illuminated another woman filling a canteen with water from an old tap and re-starting "Amazing Grace."

"Hey, you beat us to it, Celia," Irene said.

"I sneaked in when you lot were gassing," Celia said, a woman in her fifties who Irene knew always wore a long, turquoise kaftan.

"Thought the water might run out tonight, did you?" said Liz, positioning herself to be next with her two-litre bottle.

"Not really. On the other hand, it won't last forever."

"None of us have any water in our houses," Irene said. "Jack reckons the pumps have packed in 'cos no one's been maintaining them."

"I've heard the military have taken over the water," Senita said.

"Yeah, to make sure they've got enough," Celia said. "Though I've also heard that there isn't any army. They've not been paid, so they've gone home."

As she filled her container, Irene said, "I'm relieved that for at least another day we have water." Irene had found that the taps at her home brought no water, then read her note saying where a sure source was in the town. She had no idea why the church tap worked. Maybe it had a huge tank, built a century ago when farm folk in the area could use it before a deep well tapped the ground water.

Outside, the women held hands, taking comfort from each other before heading home through the chilled, starlit desert town. A fire in the suburbs added a glow to the sky and worry to the women.

"The school?" Mel said.

"Looks like it," said Liz. "I heard talk this afternoon of there being food and drink in the cafeteria there."

Mel said, "To think I spent years in there as a kid. Shame. Another part of my life gone."

"Gunshots probably came from there," Liz said.

"Might have been gas canisters exploding," Irene said, clutching at less aggressive options. "Anyway, we should make our way home now while the ne'er-do-wells get drawn to the flames."

They hugged, hoping to re-congregate the next day.

Irene had a mile to go in the dark and kept to walls wherever she could. A paper in her dress pocket held her address. Instinct told her to be as inconspicuous as possible. So it came as a shock when someone came up behind her and called her name. "Irene, slow down please."

"Oh, God, it's you, Celia. What you doing sneaking up on me?"

"I forgot to bring my address."

"Don't you live on Rushmore Street? Oh, my God, that was years ago and maybe you moved. I can't remember either. Don't you have any clues?"

"I know all these places, Irene. I used to foster kids and that took me into an awful lot of houses in Rosamond. There are clues all around me, all leading to too many houses." She cried. Irene put her arms around her shoulders.

"You'd better come home with me, Celia. We can look in the phone directory for your new address."

"So it will be. Aren't you clever, Irene?"

Irene had a sinking feeling, and sure enough, a few moments later a cracked melody of more "Amazing Grace" disturbed the cats. They both started giggling when a dog howled. A slamming door shut them up. Running footsteps stopped them until Irene's flashlight allowed her to recognise Eddie, her thirteen-year-old son. She cried with sorrow for the kids. They had such a small life and the forgetting disappeared it so fast.

"Mom, come in quickly, it's Debbie."

Irene looked at him. Confused, because most of her remaining continuous memory had Eddie as a much younger child. She supposed each morning she had to get used to a more grown-up son. She shook her head to react to his bawling about his younger sister. Her first reaction was to blame him for slamming the door and scaring them half to death.

"What have you done to her this time, Eddie?"

"Nothing, Mom, but she just sits there crying."

"Where's your pa?"

"He's not back."

A range of dangerous scenarios went through Irene's mind: the fire at the school, his talk of farm raids and tendency to seek liquor and its instant consumption. But she had a domestic crisis to deal with.

"Come on, Celia, play happy families." Irene tugged at Celia's elbow. Eddie followed them in with a long face.

"It's not that happy at the moment," he said. "Debbie won't come out of her room."

"She often does that until meal times." Irene exchanged an ironic laugh with Celia at the child-rearing clichéd angst.

Irene called Debbie's name as she climbed the stairs after stopping a second to detect sobbing sounds. Thank God they'd refused both kids' frequent whining demands for door bolts. She knocked as she pushed the nine-year-old girl's bedroom door open.

"Debs, what's the matter, darling?" Irene asked in vain as her daughter sat on her bed, arms wrapped around her raised knees making herself as small as possible. Her shoulder-length red hair tangled at the wet, straggled ends. A flickering oil lamp gave her an eerie glow, projecting odd shapes on her wall. Irene sat on the end of the bed. "Come on, sweetheart, tell your mom what it is. Has your brother been bothering you, again?" Irene put out a hand to lift Debbie's chin so her red eyes could be scrutinised. She reckoned that no matter what her children said, their eyes told her the truth. She saw fear and confusion, and by doing so, Irene trembled, wavered in her normal cool demeanour.

"Oh come on, Debs, say something."

"She won't, Mom," said Eddie, "or can't."

"I know," said Celia, who'd followed them up the stairs. "What's your favourite food, Debbie, dear? Your favourite food is?"

They all looked at the girl, willing her to verbalise her thoughts. Her lips trembled, giving the onlookers hope an intelligible word would emerge. All three closed in, making the terrified girl shrink into her pillow.

Irene erupted at Celia and Eddie. "For God's sake, get back! Celia, the phone book is downstairs in the kitchen, find yourself and get your husband to come and get you."

"I've got a husband?" Celia said. "Since when?"

"Two years... or was it three? Oh, I don't know. Find your address and my Jack will take you home."

"If he gets home," said Eddie, showing Irene Debbie's diary, which had its last scribbled entry a fortnight ago. It said:

lectric gon Pa hit Ed iM skard

A tear pearled at the corner of his eye. Irene knew he was the hardest kid at school.

She glanced a scowl at him before turning a sweet smile again at her daughter. "Now, Debbie. Where were we? Well— why not—what is your favourite food? Tell me and I'll make it for you."

"Yeah, right," whispered Eddie.

Irene used her most pleading face, pouring emotion into her own wet eyes. "Come on, sweetheart, what is your favourite food?"

Debbie opened her mouth a little and uttered, "Food."

"Yes, lovely, yes, yes. Food, food. Now what is your favourite food?"

"F-food," said Debbie, a little louder.

"Yes, dear, now what kind of food?"

"Food," said Debbie.

Eddie spoke up, "Say peanut butter and jelly, dumbass," and ducked to avoid his mother's left arm sweeping around. Turning back, Irene saw Debbie curl up once more.

"I'll bring you some food, girl, just a minute," said Irene, ushering Eddie out and down the stairs. "What the hell is that all about, Eddie? What have you done to your sister?"

"Nothing, Mom. It's the memory-loss thing."

"What, she's just forgotten her favourite food? I don't think so."

"No, Mom, she's forgotten how to talk. She hasn't written in her diary for two weeks. But you've seen that newspaper article we keep to remind us every day. We're losing a year for every week and that's eight years since it started."

"My God...the poor girl's only nine. God, Jack, where the hell are you?" Then she realized they had no power. No bread for peanut butter and jelly sandwiches; Debbie's favourite food.

"She was learning the word *food* when we kept saying it, Mom. She doesn't remember what it is. Mom, I'm only four years older than Debs. That means I'll be the same as her soon, won't I? I can't work it out, Mom." He cried, hugging her as his mother spread peanut butter and jelly and tears on crispbread for her daughter.

"Another month yet for you, son. Oh God, this is awful. It's inhuman forgetting. I'm going to bake some bread tomorrow. Damn, there's no electricity for the oven. I know, I'll build a fire in the yard. Damn it, yes. Hey, Eddie, are these twists you made today? Good boy."

"Mom, I don't want to forget any more. I can't remember how to do stuff, the TV doesn't work, or my games..."

"Games don't matter shit, you stupid kid. They never did. You still play with Tommy, don't you? And that blond kid, what's his name?"

Through tears, Eddie looked puzzled. "Mom, I don't know no Tommy. I hung around with some kids down at the mall today, but none of us knew each other. I'd never thought about memory before, Mom. Never thought I had any use for it. But it held all my friends." He burst into more tears.

Irene softened and hugged him again. She wanted to say comforting words but none came. Eddie hit it square on. The use of memory. She had her childhood memories like all those in retirement homes in their rocking chairs. Her Eddie had lost that. Forever gone. Eddie interrupted her morbid thinking.

"Mom, what's gonna happen to Debbie when she forgets everything?"

"God, son, what do you mean? I'm going to take her this snack. Here, I've done some for you, and drink some pop, while there's still some."

Ignoring the food, Eddie followed his mother up the stairs. "But, Mom, next week her memory will be when she was born. Then what? Will she remember to eat, drink and breathe?"

"Stop pestering me with such nonsense, boy." Irene gave up on the fight to stem the tears. She sat on the bed and pushed the plate at Debbie, who looked at it with crimson eyes. She grabbed at the brown-splattered crackers and shoved them in her mouth.

"Instinct, see," said Celia, who had followed them again up the stairs. "Some things our bodies carry on doing even though we don't think too much about them. Like animals."

"But will we be able to find food and cook it?" said Eddie. "We've got loads of canned and bottled food, but will we know what they are when our memory has completely gone?"

"Search me, Eddie," Celia said. "Hey, our notes and newspaper clippings aren't going to help much when we forget how to read.

"I've got stuff on my recordable player. That's what us kids were doing down at the mall, reading to our players."

"What about batteries?" Celia asked, looking at Irene who was hugging Debbie.

"There's loads of batteries in the stores but loads of players use solar like lots of other stuff. Mom, there's solar cookers in the stores. Maybe I should tell Pa."

"Good idea, son, we could leave a cheque to cover the cost for the storekeeper when he comes back."

"Sure, Mom," Eddie said, looking up at Celia, with a look beyond his thirteen years going on five. "Did you find your address, Mrs, er, Celia?"

"Not there, Eddie. Guess we might be unlisted or we haven't got a phone except the mobiles, and I can't find mine."

"We've got room," Irene said. "There's a futon in the spare room."

"Irene, you're an angel."

"Yeah, well keep low because just lately I think I'm married to the Devil."

They spent an hour munching and thinking. Irene rocked Debbie to sleep as if she was a nine-year-old baby. Maybe it was just as well each day started fresh. Irene knew she'd sink lower than a toad's belly in a dry well if she carried her children's burden over from one day to the next. A day at a time gave her little opportunity to dwell on how bad it could get. She glimpsed herself in the future but dismissed it as too incredible to contemplate. She had to be brave. Braver than her husband who'd gone wandering off again. She knew Jack's masculine aggression had put him on he-man mode; a real-life game to play.

A white light filled the room and swept away.

"Your pa's home," Irene said to her children, whether they listened or not. She eased her arm away from the sleepy Debbie and ushered her son out before Jack came charging in.

The front door slammed, shaking the thin staircase walls as Irene and Eddie started down.

"Get yorn and the kids' clothes together," Jack called up. His unshaven face glistened with perspiration, but at least his shirt had no blood staining it. "We're leaving in a hurry."

"Oh, my God. What have you done now?" Irene stayed motionless on the stairs, clasping a hand to her mouth with her other hand grasping Eddie.

"Nothing, you stupid mare. There's no water nor food left here. It's madness to stay in a desert town. You know that, don't you?" His wide eyes told her to agree while he rushed past them to get the suitcases off the top of their closet. "I got us some transportation," he said with uncharacteristic glee.

"Jack, I gotta tell you something about Debbie."

"Tell me on the way, Irene. We gotta go while it's dark."

"You've stolen a bus, haven't you?"

"No, I bought it. What do you think? It doesn't matter shit how I got it, just be grateful, fully fuelled and all. It'll get us easy to LA."

"Hang on, Jack. Cities are trouble. We've got notes about it all over." She opened drawers to grab clothes.

"Trouble because there's food and water in them, so there's fighting. We've got protection, Irene, firearms. I know you don't like 'em, but to survive, we got to take chances."

"I don't like it. The highways are blocked by gangs, we got—"

"Notes, I know, but Charlie knows back roads all over."

"I might have guessed he'd be behind this." She glared at him. They had a history with Charlie who lived on the edge of the law and had served time. She'd worked hard to keep Jack in his great technician's job by denying him access to his school friend except on bowling and card nights.

Irene, still upset with Debbie's worsened state, turned on Jack. "We'd be safer in the country. We have our kids to consider."

"Exactly. Charlie's got pals in LA. They'll look after us."

"He said that, did he? Has he checked with them, lately? Come on, Jack, it'd be everyone for themselves. Think about it."

Jack shrugged in agreement and helped her to fill cases. "Okay, where are we going? Any bright ideas?" He took clothes and toiletries off her to accelerate packing.

"My folks have a farm near Monterey. They have their own water supply from the hills." She expected him to blow up, but he stood as if in suspension, as if he was thinking about her alternative destination.

"I'll put it to Charlie. It's much farther but maybe better. Now get what water and food we got out to the vehicle." He grabbed a couple of bulging tartan cases and went outside with Eddie dragging a case with him.

"Is there anything I can do?" called Celia, poking her head round Debbie's door as Irene returned there with a case.

"Celia, I forgot about you. You heard? Good, saves me explaining. You might as well come with us. Go down to the kitchen and start piling food and full drinking bottles into bags and boxes, whatever."

Eddie ran back in. "Hey, Mom, cool transport. I wish I could tell my new friends."

"I knew he'd steal some school bus."

"Naw, it's like an army war truck. I'll get my games and stuff."

Jack came in and grabbed a box of food that Celia had put there. He looked at her, his eyebrows crept down.

"She's coming, Jack. Celia has nowhere to go."

"No way. It's no fucking Noah's Ark."

Irene stood, hands on hips. "It's a military vehicle you've stolen from Edwards today, isn't it?"

"Okay, she might be useful cooking and stuff. There's a lot of food and water already on board from the cafeteria at the base."

"Good, we're about ready then. I'm going up to get Debbie."

"Yeah," said Jack, "about time I had a long chat with that girl."

CHAPTER 24

Sunday 14 June 2015:
Banff Commercial Estate. Most people have lost eight years of memory.

MANUEL HUNG BY HIS FINGERTIPS. With the front entrance blocked by an overturned truck, he had no choice in his mode of entry into Jenkins' Pharmaceuticals.

Of course, he had tried the main hospital first. With Jat drifting in and out of a coma, strapped into the passenger seat of the pickup, Manuel had spied on the hospital on Banff's Lynx Street. Parked near the railway station and behind bushes, he used his binoculars. Desperate to get his hands on neo-Humulin or any kind of insulin, he'd broken his promise to her that he wouldn't leave the cabin. A complete turnaround: she decided her life had finished but that he shouldn't put his at risk. But emotions were stronger than logic and so after an uneventful drive to their nearest big city, he found himself behaving like a frontline spy. On the steps of the hospital sat a group of men and a couple of women. When, through the glasses, he detected National Guard olive-green uniforms and firearms, he thought he could take a chance: explain Jat's need. Caution made him hang back.

A grey, freezing mist off the river swirled around the pine trees outside the hospital adding to his obscuration from the guards. A group of cyclists passed him, forcing him to duck in his driving seat. He brought his head up to watch the six riders screech to a halt a hundred metres from the hospital. Through the mist, Manuel could see they all wore rucksacks and some bikes had panniers. A mixed-age group, but he guessed most were young twenties. He couldn't help wonder where they came from and how they were so organised? Suppose, unlike him, they remembered yesterday? There were bound to be some groups isolated in the rural areas who needed supplies and had to risk infection.

The guards had readied their weapons, which meant waving them in the air and then at the cyclists. One of them strutted out in front and shouted something beyond Manuel's hearing. He thought about them too. Take one of those soldiers. Assuming they'd been in the army for years, they'd wake up each morning in their barracks. No change there; no hint of what was to follow. Newer squad members might be missing, but after normal morning ablutions, they'd go to fill their bellies. Even if the catering staff had turned up out of habit, lived on site, or had nowhere else to go, they'd have problems. Maybe a well-stocked services base would have a year's supply of dried and long-life foods but not perishables like milk and eggs. It would only take a conversation or two to get the full impact of what ARIA was doing. Wouldn't they want to get to their families, like Jat wanted to? Sure, and they might be stopped by their commanders, if they haven't already gone family hunting themselves. No, the only soldiers left would be those whose families were unreachable or undesirable.

Mulling over such traumatic possibilities became a penalty for leaving the comfort of the cabin. His throat dried up with concern for those cyclists. Why did they risk travelling into the city unless one of them or a friend back home needed medical help? He could understand them using mountain bikes instead of motor vehicles. To avoid potential roadblocks, they could make use of forestry and mountain tracks and not run out of fuel. That was a principal reason for not driving Jat all the way to her home city of Vancouver. No electricity to work fuel pumps at gas stations and antitheft devices on modern vehicles would make it difficult for him to siphon any from abandoned cars. Whatever the reason for getting to the hospital, they might be regretting it now. One of them put his bike on the ground and his hands in the air while walking to the lead soldier.

It must be all right. They were laughing, and all the soldiers had lowered their rifles and sat back down on chairs maybe brought from the ER reception. Encouraged, Manuel climbed out of his pickup and walked a few paces forward, keeping the tall pines as cover for a little longer. As his visibility improved, he noted a large number of empty beer cans around the soldiers and many assorted bags. In spite of the cool air, beads of perspiration moistened Manuel's forehead. Those soldiers couldn't be there just to prevent the storming of the hospital by desperate addicts. The leading cyclist, who had been chatting to the soldiers, waved the others to join him. Manuel hoped they'd be suspicious, but they moved forward. Maybe it would all work out. He'd become so paranoid; worse each day.

No. Two of the soldiers, if that was what they were, had circled the cyclists, who had reached the other soldiers at the entrance steps. They'd stopped laughing. Some started waving protesting hands, others threw their rucksacks away or dropped them, and two emptied their pockets. All at gunpoint. No, not a guard duty, just a heist. He didn't hang around. Maybe he could have found an unguarded entrance.

Turning to go, his heartbeat doubled as a growl warned him off. Blood-dripping canine teeth poked out through a dark green laurel bush. The head followed as it pushed through the leaves. The dog didn't want to leave its meal of the day. Manuel had missed the small, bloated body of a child. Its swollen stomach made him think of all those people that must have picked up food poisoning because of the lack of refrigerated and fresh food. He associated Dalmatians with Disney films and middle-class homes, yet here it was scavenging; a dog that had no doubt seen the inside of more canine beauty parlours than Manuel had hairdressers, and it had turned on its provider-species as a more direct source of food. Shuddering, he edged away from the beast. Manuel guessed that as long as he kept his distance, the dog wouldn't follow. He reached his pickup but heard approaching barking from other hounds.

Before setting off, he looked again at the once-proud hospital and thought of the infant's body. Maybe a desperate parent had carried the child so far and, like him, turned back after observing the soldiers. He appreciated the wisdom of using a hospital, with all its stores and equipment as a gang base, wondered at the fate of the patients in there, and after checking Jat's wavering condition, left. He'd used the web to find the location of all the manufacturers of Humulin in its various forms within a hundred miles of Moraine Lake, and one could be found in amongst a group of industrial small-scale manufacturers on the outskirts of Banff.

"Well, Jat, I don't know if you can hear me, but there's good news and bad news about Jenkin's Pharmaceuticals. The bad news is that the only entrance is blocked and all the windows are shuttered. The good news is that it means it's not been tampered with. I just hope I'm in time." She didn't reply. Her skin damp, her shallow breath smelt of pear drops, and she made jerky movements.

Although he awoke each day not knowing this woman in any meaningful way, concern gnawed at him. He'd seen bodies on the sidewalks and gutters. Even ignoring those dying as a direct result of malicious attacks, the lack of antibiotics meant people died of abscesses and simple infections. This was especially the case where they were, away from family or any who could feed them. It only took three or four days without water for kidneys to fail but quicker for all those thousands on dialysis, or who forgot their epilepsy medication and hit their heads while falling. Tetanus used to be the main medieval killer, even on the battlefield. Modern children had the benefit of mass immunisation, as did adults, having boosters after minor injury, but most adults wouldn't. Not that the bodies he saw would have died from tetanus or lack of antibiotics just yet. Their deaths beckoned from a month or so away. The addicts though—and weren't we all addicts to something or other? Bad enough to get minor withdrawal symptoms from alcohol, tobacco, or caffeine for those without access to stores, but there were plenty of ill people who needed their daily morphine pain-controlling drugs. Clonic seizures would have incapacitated many, which left Manuel being revolted and upset seeing them prone on the pavement.

He looked again at the unconscious young woman beside him. Occasionally she stirred, rapid-eye-movement beneath her eyelids indicating dreaming or coming close to waking up. On the few occasions her eyes opened, they were bloodshot and scared. It scared him too. For all he knew, he had fallen in love with this beautiful person and she him. He didn't think he could have gotten so lucky, but who could predict chemistry? Maybe it was hopeless and he would have to use the spade in the pickup to keep her body from the cadaver-eating packs of dogs and birds he'd seen, but he had to try.

BEING ONLY A LOW BUILDING, the roof wasn't difficult to get at with the ladder he'd stolen earlier. The skylight levered open with the aid of a crowbar he'd found in the pickup. The first real problem came when he looked down. Plan A was to pull the ladder up and manipulate it over the roof and through the skylight, but then it would have to be put into reverse, slowing any necessary quick getaway. He couldn't be bothered with all that. Only one floor height—four metres. Easy. The flashlight picked out boxes beneath. Better if they were mattresses, but he wasn't breaking into a motel, was he?

By hanging by his fingers he saved at least two metres of the drop. However, his trembling fingers worried himself into changing his mind about getting the ladder. Better than broken legs. But it was too late, he lacked the strength to pull himself back up and time slipped by.

The boxes cushioned his fall, but the breaking glass made a noise like a Saturn rocket taking off. He hoped he hadn't just smashed the very insulin he'd come for. His jeans had protected his skin from serious lacerations, so he fished the flashlight out of the knapsack he had over his shoulder. He went first to the light switches just in case emergency backup electricity was available. No.

This was more of a bottling plant than a laboratory. Manuel jogged up and down aisles. Bottles he ignored since the Humulin would be past their use-by date with no refrigeration. On the other hand, if he couldn't find the neo-Humulin patches, he'd look again for phials since he doubted the ambient temperature in the building had risen above fifty for a month. The patches should have been kept in flat boxes in the refrigerated store. He found the store. The door gaped at him and his flashlight picked out opened cold storage cupboards and some boxes on the floor. It meant the place had been raided after all. Though only partially, judging by the many full boxes of patches and tablets. Maybe some responsible worker arranged for the lorry to block the door to stop further thefts. Or a local gang leader did it, intending to return for the rest later. With luck, his amnesia meant he wouldn't be back in the next half hour or so.

In desperation, Manuel rummaged through boxes, wishing he had a headband light. He found patches for every ailment he could think of. Smoking, appetite suppressants, heart conditions, cholesterol reduction, high blood pressure, low blood pressure, depression, and many others. So many, he formed a hypothesis that all the patches had the same ingredient just different labels. Suppose he had broken into the main placebo drug manufacturer. At last he found some boxes of neo-Humulin patches. Knowing they were slow release, he looked for at least one phial of Humulin to inject into Jat straight away. In a large walk-in fridge, he finally found some and bagged them too. All he had to do now was to escape.

Figuring they had to change light bulbs, he found a maintenance section and borrowed a tall stepladder and emerged back onto the roof. Blinded by bright sunshine, which had burnt off the morning river mist, he found his ladder, and with a sigh, reached ground level.

His pickup had gone. Running in a panic, he covered the empty parking area to the open gate. The industrial estate around held only an eerie silence. Featureless warehouses bordered plain tarmac streets. No houses. No people.

Drained, he sat with his back leaning against Jenkin's gate. He thought back to when he climbed out of the pickup, fetched the flashlight and crowbar out of the back, and put his bag over his shoulder. Had he locked the vehicle? He had thought so, knowing the comatose Jat wouldn't regain consciousness. If she did, she could have unlocked the doors from the inside. Suppose she woke up and wondered where she was and took off? That must be it. In her state, it would be possible to drift in and out of awareness. He hadn't thought she would be able to make decisions, let alone drive the pickup, but what other solutions were there? Some sneak thief got through the locked door, smashing a window, then hotwiring the very secure vehicles of 2015?

He groped for the keys that should have been in his pocket. Not there, nor in the knapsack. He'd either left them in the ignition, which meant he hadn't locked it. Or, they fell out of his pocket when he fell in the factory.

Starting a long walk in the hope she was randomly driving and he'd find her, tears filled his eyes as he cursed himself. He should have left a note in case she woke up. In the state she would have been in, she wouldn't have any memory of him or the cabin. She might be frightened. He remembered how belligerent and assertive she was when he found her in Lake Louise. He knew she didn't need him to protect her. Did she? She'd be all right. If only she had the drugs he had for her survival.

CHAPTER 25

Tuesday 15 September 2015:
In orbit.

EARTH FROM 200 MILES UP FILLED THE PORTHOLE. It was better than watching their library of films, and Jena Kochi could not tire of the spectacular view. She had to admit to harbouring a soft spot for *Saturday Night Fever*—her weekly Travolta fix. Her reflected blue eyes matched the Pacific Ocean. A white disc of cirrus cloud advanced on Japan. Not that she could detect its movement even though she knew it would have been spinning at over a hundred miles per hour. She watched the ominous beast, with its central eye giving small respite to anyone beneath. She could forecast the dreadful weather for the next few days in southeast Asia, but would anyone down there be alerted to her warning? If there were, they'd already have known from the dedicated weather satellites. Though after losing twenty years of their memory, people are not going to be concerned about wild-wind predictions. She had family down there in the path of that hurricane. Her father was born in Kyoto, and although she rarely saw them, she had many Japanese aunts and uncles.

Every other hour she'd have been able to gaze at the blue planet below, knowing thousands of brilliant engineers worked day and night double-checking computer feedback links, preparing science, technical, and even tourist expeditions to visit the Space Station. They'd have been monitoring the ISS crew's health and arranging flights to restock dwindling supplies. A strange detachment gripped her, knowing that only a handful of people knew of their existence. None that could arrange flights to them or fix anything remotely from Earth. Even their families had stopped answering phones and cam links.

A tear formed when she thought of her Canadian mother, Sarah, on anti-depressants and alcohol years ago. Jena blamed herself since her mother hated airplanes let alone space flights, but the urge overwhelmed Jena to take up her astro-engineering career, and she was damn brilliant at it. Since her first space flight four years ago, Sarah had refused to take Jena's calls. Nevertheless, Jena wondered how her mother fared in this memory crisis. She dwelt on the ironic possibility of the chance Sarah would lose all the bad head-stuff in a few months' time. Then, if her father managed to survive, maybe...

Fat chance. The last time she talked to her father, he'd forgotten his colloquial English and she had to drag up what Japanese she knew. She knew he'd start forgetting where he lived at around the five-week stage, because they'd moved from Boston to Cheyenne. She wouldn't be surprised to find he'd turned up at his old home and tried to contact police in Boston to no avail. She used a finger to wipe another tear, annoyed with her own frailty. Everyone on the space station had lost contact with their families.

All the more reason for grasping at the links with Ryder in Wales and Charlotte in Australia. The ISS website, hosted and powered by themselves in space but accessible to anyone who could use the Internet, monitored hits occasionally. Those hits must be others who had electricity and the wherewithal to find their web address but too wary to leave their details. The Space Station would run out of life support within a couple of weeks and they would have to use their *Marimar* craft to return somewhere on Earth. Unless they could extend their stay. Now she had decided her friends and family were beyond help, maybe they should stay up for as long as possible.

Raised voices in the command module behind her impinged on her rumination and pleasure gazing at the slow movie of rotating Earth, but she should participate in the on-board excitement. The shouting could just be a cooker over-heating Vlad's rice but then a piercing beeping shook her.

She yelled down the corridor, "It's the proximity alarm!"

"We know," Dan said, "but none of the cameras show anything closer than an old weather satellite a thousand kilometres away."

"The Earth is closer," said Vlad, tapping a button to turn the brain-damaging noise off. "Jena, you've been looking that way for the last hour. See anything?"

"No, but apart from noting a huge tropical cyclone about to sweep over Japan, I've been daydreaming. Sorry, guys."

"*Non preoccupare.* Don't worry," Antonio said, "we've all been doing that lately."

"Excuse me," Vlad said, "but for all we know, a hastily-thrown-together-supply-ship might be colliding with us."

"One with no radio, I suppose," Dan said. "And maybe pigs flew it out here. It could have been a wiring fault, again."

Jena bristled. "I can't help it. There's only so much I can do with the engineering in this fairground..."

"I know," Dan said.

"...and there's precious little wiring as such. It's all electronic modules..."

"Jena, I know."

"We've had zilch parts for months, we have minimal manufacturing facility, and no, Dan, you are not saying you know, again." They all refrained from laughing. "Okay," she said, "I'll run a systems diagnostic yet again. But I have a feeling there is nothing wrong with the proximity sensor."

Dan became serious. "Right, Vlad, send our roving cam out to cover our blind spots."

As Vlad left to his task, Jena put a hand on Dan's arm.

"I was right, Dan, there's nothing wrong with our equipment— well, not this bit. Look at the Situation screen."

"So it indicates there is something unplanned out there but not where it is. How is that possible? It must be instrumental error. Sorry, Jena, I know you are the best engineer—"

"We have up here. Thanks for your moving endorsement. I'll update my CV for a non-existent future job, but my money is on Vlad's roving cam finding some wayward satellite."

"Not quite." Vlad thumped his console bench. "We've had a visitor all right. Look here."

It was one of those occasions when a theatre-sized screen would have prevented banged heads as the four other crew crowded around the seated Vlad. But unlike the crowd-gasp of witnessing a goal, they were shocked into silence.

Glinting in the sunlight and lethal radiation, looking brand new and as if mocking them, was an alien case.

Jena recovered first. "It's just like the other one. You don't suppose it *is* the other one, somehow brought back?"

"No, it is a different case," Abdul said. "Although that side is at an acute angle from here, you can just make out a double chevron logo."

"Yes," said Dan, "the first one had just the one. Vlad, bring the roving cam to get a better look at the logo or whatever the chevron is supposed to be."

"*Nyet* problem." Vlad enjoyed playing with his million-dollar toys and soon, they had unequivocal proof it was the successor to the other case. "If anyone asks, I didn't see who left it."

"Good point," said Jena, turning and running back to her console. "The proximity sensor is indicating normal status now. See? I told you..."

"Yes," Dan said. "Now what, folks?"

"No rushing in," Antonio said, his medical training alerting him. "Just because the other case showed no emissions or harmful indications, just consider what it did once opened on Earth."

"Yes," Dan said, "we were damned lucky not to follow our pioneering instincts there, though if we had, it might have just been us infected instead of a whole planet. So, advice please, people."

"Give it a push out into a farther-out orbit," Jena said, screwing her face up.

"A moment," said her junior engineer, Abdul. "Suppose the aliens have been monitoring TV and radio transmissions from Earth. Allah, they could be one of the web users peeking at our website. Suppose the first case, when opened, was intended to emit some health-giving particles but their project has gone wrong..."

"And they want to make amends?" snarled Jena. "Send us an antidote? Are you crazy, Abdul? You are anthropomorphising, giving the devil a human heart. It's probably a double dose, hence a double chevron, to make sure no humans are left alive. Or too few in number to resist an invasion."

"Now who's letting their emotions rule?" retorted Abdul. "Why do all aliens have to be green-skinned and with evil intentions?"

"Have we known any that aren't?" Jena said, to derision.

Dan held up peace hands. "It's good to air your opinions. We need to consider all the options no matter how bizarre. And they can hardly get stranger than what has already happened. Antonio, you and Vlad are staying quiet so far, but I'd value your opinions."

Antonio, who'd been staring at the case, started first. "*Difficile.* I see both points of view. I also think it is odd they have not tried to contact us in the conventional way. Like you, Dan, I think it is likely they are monitoring our transmissions and have been doing so since the early twentieth century. So, why not contact us via a radio? Suppose they don't communicate that way? They might be telepathic and never need to use speech or ears."

Jena interrupted. "They'd have to be powerful telepaths to think each others' stupid thoughts over millions of miles, and how would they be able to focus just on thoughts from one person they wanted to communicate with? Doesn't make sense at extreme or even medium distances." She despaired at the supposed geniuses she was trapped with.

"I am only saying," continued Antonio, waving aside the fractious interruption. "Their mode of communication could be a mass one to everyone spontaneously, who knows? We don't and that is the point. *Si*? If they pick up our weak signals, attenuating over astronomical distances, they might only conclude there is some kind of technology on Earth. Not necessarily intelligent, by their standards, and not civilised. Good heavens, we cannot pretend to be civilised the way we treat our planet and her occupants."

"Indeed," Vlad said, "they probably want to exterminate us because we are vermin and they don't want us to contaminate other planets."

"See? I'm not the only one who thinks they are evil," Jena said.

"That isn't what Vlad meant," Antonio said. "If I am right, he meant they might have a point in considering humans as only worthy of exterminating. And not to occupy our spoiled planet but to prevent us spreading."

"Oh, give us a break," Jena said. "I know there are evil bastards down there, and God knows how much environmental damage, but there are a lot of marvellous achievements in music, art, and literature."

"I agree," Antonio said, "but they might not. Their interpretation of the Arts might be completely different, if it exists at all. And the same goes for what they consider to be acts of nobility. However, getting back to why they have not sent a message, we have to consider that they might have."

"True," said Abdul, "they might be operating on a different timescale to us, such that a long spiel to them arrived as a microdot on the screen or radio noise as far as we were concerned."

"Not if they've been monitoring our transmissions. Oh, I see, they might have, but only see them as evidence of our existence and not understanding them," Jena said.

"In another way," Antonio said, "the fact we haven't had intelligible messages from them only vindicates the point that they have not understood our transmissions. Hence the cases."

"Run that last sentence by me again," Dan said.

"Simple," Antonio said. "The cases are their communication to us. Or a test."

"Now you've lost me too," Abdul said.

Antonio examined his fingernails. "Suppose they were waiting to see what mankind would do with the first case as a kind of intelligence test."

"Well we fucked that one up," said Jena.

"The aliens failed our first test," Dan said. "Let us suppose the first case was an intelligence test. It assumed the most intelligent and reasoned approach to the case would prevail. They didn't take into account some idiot opening it without the rest of us having a say."

"And so," Abdul said, gleefully, "my conjecture that the second case might be to put right the error of the first could be the correct one."

"On your bike if you think we're opening it on such a flimsy hypothesis," Jena said.

"Quite," Dan said, "we shouldn't open it. Certainly not in the station."

"But you're thinking it or you wouldn't have mentioned it," Jena said, heating up inside.

"I have to consider all the possibilities," Dan said. "Including destroying it."

"Hey," Vlad said.

"Hey from me too," Abdul said, "just suppose it had the antidote to ARIA and we blew it up!"

"I just wanted to say," Vlad said, "can I be the one to blow it up, if we're going to? After all, I found it."

Ignoring him, Dan turned to Antonio again. "What are the chances it might have some kind of antidote?"

"Let us consider the options, bearing in mind the ARIA pathogen that the first case contained. If such a virus as ARIA could infect mammals so that they progressively lost memory and new information was also difficult to retain post infection, then they might be able to do something similar in a second infection. But if you are asking me if someone who has had their memory erased can pick up a new virus that would give them their memory back, I would bet my Verdi collection on saying no. I don't know how ARIA works. Biopsy studies and brain scans would have been helpful. The blood samples Ryder arranged showed a common-cold-type virus but not how the brain was affected. Are synapses short-circuited? Or are memories stored in neural webs lost forever? In that case, if a new virus in the second case allowed regeneration of the brain, it would allow that person to start remembering new information but not recall information he had already lost."

Jena jumped in. "That's probably it, isn't it? The aliens have wiped mankind's brains and sent a new set of information to replace it. To turn us all into their slaves."

"Thank you, Jena," Dan said. "I'll add your thoughts to our various scenarios of what might be happening here."

"Well thank you, sir," she said. "But I can't believe the bullshit about them realizing they've made a mistake and sent us a fucking case load of Grannie's Cure All!"

Abdul said, "I doubt if we've even got close to what is really in the second case."

"I agree," said Antonio. "It could be a different strain of ARIA, designed to halt its spread before the first one wiped out the ability of the oldest from using language. Or it—"

"I don't buy that," Jena said. "When the first case arrived, ARIA spread real quick because of the vast amount of air travel. Now nothing is flying or sailing. Incidentally, would submarine officers remember to surface, assuming one of the crew caught the bug before boarding? Just threw that in to remind us how nasty ARIA is."

"I would hope, speaking as an ex-sub commander," said Dan, "that they would keep referring to onboard computers, and in any case, they would only lose fifty days memory per day so the next day they should still all know to get to the surface. This is a red herring, isn't it? Thought so. We still have a problem, folks. What should we do with the case?"

"Destroy it," Jena said.

"Test for emissions, all the tests we have without opening or physically touching it with our hands. And take it to Earth with us," Antonio said.

"It's what the aliens would want us to do with it," said Vlad.

"And what NASA would want us to do," Abdul said.

"A vote then," said Dan, surprising Jena as he never flinched from a difficult decision, but she realized he just wanted to know for sure who would agree with his eventual decision.

"Destroy," Jena said, again.

"Take it Earthside," Antonio said.

Vlad clenched then unclenched his fist. "Destroy, I suppose."

"Take it with us to Allah knows who and God knows where," Abdul said.

"Casting vote, Dan," Jena said, curious about the sudden pseudo-democracy.

"Take it with us. Sorry, Jena, but if we destroy it, we'd never know if we killed something lifesaving."

"Wimp," she said.

Silence filled the station apart from the sharp intakes of breath, which were then held. No one should be so disrespectful to their captain.

Vlad recovered first. "Show her the door, Commander."

Dan coughed into his fist.

"Fine, just let me get into my pressure suit first," said Jena, continuing her obstinacy.

Antonio, writing in his NoteCom, said, "We are all under considerable strain."

"Don't patronise me. I've said my piece. Don't wait for an apology." Jena stormed off to the Earthside porthole again, but she could still hear them.

"Crew members have fallen out before now," Abdul said. "Shall I go and prepare the extension arm to pick up the case?"

"Not yet," Dan said. "I'm asking Jena to work with Vlad to do a full radiometer battery of tests including any emissions."

Jena shouted over from her porthole, "Keeping me busy, *sir*?"

"There's plenty for all of us to do," Dan said. "Abdul, last time we knew something was wrong because the station rotated when it shouldn't. Check for any positional abnormalities we might need to correct. Antonio, work out a containment plan for the case in the *Marimar*. I imagine the cargo bay would be the optimum place but go through the options. Jena, book us an interview appointment in, say, three hours when we're less busy."

"Who with? There's no mission control to guide us," she said.

"With you. We have issues to sort out and I will communicate what we've found, with cam shots, to both Ryder and Charlotte. They might have ideas too."

Jena pouted, but her intelligence told her she couldn't go round shouting and behaving like a spoilt child in such a confined environment. They were in a crucible and had to prevent boiling over. He was so clever, that Dan. He knew she'd know to cool down, compose herself, so they could all get on with the job in hand.

UNTOUCHED BY HUMAN HAND, and having shown no hostile intentions via radiation or other emanations, the case was stored in a sealed section of the *Marimar's* cargo bay. But Jena hadn't finished fighting as the crew prepared for another strategy meeting.

She regretted losing her rag with Dan over the case, and she damned Antonio for being right about stress affecting her stability.

Last to take a seat at their oval, aluminium dining table with only just room for their NoteComs, she budged up Vlad so she could sit next to Dan. She reasoned that she would appear less confrontational if she didn't sit opposite him.

Dan opened. "The computer is waiting for us to tell it which landing site we are to aim for in order to calculate the optimum re-entry point. Whether we select North Wales, Western Australia, or a desert island—one with an airfield and some survival possibilities—we can be away within two hours."

"Or not," Jena said.

Abdul waved exasperated hands in the air. "Last time it was you who was ready to fight us to return."

"Yeah, well, I still had hopes my folks would be around uninfected. Now that isn't likely, there's even more an argument for staying up here out of harm's way for as long as possible."

Antonio wagged a finger. "But that is exactly the problem, Jena. It is not possible for us to stay longer. Our stores of food, water, and air as well as spare equipment are dangerously low."

"That's because we haven't tried hard enough with the environment extension programme." She put her elbows on the table and continued. "I've worked out a much more efficient water re-cycling program, which makes use of solar electrolysis apparatus not yet used."

"It's untried out here," Abdul said.

"And the same equipment can generate more air, plus we can get away with a lower percentage of oxygen—even two percent less would add a week. As for food—"

Antonio interrupted, "Are you hanging onto the optimistic possibility of ARIA losing its virility before we return?"

Vlad said, "Wouldn't it be ironic if that second case needs to be opened to do just that?"

"That could always be an option later," Jena said. "Whereas, if we leave now, we commit ourselves irrevocably to becoming infected within days of landing."

"Not if we are careful where we land," Antonio said.

"Then there is the bigger picture," Jena said. "We may be humanity's only chance of surviving ARIA. We have a duty to stay uninfected and use our communication skills to co-ordinate research and survivors down there." She tried to stop smiling at her clincher, but her mouth gave her away.

Abdul wasn't taken in. "Personally, I don't want to be gasping for breath at the last minute. I'd rather have some leeway with somewhere to come back to."

Vlad laughed. "Abdul, my friend, once we leave this station, we won't be coming back."

"At least not once we re-enter Earth's atmosphere. We have barely enough fuel to have full choice of a landing spot as it is," said Dan. "However, Jena has a point. But not hoping for ARIA to die out. If the case does have an antidote, it would be irresponsible to delay using it, and for all we know, it has a shelf life of days and will be useless by next week. Her worthier point is that the case is more than just us. We must get it to people who can do something useful with it. To me, that only leaves us going to Ryder in North Wales. They have lab facilities and infection-free people who know how to use it. Anyone with a stronger argument for Charlotte in Western Australia?"

Antonio spoke up. "Charlotte is the only person on the planet who appears to have been exposed to ARIA yet not infected herself. This makes her both very interesting and a potential salvation."

Abdul said, "After talking to her more than you guys. Oh shut up. It's possible the girl she met might not have had ARIA."

Charlotte's plight tugged at Jena, but she was afraid to say too much, considering her appalling success rate in winning recent arguments. "So you're saying she isn't immune to ARIA, just lucky. That's mean."

Dan patted her hand. She glowered at him.

"I'm not writing her off as a possible medical breakthrough," Dan said, "but there would be no point landing there. We'd have landing co-ordinates, and there's a long runway but no lab facilities, and we might attract attention from demented or desperate people."

"Allah," Abdul said, "that could happen wherever we land. They might attack us thinking we're the alien perpetrators of this madness."

Antonio prodded a finger at his temple. "It isn't madness, just a loss of memory. People still have all their other mental faculties although I admit that as time passes, intelligence will suffer. And I suppose with the confusion and loss of livelihood, starvation, seeing death, knowing that they must have loved ones but not how—*si*, they would see it as madness..."

"Thank you, Antonio," Abdul said. "Lady and gentlemen, a miracle has just occurred. Our doctor has admitted an error." Even Jena joined in the tension-easing laughter.

"So," Dan said, "we land at an airfield as close to Ryder's centre as he suggests. We'll take advisement from him as to the local situation and then as to whether to land at night and so forth. Vlad, update the computer for a selection of re-entry windows, bearing in mind our approximate destination. I'll get onto Ryder. Jena, let Charlotte know what we're up to and let her know we will keep in touch. Be positive and encouraging—as if I need to say."

CHAPTER 26

Tuesday 15 September 2015:
Anafon Study Centre, North Wales, twenty-two weeks since the start of ARIA. Most people would have lost twenty-two years of memory.

"NO. NO WAY!" SHOUTED BRIAN, his blond, overgrown crew cut bristling like a toilet brush.

Bronwyn agreed. "Five astronauts? Five more mouths to feed. That'll deplete our food. I'm not cooking for five strangers."

Ryder fought back a wry smile. These two remained as cantankerous, yet supportive of each other, as they were before their absconding attempt and Bronwyn's gunshot wound.

Derek patted Bronwyn's hand. "And just them landing nearby and us leaving our perimeter to fetch them makes us much more likely to come across ARIA."

"Objections noted," Ryder said. "But it's going to happen; it has to. And with careful planning, we'll minimise the chances of ARIA coming back here. One thing we know for sure is that none of the ISS crewmembers have it. But there are other reasons why we should welcome them."

Bronwyn clenched a fist at him. "So, you are going to ignore our wishes, yet again."

"Remember," Ryder continued, "they were five of the planet's brightest people before they left Earth, and Antonio is a first-class physician."

"Even his skills are useless against ARIA," Derek said.

"There's something Ryder hasn't told you, yet," Teresa said to the group. Then to Ryder, "Isn't there, dear?" Brian and Bronwyn lowered their eyebrows with suspicion at Ryder while the rest raised theirs in interest. The teenager, Megan, sat farther back, plugged into her personal stereo. Ryder glared at Teresa, he anticipated some hostility to the notion of the arrival of the alien case and hoped to concentrate on the benefits of the ISS crew joining them.

"Thanks, dear. Yes, another case appeared on the space station." Gasps from the biology technicians showed they saw first the significance of the new development and the implications if opened in their presence.

Laurette butted in. "So, the crew might not be free of ARIA after all?"

"That isn't what I'm saying at all," Ryder said, fighting impatience at people who wouldn't let him finish. "Like the first one, they haven't opened it. It's sealed in the *Marimar's* cargo hold. No decision has been made what to do with it and won't be until it arrives here."

"This gets bloody better by the minute," shouted Brian. "You are allowing strangers to bring ARIA to us for certain."

Gustav, as a bio technician, possessed more foresight. "It could be our salvation, Brian. There would be little point in the aliens sending a duplicate virus when the first has done such a thoroughly devastating job."

Bronwyn looked confused. "I dunno how you can say that. We might not be the only uninfected. There must be loads of isolated communities. Suppose the second case is just to make sure."

"We don't have time for this," Ryder said. "Unless Brian and Bronwyn, as locals, know any better, the maps show me that the nearest airfield with a long-enough runway for *Marimar* to land is at Hawarden near Chester, fifty miles away." He waited for the two to acknowledge.

After a long pause, Brian said, "Hawarden's runway will be long enough. It's private though, no commercial flights."

"All the better. I don't suppose there would be anyone there now," Ryder said.

Bronwyn said, "Wouldn't it be better for it to land on a straight bit of beach closer to here? Fifty miles mightn't sound so far, but it could be dodgy."

"They considered that, Bronwyn," Ryder said. "Always dangerous to land on a beach, especially at night. Then there are other advantages to landing at a proper airfield."

"It can't refuel and take off again once it's buried itself on a beach," Teresa said.

"Exactly," Ryder said. "So are there other airfields closer than Chester?"

"RAF Valley might be closer, but you'd have to cross to Anglesey over the bridge with all the dangers of getting trapped, see," Brian said.

"And it's a military installation so it's harder to get into and just might have people there," Bronwyn said.

"Other airfields are too small for the *Marimar*," Brian said. "How are you going to get there and back without running into infected people?"

"Okay, so we have decided on Hawarden Airfield," Ryder said. "There's at least three road routes."

Brian scowled. "I assume you mean the coast road, the A55 dual carriageway, and a country-lane route. And there's no democratic vote on which is the best airfield? Again."

"We think the coast road might be best since there might be roadblocks, manned or otherwise, on the dual carriageway," Derek said.

"You must be kidding," said Brian, laughing at them. "The coast road goes through all the coastal resorts, including campsites—and I mean thousands of caravans."

"Ah," said Derek, "but ARIA will have cut the numbers down. I know it's sad, but we're talking twenty years of memory loss and most of the caravans wouldn't have started their holiday season back in April."

"It's a good job you have local people here then, isn't it?" said a smug Brian, exaggerating his melodic Welsh accent. "Where do all the old people go to retire?"

"Eastbourne," Derek said.

"And?"

"All right, Rhyl and the other North Wales resorts," said Ryder. "And being ancient, losing twenty years to them isn't going to count for much..."

"...compared to middle-aged and younger people," said Derek. "So we avoid the coast road."

"And avoid the gangs of pensioners," said Bronwyn with a smirk.

"Let's just have a thought for those pensioners," said Teresa. "Most would have been on medication, all gone. So the diabetics, heart conditions, anaemia, kidney problems, hypertension, those prone to infections, Parkinson's..."

"We get the grim picture," said Ryder. "No swarms of geriatrics except fit ones and there's not many of those. Even so, we should avoid the coast road. How about the country lanes. I suppose there's a problem there too, Brian?"

"Only that the lanes wriggle a lot 'cos they visit every sodding village and town. Do you want that? And then they are just tractor width in places and so might be blocked by accidents, abandoned, manned roadblocks, or trees that fell in the last five months."

Derek stood to get a drink. "Let's consider this roadblock idea. How would a group remember that they manned a roadblock the previous day? They wouldn't, unless they wrote each other memory-aid notes and stuck them on each other's foreheads. I suppose they might each wake up, realize they are hungry, wander outside, and find each other. In the conversation about what the hell's going on, they might suggest highway robbery. Some would be well brought up and resist that action, so time would be spent arguing."

"So if there are any roadblocks they are unlikely to be manned in the mornings," Ryder said.

"But they could go on through these long summer evenings into the night," Brian said. "Making very early morning, say three, a good time to move around."

"Agreed," Ryder said. "And for speed, I'm leaning towards the A55 dual carriageway. There are plenty of links between that and the coast road if diversions are necessary."

"There's some difficult strategy questions, though, aren't there?" Brian said.

"More a policy decision," Derek said.

"I'm tempted to say we'll only shoot people shooting at us," Ryder said, knowing that was what they were referring to. "But it's like if strangers breached our perimeter here. In fact, our going to the airfield is like a bubble of Anafon on the move."

"Nice image, but not quite," Derek said.

"No," said Teresa. "Ryder, you said if anyone came over the hill towards us we had to try and ascertain if they were infected just in case they had heard of us from the ISS and came here as uninfected refugees."

"Yes, but if we thought there was a good possibility they were okay, we would quarantine them in the mine," Ryder said. "How can we take the mine with us?"

"We could take the estate car as a mobile quarantine, but that would be impractical if we picked up hundreds," said Brian. "And I don't like the idea of shooting hundreds either."

Ryder had to make a decision. "We could have the estate in front and the minibus some hundred metres or so following. We have mobile phones working on our own local network like walkie-talkies. If the lead car sees people, unlikely so early in the morning, it tells the minibus and both retreat and reroute. Only shoot to maim in order to stop anyone following. If we have to. It's tough, but us getting ARIA is a slow death sentence, and if it's them or us..."

They all had no choice but to agree, leaving Ryder to go to the comms and let them know up there in space.

CHAPTER 27

Wednesday 16 September 2015:
Orbit.

"WE HAVE ANOTHER PROBLEM, COMMANDER," SAID JENA.

"What?" Dan said. "Vlad's found Santa Claus orbiting the moon?"

"Hey, that's good," she said. "In fact, he's found Santa Claus, but he's orbiting Saturn. Come and see."

Vlad said, "We can hardly see anything, but the computer says there's a new object in the Cassini Division between rings A and B. Our telescope has it as a fuzzy ball."

"Size?" asked Dan.

"How do you measure the diameter of a pom-pom? My apologies. I estimate it to be about a hundred metres."

"Any transmissions coming from it, Vlad?"

"No, Commander, not on wavelengths we listen for."

"Right, send what we have to Ryder and Charlotte. Maybe Charlotte can direct the remote scopes to it. In the meantime, get Hubble trained on it with IR, UV, X-rays, visible light, the works. I need to consult Antonio. Call me when you get anything."

Jena sat at the neighbouring console to Abdul. "Zap over the alien's coordinates and I'll handle Hubble. Extend the range of wavelengths. If they sneeze, Abdul, you make sure you hear it."

"I will if they sneeze in Morse code," said Abdul. "But they didn't talk to us before, they won't this time either. What about a radar-imaging scan?"

"Everything, Abdul. Do I have to do it for you?"

"Jena, a radar probe will tell them we've found them and they can use our pinging to find us."

"Oops," said Jena, adding an embarrassed smile.

"I'll take that as a don't do a radar scan, then."

"We could use one of the other probes already out there. Check, but I think the Cassini Saturn orbiter probe launched back in the nineties is out there," Jena said. "That way we're not sending radar pings to the alien but asking existing satellites to do it."

Abdul tapped his database. "Cassini died in 2008, while orbiting the biggest moon, Titan."

"Um, suspicious?"

"Not really, Jena, it had passed its expected life. But remember it launched its daughter probe, Huygens, onto Titan. We might be able to re-activate it. More interesting is the Jupiter Moon Mission. It reached Ganymede last year and it's active."

"Excellent, get the codes for both, the last one was managed by Darmstadt, Germany and the first from Houston. Ping the alien bastard from one or both."

"Pardon me, Jena, I'm a computer hacker whiz. If we were radar pinged, I'd be able to backtrack it to the satellite and then follow its radio transmission in under five minutes."

"The point being, Abdul?"

"The point is if a mere human can track it, a smart alien could be knocking on our door demanding to see my hacker's licence before you've seen any results."

"Not if you send the radio controls via a broad-scattered signal and ditto for the orbiters. We don't need to avoid confusion from the non-existent radio signals from Earth and it doesn't matter if others pick our signals up. No one could track them back."

"Not just a pretty face, are you? Hey, I could bounce the initial signals off other satellites to add to the confusion."

"Then fucking get on with it, Abdul." Her aggression sparked because, although the ruse she suggested might work, they had no idea how clever the aliens were and Abdul had pointed out her mistake. Out of his sight, she chewed at her fingernail—a stress habit hidden from NASA shrinks. Abdul reminded her of the possibility of the aliens finding them. Maybe they should return as soon as possible, after all.

"I can't raise a squeak out of the Huygen probe on Titan," said Abdul. "Shame, it is the closest to the alien. Shall I keep trying?"

"No, Abdul. Either the probe had a mishap or the alien shut it up. We'd better not keep trying and give them more data to track us down. What about the Ganymede probe near Jupiter?"

"It's alive and chatting but the radar appears to go right through the alien. It doesn't—"

"Not surprising. If we have stealth technology, so has the alien. Hey, I got a visual on the fuzzy-ball alien."

"Great, Jena, what does it look like?"

"A larger fuzzy ball but brown in colour."

"Jena, you don't think we've just been wasting our time, do you?" said Abdul, looking fed up.

"Why? Had you something better to do? Besides packing."

"Already packed. To be honest, I'm getting a bit nervous up here. I've never been so keen to get back to terra firma."

"All you men are wimps. I've set Hubble up locked on the alien, even if it moves, as long it doesn't shift too quickly. You do the same for listening to frequencies and transmit to Ryder and Charlotte. With solar power recharging our batteries, we should be able to keep an eye on them for years."

"Pity we haven't some air-to-air laser guns," Abdul said, but Jena looked at him as a dog trainer would a puppy that had just made a puddle.

"We could do a darn sight better than that. Gotta speak to Dan."

Dan had his head close to Antonio, making Jena sure they plotted some dire deed.

"Hey, Dan, since we know where the alien is, how about doing something about it?"

"We are," Dan said. "You are finding out all we can about it, and I've asked Antonio to do what he can in the way of the old-fashioned criminal profiling method, using what we know about both cases."

"You're joking," Jena said. "Just because the cases are conveniently human holiday size, doesn't mean the aliens are our size. For God's sake, they've probably been monitoring our TV for years and know everything about us and made suitcase-sized Trojan horses. They could be tiny or huge."

Antonio rubbed his chin. "Or have no shape at all."

"I'd like to see a gas or thought process manufacture something solid," said Jena.

"We can't rule it out, especially looking at their spaceship, assuming that's what it is," Antonio said.

"I think it is a safe bet that ball of fudge is them and I think we owe it to mankind to hurt it," she said. There; she'd laid bare her emotion but was prepared to back it.

Dan remained calm. "You know I respect your intellect and engineering skill, Jena, but to attempt to destroy the alien—"

While Jena became flushed, Antonio spoke up. "We need to clarify our options."

Vlad had completed most of the station hibernation procedures by keeping the solar panels facing the sun, so there would be plenty of electricity. This ensured the onboard computers could act as a webserver for anyone from Earth to access e-mails, message boards, pages of news and information. He also set up some of the computers to act as a mobile phone receiver and transmitter since the Earth-based ones had bellied-up.

"When do we get our re-entry window? Hello, are we having a goodbye party?"

"No, Vlad," said Abdul, "Jena wants us to have a pop at our luggage depositors. Maybe send the case back to sender, address unknown."

"Now then, Abdul, don't be facetious," Antonio said. "The suggestion possesses logic."

"Thank you, Antonio," Jena said. "We show defensive spirit. Even if we can't destroy them, maybe they will change tack and bother some other planet."

"I mean the logic inherent in giving us cover fire while we head back to Earth."

"I know we are under some stress," Abdul said, "but my dear Antonio, if we made a homemade rocket with some spare tubing, explosives, and propulsion system, it would take at least three years to reach Saturn. Or have you figured out a slingshot trajectory that will shave a few months off it?"

"And it would be like firing a popgun at an aircraft carrier," said Vlad. "Unless we convert the nuclear propulsion unit from the ion-drive on that experimental remote probe we have in the science bay. *Da*, that'll do it, but it would still take too long to reach them."

"How about using the emergency escape pod?" said Antonio, with the smug look he had when he considered he had a winning argument.

Dan shook his head. "It's for an emergency escape for five crew to reach Earth and nothing more. We can't just take it, reconfigure its programming, convert it into a space torpedo, and send it to a possible alien target."

"If it isn't their ship, it wouldn't annoy them then, would it?" Jena said. "But we have the *Marimar* to fly around in so we use the pod as a weapon."

Vlad said, "It's comforting to know the escape pod is there, but I'd much rather fly back in the *Marimar*. I vote we use the escape pod."

Dan wagged a finger. "You are all assuming it is a choice between using the escape pod or the *Marimar*."

"Oh yes," said Abdul, "there's the homemade-rocket option."

"No," Dan said, "I meant not throwing anything at the fudge ball. It would take up too much precious time; it might aggravate the situation, and if it is related to the aliens, it might be a decoy. The real alien mother ship might be round the dark side of the moon. Then there is the other strategic argument."

"Oh, I know it," Jena said. "You still think ARIA was meant to be for the benefit of mankind. You must be a demented—"

"There is a possibility," interrupted Antonio, "that the second case might immunise uninfected people like us."

"It doesn't matter what we all think, does it?" She looked at the others who gave her no encouraging return nods. No matter how logical she might think her points were, none of the others would entertain going against the gang leader.

CHAPTER 28

Friday 18 September 2015, 0230 GMT:
The A55, North Wales, 22.5 weeks since ARIA; twenty-two years,
six months memory loss for most people.

THE TAIL LIGHTS OF BRIAN'S VOLVO ESTATE GLOWED at Ryder like a monster's red eyes. The black, overcast sky and lack of streetlights freaked them all out, yet the obfuscation comforted them.

"At least we'd see other vehicles for miles," Gustav said, sitting next to Ryder in the field centre's minibus. He'd driven at a steady fifty miles per hour since getting onto the dual carriageway twenty minutes before. Ryder had seen no other vehicles; just a few oil-lamps and candles flickering behind windows. They'd agreed to use sidelights in case their headlights alerted the curious. In the gloom they'd had a couple of scares when they came across abandoned vehicles. If that wasn't bad enough, Ryder knew they were driving into a busier region and certain to be scared again.

Brian and Laurette drove as agreed, a hundred metres ahead. Without warning, the red eyes intensified as Brian braked again, making Ryder brake too.

"Now what?" Gustav said. "He's more nervous than the rabbits and sheep we've scared off the road."

"Instead of whinging," Ryder said, "get them on the mobile."

"Hello, Laurette, speak to us."

"Brian thought someone ran across the road in front."

"But you can't see him now?"

"No, but about a hundred and fifty metres ahead there is a lorry and some of its load in the road."

Ryder took the mobile phone. "Turn your sidelights off. Good. Now is the road blocked? Use your night-sight binoculars."

"Just a few packing-case-sized boxes, scattered mostly near the lorry."

"Remember what we said? A few large items can be driven around but one telegraph pole on its side would stop us."

Laurette came on. "I'm using the binoculars, Ryder. There is a clear way through. A zigzag to avoid boxes dead ahead. There is nothing going right across the lanes. But...I might have seen torchlight to the left where Brian saw someone run to."

Brian said, "We should withdraw. There's an exit to Colwyn Bay about two miles behind you, Ryder."

"I'm not sure it isn't just one person," Laurette said. "They might live in one of the cottages near the road and saw our lights from way back. In this dark, even our side lights would be visible."

"Too risky," Gustav said. "There might be a mob of them waiting to throw obstacles just in front and behind them. That is our Laurette in that car, Ryder. You have a duty—"

"Right, Brian, this is what you are going to do. With your lights still off, drive fifty metres forward slowly. Then be guided by Laurette's navigation. Don't think for yourself, Brian. That's not an insult, it's survival rally driving. So when Laurette shouts right, do it immediately."

"We should have bloody practised this," snarled Brian.

"Agreed, but we ran out of last minutes. One more thing, Brian."

"What?"

"At the point of turning right, put your lights on full beam. Scare the living daylights out of them."

"And I suppose you'll be sitting comfortably way back there to see if we get marmalised."

"I have a rescue plan too. Whatever happens, keep going, and fast. But, Brian."

"We're listening."

"Turn your headlights off once you're past them and then keep going at fifty if you see us behind you."

"And what if you don't follow us?" Brian sounded suspicious.

"That's why we have mobile phones. Any time you're ready."

"Fuck off," Brian said and accelerated.

In the pitch blackness, Ryder couldn't see Brian's car move off or the road ahead. Nothing outside his windscreen. An eerie green glow from the dashboard illuminated his whitening knuckles. He released his left hand to press a button. Gustav's side window buzzed as it slid down.

"Get the shotgun ready for a shot up in the sky, Gustav. But only when I shout 'shoot.' Got it?"

"Laurette's giving instructions. Listen."

"Lights now, dammit!" Laurette shouted to Brian.

Bright white light illuminated the road ahead, with Brian's car looking like an eclipse of the sun in the middle.

Laurette screamed, "Right! Turn right now!"

Their headlights swept right, illuminating the boxes and sent elongated shadows across the road.

"I can't see any men," said Gustav.

"Quiet," Ryder hushed, concentrating hard.

Laurette's voice again on the mobile: "Sharp left now."

Their headlights swept left, this time showing two men with pickaxe handles running at the car.

Ryder drove forward, accelerating as Laurette shouted. "They've thrown something in the road. Can't see what. Not poles; ball bearings! Have to slow down!"

Ryder shouted at the phone, "Don't stop. We're coming too."

Just as he saw their brake lights come on and the two men reach their car, Ryder put his headlights on full beam. "Shoot!"

Gustav's shotgun went off. The shot hit one of the boxes making it fly. The men ran off to the left.

"My God," Laurette whooped. "That's brilliant. Oops, the car's like on an ice rink but we're going forward. Oh, it's okay now. We'll carry on as planned."

Ryder drove straight ahead now the box blocking the way had been shot and showed evidence of being empty. They slowed to pass over and through the ball bearings while Gustav played shotgun guard out of the passenger window.

They heard Laurette remind Brian to switch to side lights as they reached fifty once more.

"Gustav," Ryder said. "You know when I said fire the gun in the air?"

"Yes, it worked really well, didn't it?"

"No, Gustav. I said in the air. You fired horizontally, at the men."

"There was air on the way. I am German, from Leipzig. My English is not so good..."

"Bollocks. Gustav, you and Laurette aren't an item, are you?"

"Why shouldn't we be?"

"She playing hard to get, then? But maybe not after you rescued her with a shot in the dark?"

"Not much gets past you, eh, Ryder?"

"Plenty, but, Gustav, next time you do exactly as I say or you're walking home. Got it?"

HALF AN HOUR LATER, the two vehicles drew up where a public road ran along a perimeter fence of the airfield. Owned by an aircraft manufacturer, it was extended for Airbus test flights, so it had the length required for *Marimar*. Gustav and Brian made short work of snipping a large hole in the perimeter fence. Laurette sat on top of the minibus as lookout while Ryder talked to Dan on the *Marimar*.

"We are lighting two fires at the end of the runway and

positioning our cars on either side of the start of it with our headlights shining down its length. That's about all we have time for, I'm afraid, Dan. Which way are you coming in? The wind is from the west at about ten knots."

"That's okay, Ryder. We have the details of the airfield in our database, and I repeat, we are coming in from the east to land into the wind. One extra thing you can do is to make sure the mobile phone you are using is on and in the centre of the start of the runway. In the absence of instrumental automated landing aids, we can use your phone as a homing device. Luckily, the GPS satellites are still functioning."

"Right, Dan. ETA eighteen minutes. See you on the ground."

They needed all eighteen minutes to get the fires lit and the cars positioned before they heard then saw the nav lights on the *Marimar* as it appeared beneath the cloud base in the east.

Ryder often travelled for hours to see a returning space flight, but now he worried. Just suppose any of the usual four million people who lived within twenty miles looked and listened. What would they think? He hoped their memory loss would mean they would wake confused but think nothing was too unusual about an experimental plane landing at Hawarden airfield. Only later in the day, after they were properly awake, would they realize their memories were haywire; maybe then they would have come to investigate the approach of a spaceship.

In spite of an increased heart rate and perspiration, Ryder was awed by the sight of the *Marimar*. Built more like an executive jet than the old, stubby-styled shuttle, it came in much faster than most jet planes. Ryder appreciated the wisdom of the pilot not putting all his lights on as he would have in normal circumstances. Of course, with no other metal birds in the sky, there was no need for alert lights.

A few seconds out, the *Marimar* put its full landing lights on and made a scary, fast-but-perfect landing. The two vehicles chased it and Ryder cursed not having one of his team get a mobile stair ready. To his surprise he saw Gustav driving one up to the *Marimar's* hatch. Then he was even more surprised to see Laurette drive a baggage belt to the spacecraft.

IN THE REMAINING DARK AT FOUR A.M. but with a hint of a lightening eastern sky, Ryder greeted the astronauts and tried to hurry them into the minibus. He'd forgotten about the case until he saw two of the crewmen carefully catch it off the rollers. For a few moments, he stood transfixed. Not that they could see the actual case but just to know that the padded, heavy bag contained either their salvation or termination tightened his stomach.

Gustav had already prepared the rear of the Volvo estate car with so much polystyrene, they had to leave white piles of it on the tarmac.

"Hold your horses, Ryder," said Dan. "I want the *Marimar* refuelled and hidden before we leave."

"Dan, even assuming we can find the right fuel, by the time we empty a hangar, it'll be daylight and we could be overrun with local gangs. Let's go now."

"Give us twenty minutes," Dan said. Ryder had become used to giving orders and being hard on people who disagreed, but he had no choice. For any normal flying around, the *Marimar* would make do with ordinary aviation fuel and they found a tanker with enough for a 75-per cent fill. The first three hangars they came across had been trashed by looters. Ryder couldn't work out the logic as he thought most people would be starving, not looking for aviation parts. Having decided to leave the *Marimar* under a net they'd found, Brian had an idea.

"Clear enough space in the emptiest of the hangars. Back the plane in and put some more trashed boxes and rubbish back."

"Excellent," Vlad said, "confused people with poor memories will ignore it."

By the time their two-vehicle convoy started back, the dawn raced them down the A55.

Coffee and sandwiches made from homemade bread and honey occupied the astronauts, and Ryder talked on the mobile again to Brian.

"I agree with you. It's too risky to stay on the A55 in the Colwyn Bay area just in case those men are able to remember or work something out. How about the coast road?"

"No. We need to head inland for a while."

AT RYDER'S REQUEST, the ISS crew brought their pressure suits and helmets. They'd changed into more comfortable NASA working clothes: pale blue, all-in-one baby-grows, as Laurette described them.

Gustav insisted on having a go at being a bus driver on the return journey so Ryder rode shotgun and phone.

Encountering those men in the road made Ryder ask Brian for an alternative route. "Route details?"

"I was thinking of taking us to Betws-y-Coed then round the back of Anafon. Apart from Betws itself, we hardly touch a village. There are loads of minor roads that go over the back mountains but not right over the moorland to the centre. Of course, if you want to walk the last couple of miles..."

"We'll take a chance on Betws then. Should get there by 5.30; early for even the hardiest."

They needn't have worried, although they did startle a few dawn dog walkers and had to inch through a herd of escaped sheep.

All the astronauts had to be awakened when they arrived at the field centre, and Ryder collapsed in his bed, the adrenaline no longer needed; the relief sedated him to deep sleep.

PEACE DIDN'T LAST LONG. It wasn't the shouting that brought his game-show-host dream to an end, but Teresa shaking him with such violence, he bit his tongue.

"Wake up, you dozy ha'peth. All hell is breaking out!"

The stress and responsibility had worn him out. He struggled to swing his legs over the bed then staggered to the refectory, but the hullabaloo rattled the windows from the outside. Ryder stood in the doorway looking out.

"We've been months in space, circling this planet and you are saying we can't go for a walk?" shouted Adbul at Brian and Derek, who each held a rifle at the astronauts.

Vlad took his turn at bellowing. "Have you people any idea at all what it's like cooped up in a tin box for so long?"

"Why don't you shout a bit louder, boys," Bronwyn said. "Did you shout at each other up on the space station?"

"'Course not," said Vlad, to a *Yeah, right* from Jena.

"Listen, if you did yell at each other in your tin can, no one would have heard you, would they?" Bronwyn continued, like a nagging schoolteacher. "Whereas out here." She waved her arms at the hills. "Just beyond those echoing hills are millions of people who all have perfectly functioning ears as well as ARIA."

Her admonishment brought silence.

Dan, Jena, and Antonio leaned back on the minibus, each with a steaming mug and saying nothing. Ryder couldn't tell by looking in their eyes whether they were laughing, annoyed, or indifferent. He'd told Bronwyn that the ISS crew were the most intelligent set of people left who still had all their marbles. He knew it would have given her great pleasure to give them a dressing down.

"Ryder, tell them," Brian said.

Ryder waved at the hillsides. "Dan, this valley might look very spacious to you, but we need to have a chat, lay down some ground rules and—"

"I don't like the sound of rules," Jena said. "We've had to live by checklists and NASA protocols for ever. I'm kinda looking forward to a taste of freedom."

"I'm sure you'd rather we all follow a few basic precautions than catch ARIA. It's as easy as meeting a stranger on that hilltop. And then we'd all have it. The end."

"Yeah, come on guys," Dan said, "let's get to business and decide what we're doing with that case."

CHAPTER 29

Friday 18 September 2015:
Moraine Lake, Rocky Mountains, five months since Manuel (55)
caught ARIA, twenty-two years of his memory gone.

THE MORNING SUN HIT MANUEL'S NIGHTMARE-TORTURED FACE. His hangover beat him up. His ears tried to shut out the irritating tapping noise from someone who was going to get shouted at when he raised enough energy. Eyelids stuck down with sleep struggled to obey opening instructions. His right arm stretched out under the sheet and found warm flesh that wasn't his.

More asleep than awake, he turned to the woman. "Anne, shall I make some coffee?" Then one eyelid inched open, like a portcullis. Confused thoughts about getting divorced from Anne ravaged his brain when he remembered her with blond hair and not the redhead turning in bed to face him. He moved a leg to find the floor as her green eyes found him.

Her scream drowned out the tapping. As he turned from the howling, Manuel caught the blue flash of wings as the woodpecker flew away. The cabin vibrated: every animal in the forest was on the run. Forest? Why was he in a forest cabin? As the screaming from the naked woman (not Anne), continued, he thought about trying to calm her down, but he didn't know how. He assumed they'd had sex by the fact he, too, wore no clothes. Nothing he could think of saying could mitigate the situation, so he found some trousers and wandered off to seek a bathroom.

An old man with almost no hair stared at him from the mirror. It wasn't him. He touched his stubble and his shiny head. He must be in a dream. A note taped to the mirror said, "Kitchen table. The NoteCom. Press Go."

The kitchen in this familiar yet unknown cabin was too neat. The table was bare. What the hell was a NoteCom anyway? A pad could be a notepad, like the ones he used as a journalist. Of course, back in his office, he used a computer to word process his pieces, like all modernised hacks in 1993. Good, the shrieking had whimpered off. He filled an electric kettle and switched it on, noting a dial on the wall indicating 60% solar charge. Something else he hadn't remembered seeing anywhere. The packaging of foods in the cupboard looked different with their plastic-like containers carrying labels embossed rather than stuck on their child-proof sealed lids; the cooker hob had touch-sensitive panels rather than knobs.

A well-thumbed *Rocky Mountain What's On* magazine lay on the fridge. Manuel shook his head at the March 2015 date. "Somebody's having a joke," he said to himself, and then the bedroom door burst open.

They looked at each other in silence, trying to figure out the who and what had happened, racking their tortured memory for unavailable clues. Finally, Manuel pointed at the bathroom door.

"The bathroom. I'm Manuel."

"I'm pissed off."

"Makes two of us." He made two coffees. No bread to toast or bagels, no fresh foods. He pulled a face at a few packets labelled *Humulin products*. Maybe his mystery woman was a diabetic. He settled on crackers and opened a cream cheese plastic container with a *Use by May 2015* warning. "Should be all right for another few years." A headache fuzzed and the back of his eyes hurt like he was catching a cold, but curiosity drove him, carrying his coffee, into the lounge. He almost dropped the coffee when he saw strange Hi-Fi-type multimedia devices. A large black mirror on the wall took some time to be recognized as a TV. More yellowing papers and magazines confirmed the futuristic date.

He collapsed into a large leather armchair.

"What the hell has happened?"

"When you've figured it out, let me know," said the woman, dressed in shirt and slacks, carrying the coffee he'd made for her. She roamed the lounge, picking up the same papers and magazines, stared at the same unremembered technology, until she sat in a chair opposite him.

"Manuel. Who are you and what are we doing here?"

"As far as I know, I am Manuel Gomez, a journalist specialising in astronomy. I recall a cabin like this in my boyhood. That was in Lake Moraine and the mags and view out the windows verify that. As to why we are here. I've no idea. Last thing I remember was going to bed in my home in Baltimore in 1997. You?"

"This has gone far enough, Manuel or whatever your sodding name really is. You must have slipped me a Mickey in a drink last night and brought me here. Messed me up and put trick stuff in here to confuse me. Where's my car keys? And my car!"

"You're nuts," he yelled back. "I'm as darned confused as you are." He stood, as she did. Two bewildered combatants.

"I'm calling the police," she screamed. "I hope you like prison food, you bastard." She had found the landline phone when she first came into the room. "You've cut us off!" She threw the phone at Manuel, who, unprepared, caught it with his forehead.

"You bitch, you've drawn blood!" His hand dived into his pocket for a handkerchief but only brought out a car key.

She grabbed for it and held it in front of her, first in triumph then puzzlement. The key had a familiar Ford logo in a clear Perspex fob with a couple of press buttons. But the working bit, made of what looked like stainless steel, was a smooth, two-inch glass rod. No familiar twentieth-first-century car key. Her face crumpled into tears as she let the key fall.

Also confused, Manuel examined it. Working with space technologies left him few surprises; he must have picked it up at one of the many conventions he enjoyed. He thought he ought to try a hand at consoling the woman but counter-advised himself. He looked for more clues by returning to the bedroom.

By his side of the bed, he found a digital watch.

0832 09:18:15

Did the fifteen represent 2015 after all? He slipped it on. He walked round to the woman's side and found a textile shoulder bag. The urge to empty it on the bed fought with the prediction of a huge fight if she walked in, so he carried it to the lounge.

"Shall we see if this bag gives us any clues as to what's going on? Look, I'm in the dark here too. I've told you my name. I can't call you 'You,' can I?"

"Please yourself, I'm out of here." She headed for the door.

"If we are where I think we are, you'd have to walk miles to the nearest town."

"It can't be far to a phone box or to the next lodge. Somewhere with a friendly face, instead of a kidnapper, rapist—"

"You still think that of me? Gee...and I made you coffee. How do you know the next lodge is occupied or the next and the one after? It might be full of real rapists."

She slowed her walk to the door but reached and opened it. "Some things are worth risking."

"Aren't you forgetting something?" He held up her bag.

"It's not mine." She frowned.

"Where's yours, then? All women have a bag; it's a law or something." He grinned at his joke and saw just a glimmer of mirth in her face, but she had good control.

"I don't know. I have a red leather bag. You must have grabbed me before I had a chance to pick it up."

"Right. Let's see what's in here." He turned it upside down on the table. Handkerchief, cosmetic containers, notebook, pens, a change-purse, card-wallet, and a cell phone fell out. She stayed at the open door, but her mouth gaped at the sight of the distinctive red leather purse. Manuel picked up the card-wallet. "Julia Tyndall of Washington?"

She rushed over, snatched the wallet and purse. "You're a thief as well."

"I think even you must be doubting these instant reactions of yours." He picked up the phone. "Well, look at this. I thought it might be a calculator, but it unfolds with a little screen. Damn me if it isn't a phone. Mine's more of a talking house brick. Look at it."

"That must be mine too," she said, more sulkily than angry. "Give it to me." She punched at it but it was lifeless.

"Would you check your notebook out, Julia, or may I?"

"Mrs Tyndall to you," she snapped, grabbing the notebook and sitting on one of the stools around the table. She spent some minutes in silence while Manuel put a plate of crackers and cheese together for her and fetched her coffee back from the lounge. As he sat opposite her at the table, she closed the notebook, looked him in the eye without giving away any expression. She tossed him the notebook.

Shopping lists made up the first few pages. Manuel looked for clues; both to find out where twenty-two years had disappeared to, and how the two of them had crashed together in this cabin. He scrutinised a few more pages. Some items made him think maybe he was in 2015:

> *KwikMart*
> *Eggs, Cheese, Bread—low fat multivit organic wholeml*
> *Mike's medication—Seratonin patches*
> *Memory bubble stick—100 TetraByte - the $20 special offer*
> *NoteCom case*

Who heard of organic low fat bread at a KwikMart? Who's Mike and patches for medication? He guessed at the computer memory components, but as far as he remembered, a TetraByte was a thousand GigaBytes. Sheesh, that's more than the whole space program uses—or used—in the 1990s. Manuel remembered the mention of a NoteCom on the bathroom mirror.

He examined a more recent page:

> *Travel toiletries*
> *Pick up flight tickets Washington 2 NY, NY 2 London*
> *Job swap documents*

Then a dated page:

> *Thurs 23 April on Dreamliner flight La Guardia to London. Everybody sick—headaches, confused. My papers remind me I'm meeting family who already have ARIA but some passengers can't remember why they're on the plane!!!!*
> *Mutiny—the flight crew ill or dead. A passenger who was a pilot flew the plane.*
> *Going back to America. Dizzy.*

> *Friday*
> *No one answers phone at home. With others I walked out of isolation hospital—staff there weren't around this morning. Going to try and get back to Winnipeg— somehow more family there.*

Manuel flipped through some scribbled pages of confusion of Julia's dreadful state and journey via lorry and car lifts, hiding out in Toronto and Port Arthur—until the last page:

> *Sept 16*
> *Banff—sticking with M. A good man. Lost his wife Jat according to his NoteCom. Heard my family aren't in Winnipeg any more. Manuel also worked NASA at Goddard but I don't remember him. He knows my boss Karen and her brother, Ryder—so do I, apparently.*

Manuel looked up at Julia. She shrugged, and he took the gesture as an apology for all the earlier bawling. "Good idea; keeping notes," he said. "If we're still here tonight, we should write a big one for the bedroom ceiling. Looks like I have some useful information in something called a NoteCom. I ought to look for a holdall. Maybe outside, left in my—our—car, or something. Any ideas? And any notion as to what ARIA actually is?"

She shook her head. Tears dropped to the magazine on the table followed by her head as she sobbed. Manuel stood, walked around behind her, and patted her shoulder as he passed to the door and out in the hope of clearing his head with a walk and finding his NoteCom. How many mornings had started with shock, horror, and reconciliation like today?

CHAPTER 30

Saturday 19 September 2015:
Anafon Field Centre. Many people outside the valley will have lost
up to twenty-three years of memory.

AFTER THE UNEASY START WITH THE ISS CREW arguing with the centre staff, Ryder woke determined to make a positive, new beginning. They'd sorted a few ground rules then split up into three tour groups. Tour one looked at the centre's facilities. Tour two took in a long walk around the Anafon valley perimeter with additional advice to keep away from the sheep and feral ponies in case they have ARIA. Tour three, led by Ryder, took astro-engineers Jena and Dan to the abandoned mine where they'd put the case yesterday.

"It's a mile," Ryder said, stuffing a rucksack. "Not far but enough to get soaked in a sudden Welsh storm. The mine goes under the mountain for at least another mile, which is why we're packing rubber boots and head-torches."

Jena pointed at the trolley Ryder had brought round, loaded with the white NASA space-pressure suits. "I assume you want these to act as biohazard protection suits for when we open the case?"

Ryder tried not to stare at her. Her slim features and model-like Euro-Asian face matched an ideal-woman formula in his hormones. Her deep blue eyes shone, but he hadn't dared be drawn into them.

A clearing-throat cough later, Ryder responded. "Yes, even though they won't fit all of us, they're better than our thin disposable suits."

To his astonishment, once ready to go, she linked arms with him as they set off. He glanced back to check Teresa hadn't seen them. Then he remembered she led the valley and perimeter tour with Dr Antonio Menzies and Vlad. Of course, she had binoculars...

It must have been her being cooped up for so long that put Jena in an exuberant mood as she pulled Ryder along. He'd not been chatted up by an American woman before.

"Come on then, what's all the goss?"

"Pardon?"

"Let'r rip, Ryder. Are you and Teresa serious, married and with children?"

"Good Lord, no. But, we—"

"I didn't think so. Nor am I, and I am delicious, aren't I, Dan?"

She turned to her commander, who pulled the luggage trolley along the rough track.

Dan looked up, shaking his head in a mild rebuke at her outrageous flirting.

"Just agree, Dan. Actually, he never makes a decision along lines I suggest, so I'll have to rely on your judgement. Am I gorgeous?"

After another cough. "I thought you astronauts would have trouble walking after being in orbit so long. Have you been exercising up there?"

"Ryder, you must have been eyeing me up. I don't mind, did you think I would?"

"No. Yes. I mean—"

"Leave the poor man alone," said Dan. "That's one of those 'have you stopped beating your wife' questions. This is a beautiful valley, Ryder. Incredible, isn't it, Jena?"

"To be honest, the bleakest of wide-open moorland would feel like heaven compared to that tin can with four morons. No offence, Dan."

"We chose this valley because of its difficult access rather than any intrinsic beauty but, yes, we're lucky to be in one of Wales's best kept secrets."

Dan beat Jena to another question. "How many intruders have you had to kill?"

Ryder raised an eyebrow.

Jena said, "Hey, why the surprise? Oh, I get it, you told the centre group you all had to be tough on strangers and they objected. Yeah?"

"Nothing gets past you, does it?" Ryder said. "You guys are used to making life-and-death decisions. Trained to be hard, whereas my friends have had hardness thrust open them."

"So to speak, eh Ryder?" Jena said, laughing. She spotted the mine entrance and disengaging Ryder's arm, broke into a jog.

"Take no notice of her. She ate men for breakfast before our ISS mission. Then had to behave, cooped up with four men married to their work. Well, except for Antonio, but Jena isn't his type."

Ryder laughed. "And who is his type? Vlad?"

"No. Antonio isn't gay, as far as I know, but he's attracted to European women with unusual features."

"Hah. What? Like no eyebrows or long noses?"

Dan looked away. "More like straw hair, freckles..."

Ryder stopped walking. He didn't need to say that Dan had just described Teresa. Even less did he want to mention their rocky relationship. On the other hand, their relationship thrived on friction. He smiled more when he concentrated on physical problems to solve rather than second guess what Teresa wanted. Relief at reaching the mine entrance washed over him.

"Jena!" He had to shout at her. "No, don't hit the padlock with a stone. I have a key."

Dan shook his head as if to apologise for the lack of behavioural control over his crew. Ryder acknowledged the gesture with a knowing look. They'd both had to deal with difficult people.

"If you had broken the padlock, you wouldn't have been able to get in—"

"Nothing can stop me getting what I want, Ryder."

"—without security cameras seeing you, and by the time you came across the next locked gate, you would have two or more firearms pointing at you."

"Excellent," Dan said. "And as we discussed earlier, it's safer to shoot first and ask questions after, so give it a go, Jena."

"Maybe not on this occasion," she said, taken down a notch. "You don't want us suited up for this excursion, do you?"

"I'm going to show you the emergency isolation facility we've set up here, for what it's worth. And where we've hidden the case."

Ryder looked forward to this little tour. He knew aspects of it unnerved those unused to grubbing around in a dark, subterranean world. He and Brian had set up a string of lights powered by a small hydro-generator embedded in a nearby mountain stream. Not enough to read by, but enough light to know when to duck or step around bottomless pits. Augmented by their head torches, the dim lights allowed the three to stow the suits in waterproof bags near the entrance.

"Hey, Jena, let me go first," shouted Ryder, as she darted like a rabbit into its hole. She let him catch up.

"I thought you were going to do that typically English tour where you led from behind," she said. "What kept you?"

"I had to relock the gate behind us."

"Impressive," Dan said. "Do we need to watch our heads?"

"Absolutely. It goes in more or less horizontal, but the miners must have been only five feet tall a couple of centuries ago, so watch the ceiling, the floor and the walls. There are rusty iron brackets waiting to catch your head. Follow me."

Thirty minutes later, they'd reached a gap in the left wall.

"We are going into a small gallery on your left," Ryder said. "There's a small step but it means the floor is dry. Here we are."

Contrary to the low tunnel on the way in, this room had at least a twenty-foot headroom. The extra volume allowed other senses to taste the air. A slight musty smell from bat droppings and the ever-present dampness took the edge off considering the mine as a holiday destination.

"Cosy," said Jena. "A home from home. Hey, cute armchair and, my God, beds. Is this your secret love nest, Ryder?"

"I guess this is a kind of isolation dormitory in case anyone gets infected," Dan said. "Excellent, Ryder. You have a heater, fridge, water filter, first aid..."

"Hey, now this is luxury," Jena said. "A computer! For playing games?"

"Why not?" Ryder said. "They'll need to pass the time."

Jena wore a look of disgust. "Give them a pack of cards. What a waste of a resource."

"Am I right in thinking it's networked to the centre?" Dan said. "So it can be used for communication? Cell phones won't work this deep in the mountain. This webcam works too? Of course it would and the medical sensors. You've thought of everything. Cool, huh, Jena?"

"Got you," said Ryder to Jena, who had stood with folded arms while the two men's voices echoed.

"Fancy thinking it was for games," Dan said and then laughed with Ryder.

"Shut up. Shaddup! You'll have the whole goddamn mountain shaking to bits," she cried then laughed too.

"It's not finished and so far not needed. Both of you come over here and give me your head torches." Ryder led them to the centre of the room. After a moment, the lights went out. If Ryder was expecting a scream, a shout, even a gasp in the complete pitch blackness, he had to be disappointed.

"Cool."

Dan said, "Astronaut training is pretty tough, Ryder."

After a minute, Ryder said, "Few people experience total blackness in their lives. Outside at night, with no mains electricity, a moonless overcast sky will still have a glimmer of light from the odd lamp. Of course, we don't see complete blackness. There are often floaters or something stimulating the optic nerve, making us see spots. Yes?"

"Can't say I do. How about you, Jena?"

"Nope."

"Must be because I'm older than you two, I suppose," Ryder said, putting the lights back on, and then he saw their smiles. "Touché, bastards."

When the laughter reverberated away, Jena looked under a tarpaulin. "Where have you hidden our luggage, Ryder?"

"This way." Ryder returned to the gallery. He couldn't resist looking back down the thousand metres to the mine entrance. A fingernail of bright light. A sight that gave him both inexplicable elation and a tinge of entrapment.

After another hundred metres walking and fending off an increasing frequency of jutting rocks, he stopped and looked back once more. He could no longer see the mine entrance. There must have been enough of a kink to deny him the exit light.

"Careful here," Ryder said, with Dan and Jena on either side. At their feet was a sharp edge to a deep pit stretching side to side and ten metres in front. Light bulbs lit down and up, casting shadows between illuminated rock segments.

"Wow," exclaimed Jena. "It looks like a bottomless pit. This is beautiful, Ryder."

"It sure is," Dan said. "Takes your breath away, the soft yellow mixed with cold greys and spooky shadows. People would pay to see this. Amazing. I take it this is where the tour ends. I can't see an easy way round."

"We have to get across," Ryder said. "Because the case is in a cavern on the other side."

"A hidden bridge?" Jena said.

"Watch and be amazed," Ryder said. "It's surprisingly easy to jump."

"No way. You'll kill yourself. And I'm only just getting to like you."

He laughed, took a few steps back, ran to the brink, and jumped. He landed in the pit, but it was an illusion. An inch of water. The pit was a perfect reflection in a shallow pool of undisturbed water.

The two astronauts, after their initial shock, laughed and then jumped too, splashing like children at the seaside.

Across the pool, they rounded a bend to an end cavern. It had similar equipment to the isolation room, with the addition of a padlocked steel cage. Although used by miners to store their more valuable tools, it served the new owners as a safe. The padded container looked no different than when they enclosed the case with it out in orbit. A light and a camera looked at it from high up on the wall. Ryder waved and thumbed up at the camera.

"Derek is monitoring it, especially since we would have triggered a couple of motion-sensor alarms since entering the mine."

The three stood looking at the wrapped case.

Dan started. "We didn't get round to discussing what to do with this beastie."

"I know what we should do with it," Jena said. "Throw away the key to that padlock."

Ryder dragged over a couple of wooden chairs to add to the one facing the case's prison. They all sat while Ryder extracted a flask of hot coffee and Bronwyn-made biscuits from his rucksack. They munched and sipped in quiet contemplation.

"It needs to be opened and soon," Dan said.

"I agree," said Ryder. "It could be mankind's salvation."

"Or its end," Jena said.

Ryder said, "Certainly humans are going to be wiped out in a year or so at the present rate. People have dropped like flies with the lack of medication to overcome their pre-ARIA conditions and post-ARIA epidemics. Soon, there'll be none who can read or remember basic skills."

Jena offered a wry smile. "They'll still be able to make babies."

"Yes, instinct and hormones will see to that," Dan said. "But ARIA means the day after, they'll forget they've had a baby, or where it is. They'll wonder why they're sore, look for a reason and, with luck, find a baby in a cot. How many babies will starve to death within days? Or fall prey to the packs of dogs we've heard about?"

"That's sure worse than when humans dropped out of the trees," Jena said.

"Yes," said Ryder. "Those early humans were able to remember what they learned."

"If it's just down to us uninfected humans to regenerate the race," said Jena, edging her chair closer to Ryder. "We'd better get started right away."

"Umm," Ryder said, "you have a point. Are you ready to be a baby factory?"

"Oh my God, I hadn't thought this one through." Jena edged her chair equidistant from both men.

Dan added to her angst. "Of uninfected people, we only know of this group in North Wales and Charlotte, on her own in Australia. How many is that?"

"Fourteen altogether," Ryder said. "According to the biologists here, that is too small a base for a sustainable population regeneration since only four women here are of child-bearing age. I'm afraid I don't fancy driving all the way to Australia to get Charlotte pregnant."

"We could store eggs from the women before we make them pregnant," said Dan. "Then use our sperm and cloning technology to set up a kinda human embryo factory to impregnate the four women with, say, six at a time."

Ryder, sneaked Dan a sly wink. "Then the women would have to be more or less permanently pregnant with sextuplets."

"Who would look after all the infants?" Jena was aghast.

"You women, of course," Ryder said. "We'd be needed doing other physical work. Women are the natural child rearers. Of course all this might be unnecessary if, somehow, ARIA could be reversed or at least stopped in time."

"Could be worthwhile seeing what's in this case, then," Dan said, winking at Ryder.

"You fuckers," Jena said. "All this baby-factory stuff was just a ploy to get me to agree to opening the case. As if you needed my blessing."

THEIR RETURN TO THE CENTRE CORRESPONDED WITH LUNCHTIME. Teresa's perimeter tour group entered just as the other two groups finished their soup. Ryder looked up to see Teresa, who had linked arms with Antonio. Her face bright and smiling more than he'd seen for a long time. He fought his immediate urge to run out and pile into Antonio. If he wasn't going to hang on to Teresa, it was because he and she weren't right for each other. The fact that they had not considered getting married put strength to that argument. Nevertheless, as leader of the group and her lover, he cared for her. But for the time being, he had more critical decisions to make. He should be grateful she smiled, mostly.

After lunch, Ryder took Dan and Jena out on the perimeter run. They were keen to breathe fresh air as well as inspect their security from the possibility of crazed local invaders. He had a strong urge to do the whole tour by walking, but Jena had spotted Brian's quad-bike and her playful side obliged her to insist on using it.

"Have you heard a quad-bike in action, Jena?" Brian, held onto the key, while Jena tried to grab it off him.

"Of course I have. Everyone has them on my beach in LA. No one would consider moving across the dunes without one."

"I thought you lived in Boston." Ryder had studied the biographies of all the crew.

"Oh, come on, Ryder. Stop being picky."

"It's not that I mind you having a great time."

"Great," Jena said. "Brian, hand 'em over."

"But we try not to generate noise that might bring unwelcome visitors."

"Antonio said the perimeter tour took four hours," she said.

"Hey," said Ryder, "if you've something better to do, don't let us keep you."

"Actually, I might have. You boys go for your hike."

Dan took Ryder to one side. "It might not be a good idea to leave Jena to her own devices. You might have noticed that she's a bit…"

"Volatile?"

"Excitable. Ryder, I know the quad-bike would be noisy, especially up on the ridge where the sound would travel all the way to Ireland, but I'd rather have her with us than not."

"Hang on a moment," said Ryder, and ran into the centre. Moments later, he came out with Megan's mountain bike. It had the latest puncture-proof tyres, thirty-six gears, and ultra-smart suspension system.

Jena snorted in derision but after a little consideration, tried it out around the centre car park. "Pretty cool. Give it a go, Dan. On the other hand, you can't—it's all mine."

"Actually, it's *me* who's allowing *you* to ride *my* bike," said Megan at the doorway.

"Oh, thanks, Megan. Does it do zero to twenty-five thousand in ten seconds like the vehicles I'm used to?"

"Only downhill. Brian's fixed the hooter."

"Great. Hey, the hooter doesn't work. Ah, that's what you meant. And I suppose he's taken the playing card out of the spokes as well, the spoilsport. Hah! Don't worry Megan, I'll bring it back in one piece."

"Before you go tearing up the valley," said Ryder, "there are a few ground rules such as keeping below the ridge, keeping quiet, get on the phone if you see a stranger within the perimeter, keep within sight of us at all times—"

"Haven't you got one of those retractable child leashes to put on me?" said Jena

"I'll just have to trust you. Phone?"

"Yes."

"Helmet?"

"Get lost." She bombed off down the narrow lane.

RYDER AND DAN FOLLOWED ON FOOT. The valley had few trees. Bracken and grasses clothed the rocks, allowing a clear view for several miles. Ryder regretted letting Jena escape by mountain bike. There was no way she would keep them in sight, and they couldn't catch up. So, they turned uphill off the track to gain the ridge. Their view of the whole valley would be uninterrupted, and with care, they'd be able to use their binoculars on the next valley.

Dan had to keep stopping. "You've no idea what this hike is doing to my lungs and legs."

"I've some idea, Dan. I used to spend too long cooped up in offices and studios. It's only recently I've had the benefit of all this fresh air, the aroma of that lavender we've just brushed through, watching bees visiting the heather blossoms, and just gazing at the eddies in a mountain stream."

"No, Ryder, I mean I've been in low gravity and little exercise-mode for so long, I can't keep up."

"Oh, sorry, Dan. Head for that rock; we'll rest up."

They sat and trained their glasses on Jena. A mile away, she'd left the rough lane to explore the stone remains of ancient hut circles in the valley floor.

"Before we arrived here, feral ponies wandered throughout this valley. Just a small herd but no doubt they assumed it belonged to them. Luckily, we only had to patch a few holes in fences to persuade them to find other pastures." A splotchy brown butterfly alighted on a sun-warmed patch of rock near Dan.

Dan leant towards it. "Well now, little fellah, do you have ARIA? I guess it would be pretty difficult to compute its memory loss."

"Since the butterfly stage only lasts a week or so, it would lose its adult memory in four hours. What would it have to remember anyway? Instinct tells it to drink, fly erratically to avoid predators, warm wing muscles on a sunny stone, mate, and lay eggs. I think it must be one of the fritillary butterflies Teresa's excited about. They're becoming rarer, though whether it's global warming or habitat loss—hey, I suppose ARIA will result in them increasing. I'd like to show you the ridge. Shall we go?"

Dan took one more lingering look at the butterfly. At the ridge top, he gasped. Both out of breath and in awe of the view.

"On the horizon to the north is the Irish Sea with Anglesey to the northwest. That milestone you're leaning on is Roman. You see a sunken grassy track here. It links ancient forts."

"There's a hell of a lot of history here, Ryder. Are we witnessing the end game?"

"I've often thought that while strolling around up here, hoping I won't see any strangers. Yet, I get a pang of hope when I see a curl of smoke from a chimney. I certainly didn't expect to see any more airplane trails."

"Sure is peaceful up here. No doubt in contrast to the chaos and mayhem in the coastal cities. We need to put our mind to opening that damn case. It might be the last hope for any of us."

Ryder agreed. "We'll walk along this ridge for a while. I'm looking but can't see any strangers, but you never know who, behind curtains or a bush, might see moving shapes along a skyline. We're hidden for a mile, and then we'd better nip back down into the Anafon Valley and head towards inspecting our security gates."

"We're not going to be scaling Mount Everest on the south side of the centre, are we?"

"Llwtymor Mountain? Not today. There are the remains of Second World War aircraft up there."

"This one little valley is a gem of a place, Ryder, and yet you say hardly anyone rambled over it on a daily basis before ARIA?"

"Gets to you, doesn't it? Especially poignant now. See our new wire fencing between the gaps in the stone wall? It wouldn't keep anyone determined out, but hopefully the signs will deter them."

"Yeah, I wondered about the 'Active Firing Range' notices. Neat."

They kept their heads below the skyline as they hiked west until following an old sheep track back down to the small lane. They soon came to a new gate.

"This is the second gate a vehicle would have to go through to reach our centre. See how there's a rocky bluff from the mountain on this side right down to the road and a steep slope down to the river on the left?"

"I've waved at the camera, Ryder, but is anyone watching?"

"*Si* there is, Commander," said a tinny voice, from a speaker.

"That you, Antonio? I thought this gatepost had an Italian accent," said Dan. "Keep your hands off my dinner."

"Ah, Dan, I let my hands take what they can, but I'll leave your pasta alone."

Ryder walked up to the microphone. "Is Teresa there?"

"I will seek her out."

Ryder imagined his grinning face.

"No, don't bother. I'll catch up with her later," said Ryder, but Antonio had been replaced by Brian.

"Everything all right at the gate, Ryder?"

"Yes, Brian, see you later." Ryder stood, hands on hips. "How did you keep your hands away from punching Antonio on board the ISS?"

"Never needed to. My wife left me two years ago. If he tried it on with Jena, it wouldn't have bothered me as long as the assignments were on target. Are you unduly worried about him and Teresa?" Dan gave the gate a tug to check how solid it was and noted the razor wire along the top.

Ryder test-kicked the bottom spar. "Logically, we need to adjust our emotions to fit the new situation."

"Easier said than done. Though it looks as if our Jena has the hots for you, or haven't you noticed?"

"Yeah, well. Teresa's hard enough to handle. Could I control Jena? Isn't she making a play for all the new men here at Anafon? Just asking?"

"Nope, I reckon she goes on full broadside for one target at a time. If you want my advice, let her have you."

"What? Dan, that isn't the kind of well-brought-up Godly advice I'd expect from you."

"Hell, it's just practical, Ryder. If you don't, she'll keep on and on. Anyway, she's darn bright and a lot of fun, I guess. Difficult and independent too. Want a hot-water bottle or a wild cat?"

"All this relationship stuff does my head in. Haven't much time for it now, have we? Let's consider the case again."

"Fair enough. The mine is isolated and you have sensors and remote operating facilities to check the case out during its opening."

"You do remember the problem opening the first case by remote handling?" said Ryder.

"If I recall correctly, it wouldn't open until a human got real close. I wonder if it was the warmth—an infrared sensor—or has it a human-contact sensor beyond our technical experience? It would have helped to have had a detailed analysis of the case after it opened. I know the situation became rapidly confused with the breached containment protocol, but before memory loss took over..."

"No, Dan, the memory loss is effective immediately. Within one hour of being in the vicinity of the open case, you'd lose two days of memory. So if his new headache and confusion let him, the techie would think—*what case*? The Edwards contamination started slower, but the case wasn't opened there. Further infected people don't display memory loss until after sleep."

They continued walking, talking, taking delight in the aromas from the heather, damp soil, and that nostril-widening experience with clean air. Ryder leapt on a waist-high boulder and eyed his binoculars.

"Hey, Dan, I can't see Jena anywhere. Have you?"

"No, I'll try her cell phone. Good job you people have set up a narrow-band local network. Nope, turned off. She must be back at the centre."

Ryder used his own phone. "The centre hasn't seen her either, but Brian said he'd use the cameras, and if necessary, the flying cam on a drone model airplane."

"My God, you are prepared."

"She gave me the impression she wasn't used to off-road biking. Suppose she's had an accident and is unconscious?" Ryder's irritation of her had transformed to concern.

"How much daylight do we have left?" Dan said. "We could split up and go along both sides of the valley."

"It's four, so we have at least two and a half hours. I don't want to lose you too. Stay with me and I'll get Gustav and Brian to nip out while the women operate the remote webcam."

After fifteen minutes with no sighting, Dan, puffed again, said, "Are those paths easier?"

"You're looking at sheep tracks, they'll go anywhere. Hello, I'm getting a call from Megan."

"Hi Dan, it's all right, I caught a glimpse of Jena round the stores area back here at the centre."

"Excellent. Thanks, Megan."

"Hang on there, Megan," said Dan, asking Ryder for the phone. "Did she bring back your bike?"

"I suppose so."

"Megan, do me a huge favour, kid, and look?" asked Dan.

"Cor, I don't know. I'm peeling bloody spuds here. Oh, all right then. It's not far, I suppose. Be right back."

"You are a star, Megan," said Dan, as he and Ryder listened to Megan's objections, Welsh-accent banter and heavy breathing. Ryder raised an eyebrow at Dan but acceded to the commander's more insightful experience of Jena's character.

"Right. I'm where my bike is kept."

"And?" Dan had to drag it out of her.

"She must have put it in the wrong place. Shall I have a look around for it?"

"No, Megan," Dan said. "Get back to your potatoes, but thanks." He turned to Ryder. "There's no point in Megan spending time looking for a bike Jena is still riding. Megan probably did see her. She went back there for I don't know—a drink, her camera, a Band-Aid for a grazed knee?"

"Pity," said Ryder. "I was hoping to call off the search, but I suppose we'd better continue it until someone else spots her and reports an actual live sighting. It makes a worthy exercise, anyway."

"All this hiking is sure giving me a monumental appetite," Dan said. "I hope Megan has—hey, what's that cloud?" He pointed south where a brown cloud grew from the base of Llwtymor Mountain. Before Ryder could react, they both heard a deep, booming crump sound. Ryder trained his binoculars but intervening hilly ground obscured the exact source.

"I have a nasty feeling about this."

"It's from the mine, isn't it?" said Dan, his query punctuated by another rumble and a fresh dust cloud. Ryder's mobile phone bleeped him.

"Ryder, it's Brian, explosion at the mine. The cameras and sensors have blacked out. We're on our way."

"Brian, hang on. Don't enter the mine," shouted Ryder at his phone.

"I'm not bloody stupid, Ryder. I know there could be more collapses."

"It's not just that, Brian. The case. We won't know if it is damaged or what it might release. If you can access the mine entrance, there are bio and space suits in large plastic bags. Let the ISS people have their own custom-made suits and we'll have our bio suits and—"

"Like I said, I'm not stupid—what?"

Bronwyn's voice came across. "He hadn't thought of that, Ryder. Thanks. See you there."

"Good, but I need to know that at least two people are monitoring cameras and comms at the centre—don't all of you go."

CHAPTER 31

Saturday 19 September 2015:
Anafon Field Centre.

LARGE BOULDERS OF GREY FINE ROCK NOW PILED AROUND THE MINE'S
ENTRANCE. Ryder's heart sank when from a distance, he saw people
coming out of the entrance after he'd demanded no one went in.
Wisps of smoky dust escaped from the gaping mouth and puffed
upwards.

Ryder and Dan ran the last hundred metres. Antonio and Adbul
were being helped out of their suits by Vlad and Gustav.

"Taking them off?" Ryder was ready to assert himself.

"*Si*, sorry to disobey orders, *capitano*," Antonio said.

"I should expect more resp—" Ryder continued, but Dan touched
his elbow to alert him to what lay in the grass by the side of the mine.
Megan's bike.

"Did you locate Jena in there?" said Dan to his men.

They shook their heads. Abdul said, "That's why we went in as
soon as we were suited up." He looked at both leaders for approval.
"But the roof has collapsed about a hundred metres in. Impassable."

"Jena was in there when the roof collapsed, then," said Ryder.
"Damn."

"She might be trapped and not crushed," Gustav said. "We should
prepare to clear a crawl-space through the rubble."

"I'm glad you said 'prepare,'" Ryder said, "because not only do we
need to bring up roof support materials, we need to ensure we are
not contaminated by the case."

"I like this man," said Dan, to his crewmen.

"I thought you might. He's as methodical and as slow as you," said
Antonio, ducking as Dan threw a handful of gravel at him.

"You can fuss and make plans," said Abdul, refastening the Velcro
on his suit. "I will be making a start. No matter what you say." He
disappeared into the mine entrance.

"Okay, there are preparations we can do quickly," said Ryder,
flipping open his phone. "Brian, get the trolley ready and hitched to
our smallest vehicle. Load up some materials suitable for shoring,
crowbars, ropes and winch cable, and extra torches. Thanks.

"Antonio, I suppose the overhead lights are out?"

"Blown by the vibration."

"Right, Brian, are you still there? A box of light bulbs too. Okay, Antonio, you might as well get re-suited and follow Abdul. I want people working on a buddy principle. Understand?"

"*Si*, Ryder, *il Duce*," said Antonio.

"That's enough, Antonio," said Dan, going over to help him suit up and shut up.

After Brian arrived, they made short work of unloading the equipment and cleared enough rubble to get the trolley in with a winch cable.

Ryder took Brian to one side. "I don't suppose anyone was looking at any of the mine cams when the roof collapsed?"

"Afraid not, and we don't record. Waste of time and resources. I'm concerned about how it happened."

"I'm no expert in mine stability, Brian, but I would've thought that if the mine stayed intact for two hundred years, it wouldn't have collapsed just because we turned it into a furnished let."

"Well, the way I see it, Ryder, all mines collapse sooner or later. You can't just dig a mine and not expect millions of tons of annoyed stone to press down. And why not, when some idiots start drilling and knocking bolts in the walls and ceiling?"

"Dan and I heard two loud noises. I suppose the roof collapse would be noisy, sudden, and create an echo around the valley. Or did you—"

"Ryder, as you know, I was at the centre, only a mile away from the mine. I worked in the quarries years ago. I'd swear I heard an explosion followed by the roof collapse."

"It gives us two possibilities."

Brian's soft Welsh accent belied his words. "Only one from where I'm standing. That cow, Jena Kochi—Chinese isn't she?—blew the case because—"

"Go on, Brian. I'll overlook the racist bigotry for the moment but give me a reason why she'd destroy the case?"

"Everybody knows the Chinese would want the case for themselves. She's probably been in touch with them and followed orders."

"Good grief, you're unbelievable, Brian. Scary."

Brian folded his arms and set his face to withstand criticism with no grace.

"Brian, Jena Kochi has a Canadian mother and lives in the US...with a Japanese father."

"S-sorry, Ryder. She must be under there and I'm blaming her. Excuse me. I'll get on with fixing the lights and power cable."

Ryder watched him go but with mixed feelings. Brian might be a racist, but he could be right about Jena blowing up the mine. Explosives were kept in the stores at the centre, where Jena was seen before the mine blew. She wanted the case destroyed. The loss of contact with her family had unhinged her. He sat on a rock, sending a beetle scurrying into the heather. Jena had too much intelligence to open the case or to attach explosives to it since the virus might survive. She tried to seal it in by blowing the roof down. He stood and walked over to Dan, who was emptying the first trolley load.

"Dan, would Jena know how to use explosives?"

Dan's face showed no surprise. "Her astro-engineering qualifications involved plenty of explosives. She was a brilliant engineer."

"Then, Dan, she *is* a good engineer," Ryder said. Both men looked for her around the valley and up the mountainside.

Dan took out his cell phone. "You can come down now, Jena. You'll miss dinner."

"Don't you think she should be sent to bed without her dinner?" said Ryder.

"No, she's ten times more irritable when hungry. There she is."

Grubby but with a raised head, she strolled down the mountain to the waiting group. Brian rushed into the mine to tell the rescuers to forget Jena, but to keep going for the case.

Ryder turned his back on her. "Dan, put her under arrest."

"Miss Kochi," said Dan, "consider yourself under arrest."

Megan had already rescued her mountain bike, so Jena walked past the men and carried on down towards the centre.

"Aren't you going to sort her out?" Brian said.

Dan and Ryder looked at each other. How do you admonish a woman as crazy as a hornet-stung bear? In their favour was that she couldn't get at the case now.

Ryder said, "You don't suppose she..."

"Took the case out first? You thought the same thing?" They jumped in the Volvo and drove after her.

"You talk to her, Ryder, she has a soft spot for you."

"You're kidding." It was too late to argue. They'd caught up with her.

"I don't want a lift."

Dan drove off leaving Ryder walking with her.

"You've caused us a lot of difficulty, you know, and worry."

She stopped walking. "You were worried about me? Oh, Ryder."

"We assumed the case had reached a critical phase. When we saw Megan's bike, we thought the case had exploded with you in there."

"What makes you think the case might explode? The first one didn't."

"The first was opened within three days of you finding it. This one was found a week ago. Maybe there's a time limit. Did it look all right to you?"

"I didn't see it. I only blew the roof supports a hundred metres in. You know the case is evil. Satan's blight. I wouldn't want to get near it."

Ryder considered she was telling the truth, so she hadn't moved the case. But there had to be an element of doubt. It was worth continuing the tunnelling to reach the case but also to search the mountainside where she'd been.

"You are coming in with me, aren't you?" Jena said to him. "I might have a concussion and I want you with me, Ryder. I don't think the others like me anymore. You'll help me shower all this rock-dust off me, won't you?"

AWKWARD SILENCES PREVAILED OVER DINNER. If Jena had the sensibilities of a normal person, she would have withered under the evil-eye stares, and haemorrhaged from stabs in the back. However, she remained aloof, secure in her belief that she had saved them from a fate worse than ARIA.

Teresa cornered Ryder in the stores where he was conducting his own inventory of their remaining communications and electronic equipment.

"She's a complete crackpot, Ryder. What are you going to do about her?" She frowned at him with all the body language of a poised mountain cat.

"What do you think we should do with her?"

"Hey, you're the centre leader. That bitch has jeopardised our future. She's a liability. You've always said that to survive, we have to be tough."

"That's true, but I'm not going to put a bullet in a healthy person just because she's temporarily freaked out."

"You mean because she's a child-bearing-age woman and you fancy the pants off her. Why, Ryder, you could put her into solitary with you holding the only visitor's ticket."

"And what about you and the Italian doctor? I don't see you batting his wandering hands away."

"You wouldn't understand. Romantically, he's a million miles ahead of you."

"Teresa, be careful of him. He's sly and a creep. At least with me, what you saw is what you got."

"Listen to you, Ryder. All pompous and above us all."

"If you say so." He was hurt by her barbed comments, but he held back. This community was too small to let bickering get the better of them. Survival was in the balance, and all Teresa wanted to do was score points.

"So what are you going to do with the mad bitch?"

"She can't damage the case anymore, so chill out. I'm in here looking to see if we have an electronic tag we can put on her. Come to think about it, you might have one in your biology equipment?"

Teresa went to a blue plastic container, checked the list of contents printed on the top and waved at it. "Help yourself, but are you sure she wouldn't prefer fluffy handcuffs and for you to whip her ass?"

Again, he held back from retaliating; he had memories of such an S&M scenario with Teresa less than a year ago. She looked at him, letting him know with a wistful look that she remembered that night too. Gone and lost forever.

"Oh, there you are," called Brian from the entrance of the storeroom. "Megan reminded me about something on Llwtymor that might interest you, Ryder."

Glad of the distraction, Ryder followed Brian into the refectory where a hot, black coffee helped him focus on the large-scale map. Brian's grubby finger jabbed at a point halfway from the valley floor to the summit.

"There's an air shaft for the mine that comes out at this spot."

"Really? How does Megan know that? There are no paths around there."

"Fishing," Megan said, who stood behind Ryder.

"What?"

"My dad used to fish the lake, and he brought me. I hated fishing so I wandered all over. Found a propeller blade once. There's an iron grating in the ground up there. Dad said it allowed fresh air into the end of the mine."

"Why couldn't we see the light from it when we were in the mine?"

"Brambles."

"It might not be straight all the way down," said Brian. "But we can find out."

RYDER CARRIED A RUCKSACK AND CLIMBING ROPE, following Megan and Brian up the rough mountainside. Brian had brought a pneumatic bolt cutter that cut through a rusted padlock. Dan and

Ryder pulled up the screeching grate until it dropped on its back, crushing thorns. Brian dropped down a lead with a powerful battery lamp while Ryder readied a fish-eye webcam to follow it down on a cable attached to a laptop on the surface. His heartbeat decelerated with relief when the cage with the case showed up on the screen. The group applauded Megan.

"Can we stop working on the tunnel, now?" asked Brian.

Ryder scratched his head. "I suppose so. For all we know, there is a mile of excavating."

"We wouldn't have enough shoring materials anyway," said Brian, relieved to forego more rock clearing.

"So what happens with our time-bomb down there?" said Dan.

"I could get it," Megan said.

"No," Ryder said. "It's safer down there."

"Suit yourself." She stomped off. Brian walked after her.

Antonio said, "Any of us could be lowered and either fetch the case or..."

Ryder pondered and said, "We could be lowered through this aperture and get stuck halfway down."

"I'd be willing to take the risk," Antonio said. "Then of course, if I do get stuck..."

"There'd be one less to feed back at the centre," Ryder said. They all laughed but Ryder meant it.

Dan and Antonio exchanged knowing looks.

"Antonio talked something over with me last night, Ryder," said Dan. "He's volunteering to open the case, alone. Equipped with enough provisions and comms for as long as we think necessary."

Ryder looked at Antonio as if he'd not seen him before. There in front of him was the man making a play for Teresa, hence the lowest form of scum. Yet, he was volunteering for the most dangerous job left on the planet. The opened case could explode, but more likely emit fumes or a virus to complete the task of the disastrous ARIA.

"I'm astounded and incredibly impressed," Ryder said, "but there are many technical issues to resolve."

"I know," Antonio said, "and some made more complicated because of this access point. For instance, how are we to ensure the contents of the case do not escape through this chimney—since that is what it would become?"

"And getting down there, if it is possible without dislocating all your bones, will be easier than the return journey," Ryder said.

"Once down there and after exposing myself to the case, I could occupy myself—in between reporting to you—by clearing a horizontal route through the collapsed roof."

"We might end up losing you under a fresh fall and we'd be back to square one," said Ryder. "I know we couldn't force you not to do what you want, but your health and safety wouldn't be just about you."

"Don't insult me, Ryder. This is a magnanimous situation. With no family left alive and being a physician, I am best placed to help everyone here."

Ryder didn't feel inclined to apologise for his patronising warning. He was used to saying the obvious to some of the centre staff and erred on the side of caution, knowing some would be offended.

"Let's sort out the details back at the centre," he said, knowing Teresa would accuse him of engineering the situation. He could see her wagging finger whooshing through the air, her nagging voice accusing him of throwing her incipient lover down a well. And the joke was that Antonio had thrown himself down. But then maybe he'd been too hasty with the good doctor. After all, his own relationship with Teresa had been rocky for months, and it would have freed him to take up other opportunities. What was he thinking? There were only two other possibilities, Laurette, who had her talons into Gustav, and that crazy, yet mysterious sorceress, Jena.

CHAPTER 32

Tuesday 22 September 2015:
Llwtymor Mountain mine.

AT THE BASE OF THE AIRSHAFT, ANTONIO PEERED INTO THE WEBCAM. "Don't forget the champagne on the next drop."

Ryder frowned at Derek, who had been appointed full-time Antonio monitor.

"I think and hope that's another of his jokes. I humour him, Ryder, more than I would you or any of the others because, by God, I wouldn't want to do what he's going to do."

Ryder was pushed out of the way by Megan so she could lower a tightly-rolled sleeping bag, airbed and foot pump all in one bin bag.

Brian and Abdul had set up Antonio's electrical supply, running both a cable from the centre and a car-battery backup trickle-charged by a small wind vane. Solar panels would be ineffective on this north-facing slope. Antonio insisted on a measure of short-term self-sufficiency in case of some disaster at the centre. Water was more difficult to organise. The centre had a filter system using local stream water, but it wouldn't stand storing for weeks without the few bacteria becoming millions. Antonio needed piped water and his own filter along with purification tablets.

Megan trudged off to winch up another load from Teresa, who'd organised a pile of supplies at the base of the slope. From so high up, with so much vegetation and boulders in the line of sight, Ryder couldn't see her. He wondered over her turmoil with her new friend shutting himself away for at least a month's quarantine after the case exposure.

"Watch your back, Ryder," Vlad said, carrying a space-age-looking aluminium cowl to go over the airshaft once they'd finished lowering provisions.

"Are you sure that will work?" Ryder said, fingering the louvers around the cubed piece of modern sculpture.

"No idea," Vlad said.

"He's kidding," Gustav said. "It will prevent rain and animals getting in, let air in and our patent wet-filter system will, hopefully, strangle any alien virus that makes it to this point up the shaft."

"Will it strangle Antonio, if he comes up the shaft?" Ryder said.

"It will be locked from above and below, but he could get out when he needs to via the winch and using tools he has."

Ryder took the Ukrainian away from the shaft for a short walk. "Vlad, the acoustics in that shaft will let Antonio hear conversations at the top."

"So?"

"I thought we laid down the specifications such that he wouldn't just be able to winch himself up and get out without us letting him. There's a danger he might become infected and contaminate us, otherwise."

"Ryder, you have to allow him to get out in an emergency. Suppose after heavy rain, his bit of the mine gets flooded or we get ill and can't get provisions to him? We can't let him die down there."

"The point of quarantine is that it's us who decides when he's to come out." Ryder could feel his cheeks heating but hoped Vlad didn't notice.

"Don't worry. I'm sure he wouldn't without our say so." Vlad returned to fixing the cowl, leaving Ryder seething, then following, plotting another failsafe device. He could understand Vlad being reluctant to trap Antonio in the mine: he'd been with him in a spacecraft for so long. He was like family.

Ryder had to plan for the bigger picture and protect what was left of mankind. He would sort it out with Brian, but he could see where they could fasten the cowl to the grating so that Antonio could only emerge with help from the outside. Keeping it from the others shouldn't be too difficult, and he had no problem letting Antonio out once a quarantine period was complete. If a disaster befell them at the centre, then Antonio would have a problem and might die, but he must have taken that into account when he volunteered. It would not make sense to let him contaminate them if he developed another version of ARIA.

EVERYONE STARED AT THE LARGE MONITOR, watching Antonio's progress. The camera was set up at an oblique angle to see both Antonio and the cage containing the case. He wore a bio-safety suit. Ryder wasn't sure why he didn't wear his space suit, or conversely, why wear any protection when he was there to be exposed?

"Idiot, we don't know what's in the case," Teresa said. "We know he's there as a guinea pig, but there's no need for him to suffer incidental damage."

Ryder could see her point, impressed really, but impatient to witness the events.

Antonio's voice came over clearly. "It's now or never. *Si*? Opening the padlock now. There's dust covering the padded bag—*grazie*, Jena."

Ryder looked round for her. She sat at a table, her hands propping up her chin. Their eyes met and she stuck out her tongue. He returned the compliment. He turned to find the image of Antonio unzipping the bag, revealing for the first time on Earth, the gleaming mirror-like surface of the case. Yet, not a case in that it had no handle, but small and light enough to be carried in outstretched arms.

"*Osservate*, the logo is flat to the case when viewed from the side, but as you move, it appears as a solid protruding object with a golden glow. A double chevron whereas for the first case, a single black chevron. Giving us hope, *signore e signori*, that this one is a second part to the first. I know what some of you think. That this is a final end to us all, but I believe this will undo the damage of the first. They are more advanced than us. This is to both rectify and move on to something wonderful."

"Typical bloody Italian," Brian said.

Antonio continued. "I believe the first case wouldn't open if merely touched by remote control, but that is what I am going to try. I am placing the case, logo upwards, on the table, using the bag so I'm not actually touching it. This is an aluminium rod I am going to press on the logo.

"Nothing happened. The next stage is to try a probe made of an organic substance. So, here is a wooden probe I am to use."

"Probe, my arse," Bronwyn said, "it's my long stirring spoon!" Everyone relief-laughed, including Antonio and Jena.

Antonio looked round at the camera. You could just see his eyes through the clear plastic headpiece. "Sorry, Bronwyn. Megan said it'd be all right. She said you didn't need help stirring things."

"I'll want it back."

Antonio pressed the wooden spoon down on the logo but nothing happened.

"The next step is to touch it myself. I'll attempt it first with my bio-suit glove on. Here I go...nothing. I'll try with more force. Note how the logo appears to show through the glove as if there is a holographic light source in the case exterior. Clever technology, *si*? I press hard and nothing changes.

"There is only one test left, *buona fortuna* to all, yes?"

Bronwyn called out, "Don't, don't, Antonio!" Then she pushed her chair back, stood, and rushed to the kitchen. "I can't watch."

Jena said, "Yeah, come back in, Antonio, have a cup of tea. Forget the case before you have no choice."

Everyone else stayed mute, transfixed by what might be the greatest moment in human history—or the second greatest.

Antonio waited a moment then said, "I'm stepping back three metres. Now I'm removing the protective outer glove off my right hand. Now the latex under-glove. This may be *arrivederci*.

"Nothing has changed on the case. I'm reaching my hand out so that it is within two metres. Nothing. One. Nothing.

"I now hover my hand over the logo without touching it. Twenty centimetres above. Nothing. Ten. Ah—the logo has vanished. I hear a small, high-pitched buzz. I'm removing my hand and stepping back. There. The logo remains absent and the sound persists. See that bright blue light around the edge of the case? And the lid slowly opens as if there is a hinge opposite to me. I am stepping back another metre to let the camera zoom in and the sensors work."

The camera showed six translucent blue bricks.

"Is the colour affected by the low light intensity in the mine?" Derek said. "Only, the first case had bricks of a funny lilac colour, didn't it?"

Ryder said, "Yes, although they had a greenish tinge to them, like a badly-coloured toothpaste. We are seeing a difference in colour. Can you confirm their blue colour, Antonio?"

"I'd say they were a sky blue as if they had an internal light source."

Antonio lowered a thin wire boom over the case and sat well back. Within minutes, Gustav had some results. "No change in background radiation. No change in temperature though light intensity has increased."

Jena swivelled her stool to work at the computer near her. They'd set up a live link to Charlotte. The signal bounced around the satellites.

"Charlotte says, 'Good luck to you, Antonio,' silly mare," Jena said.

Ryder walked over to her and spoke into the mike. "Hi, Charlotte, thanks for your good luck." He glared at the pouting Jena. "And keep an eye on any unusual activity such as radio bursts from our visitors at Cassini. Cheers."

Antonio manipulated a small Perspex tube over the case. "I'm running my gas analyzer, for what it's worth."

Ryder knew the same apparatus pulled in any viruses emitted from the case. Those could be passed over gel microscope plates and studied for unusual pathogens similar to the one Julia Tyndall found at Goddard.

"When I find something on the slide, I want it to be called Antonio's Bug."

"Still the funny man. No ill effects?" asked Abdul.

"No, and the gas analyser isn't showing anything. *Un momento.*"

The next twenty minutes saw no change. Megan excused herself to help Bronwyn in the kitchen, and Brian left to check a loose connection on a gate.

Teresa's computer sounded an incoming message alert.

"It's Charlotte. She says the ISS is relaying a radio signal."

Dan ran to the computer station controlling the ISS webserver.

"Yep, there is a 2.6 seconds-long repeated signal being picked up by the radio antennae pointed at the brown fuzzy ball."

"Good God," Ryder said. "Is it intelligible?"

"Actually it's not beamed directly at the ISS but in this direction too," Teresa said, passing on information from Charlotte.

Dan fiddled with a virtual connection to the ISS control panel. "It isn't a 'how are you doing' message. Just garbage, but exactly the same garbage every 2.63 seconds. You know what I think?"

"Somehow, it knows the case has been opened, yet it needs us to relay a code to it," Ryder said.

"It could be that some alert could get from the opened case, through the cave rocks, and off to them at Saturn," Derek said, "but they can't get a more sophisticated radio instruction code back through all that hard rock. So—"

"They send it to the ISS and us, hoping we'll pass it on," Ryder said.

"Do we?" Teresa said.

"This is a first, isn't it?" Derek said. "The aliens effectively asking for our help to activate something?"

"Not really," Ryder said. "They needed a human to agree to open both cases. However, I agree there is a subtle difference in that they need us to take an extra step. What does that tell us?"

"You're going to say that it means they expect us to cooperate with something that is going to be beneficial to us," Teresa said. "Or it could mean they realize we're too curious to have restraint. Tell them to go to hell."

"Hoorah," Jena said, finding an ally.

Dan turned to Ryder. "I presume it's a code that would unlock something else in the case. As far as we know, they hadn't used radio before, but we weren't listening for it back in April. As Derek suggests, the case is inside a mountain, they need us to relay it on."

Teresa, who had become agitated walking around, said, "We should ask Antonio. Give him the option whether he wants the message or not."

Ryder ignored her. "What does the message sound like?"

Teresa shouted, "Is anybody listening to me?"

Derek twiddled with a sound analyser. "Sounds like static in repeated bursts. It's never going to make any sense to us. It is probably alien machine code talking to another machine. Except that the receiving machine should be the case."

Megan had come in to find out why Teresa was shouting. "Does that mean the alien ship is a machine? No little green men in it?"

Dan put an arm around her shoulders. "No, Megan. For instance, when you talk on your phone, your message goes through the air as coded data to be received by someone else's phone. You're not a machine, but your phone is."

Megan brightened. "So there might be little green men on the alien ship out at Saturn who are phoning their luggage in the mine. Can't you get through and phone your Space Station instead to pass on the message?"

"You got it," Dan said, who turned to Teresa. "We've not overlooked what you're saying, Teresa. But he's volunteered for this job."

"Exactly," Ryder said. "We need to send on the code for the case to respond and for Antonio to report any effects. That's what this is all about."

"Suppose the code is a signal to detonate it?"

"They're not likely to have sent a bomb. What would be the point?" Dan said.

Teresa clenched her fists. "Suppose they know this group is the last uninfected group on the planet. They've obliterated humans without contaminating the environment with ARIA but need to take more direct action to see us off."

Jena said, "I hate to pour cold water on your theory, Teresa, especially since I didn't agree with bringing the fucking case here. But there are bound to be hundreds if not thousands of uninfected groups. Think of all those isolated mountain villages in the Andes, Himalayas, even the Rockies. They don't all have international airports, railways, or motorways. Intended visitors with ARIA would have forgotten where they were going long before reaching their destination."

"Okay, I accept that," Teresa said, clearly annoyed Jena would appear to support Ryder and Dan. "But apart from the single person Charlotte, no other group have been in touch with the ISS website."

"There have been others logging in," Vlad said, tapping at his console. "Five unknown contacts in the last three months. When someone looks at our website, it is logged. One could be the aliens, but I'd expect them to be able to scan it without us noticing."

Dan said, "We should alert Antonio and give him time to suit up."

"Do you want to tell him, Teresa?" Ryder said.

"Oh, you'd like that, wouldn't you? Let me tell him he's about to blow up." She ran out of the room.

"He knows anyway," Vlad said. "He's been listening in. Thinks it is very funny, don't you, Doc?"

"Bring it on, Derek, after I've finished with my visor and gloves."

"Okay, say when." Derek set up the signal and waited with his finger over a touchpad, waiting.

"Just a minute," Jena said. "I'm getting Teresa, let her know Antonio is all right with this."

The others waited for stretched minutes. The two women returned.

"Ready, Antonio?" Derek said.

"As ever."

"Counting down. Three...two...one." Derek tapped the touchpad, sending the short radio burst to Antonio's receiver. Speakers in the centre and the mine played the sound although it came over as a grandfather's wheezy cough.

The case looked no different after the signal, nor five minutes later.

"How are you feeling, Antonio?" Dan said. "The instruments show no change. But unless you talk to us, we've little idea about how you feel."

"An anticlimax, Commander. I'm beginning to wish I'd brought more books to read."

"Don't get complacent," Ryder said. "Suppose the case is waiting for you to remove a glove or your visor."

"I could try asking it. Hang on. Hey, case, *Ciao*! Are you waiting for me? No answer, Ryder. I am removing my headgear. I'm far too hot anyway. I'm back as far as I can get. On the count of three: one...two...three. Nothing different. I will walk slowly towards the case. From the case I am three metres...two metres...one. Maybe it needs me to actually touch or breathe on it. I'm removing a glove. There. Nothing. I am going to hover my hand over it like I did before the radio signal. Here goes. Twenty centimetres above it. Ten—*che cosa!*"

Ryder saw Antonio reel backwards as a shock-wave emanated from the case—like circular ripples from a stone thrown in a pond, distorting the image. As Teresa screamed, a tremor rippled through the centre.

Dust fell from the ceiling, but the lights stayed on.

"Antonio, are you all right?" screamed Teresa. The monitor showed Antonio sitting on the floor.

"I need the kiss of life, Teresa," he said, before getting to his feet. He approached the case. "Anyone want to see that again?"

"No, Antonio." Dan said, "A shockwave came from the case and went through us here. God knows where it's going."

Vlad tapped at his console. "It reached us 2.3 seconds after Antonio said 'che cosa.' That's a horizontal velocity of 1,565 miles per hour."

"Quite slow, then," Abdul said, to Ryder's surprise.

"Yes, earthquake waves are much faster," Vladmir said. "It's a pity the seismograph centres around the world are all offline. We've no way of telling if it petered out a few miles away or maintained itself for a complete wrap around the planet."

"We'll be able to tell in sixteen hours' time," Abdul said.

"Oh, yes," said Vlad. "It will take that long for that slow wave to circumnavigate the globe. I wonder if we have anything on the ISS."

"I've just been checking," Dan said. "We have sea-surface radar imaging continuously for oceanography research. It wasn't turned off or redirected, but it'll take me some time to detect any additional ripples."

CHAPTER 33

Tuesday 22 September 2015:
Anafon

DEREK STOOD AT THE LAB DOOR AND SHOUTED, "WE'VE HAD ANOTHER ALERT FROM THE ISS!"

"Can we take any more?" Laurette said.

Megan and Bronwyn came in carrying mugs of strong coffee.

"Is it another signal?" Ryder said.

"No," Derek said, taking his time sitting while tapping at his console. "The Hubble was programmed to send us an alert if there was any change to the image of the alien ship."

"So, instead of a brown fuzz ball, it's now a standard flying saucer?" Abdul said.

"It's still fuzzy, but it's on the move. There, I have an image."

"Derek, it looks the same," Ryder said.

"Its movement is slow, only just over five thousand miles per hour, but it is accelerating. There is an ion trail."

"Oh God, they're coming for their protégée," Ryder said.

"No," Derek said, "the trail shows they are going out of the solar system."

Jena said, "It could mean they are leaving to go round Saturn in a slingshot, through the Kirkwood Gap, to come back here."

"Good point," Abdul said, grabbing a seat at a console. "I'm downloading the Hubble data and running a program. Give me the time it takes to drink half your coffee."

"Is it good news they're leaving?" Teresa said. "It would imply their task is done. The main invasion force could be on its way."

"Or it could mean they've tried a biology experiment and they've received enough data. Happy or not, they're off to report back," Gustav said.

"You make it sound like all this has been a school project from Alpha Centauri," Ryder said. "More likely an attempt to help that's gone horribly wrong. I wouldn't be surprised if they are the same aliens who brought the first amino acid life-building blocks to our planet."

"I thought life rode in on the tails of comets," Abdul said.

"Or even from God," Bronwyn said, as she collected dirty mugs.

"God might have told the aliens to bring life here a billion years ago," Ryder said, teasing Bronwyn as he gave her his mug.

"Finished the first run-through of the data," Abdul said. "It's not on a slingshot route. It's heading out of the solar system at forty-five degrees to the ecliptic plane. No, it's not going to Alpha Centauri, but it might change. It's gone. Hubble has lost it."

"Told you we should have sent a rocket to it," Jena said. "We could have planted a homing device on it."

BRIAN CHARGED IN THROUGH THE LAB DOOR. "Why is no one answering the bloody phone?"

"Sorry Brian," Bronwyn said. "I'm on office duty, but what with all the excitement..."

"Never mind that, there's trouble."

"I know, Brian love. Did you feel the earthquake up on the road?"

"Earthquake? What bloody earthquake?"

"Interesting," said Vlad, tapping on his console. "It must have attenuated really quickly. A controlled local event."

"Don't you go believing my stupid husband. You'd have to knock his legs from under him first." Vlad stopped calculating.

Brian glared. "No, listen. Ryder, there's people on the lane."

"What? Why didn't you say? Which side of the double gate?"

"The other side. I don't think they saw me. They were about half a mile, on foot, away from the gate. The zoom on the south hill camera should have them."

Derek tapped his computer and the screen flickered to show a long-distance view of the two gates a hundred metres apart and the winding, narrow lane going down the heather-covered slopes. A small group showed on the lane.

"Awful timing," Ryder said.

"They might just go away," Dan said, "having two razor-wired and locked gates is a pretty good deterrent."

"We can't take the chance," Ryder said. "Abdul and Vlad, get tooled up—you know where the firearms are—get me the updated AK4S rifle and ammo. I'll meet you out front in the Volvo Estate—it's quieter than the other vehicles. Derek, monitor us; keep a special eye on the other cams and sensors in case there are others."

"It's very unlikely that infected people could organise a co-ordinated raid, Ryder," Dan said. "But you're right to be prepared. I'll stop here to talk to Antonio, with Teresa and Jena."

"Yes, fine, but have your weapons on you. Gustav and Laurette, arm yourselves too, and do a continuous close patrol of the centre.

Everyone keep their mobile phones on."

"What about me?" Brian said. "They might be Welsh speakers."

"Good point." Ryder noted Brian already had a pistol in its holster at his waist. "Come with us."

Vlad said, "I'm coming in case they speak Russian, and Abdul—"

"Funny men," Brian said, leaving to have a word with Bronwyn.

"Have I missed anything?" Ryder said.

"Antonio?" Teresa said. "What do you want him to do?"

Ryder looked at her, confused. "He *has* to stay down there. Derek, Dan, and you will be here to keep talking to him. It would be a good idea to ask him to shut the case, put it back in its padded bag and lock it in its cage."

RYDER PARKED THE VOLVO TWO-HUNDRED METRES FROM THE GATE. A bluff of the mountain hid the lane on the other side. A laptop screen in the car gave him a clear view from the camera on the hill. He zoomed in on four people in the lane. It wasn't possible to tell their gender. They'd dropped large bags on the ground.

"It looks like they've seen our gates and are discussing whether to breach them," Brian said.

"It was always a risk that creating a barrier would indicate there was something worth protecting," Ryder said. "Vlad and Abdul, go up on the right with those telescopic sniper rifles. Find a good spot to cover the gate, the slope down to the river, and the lane. Don't shoot unless I say." They all checked their radio headsets.

"This is a shoot-first situation," Abdul said. "You can't stroll up and shake hands, can you?"

"No," Ryder said. "But we have a strategy worked out. I repeat, don't shoot unless I give the order."

"We shoot if you're dead and can't say?" Vlad said. "*Da*, at that point, we're allowed to use our initiative."

"I'm turning into a control freak," Ryder said.

Once they left, Brian whispered. "We really going to kill those innocent people who are just looking for food?"

"You know the drill. We have to deal with certainties. If they're about to breach the first gate, we stop them, and try to ascertain if they are infected. Just in case they are a group who've been holed up somewhere like us—unlikely, but we give them a chance. No time to argue now. We get down on the ground on this side of the nearest gate to us. I'll be on the right, you the left. I'll have the mike linked up to speakers near the other gate."

Ryder wished he'd arranged for hidden mikes on the lane, but he couldn't think of everything. For all his precautions, he bit his knuckles. He doubted the group in front were armed.

Two of the strangers wore army camouflage trousers and jackets. It didn't mean much, but it heightened Ryder's tension in case he had to deal with combat-trained invaders. Two wore blue jeans and the sort of yellow jackets road workers wear. A fifth person, all in black, appeared behind them, running up the lane. All had shoulder-length hair. Ryder thought he saw beards on three.

"Brian, do you recognise any?"

"They're not local."

Ryder said into his radio mike, "The shorter one is female and the others male. Agreed?"

Vlad said, "All male. One of the non-bearded has big shoulders and struts around like a man. All late twenties to mid-thirties."

"Agreed on the ages," Abdul said. "Which means they all have the memories of children to teenagers. So maybe not very mature."

"More likely to fight silly odds than walk away, see?" Brian said.

"Don't be too sure," Ryder said. "It could be that they've survived their scavenging existence by running away when the situation became difficult. I hope so."

He breathed out a long, relieved breath when he saw the group turn and walk down the lane.

Brian stood. Agitated, Ryder waved at him to get down again, forgetting he could speak without shouting.

Just as Brian settled, Ryder saw the group bend down in the road and then start back.

"Vlad, speak to me."

"They've picked up a big piece of wood, holding it like a battering ram."

"I see them," Ryder said. "Vlad and Abdul, train your weapons on the two nearest you, they both have army uniforms. If you have to shoot, do it to kill. We don't want wounded combatants wandering."

"All of us astronauts have had military training."

"Of course, Vlad. Excellent. I'm going to talk to them."

The man in black made the others hold the battering-ram horizontally. Ryder would've put the base of the ram under the bottom bar near the hinge and using a boulder, lever upwards. They were going for the more obvious, but wrong, solution of trying to batter a super-strong padlock and reinforced bolt section of the gate. Again, if Ryder was going to do that, he would have had them stationary, near the gate, and swing the ram at it. But they were going to do a running battering-ram, which meant they would miss the lock and just crumple part of the gate. He waited for them to get back with the post, then just as they were about to run, he shouted into the mike.

"Stop! Stop!"

The group stood, paralysed. As if they hadn't heard another person for weeks. If they had ARIA that wouldn't matter for they'd only remember normality. But they'd woken into trauma, and he needed to add to their shock.

"You are breaking into a restricted area. Put down the post."

Two of the group let go, so the wood started to fall. The man in black looked up, then around. Maybe he thought someone was shouting in person nearby rather than a loud speaker.

"Let's be seeing you," he called. "Show your fucking self!" The two wearing jeans started back down the lane. "Oi, come back here, you two scumbags! What was your names again?"

"What is your business here?" called Ryder, through the speaker.

The man in black looked again then spotted the speaker where it had been bolted into a dry stone wall at waist height. He picked up a rock and smashed the speaker.

"Maybe a shot over their heads would scare them off."

"For heaven's sake, Brian, how many times have we been over this? Just scaring them is no good. Worse than no good. They'd probably come back but at night or in the pouring rain, and maybe get through. We have the element of surprise. Listen, they're talking."

The two runaways had returned. Clearly, they were afraid of the man in black, or knew they were dependent on him for their food.

One of them said, "What? The voice said to stop."

"This is the voice, scumbag." He hit the speaker again.

"My name is Robin and he's Andrew," Scumbag said.

"And mine is Batman. Now, scumbag, pick up the fucking pole so we can bash in the gate. That goes for you, woman."

The speaker still carried Ryder's voice. "Put down the post!"

"No!" shouted Batman, who let out a long, loud moan, which could have been a war cry in another millennium. Then he shouted, "Right! One...two...three!" He pushed the one called Andrew to encourage the others who ran with the post at the gate.

"Stop!" hollered Ryder, and again the group faltered.

One of the army-uniformed men shouted, "We'll stop if you give us ammo. Give us ammo!"

"Yeah," the other army man shouted, while Batman hit the first. "Give us ammo, we've only got grenades. See?" He picked one out of the olive-green bag on the ground and waved it. Batman grabbed it off him.

"You prick. Hey, I forgot about these. Right, everybody back a bit." He pulled out the pin and placed the grenade under the lowest bar of the gate before he took a few steps back.

"Oh my God," Brian said.

Ryder echoed that thought as he dared to look. Batman must have decided he needed to relocate the grenade and went back to it. The grenade detonated. The blast hit him in the middle, throwing him back and in the air, doubling up as shrapnel shot through his body. Although shrapnel, flesh, and shock must have hit the others, the two army men threw themselves forward, ran through the remains of the tangled gate, and waved grenades. The one Batman referred to as "woman" ran for the grenade bag, and Scumbag started running down the steep slope on Brian's left to the stream.

Ryder shouted, "Shoot now!" One of the army men fell backwards, with a shot in his chest. The other clutched an arm and ran off to his left, away from Ryder, ducking low, putting him out of shot of Abdul.

The woman had dived for the bag with the grenades. Ryder lined up the telescopic sight so the cross-hairs centred on the woman's stomach. The largest target and most likely to get a hit if she moved. With his own stomach threatening to revolt, he pulled the trigger for a single shot. She staggered back with the bullet's impact, but threw herself forward again. It was the first woman he'd taken any kind of violent action against. The first woman he'd fired a weapon at. The first person.

He smelt the cordite but tasted acid in his mouth.

Unlike on the old westerns, people didn't die straight away with a single bullet; nothing so neat. Then he noticed Brian running down the grassy slope to his left on an intercept course with the remaining man, referred to as Scumbag. Ryder shouted at Brian, even though he wondered why his own weapon wasn't working properly, and the woman busied herself looking for more weaponry.

"Brian, stop where you are and shoot him!"

Ryder remained lying on his stomach while he tried to remember the little training he'd had on unjamming his rifle. He looked up to see the woman slump over the bag with part of her head missing.

"I've got him—her, whatever," Vlad said, in his earpiece. "I'm helping Abdul find the other army bloke."

Ryder had no choice but to stand and look down the steep grassy incline for Brian. He could see the stream in the valley floor and hoped the two of them hadn't crossed it into the forest of conifers up the other slope. He saw a flash of reflected sunlight near a jumble of boulders and feared the worst.

"Brian, talk to me."

"I'm a bit busy," Brian said, adding grunts. Ryder stood on a boulder to see better and staggered as he picked up a whiff of cordite and burnt flesh that had drifted from the first grenade blast. He regained his footing on the lane and caught a glimpse from his right of Abdul making his way down the slope towards him but with his automatic Bren gun trained to the north.

"He's over here," Vlad said, "about two hundred metres from me. I'm waiting for a clear body shot."

Ryder heard two rapid shots and ricochet, but with the mountains around couldn't be sure whether it came from Vlad, Abdul, or Brian. "Who shot who then?"

Abdul spoke, "We both shot the other army bloke. Do you want to go assist Brian while I return up the bluff to be with Vlad while we guard the lane approach and the north off-road track? Others might be attracted by the gunfire."

"Good thinking," Ryder said. "And good work. I can't actually see Brian and he isn't saying much. I don't suppose either of you can see down into the valley floor from your position."

"No. Do you want me to climb higher up? I can see anyone down there from the ridge," Abdul said.

"No, stick to your plan. I'll edge over from the lane and see what I can."

"Ryder, this is Derek, you receiving?"

"Hello, Derek, you want an update?"

"No, we've heard everything and seen much through the cameras. Speaking of which, we have the mobile cam on the drone-airplane over the valley approaching you. I'm sorry to tell you that Brian has been in hand-to-hand combat. He's lying wounded in the stream. The other man called Andrew or Scumbag isn't moving, about five metres from him."

"Bugger."

"Too right, Ryder. Worse. We couldn't stop her. Bronwyn's on her way in the pickup. She's suited up in a biohazard suit and has her first-aid kit and more suits."

"Yeah, I forgot about those, didn't I?" Ryder said, though it was only partially true. He was no expert but worried that the breathing apparatus in the biohazard suits might not be effective against ARIA unless they also wore the medical air tanks, and they only had one of those. The space suits, though more cumbersome, offered far more protection but were custom-fitted.

He fought the urge to go down the slope to help Brian until Bronwyn and Laurette arrived with the suits and first-aid kit.

He spoke again to Derek. "While it's already in this area, Derek, send that drone to follow the lane to the village and back. It would be useful to see if there are people. Here comes the pickup. See you later."

A distraught Bronwyn leapt out of the pickup. "You haven't shot him yet, have you? Please, Ryder, don't kill my Brian!"

"No, Bronwyn. I'm not a monster. We still have a bit of the mine entrance we can use as an isolation unit."

He clambered into the plastic-smelling suit and before hooding up, called Vlad. "Any signs of activity? I'm about to suit up and help get Brian patched and taken to the mine entrance."

"We see a line of smoke several miles away on the coast but nothing appears to be moving here. We'll stop until you've finished."

Derek also reported no movement spotted by the plane so Ryder pulled up his hood and was pleasantly surprised to find a medic-air supply unit tubed into it with a miniature compressed air unit at the waist. A digital output showed twenty minutes' worth of air with a simple switch. He followed the two women down the slope. Brian sat up against a rock, holding large dock leaves to his left side. His trousers were bloody but it could have been from his assailant who lay face down in the stream a few metres away. Bronwyn was persuading him to move his hand so she could open his shirt and apply her nursing skills.

Laurette squatted nearby with a large green first-aid bag.

Brian lifted his desperate eyes. "Sorry, Ryder. He surprised me with a knife, the bastard."

"No need to apologise, Brian, you stopped him getting past us. Concentrate on living."

They patched him up as best they could and placed him in the back of the pickup, packed in by bags and boxes. Before they left for the mine, Laurette spoke to Ryder. Normally, he'd relax to her soft French accent. "Brian has a deep laceration just below the left lowest rib."

"Kidneys?"

"Brian has a doughnut buffer zone. But he might have internal haemorrhaging. In hospital, he'd have a scan, but all we can do is antibiotics..."

"You're implying that you could do an exploratory operation to find and stitch up internal damage. But..."

"We have precious little facilities for that—as in anaesthetic, compressed air for everyone operating so we don't breathe his air. *À propos*, that was a superb idea to give Brian the sealed head hood and air supply with output bag so we didn't have to wear one."

"It might not be foolproof. How's Bronwyn?"

A small smile. "Once she had some work to do on him, she calmed down. Something will need to be done with the bodies, you know. Besides flies and vermin, dogs will find them and look for more."

Ryder had been thinking about that. "Laurette, in your medical experience and being the highest-qualified biotechnician, ever..."

"You said that to Gustav, once."

"The snitch," Ryder said. "Anyway, do viruses die when the host dies? I mean are those bodies safe for us to handle without biohazard suits?"

"Maybe, after, say, a day, but what else do they have? AIDS, hepatitis? There's lots of blood and gore around, Ryder. I'd want to be suited up."

"Thanks. Always with the spot-on advice."

"*Oui*, save your soft-soaping for your new girlfriend," she said, her eyebrow raised.

Ryder didn't know whether to interpret it as a good-luck-you'll-need-it-look or as a remonstration for falling out with Teresa. As if it was his fault she'd fallen for Dr Cinzano Bianco. It must have been the latter because as his thoughts reached Antonio, she spoke again.

"Pity that a first-class physician is locked up in the mine, *n'est-ce pas?*"

Ryder agreed. After a little more thought, he tapped at his phone again.

"Gustav, get the pickup after Brian's been taken off it. Collect Abdul, Vlad, and Antonio's space suits, a reel of barbed wire, shovels, and bring it all out here."

"Antonio's suit?" said Gustav. "Is he...?"

"No, it's for me in case the disposable one I'm wearing falls apart. I can't expect people to shovel that shit if I'm not prepared to do it myself."

STILL WEARING HIS PROTECTION SUIT but not trusting it entirely, Ryder examined the twisted gate. Most of the blast had passed harmlessly through the gaps in the bars. Enough, along with shrapnel, had hit the galvanised steel tubing, twisting the lower bars and breaking two. Putting his hand on the gate, he pulled and it scraped the gravel as it opened. It wouldn't take much to do a temporary lock-up to deter casual wanderers—unless they too carried an arsenal in their hand luggage.

He heard footsteps scraping the loose stones on the track round the bluff. He threw himself behind a rock to the right. His rifle was on the other side of the lane but he'd be in view if he went for it now. Salty sweat stinging his eyes, he whispered into his phone.

"Abdul, Vlad, can either of you hear me?"

The footsteps became louder and faster, accompanied by a shout. "Ryder, where are you?"

"Damn," Ryder shouted. "I thought you were more of that group. Bloody hell, I can feel my pulse going like the clappers."

Abdul held out his hand. "Oh dear, Ryder, we are so sorry. Shall we get you a chair, a cup of tea, biscuit...?"

Ryder took his hand to haul himself up. "I suppose you did some extra exploring on that old Roman road?"

"We saw an ancient signpost. If I was Dan, I would be saying how amazing that we've just walked a track others have walked for over two thousand years."

"So?" said Ryder, rubbing an elbow from his fall.

Abdul grinned. "The route I used to do to my school in Al Wakrah, had been walked on for six thousand years."

"Hey, my friends," Vlad said, "I come from an ancient village near Kiev that too goes back over six thousand years."

"I bet there is a two million-year old footpath in Olduvai Gorge," said Ryder. "And how quick will all the paths crumble as Nature takes them back? As a young man interested in the environment, I always thought the human race would end by its own stupidity. Not so much blowing each other up, but by unleashing some pathogen or other without a cure. It never occurred to me it would come from space."

Abdul looked round at the grisly mess near the gate, and the two bodies a few metres farther down. "Bury or burn?"

"Ironic, isn't it?" said Ryder. "There are people dead all over the place out there, with no one in authority to organise disposal. Most rot where they fall. Animals will feast on some but not all. I swear I sometimes smell the putrid odour on wafts of air."

"I too, since walking around up here, not at the centre. We are lucky there," Vlad said.

"I don't suppose you found a convenient hole in the ground when you had your ramble," Ryder said. "No? There's a farm down the lane. It will have somewhere to put these corpses so scavengers can't get at them and passers-by won't see them. Gustav has brought your suits."

To Ryder's surprise, Dan disembarked from the passenger side wearing his suit and he saw Gustav wore Antonio's suit.

"I needed to come out from behind the computer, Ryder. You go back and handle those women; it's your turn."

"Very well," Ryder said. "Now, don't forget there are two bodies besides the three here and—"

"Ryder," Dan said, lifting Megan's bike out of the pickup. "Here is your transport back. Let *us* get on with it."

"Right," said Ryder, who hadn't ridden a bike for years and didn't want to show himself up. The first heavy spots of a shower splattered the rocks. "With luck, you'll get drenched."

"It'll save us having to wash the road down," Abdul said. They all waved Ryder off as he, on the bike, wobbled round the bend.

EVEN THOUGH HE NEEDED A SHOWER, fresh clothes, and a strong cup of tea, Ryder kept his suit on to see Brian. The roof collapse left the first 150 metres intact, which meant it had power and was dry. They'd set up an area near the roof collapse where Brian slept, with a camera keeping watch. Laurette, suited up, had just checked on his condition when Ryder entered the mine.

"He'll pull through," she said. "The bleeding has stopped and all his vital signs are normal."

"Great, and?"

"*Un peu* confused but most knife victims are traumatised. We'll know better when he's had a long sleep. Ryder, was it necessary to kill those people before finding out if they were infected?"

"Laurette, they were memory confused. We had little opportunity to ask them for biological samples or to fill in a questionnaire. If Brian has it, we made the right choice."

CHAPTER 34

Wednesday 23 September 2015:
Anafon, breakfast.

AFTER ALL THAT ENERGY EXPENDITURE, Ryder should have slept well the night of the action, but he couldn't. The gunfire and grenade must have been heard in the local village, and the nearest town, although the valleys and mountain sides played acoustic tricks so maybe not. He'd spent an hour with Derek examining the flying drone camera shots of the nearest village.

"There," said Derek, using the cursor to point at a shape in a doorway, another at a window, and a definite human couple crossing the A55 dual carriage at the coast.

But several corpses littered the lanes, fields, and a car park. Many house doors were open and windows smashed.

"Not the quaint tourist honeypot it used to be," said Ryder, before scanning the other cameras and checking the status of sensors. The cameras with Antonio showed him cooking pasta on a camping stove. The sensors in there indicated nothing unusual, making them wonder what the micro-earthquake tremor was all about. Brian's camera showed him asleep. Vital signs showed an eighty-beats-per-minute pulse and raised, but not dangerous, blood pressure.

"The ISS crew did a fine job clearing the bodies," Derek said. "I did a midnight shift check out there. The rain washed most of the blood away too, so I hope no one is drinking the stream water in the village this morning."

Bronwyn brought them both steaming mugs of black coffee and toast.

"Thanks," Ryder said, wondering if she'd spat in it. A horrible thought, but he'd heard from Teresa that she blamed him for her Brian's contact with the infected outsider. "He's had a good sleep."

Bronwyn, red-eyed, nodded.

"I did try to stop him," Ryder continued, but with regret since it sounded as if he was shifting the blame. "What I mean is—"

"Ryder," she said, in her Welsh lilt. "What's done is done. If he hadn't stopped that bugger, we'd all be ill now, wouldn't we?" Tears welled up once more. Ryder put down his mug and hugged her. Derek made it a group hug, with tears of his own.

"One of my friends, Manuel, in the States, found having the basics written on a pad helped him each morning," Ryder said.

"I know. Teresa's already done one on the computer. It's been printed and waiting beside him now."

After Bronwyn left them, Ryder said, "I'm not number one round here, then."

"Ryder, I was your boss for years. Unpopularity comes with the territory. To be honest, Brian is lost to us now. From my old personal-management viewpoint, he's a waste of our resources and energy. Of course, he is still our friend and cannot be deserted—"

"Unless it comes to an issue of his survival put against all of the rest of us," Ryder said, knowing he could be frank with Derek.

"Quite. But we should be more concerned about Antonio."

"I thought I hid my feelings about Antonio rather well."

"No, you haven't, and I wasn't thinking about your green-eyed monster. We know a shockwave emanated from the case, yet the tremor was probably not intended to harm anything. So I've expected a condition change in the man who triggered it."

"But Antonio has not changed."

"We don't know that for sure, do we, Ryder? All the vital signs we measure are within normality, but we've made a monumental blunder in our planning."

"I can't claim to be infallible. I was a documentary maker with space expertise. We had to make urgent preparations. For all we knew, there was a use-by date on the case."

"Calm down, Ryder, I'm not blaming anyone. If we start pointing fingers to apportion blame in this extraordinary situation, our arms would get interlocked. What I refer to is that we are not monitoring his memory functions. I've done psychometric studies at uni. We've relied on him telling us how his memory is, but we should have done a battery of word, number, shape, and concept-recall tests to compare before and after the case being opened."

"Of course. How stupid of me to overlook it."

"You know the next step?" Derek said.

"After a week or so, he needs to be exposed to ARIA to see if he is immune."

"Right. Did he know this?"

"Of course he did," Ryder said. "Surely? Why else be exposed?"

Bronwyn passed them on her way back to see Brian. Ryder and Derek hadn't noticed the monitor showing Brian reading the information sheet Teresa had typed up for him.

"Give him our best wishes, Bronwyn," Ryder said. "Take no chances. You're more helpful to him as a fully-functioning person than an amnesiac yourself."

"And more useful to you."

AN HOUR LATER, Antonio thumbed up at the camera and at Derek's request gave a perfect account of what happened the previous day, indicating no lapse of memory.

Bronwyn returned to the refectory from the mine and threw her air cylinder on the floor in front of Ryder and Dan. "Why don't we have any compressed-air-making-equipment here? We've nearly run out of it." Sobbing, she slumped in a seat at the table.

Laurette came in behind her. "Brian has no memory of last month. I hoped it might be attributable to trauma, but *non*. We have only one hour compressed air for our biohazard suits."

Dan whispered to Ryder. "We have some in our spacesuit packs."

"No, Dan. We might need them for more than visiting the sick. But it can't be that difficult replacing compressed air for those cylinders, can it? I'll ask Gustav."

"We're missing a trick here, Ryder," Dan said.

"I know. We're supposed to eliminate the ARIA-infected person, even if it's one of us. The risks are too great."

"No. I mean we should put Brian in with Antonio. Two reasons. It would be useful to know if Antonio is now immune to ARIA and to see if exposure to the case has any effect on Brian's memory loss."

Ryder felt annoyed for not thinking of it himself yet, while sipping an orange juice, was relieved Derek had. "Of course. How?"

Derek picked up his coffee and then put it down as if he couldn't drink and think. "Yeah, the natives around here are getting restless."

"I don't think we'll have any problem with the pro-Brian group since he hasn't anything to lose with this development. But Teresa will go ballistic when I tell her we're going to give Antonio an infected visitor."

"Surely not," Dan said. "It's what he volunteered for. Finding out the secrets of the second case."

"Yeah, you're right. Teresa will be so cool about it."

ABDUL AND JENA BUILT A VALVE with a bicycle inner tube and a car-tyre foot pump, which worked well to put thirty minutes of breathable air, tasting of rubber, into the small air tanks on the biohazard suits. Vlad and Abdul walked Brian up the mountain and down into the shaft to greet Antonio.

Ryder thought it best to keep quiet with the others in the IT lab eagerly awaiting developments. Antonio refused to wear protective gear and helped Brian to his only easy chair: a padded deckchair belonging to Brian in the first place. The doctor, glad to practise medicine once more, soon had Brian's dressings off.

"*Ciao! Buona,* you've come to my surgery, Brian. This needs stitches and, *guardi quello*! I don't like this. Looks like septicaemia. Have you witches given him Amoxycillin-14? I'll give him some out of my box anyway."

"*Qu'est que ce?*" Laurette said. "Septicaemia cannot be diagnosed yet. If his wound is infected, it'd take another three days for symptoms to show. *Regardez*, the monitor is showing Brian's temperature to be normal. He'd have hot flushes and really feel ill."

"Laurette," Dan said. "I don't think it's you. He hasn't had enough doctoring to do for a while, that's all."

"I hope he isn't getting my Brian as worried as he's getting me," Bronwyn said, whose red hair had its silver strands multiply overnight. She tapped the console mike switch. "Brian, how are you, love?"

"Are you cooking kippers in here, Doc? It's still bleeding, isn't it? Bit chilly."

Gustav leant forward. "Is he rambling or just giving an experience-to-speech account?"

Jena said, "Childhood smells is an early symptom of ARIA."

"Brian loves kippers," Bronwyn said. "We have them all the time."

"No you don't," Megan said.

"Time you went to bed, lady," Bronwyn said.

"Just out of interest, when was the last time?" Dan said. "And what are kippers?"

"Smoked herring. We last ate them on holiday in the Isle of Man. Famous for them, you know."

"Auntie, you haven't been there for three years."

SATURDAY 26 SEPTEMBER 2015

"Good news and bad news. Which do you want first?" Antonio said to Laurette at her early morning shift. She'd already called Derek to sort out an IT problem. The frequent gales and heavy Snowdonia rainfall played havoc with cables and connections.

"Good news, Antonio. Leave the bad for someone else's shift."

"In my opinion and from memory tests I subjected him to, Brian had not lost any more of his memory since the three days he came in here."

"That's incredibly good news. Fantastic, and because of the case."

"I wouldn't say that."

"What do you mean?" Laurette said. "What wouldn't you say?"

"The halt in Brian's retrograde memory loss might be due to his exposure to the case. Or it might be due to my exposure days before. In other words, I have something, undetectable by our feeble sensors, which stunned the ARIA in Brian."

Jena had come in and overheard. "Antonio, I don't suppose Brian has recovered any of his lost memory."

"You remember, Jena, he came in here within forty-eight hours of him catching ARIA and he was ill, confused. He had lost two months. But he remembered new information. Each morning until today, he woke up, saw the mine walls, and screamed."

Jena looked puzzled. "Antonio, I can understand why an ill person would wake up in there, think he's in hell and scream, but why not today?"

Antonio said, "Brian died in the night."

THE SHOCKING NEWS UPSET EVERYONE EXCEPT ANTONIO. Ryder found Scary Jena at a computer, adding to a diary of every notable event. Not a book as such, but a multimedia event. The first images of the case, movie files of their landing at Hawarden, and the fight at the gate, which Ryder didn't want to review. Weird art by Megan, songs by Bronwyn and Brian, and poetry from Vlad—in Russian.

"Sorry to interrupt you, Jena," Ryder said.

"You're the first ever to interrupt me with this journal, I will make a note of it."

He sat on a stool and gave her a chocolate bar from his secret store. "Jena, you know him well. What do you make of Antonio?"

"I don't know him that well. What are you implying?"

Ryder stood, shocked. "I didn't mean anything sordid, for God's sake!"

"And why shouldn't we have been? Are you saying there's something wrong with me?"

Ryder's face heated. "No. Of course not. I can't win here can I? Can we start over?" He didn't know whether to sit again or walk away.

"Ryder, you are so easy. Sit. How can I resist teasing you? How can I resist you? Oh, you want to know about Antonio. Yes, he's cracked, hasn't he? Is that what you wanted to know?"

Ryder, relieved, made himself comfortable—just—on the stool and waited for elaboration. He dared not prompt in case it became a trampoline for more verbal gymnastics. He didn't have to wait long. Once Jena's spring wound up, off she went.

"Highly intelligent, but self-effacing, dry sense of humour, and teased everyone a little. That's how he was before he turned into an unbearable asshole."

"That's what I thought. Of course, having lost your family then volunteering for a suicide mission would unhinge most people."

"Ryder, we've all lost family, though one of the reasons Antonio volunteered was because he wasn't close to any of his: wiped out in a Naples riot while we orbited."

"There's something more about him, isn't there? Even if it's not solid fact, I'd like to know."

"All right, but this is known only to Bronwyn and myself. She insisted on a last look at Brian after Abdul and Vlad brought him out of the shaft. They said they were to take him to the farm, where the other bodies were put—apparently in a cess pit?" Ryder waved her on. "They let her see Brian's body once she'd suited up. She asked me to see too, which was a damned nuisance, but after I suited up, I went to look at what she'd found."

"Which was?"

"Funnily, my two crewmates hadn't noticed, but Brian had purple marks around his neck."

"Front, side, or back?" Ryder said.

"We're not stupid. He was strangled."

"What did Bronwyn say?"

"I convinced her they were from the harness being too tight when they hauled him up."

Ryder's mouth was dry and he looked around for a drink. "I might be convinced of that."

"Ryder, you ignoramus, he'd been dead for at least two hours, more if he'd died like Antonio said, in the night. So there wouldn't be any post-death bruising." She passed him her paper cup of coffee.

"I know that. All right, so you reminded me. This adds to our impressions of a very different Antonio."

"One that isn't very nice."

"You know what he's going to suggest next, don't you, Jena?"

"You're not serious?"

"He considers himself to be a medical catalyst to stop ARIA." He sipped the coffee. It was rum flavoured.

"Ryder, he said himself it could have been the case and not him that stopped ARIA."

"He slipped up there, Jena. He'll convince himself there's nothing to fear from the case. And nothing from him."

"No way," Jena said. "He's a doctor, he knows how long clinical trials last. He needs to be in there for weeks before we can be sure he's safe."

The rum left an unpleasant aftertaste. "We don't work with a pharmaceutical industry contract here. He'll consider speeding the formalities up a bit."

"Hey, Ryder. You know I opposed bringing the case to Earth and did my best to stop it being opened."

"I had kind of noticed, Jena." He walked over to a tap and filled a paper cup wondering how many were left.

"I was adamant that if Antonio was going to open the case, he wasn't emerging for a long time. He could have a variant of ARIA, one which won't manifest itself for weeks."

"Another thing, Jena, and I'm afraid to mention this but here goes: He's been exposed to the case. Brian was exposed to both him and the case, but Brian was an ARIA-infected person."

"Oh no, I see where this is going. Ryder, are you asking for a non-ARIA-infected person to volunteer to be with him?"

"I'm saying *he* might."

"Noble of you not to volunteer any of us. By the way, I noticed you'd made sure he couldn't get out of the shaft by himself—by locking the cowl to the grating."

"Self and group preservation are pretty strong urges in me at the moment."

"I was kinda hoping," Jena said, "you had other urges too."

"Maybe I have."

She stopped typing—she'd hardly stopped writing her journal throughout the conversation. "Well, I have an hour before my perimeter-check duty starts, lover."

"Oh, shame, Jena. I have a meeting with Dan, now."

She threw the beaker at him, but he was expecting it and ducked. The brown liquid splattered Megan, who was passing. Megan shrugged and walked on by. Jena, horrified, left her console to apologise to Megan when Ryder stopped her.

"You are so easy to wind up, Jena."

"*Touché.*"

CHAPTER 35

Tuesday 6 October 2015:
Anafon, early morning, twelve days since Brian's death. Most people outside Anafon will have lost up to twenty-five years of memory.

JENA HEARD TERESA KNOCK TWICE on the pine bedroom door and enter without waiting for Ryder to respond.

She raised her head, leaving an imprint on Ryder's arm.

"Oh, hi, Teresa. Don't tell me you're bringing us breakfast in bed?" Jena admired the way Teresa fought and controlled her demons. Her partner of five years, fiancé for one, had swapped beds, and Teresa's own Latin lover was on a suicide mission. Jena's Oriental eyes looked at Teresa's fair hair and cool green eyes that said "bothered" on the outside but hurt inside. Teresa had told Jena about Ryder always having had the hots for Hentai Japanese cartoon girls with sleek black hair, insatiable libido, and incongruous blue eyes, then one dropped out of the sky.

The two women finished exchanging unsaid emotions. Teresa said, "Antonio is in the kitchen. I found Bronwyn making him and Vlad a big breakfast, so it's too late to talk about isolation."

Ryder, bleary-eyed, rubbed the red imprint on his arm and said, "Damn that arrogant Antonio—sorry, Teresa. I suppose what's done is done. I'd better get there."

He waited for Teresa to leave but she stood at the door.

"Do you mind?" he said to her.

"It's nothing we haven't seen before," Jena said, who couldn't repress a smile.

"No," said Teresa. "Nothing much at all." She left, leaving the door open.

Jena threw on a large T-shirt and followed a grumbling Ryder, hopping to complete the donning of his jeans on the way to the refectory. They found everyone, except Derek, who watched cameras and sensors. Abdul was out on patrol.

Jena hesitated at the entrance to the refectory, the double doors still swinging after Ryder had barged through. This was one of those make-or-break moments. She could have turned, left the centre through a window and walked away, took a vehicle, anything but to have been infected by something they'd not understood.

Sighing, she pushed the door and walked over to the range to have a coffee offered by Bronwyn.

"You and Dan might as well stop shouting," Antonio said, taking another sip of coffee. He held it up. "Beee-utiful, this, Bronwyn. *Bravo*."

"It's not surprising we are annoyed with you, breaking your agreed quarantine time," Ryder said.

"Get over it," Antonio said.

"You've no idea if you've some secondary infection, undetectable at present but—"

"You should have been down there, Ryder. Grim, not at all the peaceful haven I had imagined. Not the hermit cell for uninterrupted contemplation. I had visitors, you know."

"What?" said Dan, "What visitors?"

"One in particular," Antonio said, looking round at everyone in turn as if trying to identify someone. Teresa shifted in her seat while Jena shook her head at the charade.

"With beady black eyes and no clothes, hah!" he said.

"There was a pair of rats in the mine then," Jena said. The others groaned.

"I thought," Antonio said, "that if a rat could get through the roof fall rubble, then it was not impossible to make an Antonio tunnel."

Jena noticed Derek shake his head at Ryder. She knew Derek had been brilliant at monitoring Antonio's health and activities with the cameras and sensors. So the tunnel talk was a bluff to put them off how he escaped. She knew Ryder had re-locked the grating after Brian was pulled out. It was possible Antonio had some cutting gear, and he had a winch system to get himself up to the opening. That left two people with a personal interest in Antonio. Bronwyn had gone soft on him since she assumed he'd helped Brian in his dying days. Maybe she should have told Bronwyn that Antonio strangled Brian.

She saw Teresa playing with her empty cup, turning it over, lifting it to gather the coffee-residue aroma that somehow smelt better than the taste. Recognisable behaviour of someone trying to be absent: not participating in the discussion and hiding her face. Still had a crush on the not-so-good doctor and undid the padlock for him. Damage done, so they might as well move on. And so she did, taking a place at the table opposite the doctor.

"So, what now, Antonio?" Jena said.

"I've missed your enigmatic questions, Jena. What do you want to happen?"

"Me? I want—"

"All this to go away? Sleep and wake up to find all this was a dream."

"Are you our nightmare, Antonio?"

"I am your saviour, Jena. You all are now immune from ARIA because of me. Shame about all those who already have it. But there's nothing to stop you strolling down the road to the village or Conwy."

"What is all this really about then, Antonio?" Dan said.

"Ah, are the aliens preparing Earth for their occupation? Maybe. Have they tried to help us better our feeble brains and made a few errors? Perhaps. There might be a third option. And it could be a... ah, Bronwyn, another cup please, *per favore*."

Ryder and Dan pestered him for the third option, but he teased. Jena found them guessing and brainstorming between them in the office.

"Don't torture yourselves, you two," she said. "It's another wind up and we'll get plenty more from him, you'll see."

"You might be right," Dan said. "But even without him, we have to think and plan for what those damn aliens really want. Whatever bad vibes you have about him, Jena, he is the only link we have with the second case. Some facts are clear. He was exposed to the second case without obvious ill effect so far and exposed to Brian as an ARIA victim yet hasn't lost his memory."

"There's only one way to check if we are immune to ARIA," Ryder said.

"Count me out on that one," Jena said. "And I don't want you going for a sociable stroll into the village. Don't come back if you do."

"And I thought you two were getting on so well," Dan said.

"We are," Jena said, then turning to Ryder. "Aren't we?"

"Absolutely, that's why I'm not going to go wandering into the populated wilderness to test our supposed immunity. We have a protocol for that anyway."

"One of the protocols you listed before we arrived?" Dan said. "What is it this time? Anyone who meets someone who might have ARIA has to keep away."

"Close," Ryder said. "But they can phone to report progress or return to the isolation unit at the mine."

"Watch out," Jena said. "I wouldn't put it past Antonio just to take Teresa or Bronwyn out of the gates for a paddle at the seaside, irrespective of protocols."

"If he does, he'd have to send a postcard back, because I wouldn't want to see him again," Ryder said. "You know what else we should do?"

"I think you'll find Laurette and Gustav are already looking for spurious anomalies in blood samples," Jena said.

"It's like living with telepaths around here," Ryder said. "And that's before any ARIA or related exposure."

Jena sneaked back into the kitchen for a coffee refill, hoping to keep contact with Antonio to a minimum.

"He's gone for a lie down," Bronwyn said, pouring the thick liquid into the three mugs. "Hadn't had much sleep while in the mine, poor thing."

Jena was on the verge of telling her how she thought Brian died but scalded her lip on the mug. "Bronwyn, you've made this with hot water, again."

"Well, I have to—oh, you're joking, aren't you? It's funny about the doctor, though, isn't it? He had tea for his breakfast drink and he always had coffee before."

"He's been through a lot, Bronwyn," Jena said, although Bronwyn's observations made her think.

"He said he wanted Camomile tea because it was his first ever hot drink—fancy remembering that."

"He might have been told that a thousand times by amused relatives."

"And he said that was an October Tuesday, the first Tuesday of the month, Jena, when he was eighteen months. And that the second hot drink was hot lemon water the following Wednesday. He'd moved on to chicory coffee the day before his second birthday."

"I wish I had such a detailed memory, Bronwyn," Jena said, thinking what a contrast to ARIA. And that although those victims still possessed diminishing childhood memories, only rare people would remember trivia like that.

She rushed back into the lab to check biotech progress.

Gustav waved despairing hands in the air. "He won't let us take any of his blood."

"What?" Jena said. "He has to. No choice, Dan and Ryder made it so, so to speak."

Laurette fiddled with a pipette. "Once he's thought it over, he'll let us, *oui*?"

"How much do you need?" Jena said, hatching a plan.

"Just a pin prick would be enough to show if anything like ARIA is there," Gustav said. "Why? Are we going to get him?"

"*Non!*" Laurette said.

"Gustav," Jena said, "bring a blood-sampling kit."

Out in the corridor, she waited for Gustav, hoping that Laurette wouldn't come since she might cause more trouble. He came out. His light brown, shoulder-length hair, and his exuberance, gave him the airs of an undercover cop on a mission.

Jena frowned at the sampling kit. "Antonio is asleep. Is it possible to take a blood sample without disturbing him?"

"I get it. You want the evidence of what's happening to him before he can refute it."

"Something like that. Is it one of those thumb-prick gadgets?"

"Don't worry, I'll do it. Lead the way to the prick for a prick."

Antonio slept fidgety, face-down in an eight-bed dormitory. Jena and Gustav snapped on surgical gloves. She placed her hands above Antonio's back so as to push him down if he woke up. Gustav held a sampler the size of a matchbox against the back of the doctor's bare upper arm. Six tiny needles darted in, sucked for a moment, then withdrew. Gustav stood and turned to go, but Jena bent to look at the sample point. She could only just see the six red dots. Her heartbeat leapt as Antonio groaned and started a roll. As Jena jumped back, she watched the doctor rub at the spot, but his eyes stayed shut.

Back in the lab, Gustav offered the sample to Laurette, who took it, giving Jena a look of knowing that it pulled her inexorably into the conspiracy. Within three minutes she said, "Yes, he has an anomaly but different from Brian's before he visited the doctor. The ARIA virus was spotted by Julia Tyndall, if you recall. She was Karen's chief biotechnician at Goddard, and although she had had ARIA for a day, she was able to send an image of a spiked sphere about thirty nanometres across. Looked like an adenovirus, possibly a viral pathogen. Now the beastie we found in Antonio is similar but with nodes between the spikes."

"So with the convention of naming viruses after their discoverer, we have the Tyndall virus," Gustav said.

"*Continuez*," Laurette said, with a glimmer of a smile.

"All right, the second case virus should be called the Pain-in-the-butt virus. No? ARIA is the effect of the Tyndall virus, so we'd need a suitable acronym for the second."

"I think we need to wait to see what the full effect of the Laurette-Gervais virus is, don't you?" Laurette said. Jena could see in her face that she was fighting the proud moment of having a virus named after her. If only scientific papers were being published.

Jena patted her on the back.

"Good work, Laurette. Well, you found that new virus in the blood of Antonio. And our blood?" Jena said.

"Normal," Laurette said. "Antonio's blood shows something like ARIA, call it ARIA2 for now, which might make him immune to

ARIA. Our blood doesn't. But, of course, it might do later. We need to retest every day or so."

"So if we walked into locals out there, we'd get ARIA, but he wouldn't?" Jena said.

"Not as simple as he said, is it?"

"No," Gustav said. "We've only been in contact with him for a couple of hours. It might take days to develop."

"And I suppose it might need us to be exposed to the case first, followed by exposure to someone with ARIA, like he was," Jena said.

"Either way," Gustav said, "it was premature of our doctor to encourage us to go sightseeing."

"More likely it was disingenuous of him," Jena said. "He wants us to catch ARIA."

"*Incredible.*" Laurette waved an arm. "He's one of us. Why would Antonio want to ensure we had a slow death from ARIA? He'd be the only one left alive."

"Maybe that's his plan," Gustav said.

Jena leaned against the bench examining a printout of the ARIA2 virus. "Or the plan of the changed Antonio. Perhaps he isn't in control of his actions. The infection he carries was spat at him from another species. Who knows what mental deviation it might produce?"

Laurette looked away from a viewer. "There are culture and other tests, Jena. Do you want me to inform our twin leaders, or do you want to sneak off to them without alerting our sleeping demon?"

Jena reached for the door just as it swung in. Antonio's face contorted with rage shouted, "I know what you've done! I specifically denied you permission to take any samples from me."

Jena recovered and said, "It's not all about you, you bastard."

"It *is* about me. *Dio mio*, you are so insignificant. I piss on you. All three of you."

"Can you hang on while I get a sample beaker?" Gustav said. He laughed at his own inappropriate and mistimed joke.

Antonio lunged at him, but Gustav ducked and threw himself down behind a long lab bench. Jena yelled, "Stop!"

Laurette screamed as Antonio picked up a retort stand and lunged at the microscope array. The microscope crashed to the floor while Laurette's screams went through the roof. The swing doors crept open followed by Bronwyn pointing a shotgun.

It had the desired effect in some ways. Laurette had run out of clamour, and Antonio reverted to hysterical laughter while collapsing on the floor amidst broken glass.

"*Mi scusi*, my good friends. I'll help clear this mess up and I'll pay for replacements. Hah! Pay for replacements, that's a good one, is it not?" He rose and staggered out.

Jena whispered to Laurette, "He thinks he's destroyed his sample before you could examine it. Don't let on just yet. I know it's unlikely, but there wasn't any trace of alcohol in his blood, was there?"

"Jena, there's not been a drop in the centre for weeks—unless you know different—but I didn't test for it. I could do though."

"I don't fancy taking another sample." Jena could feel her heart pounding from the fracas and didn't want any acceleration.

"His blood is on the floor from where he broke the slides."

Ryder rushed in from the kitchen followed by Abdul, who said, "I just returned from patrolling the perimeter. We watched smoke from bonfires, house chimneys."

"Yes, but from miles away on the coast," Ryder said, looking concerned at the blood-decorated glass on the floor. He held out an arm to comfort Jena.

Abdul toed broken glass to one side. "I saw two, several miles apart and one from the nearest village. What's its name? Aber-gobbledygook."

"Abergwyngregyn," Ryder said. "We gave you a map so you could give an accurate report. Three miles isn't far."

"It is autumn now," Jena said. "People need more fires to keep warm. It doesn't mean they are creeping in on us. We have something else to report. Something important. About Antonio's blood."

CHAPTER 36

Tuesday 6 October 2015:
Anafon

WHEN ANTONIO AWOKE FROM ANOTHER DAYTIME SLEEP, Jena noticed everyone being wary of him. She couldn't avoid him: his maniacal character was more virus than a reaction to being isolated. They had to know if it would happen to them. Megan was the sole member of the centre who didn't break out in a cold sweat at the sight of him.

Abdul and Vlad played poker in the refectory when Jena saw Antonio stagger in, half-asleep. She saw Dan sitting, reading a book. He looked up but didn't move. She had told him about the presence of a new virus in Antonio's blood.

"Hey, Antonio, make up a threesome. I'm getting bored with this Ukrainian's crazy playing," Abdul said.

Antonio stuck out his bottom lip as if thinking about acceding while he filled a large glass with water. He buttered some freshly-baked bread and leant against the counter, stuffing his face, watching the game. It could have been the aroma of Megan's bread-making that drew him from his bunk; it generated saliva in everyone.

Megan came out of the kitchen, saw Antonio, and rushed back in again. Within a minute, she had emerged with a jar.

"Antonio, try my homemade blackberry jam."

"What? You've made this from the blackberries you picked yourself?"

"Yeah, well. They were going to waste around here with just the birds eating them."

Jena watched from across the room. She'd seen moon-struck looks like that before.

"Megan, you are a star," Antonio said, giving her a kiss on her forehead.

"Antonio, put the staff down and let us take your money," Vlad said.

Jena was amused at the stake money. They'd found a cash drawer in the office with hundreds of old pound and silver coins. No use to anyone now except to play with.

"Come on, Doc," Abdul said, "we're playing—"

"Seven-card stud, I can see that. There's no point."

Vlad was on the third betting round, so each player had four cards each played face up, and three down. Each tried to bluff the other with winks, grins, and groans. Apart from the played face-up cards, neither had revealed their cards to the spectators. After watching for a few minutes, Antonio spoke up.

"It is obvious that you, Abdul, have the better hand with two sixes, Queen, seven, three, and two Kings to choose your five-card hand from. Vlad, I'm afraid, has two Jacks, two tens, two fours, and a two. Shame. But too predictable. Boring. I'm going for a walk." He left. Dan followed him out.

Abdul scowled. "How did he know my hand?"

"And mine. Jena, were you waving your make-up mirror around, again?" Vlad risked a thump, knowing she never used cosmetics. She looked around, but there were no mirrors in the room.

Abdul persisted. "So, he worked it out from watching from the first deal."

"And he saw me shuffle the cards when he first came in," Vlad said. "Has he got magic eyesight, now, Jena?"

"I believe some card sharks and illusionists can train themselves to memorise a pack when it's being shuffled," she said. "I've never known Antonio to be interested in cards or magic tricks on board the ISS."

"Nor me," Abdul said. "What's the odds against him getting those hands right, Vlad? You're a better probability theory man than me."

"There are over four million combinations of any seven-card hands. You know, I don't feel like playing any more. Sorry, Abdul."

Jena walked past the two would-be winners and followed Dan and the doctor outside.

Though still overcast, the usual Welsh drizzle held off. Dan and Jena scanned the valley and mountainsides for signs of people, sheep, feral horses, and dogs; in that order. They'd have work to do, with rifles, had they spotted any.

Antonio turned. "Ah, Jena. Sorry about earlier. Not myself, you know."

"I understand. Really," she said and risked linking arms with him to put him at ease. All three strolled towards the lake, a few hundred metres away.

Dan risked a direct approach, "Antonio, you have the opposite of amnesia."

"There's an interesting concept: the opposite of amnesia. Does that mean I remember more than I knew? You might be right in some ways, Dan. I remember things I didn't know I knew. Like all the medical notes I'd ever made. You know, it is hard for medical students. So much recall of anatomical trivia and procedures rather than problem-solving. But now I only have to think of, say, hypertension, and I can see all the pages of my notes, the screen data, case studies. I wish I could have done that for my finals."

Dan stooped to pick some bilberries. "You didn't do so bad, if I recall your record. You came top in your year."

"*Si*, but to have had a hundred percent. I could do that now. Hah! That would show those pompous asses at Milano."

Dan looked at Jena as if he was willing her to take an interrogative turn. "Antonio, what would you like to do to those tutors who annoyed you?"

Dan's dark, bushy eyebrows lowered so much, Jena couldn't see his recriminating eyes. She assumed she played the bad guy and he the good. Oh well.

"There's plenty I'd do. There was a know-it-all woman from Torino. She wore such tight clothes to get us steamed up—even the women students—then she'd have killing put downs. *Si*, I'd take her down all right. Tie her to a chair. Remove her clothes with my teeth...hah!"

"Steady on, Doc. You're in the presence of a lady." Dan gave Jena a wink. Her question revealed more of Antonio's depravity.

"Oh, Jena can take it. I bet Ryder is having the time of his life with you, isn't he?" Before Jena could answer, Antonio fell to his knees on the slate chippings path, clutching his head.

"*Madre Teresa*, why don't they go away? Go! Go!"

Jena put her hand on his shoulder. "Who do you want to go away, Doc?"

"The demons in my head. I want to remember things at the right time not all at once." He lay on his back on the wet path, beating the stones with the palms of his hands. "You're right, Dan. My memory is perfect. I have to work hard to try and stop recalling every minutia of my life. I have to exert energy to block my first words, first steps, biting my mother's nipples to stop her pulling me off her after a suckle, being born! And—*Dio mio!*—before that!...I have to stop it. But I can't. It's like that trick, Dan, Jena. You know when someone tells you to not think of a pink elephant?" He lay there, quiet for a moment, eyes shut while Jena had a mental image of a pink elephant and tried not to.

Antonio sat up. "I am enhanced, aren't I? An enhuman. Hah." Then he fell back down in the wet again.

Dan sat cross-legged on the wet path beside Antonio; an act that impressed Jena, but she just concentrated on hearing better from her vertical position. She noticed Ryder had come out of the centre and was walking towards them. She held up a hand to wave and indicated that this wasn't an emergency, although in some ways it was.

Dan adopted his commander's voice. "Antonio, you've been through a lot. You have a new virus, which while not destructive, is kinda supercharging your brain. Maybe all the poor connections we usually have blocking memories have been cleared for you. But it needs time to adjust. I bet in another couple of days you'll be fine. At least you were functioning logically when you put the case safely away. Now, come on up, or we'll both get dropsy or whatever these wet Welsh hills give you."

Ryder held out his hands to Antonio and helped him up. "There's a message from Charlotte to say she'll be live in ten minutes and has some exciting news."

On their way back, Jena updated Ryder, who said, "Did you believe any of that?"

"Not about Antonio coping with his enriched-humanity anymore than Dan did."

GUSTAV AND LAURETTE LEFT TO PATROL THE PERIMETER and Antonio hit his bed again. Ryder joined the rest clustered around the computer to greet Charlotte. The ISS linked with a NOAA satellite allowed the signal to pass to and fro. Derek logged in during the potential communication window every day but Charlotte responded only when she had news. Ryder knew most of her news was that she'd seen no one, the small town was deserted, as was the once thriving USAF base in Australia. When she did see anyone, she kept out of their way. At Laurette's request, she'd searched the base for a microscope to examine her own blood.

"Hi, gang," she said, as her image flickered on screen. "Sorry to read the messages from you about Brian, but it's good news about Antonio, isn't it? Wow, you must all be so chuffed."

Ryder looked at Derek, not wanting to tell her what they thought, outvoting Jena on letting Charlotte have all they knew.

"I've been thinking about my alleged immunity to ARIA. I could just have been lucky and not been near enough anyone with it. I can't find a microscope. Is there any other test I can do?"

Dan leaned towards the microphone. "We'll get Laurette on to you tomorrow. Was there any other news? You indicated there was."

"Yes, there is, as we expected, another group who've been on the ISS message boards, have been bantering with me overnight, so Derek won't have got it yet."

"Those strange IP addresses that log in but say nothing?" Derek asked.

"One of them is. Anyway, there is a group of New Zealanders and local people on a remote island in equatorial Pacific. They've had no visitors since March this year except the odd boat whose crew is also uncontaminated."

Dan's face lit up. "That's the best news we've had since we heard your sweet voice, Charlotte."

"Aw, Yankee, you big flirt, lover boy," Charlotte said with an exaggerated Australian accent. Everyone laughed except Dan, who'd flushed deep pink.

Ryder took over the mike. "Charlotte, if Dan could stop choking to death after that, he would have liked to ask the name and location of the island?"

"Dunno that myself, Ryder, just like I don't know where you are. I'm the only one anyone could send a postcard to. Not that it would be delivered for a while."

Derek took over the microphone. "Charlotte, I've been going through the message board, I found a message from some Kiwis. So that's them?"

"Sure is. Hey, you can't track them backwards to their satellite dish, can you?"

"Afraid not, but it means we can talk to them like we do for you if they have a standard voice setup on their system."

JENA FOLLOWED DEREK TO HIS OWN CONSOLE, leaving the others nattering to Charlotte.

"You can, can't you?" she said, noticing Ryder coming over too.

"You think I tell lies?" Derek said, looking offended.

"Sorry, I just—"

"Got you!" he said, and she hit him on the shoulder. "It doesn't mean I can track them, but there is a way using the ISS equipment and a NAVSAT-GPS satellite, but only when they are on-air, and depending on the type of upload equipment they use. I can set it up and wait for them to leave a message on the board again."

"I'm not sure we should," Ryder said, who'd followed them. "They might have the equipment to tell they're being traced through that GPS satellite and decide we are untrustworthy."

"There's no logic there, honey. After all, if they see we've located them, what are they going to do? Pack their bags and go where? They must be on a secure and safe island—they wouldn't want the risk of finding somewhere else."

"Good point, but it puts our relationship on a sour starting point. Let's try negotiating with them first."

"With the aim of what?" Derek said. "Are we really going to leave here and hitchhike to the Pacific?"

"It looks like a good option, considering our insecure future here," Ryder said, and basked in the pleasure of seeing Jena grin.

"RAROTONGA," DAN SAID TO JENA AND RYDER as they returned to the others crowding the console. "Charlotte has just been chatting to us. They want to talk to us direct and they've agreed not to ask for our address given our vulnerability here."

"Rare what?" said Ryder.

"Rarotonga is a small Pacific Ocean island almost on the equator," said Dan. "One of the Cook Islands."

"How come you've become an instant gazetteer, Dan?" Ryder said. "Just a minute, aren't they all atolls and about to be swamped with the rising sea level from global warming?"

"I'm surprised at you, being in the media. The population were temporarily evacuated last year because its volcano grumbled. A few stayed behind manning the new combined optical and radio observatory there. It isn't a sea-level atoll like most of them. In any case, the sudden demise of industry and vehicle emissions will have already reduced carbon dioxide levels. Global warming is slowing down." He grinned at this benefit of ARIA.

"I hadn't thought of that," Ryder said. "Do you think the aliens might be some sort of intergalactic green police?"

"Unlikely," Dan said, taking Ryder's quip more seriously than he intended. "But they are close to wiping us out without damaging the planet."

Jena held her nose. "With the exception of a few million rotting bodies."

"Hey, look at the time, 17:00 hours. Jena, we should have left for a tour of the estate."

"We can go from here, up the slope to The Drum mountain on the old Roman road.

"It'll be dark by the time we get back, so we need torches, rifles—"

"Sandwiches. Ryder, how come our shifts are during dinner?"

"We'll be back in time for briefing."

"Whoopee, you know how to swoop a girl off her feet."

"Yeah, sorry, Jena. Maybe we can go down to the pub instead. A tropical island is like a dream too far."

Jena thought for a moment. "It would mean driving again to that airport we landed at, a refuel, say somewhere in Canada..."

"Canada? Is that on the way between here and the mid-Pacific?"

"The shortest distance is via one of the Great Circle routes, which from here would cut across Canada. In fact, it would be the only large country to pass over, so we'd have to land at a major airport and refuel. How do we arrange that without bumping into anyone? So, yes, maybe it is only a dream."

"Hey, Jena, collect our rucksacks and the weapons, will you? I've just got a little job to do."

THIRTY MINUTES LATER JENA AND RYDER reached one of the highest points of their perimeter. The clouds had cleared, giving them a surprise early-evening light. An enchanting golden glow sent sharp shadows marching across the otherwise bright green valley. Bursting out from the last cloud in the west, the brightness made Jena shield her eyes. The Anafon lay before her as a valley of stark optical contrast as one side sunbathed and the other fell asleep in the dark. She sat on her rucksack absorbing the desolate grandeur while Ryder checked a CCTV post and nearby fencing.

She used her binoculars, looking for anything that moved.

Ryder pointed at a track to the northeast. "It's quite possible intruders would come this way rather than up the lane from the village."

Jena smiled when she saw that the low sun had projected her shadow way down the grassy slope as if she were a giant. "I suppose we're vulnerable."

"But are we more vulnerable with time or less? As the months pass, there is an increased chance of random-movement opportunity to find us, but then they'd be less organised."

"Ryder, I bet there are plenty of people out there in isolated farmhouses who might have escaped interference from marauding gangs. They might employ strategies to keep their minds alert, especially those old enough to have skills and survival memory but not so old as to be infirm."

"You're right, which brings me to one such case like that. I've talked to you about Manuel?"

"The NASA media mogul. I've met him on a couple of public-relations events, but he was much more of a friend than a colleague to you, wasn't he?"

"Last time I managed to talk to him, he'd managed to get to an isolated tourist log cabin. Infected, but like we were saying, coping by using a NoteCom to update himself each day. He'd picked up a female companion too."

"I know it's grim, honey, but there's no point dwelling on past friends and family who are both way out of reach and dead by now. I know it's hard but..."

"This log cabin is near Banff, which has a long runway at its airport, and in western Canada. Ring any bells?"

"Interesting, and yet it hammers my alarm bells. Are you suggesting we attempt to use Manuel for the refuelling stop?" said Jena, refocusing her binoculars on a newly spotted wisp of smoke to the northeast.

"Sadly, I haven't been able to contact him for a while. He has a satellite Internet receiver. I have the IP addresses of his PC and NoteCom and can tell they've been turned on. It gives me hope that I'll chat to him. You seen that smoke?"

"I get it. Neither of you are around at the right time. We can't take him with us; he must be one of the first to get ARIA. I'm looking at it now, Ryder. There are brown and blue tinges with bursts of red flame in it. Too pretty for chimney smoke or a bonfire."

"He's lost over twenty years' worth of memory, but at fifty-four, he'd have enough knowledge to help us at the airport. I left a few messages on the ISS message board. But I tend to leave it to Derek to let me know when Manuel replies. I reckon it's a building on fire. So many different combustible materials are going up over there."

"Okay. I'd say that he's a likely way of getting us refuelled so we could get to Rarotonga. When we get back, we'll take turns pinging his systems. Hey, can we buzz his speakers with a signal?"

"I'll give Derek a call now. Looking at that fire, the sooner we are out of here..."

"No arguments there," Jena said, shocking herself with such a rare phrase. "But I hope you know of another airfield with a strong likelihood of available aircraft because that smoke means people between us and where we left the *Marimar*. Pity, because we know she would do the job."

"No, you don't," said Ryder, risking a dig in the ribs. "It might have been discovered and trashed, and it's not been for a check up since you took it to space and back."

"Okay, let's suppose you're right, where else?"

"Valley. It's a large RAF airbase on Anglesey. If you look over there," he pointed west, "and made a hole in Llwtymor Mountain, you'd be able to see it. At around thirty miles, it's half the distance to the *Marimar*."

"What? Why did we go so much farther when we landed, then?"

"Valley is military, and back then, it stood a better chance of having people with guns pointing at us than now. Anyway, I'll see if I can get Derek to buzz Manuel."

Ryder's mobile phone startled him just as he tapped at it to ring Derek.

"Hi, Derek, I was just calling you. What's all that racket? I can't hear you. Are you having a party?"

Jena grabbed her mobile, thought for a second, and called Dan, while turning to look at the centre. She tried to use the binoculars with one hand, but couldn't steady it, so she put the phone on a boulder. As soon as she brought both hands up to concentrate on the centre, she heard Dan answer the phone. She let the binoculars dangle from her neck just as she thought she saw someone open the centre door.

Ryder looked at her. "I can't hear Derek talking with all the din going on down there. You talking to Dan on yours? Can he ask Derek—"

Jena gave him her pitying look. "You are an idiot sometimes. Something's going on down there and it can only be because of one person." They both put down their phones to focus on the centre.

CHAPTER 37

Tuesday 6 October 2015, 18:00 hours:
Anafon Centre. Most people outside Anafon will have lost up to twenty-five years' memory.

ANTONIO KNOCKED HIS HEAD AGAINST THE REFECTORY WALL as if the blow would dissipate the skull-tightening pain he'd developed. If he had a drill to hand, he would have trepanned a hole to let out the demons. His brain annoyed him. He'd always a good memory, but being able to recall everything was too much. Huge movie reels of his experiences would flood his consciousness, whether or not they were significant or relevant to the moment.

"It's all your fault," he said to Dan. Since he'd smashed the microscope and obliterated his blood sample, he'd noticed the commander following him, like a poorly-trained spy. But he had detected Laurette's mind telling him she'd already run the analysis and found a virus. He couldn't read thoughts, but he could sense the tenor of their cognition—the intent behind their false smiles.

"Antonio, you are in turmoil. I understand."

"You have no idea. You should not have brought Brian to me when you did. It was too soon after my acceptance of the case's gift, transcending my being to a superhuman—enriched human, beyond your experience."

"You agreed to have Brian. It was to expose him to the case to see if it would halt the retrograde nature of his amnesia. It did. We suggested you should suit up. You said it didn't matter. Do you really consider yourself an enriched human?"

"I wouldn't go as far as to call myself Superman." He laughed like a demon. "My strength and body functions are no different than before, but I have a mental acuity and other functions making me an enhanced human."

"*Mon Dieu*, Antonio," Laurette said, "you're more egotistical, that's all. A bighead-human."

Antonio saw Abdul and Bronwyn trying not to laugh.

"Shut up!" Antonio bellowed at them. "Sheep, all of you."

Dan spoke to the rest. "You aren't helping. Haven't you got work to do?" Bronwyn, stifling a laugh, ran into the kitchen. Dan turned to Antonio. "Are you saying you wouldn't have this turmoil in you if

Brian hadn't been brought to you?"

"You did it to test me."

"That's unreasonable, and if you could read my mind, you'd know I tried to help you."

Antonio sneered. "You're too cunning to let me know what's going on in your commander's head. You hide so much up there." He used his right forefinger to poke at Dan's forehead, making him stagger backwards into the wall.

Abdul jumped up, making his chair fall back with a crash.

Antonio spun round with his arm still extended. He flexed and jabbed out his right arm once more, and even though Abdul stood two arm-lengths away, he staggered back as if punched. Three mugs on the nearest table tumbled away as if Antonio had a telekinetic force emanating from his fingertips. A silence gripped the room, broken by a laugh from Antonio. He grinned, knowing his superior abilities were being revealed one by one to the mere mortals before him.

Antonio's smugness was short-lived as Bronwyn stormed through the swing doors from the kitchen and threw herself at him. He stood his ground as she punched him in the left arm.

"Laurette's just told me!" she shrieked. "You killed my Brian!"

"He had no future."

Bronwyn screamed, and with a short kitchen-knife hidden in her left hand, slashed at his face. He sensed the attack through her rage, but not in time to stop the blade lacerating his right cheek, causing an instant spurt of dark-red blood. He pushed her away and ran down the refectory towards the kitchen.

"Bronwyn, you shouldn't have," said Laurette at the kitchen door, stepping sideways to avoid Antonio.

"He killed my Brian."

Although Antonio heard her, a deep pain jabbed at his brain. Not the cut, it was nothing, except a red mess on his white shirt, but his head meant something more sinister. Through his agony, he detected snippets of brainwaves from the others. Their fear reasoned he'd dashed into the kitchen for the first-aid box. The fools hadn't bargained on him ignoring the green box. He reached for the cupboard down on the left. The loaded shotgun leapt into his clutching hands. The cool steel represented the solution to his problems.

Antonio looked for the revolver he thought was kept in the kitchen. He muttered to himself, "As contaminants, they should be eliminated. A danger to the cause." He had a notion that along with being impregnated with the new, enhancing virus, some data about the source had shot into his brain. His head hurt too much for him to work it out—maybe later. He supposed a coded brain transmission might have occurred when the case first opened, which made him more special than Brian was, but he couldn't be sure. The only thing of which he was confident was that he had a duty to destroy the centre occupants. He'd have to give up on the revolver—it was either too well hidden or one of the others had it. He'd have to take a chance.

He looked through the small window in the door. In the refectory sat and stood the tea and coffee drinkers, stabbers, and village idiots, all ripe for disposal.

Antonio readied the shotgun, kicked the door open, and marched in blasting away.

Dan had been sitting facing him and caught the full blast in the chest. Splatters of his blood and stray shotgun pellets caught Bronwyn, who had sat beside him. She fell, spinning. Antonio's second shot was aimed at Vlad, but he had a moment to duck, so just his scalp and some bloodied brains splattered the air while the main shot hit Laurette, sending her backwards into the lab. The opened lab door revealed Derek, who had started to level the missing revolver at Antonio. They fired together. Antonio spun to his left, from a hit to his upper arm, but Derek doubled up as a hole opened in his abdomen. The odour of cordite and burnt flesh pinched his nose. He staggered outside looking for the others.

"*Un minuto,*" he said, even though no one was there to listen. "That bastard Abdul was in the refectory...fuck, fuck, when that cow, Bronwyn, stabbed me. So where did he go while I was in the kitchen? Jena and Ryder are...fuck, fuck, out of the way in the valley. I'll get them when they return. Teresa and Megan must be hiding here." He checked the magazine, turned, and re-entered the centre, ignoring the blood oozing down his right cheek and neck.

Abandoning the use of his bloody left arm, he shouted. "Where are you, Abdul? I have a surprise for you...fuck, fuck, where are you? I'm not going to hurt you! Just kill you! Hah! Did you hear that, Abdul?"

He heard a crash from the lab, so he charged in. Derek's body lay to the left and a streak of blood led to the right. "So, Bronwyn. Are you a little poorly? Fuck, fuck. Teresa, you are in here too. I can sense you, smell you, suck out your thoughts. Hah!"

He ran to the right along the blood trail, but the lights went out, and the long room with its benches and computer screens created a difficult place to find people who insisted on hiding. Another set of doors led through the back to the outside stores.

Antonio sensed the presence of Teresa and Abdul outside. Synapses fired in his brain, forcing both pleasure at his discovery and anger that they hid from their necessary destruction.

"Got you, got fuck, fuck you!" he shouted as he crashed through the doors, his shotgun levelled. A newly acquired instinct made him dive as a scaffolding pole slammed onto his back, followed by Teresa and Abdul running back into the centre.

"You can't fuck, fuck escape. *Non lo permetto*!" He turned to find they'd shut and locked the doors, leaving him in the outside storage area with no access back in or out of the centre complex. The single-floored building had its roof razor-wired to keep visitors out, and there Antonio found himself trapped. Nonsense, it merely slowed his progress. Picking up the scaffolding pole, which would have crushed his vertebrae had he not been superior, he swore-assisted it to punch holes in the door until the lock gave way. He could have used the shotgun but the irony of using their weapon had given him more satisfaction.

He didn't need his telepathic-like abilities to know they wouldn't be hiding in the lab when he re-entered. He knew they'd have made it outside to hide—the cowards. But once he was out there, he'd be able to track them down and they'd not want to leave the security of their precious valley. Hah! Fuck, fuck.

Checking his gun, again—obsessively—he approached the door to the outside. Hah! He detected their presence behind the boulders up near the lake. He'd pretend he didn't know the cowards were there. Wander over to the higher ground at an oblique angle and blast the fuckers by surprise.

He sneaked the door open and crept out. A bullet hit him in the chest, and one in his right arm, sending him staggering back into the centre. As his life energy ebbed, he worked out that Jena and Ryder had fired their rifles from the other side of the lake. Fuck. And Gustav shot him from inside the pickup. He'd forgotten all about him. They'd fucking won. Hah! Had they really? Fuck, fuck.

CHAPTER 38

Tuesday 6 October 2015, late evening:
Anafon Centre. Most people outside Anafon will have lost up to twenty-five years' memory.

IN THE REFECTORY AND FIGHTING A STRESS HEADACHE, Ryder blurted out, "What a bloody mess." Bronwyn lay on the floor with Teresa kneeling beside her with Gustav. Megan was making strong coffee for the survivors. Ryder looked at Abdul and Jena who, like him, were struggling to delay reality-denial sleep, slouched on canteen chairs at a table. He fought to keep his senses. He hoped his mighty headache was stress related rather than ARIA.

"There's no need to keep repeating that it's a mess," Jena said.

"Leave him alone for once, can't you?" Teresa said, tending to Bronwyn, who'd suffered shotgun wounds to her right side. In pre-ARIA circumstances, there would have been certainty of her surviving. Ryder knew the chance of her picking up a wound infection was high. They'd stemmed the flow of blood but had no idea of any internal haemorrhaging.

"Let's have no arguing now there's just six of us who are able-bodied," Abdul said.

Ryder saw Megan shooting Abdul a stern look, but she had suffered too much to say anything.

"Let's get this right then," Ryder said, ignoring the percussion orchestra in his head. "Of those alive, Bronwyn has actual bullet wounds, and no one else has anything more than grazes, cuts, and bruises? In that case, we need to evacuate this place as soon as possible. Gustav and Abdul, get the case out of the mine. It's shut and sealed in the padded bag, but if you want to suit up..."

"Just a minute," Jena said, "we could leave it in the mine. No one else knows it's there. Taking it with us just increases the chances of catastrophe on our journey, whether we reach Rarotonga or only Abergoggle-whatever."

"Here we go again," Gustav said. "Jena, it might be needed, if not by us, then by others."

"It's too fucking dangerous, Gustav. Let's bury it in the mine."

"Gustav is right," Teresa said. "We have to accept that the case contents have halted Brian's memory loss. And I know you're going to point at Antonio, but we don't really know what went on with him."

"You're damn right I'm pointing at that freak. I'm sure Ryder will back me up," Jena said, looking at him for support.

Ryder shook his head. "Sorry, Jena. Abdul and Gustav, we've no time for debates. Get on with it."

Ryder didn't want to embarrass Jena in front of everyone, but they had to evacuate before anyone decided to investigate the shooting. Like the others, the trauma was hitting him in the guts, making logic difficult, but he had to try. The echoes must have reverberated for miles. He had to busy himself in the lab, trying to contact Manuel and gather equipment. The survivors included three ISS crew who were all experienced pilots. He punched the phone for the kitchen.

"Megan, will you load provisions and bottled water into the pickup?"

Between sobs, Megan blurted back into the phone, "I'm in here getting a drink for my aunt. Do your own jobs."

"Megan, we have to help Bronwyn by getting her to safety. To do that, we have to leave. I know you're upset. We all are. Please help."

Jena came into the lab. "Do you want me to collect the ARIA and second-case evidence together while you play?"

"I'm collecting IT equipment that will be damned useful and rigging up an automatic-retry message for Manuel." He avoided looking at her eyes, which were no doubt mocking him. "I'm evading contemplating the way our friends died. Especially Derek. We went back to my first year of work."

"We'll all need therapy. It's forgivable to neglect confronting our demons now, but keep on going against me at your cost." She blew a kiss at him, which Ryder accepted as if it attacked him.

After he'd done all he could with the computers and loaded his considered bare minimum into the boot of the Volvo estate, he helped Gustav move the bodies to a storage building outside. Megan finally came to help too.

"It's okay," Gustav said. "We two strong men can manage."

Megan insisted. "You'd better not be suggesting that I'm a bloody weakling."

Gustav held up his hands. "I'm sure you eat rocks for breakfast." Ryder pulled a face. The poor man would have rocks in his muesli tomorrow.

"So, now you're having a go at my cooking. You can make your own sandwiches from now on." She used a trolley to move Antonio's body, blood dripping. After draping a tarpaulin over the body, she turned to Ryder and pulled him outside. "What are we going to do with Bronwyn? She's too ill to be moved out of her bed, let alone go on a journey to whatever airfield you and your new bitch have decided to go to."

"It's only RAF Valley, not far. I'm ignoring your rudeness. I'll come and chat to her."

Ryder followed her to the small dormitory—now with an antiseptic aroma—shared by Megan and Bronwyn. The fluorescent strip light cast a harsh brightness in the room. Bronwyn lay propped up by blood-stained pillows. Barely awake, her pale skin glistened.

"Hello, Ryder, you finished your holiday here then?"

"You could say that."

"Don't forget your travel-sick tablets, Megan."

"I think Megan could stay here with you. You're going to need a lot of looking after."

"No, Ryder. Although I'm not leaving Brian, I want to know Megan is with you and the others."

"Good God, Bronwyn, I hope you aren't thinking we're off to a sure safe place. We might not make it to the airport. Our refuelling in Canada might not happen. We might land again in that Pacific island and find everyone has ARIA after all."

"No problem," Megan said. "We'd open the case at them and they'd stop being infectious."

"We don't know that for certain. Just that Brian stopped forgetting things and the virus in his blood changed. But if Bronwyn insists, I suppose we'll have to have some more weight," said Ryder, dodging the pillow Megan threw at him. "We'll put off leaving until you are well enough to come with us, Bronwyn."

THAT NIGHT, RYDER MASSAGED JENA'S SHOULDERS with lemon-based aromatic oil. A knock on their door, followed by a Teresa cough, interrupted them.

"She's perfected her sense of timing," Jena said, throwing a dressing gown on. Ryder didn't bother, and wearing nothing, yanked the door open.

"No need to dress on my account," Gustav said, who stood with Teresa.

Ryder grimaced.

A couple of minutes later, the four of them shared hot chocolate drinks in the refectory. Ryder tried to assess the composure of Teresa, whose red eyes gave away her loss. She was very fond of Laurette, and latterly, Antonio. A whirlpool of emotions. Gustav had shown them how strong he could be, his face immutable and stolid. Jena must have had angst for the murder of Dan, but she fought it well. Ryder couldn't tell whether her bravado came from astronaut training or bloody-mindedness. He fought his own torment with Derek's death. The whole situation was likely to worsen.

Teresa opened the discussion. "If we take the case to Rarotonga, we may be missing out on a big opportunity. By the time it is examined under intense lab procedures and security conditions down there, it will be months before the new virus would come back to Europe."

"So, what are you saying? Expose some ARIA victims here, before we whip it away to the other side of the world?" Ryder said.

"Exactly," Gustav said. "If ARIA-2 infects one person with ARIA, it might halt their memory deterioration. Then if they are infectious..."

"A lot of ifs," Ryder said.

"I can just imagine the practical implications of doing this without exposing ourselves," Jena said. "But I've been thinking along those lines too."

"I'm not opposed to the crazy idea. After all that we've been through, I haven't a clue of the difference between normal and bizarre. But suppose they react badly?"

"Then they aren't worse off," Teresa said. "We know that without this additional virus, they will continue to lose memory until they die via their own or others' neglect."

"Antonio?" Ryder had a nightmare vision of a world populated by psychopathic crazies. The Welsh hills would resound with weird animal cries, and they wouldn't be sheep.

"Right," Gustav said, "suppose they react like Antonio and become psychopathic? They might end up killing each other. This time next year, they'll all be dead anyway. Whatever we do, or don't do, is risky, but the case gives them, and so humanity, a slim chance of survival."

"You're right," Ryder said. "But, how the hell are we going to do it?"

Gustav spoke up. "Let's go for the simplest solution. Two of us suit up and go, with the case, into the nearest village at night."

"Why at night?" Teresa said.

"Because it is easier to see which houses are occupied," Jena said. "Especially just after dark before too many have gone to bed."

"Exactly," Gustav said. "So it's too late tonight. Tomorrow evening, I'm going out with the estate car down the lane to the village and—"

"No, you're not," Abdul said, who'd come in from his patrol shift with Megan. "Jena and I will go because—"

"We have the space suits and more brains," Jena said, holding up her hand for Abdul to high-five.

"You do have fitted space suits," admitted Gustav, winking at Ryder. "Not sure about the brains." He ducked as Jena threw a biscuit.

WEDNESDAY 7 OCTOBER 2015, 19:30 HOURS

Jena and Abdul drove all the way through the village without witnessing a single light behind a window. She spotted a dozen bodies on pavements and in the road.

Jena used her phone. "Ryder, we're going onto the dual carriageway and heading east to Conwy. We're bound to find some live ones there."

"Maybe you should abort mission and return."

But they continued. Gustav gave directions. "I've been here with students. Conwy is circled with a medieval stone wall. Head for the large houses on the left, with large gardens with hedges."

They parked in a dark side street then they fixed helmets; incongruous on a Welsh street. Armed with guns and the case, they rounded a corner and saw oil lamps in two windows of a large detached house. Sneaking up the path, Jena hesitated and tugged at Abdul to stop. They couldn't just open it on the doorstep and ring the bell, risking the householder stumbling on the case or taking it in.

Jena whispered. "There's a low hedge near the door." She opened the case on the side of the hedge away from the door and waited for a few minutes for the blue blocks to emit particles.

"To think this might be the start of a diffusion of more sanity for the planet or the acceleration to the end," Abdul said. "I hope they don't notice the blue fluorescence."

"If they look as if they're going to touch it, we'll have to point our guns at them and tell them to go in the house while we run off with the case. Right, who's going to play Trick-or-Treat?"

"Isn't it Knock-and-Run? Although, we're only hiding, and we are giving them a treat," said Abdul. "All right, I'll do it."

Jena suppressed a laugh at the ludicrous vision of a NASA spaceman in full suit sneaking up to a door, knocking on its letterbox, and running back to her in the bushes.

"You could have just lobbed a stone at the door, you muffin."

"Now you tell me."

A moment later, the door opened and an angry, elderly man in a dressing gown stepped out on the path. "Who's there? I bet it's young Robbie, ain't it?"

A woman in her thirties came out. "Come on, Daddy, it's cold out there." She joined him on the path, put an arm around him, and together they returned to the house and shut the door.

"I'll count that as a success," Jena said, as they retrieved the case and turned out of the gate. Across the road, The Glyndwr Arms released sounds of talking. Dim lights escaped through curtains from hurricane lamps.

They peered in through gaps in the curtains. Abdul said, "Four—no, five men and two women. They're having drinks as if nothing has happened."

"Probably a bit like that father and daughter back there. She's lost twenty years, called the crotchety old feller, Daddy, and cuddled him like a young girl might. Are we up for it? Seven birds with one stone?"

"I'll hold the case open while you point both hand guns, although the sight of us might freak them into a catatonic trance."

"Shall we ask Ryder first?" Jena said.

"He'd refuse permission."

"We could ask, let him refuse us, and do it anyway. It would really piss him off," she said, grinning behind her visor.

"I thought you liked him."

"So?"

They burst through the double doors and stood there facing the drinkers. Most were senior citizens with slow reactions. A middle-aged man about to sip from a bottle hesitated as if frozen. Abdul put the case on a stool and opened it. The six blue bricks shimmered. The drinkers' eyes flitted between the mesmerising contents of the case, the astronauts' space suits, and Jena's guns. One of the men let his bottle slip out of his shaking fingers. It smashed on the floor sending a jet of liquid shooting back up. Jena took pleasure from the beautiful application of Newton's Third Law of Motion: for every bottle of beer hitting the floor, there is an equal and opposite fountain of beer rocketing up.

Jena spoke, her American accent adding another oddity to the occasion for the drinkers. "You will find your memory loss will stop, and you'll start remembering things from now on. Breathe on others, spread it around. When we leave, lock the door for at least half an hour."

Abdul closed the case and said in his equally strange Qatar accent, "We'd buy you a round, but we haven't any money. Have a drink anyway."

They ran to their car. In between bursts of relief laughter, Jena warmed with the thought they might have done some real good. But then she remembered the aliens were responsible for both cases. Had she been an unwitting accomplice by implementing an awful plan?

SATURDAY 10 OCTOBER 2015, 03:00 HOURS, AFTER ABANDONING ANAFON.

Both vehicles hid behind a low hill while Ryder trained night-sight binoculars at Menai Bridge. They had seen no one on the way, not even candlelight in windows. RAF Valley was on the island of Anglesey across 300 metres of grey Irish Sea slopping back and forth up the Menai Straits. Beautiful in the moonlight following an earlier rain, the suspension bridge glistened metallic green. Nineteenth century graceful catena curves and vertical steel ropes tried hard to sooth the troubled minds looking out for trouble.

"I don't like it," said Ryder. "There's a barbed-wire barricade at this end. Okay, we have bolt-cutters, but I can't see the other end of the bridge. Abdul?"

"I see obstacles on the bridge but no more than the surprising amount of debris on the road all the way here. It's too dark, and the curve in the surface of the suspension bridge stops us seeing the end."

Ryder remembered something. "There's another bridge. Britannia was road and rail but used only for the railway for years."

"Let's have another look at that map. Yes, the railway goes all the way into the airfield."

"No," Ryder said, "we can't drive on the tracks. The wheelbases on our vehicles are wider than the 4-feet-8.5 inch-railway gauge, so we'd be driving over the sleepers. It would be a hell of a drive."

"I'm up for it. Both vehicles have excellent suspension. The pickup in particular can have the wheels dive into holes without the chassis deviating."

"Abdul, we have delicate computers on board and the case."

"Ryder, the computers and case are tough enough. Are you?"

"You think it would be a soft option to go across this bridge and stay on the roads?" Ryder checked his anger with Abdul. He found that lately he was apt to boil over too easily. The deaths and increasing danger must be getting to him. "Let's have that map. Maybe you have a point. The railway hardly touches any villages."

Ryder smiled as he could tell that Abdul had sensed a rare point win over him.

Abdul said, "We could put it to a vote."

"No need, Abdul. We don't want them to think we aren't decisive, do we?"

A LARGE PADLOCK LOOKED AT THEM. Gustav wielded his favourite toy. The turbo-assisted, long-handled bolt cutter was eager to get to work, and even with the caveat of Ryder's shushing, the heavy-duty padlock had its steel U-shaped shaft sliced. A sharp crack echoed off nearby grassy banks, but Jena caught the steel debris in her hands to prevent further noise.

"Well caught," Gustav said. "Now squirt the lubricant on the hinges and we're in."

Ryder and Abdul patrolled with loaded rifles and night sights during the operation to allow the vehicles onto the tracks. Soon they were all aboard. They had opted to straddle one rail. Ryder drove the pickup and struggled, losing his fight with the wheel. Gustav drove the estate car and pulled away in front of him. In spite of the relative security of not driving on the roads, they agreed on using sidelights rather than headlights that might have attracted more than moths.

Teresa sat next to Ryder, with Abdul in the seat behind, along with Megan. Bronwyn rode for the extra comfort in the estate car with Jena and Gustav.

"Ryder, you would find driving a lot easier if you drove faster," Teresa said. "Look at Gustav, he's leaving you for dust."

"It's not a race."

"Granted, but a bit more speed would allow the wheels to skip over the smaller gaps in the ballast between the sleepers. For God's sake, try it, man."

To his surprise, the pickup did ride with less walloping at a speed of thirty, as opposed to twenty, but it still rocked around, creating worrying banging and crashing noises in the rear.

Jena's voice came over the phone. "Ryder, you haven't engaged the turbo-assist suspension, have you?"

"What's she talking about?" He glanced at the eerie back-lit green dashboard.

"And I thought you two were entwined in thought and deed," Teresa said.

"Funny. Hey, you drive this contraption more than me."

"It's this lever, but it's engaged so I don't know why it isn't working. Any ideas back there, Megan?"

Megan undid her seatbelt and leaned forward between them. "Gotta have four-wheel drive on," she said, sat back and put her headphones back on.

The pickup lifted and sailed across the sleepers.

"Hey, I'm impressed with this suspension," Ryder said. "Why did no one tell me this before? It would have made cross-country driving in the Anafon Valley so much easier."

"Figures," Teresa said. "You don't ask for any advice in case they think you're as weak as I know you really are."

"Come on, Teresa, we've been falling out over trivia for over a year. You can't blame Jena for that."

"She's just a bitch-on-heat that happened to be in front of you at the right time."

Ryder was about to reply when Jena came on the phone. "This bitch thought you ought to know we're coming up to the bridge and stopping for a reccy."

"Was your phone on all that time?"

Teresa played with it. "So?"

"THIS IS GOING TO BE SPOOKY," Megan said. "Do we *have* to drive underneath the road bridge? It'd be like in a tunnel."

"That's where the railway lines go," Ryder said, looking through his binoculars at the double-decker bridge and not seeing any sign of movement on the road above or lines beneath. Both, however, were barricaded with gates and rubble.

"Do you think the Anglesey islanders were trying to stop ARIA-infected people crossing?" Abdul said.

Ryder talked as he peered through the eyepieces. "It might have slowed ARIA by a day or two, but the ferry from Ireland would have been disgorging infected people unless they also laid a minefield out at sea."

Gustav had his own field glasses. "In our favour is that no motorised traffic has passed for months."

"No, they'd still be on the island," Jena said. "Some would boat across the straits or clamber over those barricades."

"We could cross by sea, if we could find a boat," Abdul said.

"Probably quicker to make a dent in that heap of rubble than winch ourselves over it. Pity we daren't use explosives," Ryder said.

Gustav stood on the pickup's bonnet. "I can see where we can hook the pickup's winch cable on a strut the other side of the rubble and take it over towing the estate car."

The women took up armed-guard duties while the men sorted the winch.

Gustav drove the pickup right up to the mound and released the winch reel at the front. Ryder and Abdul took the cable over the mound and hitched it over a bridge support. The winch rewound its cable while Gustav put the pickup into first gear and applied a gentle acceleration. Jena drove the towed estate car behind.

Ryder watched the taut cable and checked their cable connection round the strut. "It's too noisy."

"Sounds worse under here than out in the open," Abdul said, waving Gustav on towards him. "Look, it's nearly at the top. Doing well."

The pickup rounded the top and started down, putting a greater strain on the nylon towrope pulling the estate.

They stood around, looking pleased with themselves.

"Problem, people," Abdul said.

"Not another," Ryder said.

"Ryder, you know you said we weren't to use side lights while crossing the bridge in case we were seen from the island?"

"So?"

"I see the problem," Jena said, walking along the sleepers a few metres. "One of us needs to walk in front with a torch. There's a narrow surface a foot or so wider than the rails then planks."

"It's been only seven months since this was a busy mainline route, so as long as we take care, it should be all right." Ryder couldn't bear the thought of going back.

Gustav faced Ryder. "There's no way we can safely drive at thirty over this. A wheel might skid on a plank or break one."

Teresa brandished a flashlight. "I'll walk in front. There are no bends so you should see my torch."

Gustav followed her in the estate car at walking pace. Being unable to see the stars or moon overhead, along with the more rickety travelling, made the journey feel more hazardous than in the open.

Abdul phoned Ryder from the lead car. "Teresa says she can't see a mound at the other end but there is a gate. No big gaps in the driving surface so far."

Ryder's stomach lurched. The drive took on the gut-churning experience of a fairground ride-of-fear where the driver had no control over the direction, couldn't see very much, and could be spooked by the unexpected.

Ryder looked left and right. Even a single candle at night should have been seen miles away. In the mirror, he thought he saw a red light but realized it must be a reflection of his own rear lights.

"Look out!" Megan called.

Gustav must have braked. Even at just over walking pace, it took him too long to apply the pickup's brakes, so they collided with the estate car, making it lurch. Ryder jumped out and ran to the front, imagining Teresa lying in the road.

She was a few metres in front, waving her torch at a hole in the ground.

Gustav called out of his driver's window. "I know you want us to get there, but there's no need to push." He had a grin, as did everyone else: so pleased to see Ryder at fault for once.

Abdul laughed as he walked round to the rear of the pickup and pulled out a rectangular sheet of tough PVC used for off-roading, and placed it over the gap.

"And you can shut up," Ryder said to Teresa, who'd joined in the stress-relief merriment.

"You have to stop again," she said.

"Another hole?"

"The barrier in front. Looks like several large gates you see around building sites. They're chained together so shouldn't be difficult to get through."

Gustav cut through the chains, and they used the pickup to push the gates down. Ryder was afraid of the noise of crashing metal. People might wake and think there were vandals rampaging or a train crash, one of which was true.

Away from the bridge, Ryder could see the moon and stars once more. He tried not to think of the latent terror lurking in the silhouetted landscape flitting by. The demon-looking trees threw their branches menacingly. Gusts of westerly winds grabbed their leaves and hurled them into the air. Many splattered across the windscreen.

Ryder lifted his spirits where he could by absorbing the monochrome scenery. Megan sat beside him, Teresa in the back with Bronwyn. Jena joined the two astronauts in the estate.

Unlike the stomach-gripes he had driving on the road towards the Chester airfield, they drove in relative safety. Away from the trees, they had miles of mostly flat and undulating fields on either side, with an occasional sight of the ocean on their left.

Teresa's phone beeped. "Hey, I hope you two aren't quarrelling back there." Ryder heard Jena laughing.

Teresa snapped, "Don't you know which way to go?"

"You know there's only one railway line all the way," said Ryder, then shut up knowing he'd best not get in the way.

Jena spoke up again. "This is a courtesy call to let you know there's a tunnel up ahead. Could be trouble. Teresa, do you want to run ahead again?"

"Stop just inside the tunnel, leaving room for us behind you," said Ryder.

They could easily flood the tunnel with vehicle headlights but that might give them away.

Ryder and Abdul used dimmed torches to walk in the tunnel. They stumbled on the uneven ground. They were both man enough to ignore the scurrying rats, but their noses twitched at the stench of a rotting corpse. They didn't wait to investigate whether the odour came from a dead human, but rushed the remaining 200 metres to see moonlight again.

Heading towards the semicircular exit, Ryder's torch picked out a pair of eyes, and then another, and so did Abdul's.

"Gustav," Ryder whispered into his phone. "Bring the estate up here to collect us. Quickly. There are dogs."

Abdul and Ryder turned their torches off but knew the dogs would still detect them. They walked to the side of the tunnel and stood with their backs to the grimy wall. Ryder could smell the mix of diesel and soot.

He heard a growl and then another.

"We could shoot them," Abdul said. "I know it would make a noise, but maybe most of the sound would stay in the tunnel. Anyway, who's going to come running in the middle of the night when they know a pack of bloodthirsty hounds are at large?"

"We'd just need to kill one. One dead dog is food for the rest." Ryder said. "Where's that car?"

A developing lump in his throat, he scrutinized the three dogs, which became four. More came, edging forward, emboldened by hunger and sensing the fear in the humans. He realized he hadn't brought his rifle. "Abdul, shoot one of them."

"Can you use yours, Ryder? Mine's back in the car." One, then two of the dogs barked while the others growled.

"Stay, boy!" shouted Abdul. The dogs moved closer.

"I don't think they speak English in Anglesey. Did you bring your knife?"

"Penknife, but one of those beasts would be able to take my hand off before they noticed the blade. Do you think Gustav's stalled the car?"

The dogs, all barking, were only two metres away.

"Let's shine our torches in their eyes."

"Yes, blind them to death," Abdul said, putting his torch on full power. It stopped the dogs from advancing but they barked louder. Ryder noticed a couple at the back edging round. He tried to dazzle them but they continued. Another minute and the they were going to be dinner. He shone his torch at the nearest dog while he called Jena.

"What the bloody hell's happening back there! We're about to be eaten here. Jena? Speak to me." He tried to listen to her response, but the situation didn't offer a two-way conversation with his ears full of a cacophony of hungry barking.

"They aren't responding. I hope they haven't been attacked back there."

"No, he's stalled or run the car into the tunnel wall. It'd help us now if they put their headlights on full. Get back!" Abdul yelled as one of the dogs tested its luck with a snarling lunge at his arm.

Ryder picked up a handful of stone chippings and threw them at the nearest dog. It yelped with surprise. Ryder was shocked to hear the dog's snarl transform to one of a puppy's whimper. But it hardly lasted two seconds as it leapt at him, this time with spittle flying from its bared teeth. Ryder fell on his back, his brain telling him to strike the dog with the torch, his only weapon, but he needed both hands to hold the beast's gaping mouth from biting his face. Its fetid breath made Ryder retch. Drool splattered his face and his leg kicked with a sharp pain. He heard Abdul shouting, but couldn't make out words.

It was a matter of moments before they both died ignominiously on the grimy shale floor of a railway tunnel.

A shock of bright light followed by explosions behind him gave Ryder instant relief as the dog vanished. Dazed, he lay back and looked to the right to see Abdul sitting up against the wall, looking and shouting at him. Ryder's ears buzzed with more bangs and dogs' yelps, so he couldn't hear what he was saying although his hand gestures and mouth said "stay down." No argument there.

"YOU DID WELL TO LIE DOWN," Jena said, applying more antiseptic wipes and plasters to Ryder's wounds. "One of my bullets might have found you instead of the dog."

"Don't think we're not grateful, but what kept you?"

"You told us to stay put until you called."

"We kept phoning."

"We thought you might have been. Gustav suggested the tunnel might have interfered with the phone signals. Teresa reckoned she could hear shouting, barking or whatever. But maybe she didn't and she was tired, so we waited some."

"You're kidding."

"Anyway, Gustav and I decided to investigate, drove the car halfway. Turned the engine off and heard the racket. Turned on the lights and walked in blasting like Clint Eastwood."

TWENTY MINUTES LATER, THEY MET ANOTHER BARRIER. A double set of impressive 10-foot high wire gates where the railway entered the airfield. As Ryder decelerated the pickup, he saw Abdul's dark shape against the predawn. He stood on the roof-rack of the estate car, peering through his binoculars. Moments later, Ryder walked up dangling his own night-sight glasses.

"Several aircraft that should do," said Abdul.

"But do you see people, lights, smoke, or bloody dogs?"

"Nothing. Except what might be a wisp of smoke from a building over to the right on the opposite side of the runway from the planes."

Ryder stood on a boulder and focussed at the same spot. "What else could it be? Condensation from a hot-water system? Too far away for us to be able to see cigarette smoke. How far?"

Abdul flipped a switch on his sights. "Exactly 231 metres on the range finder. Shall we try to sneak around the outside of the fence to get a closer look?"

"No, we'd lose too much time. We'll get these gates open, head for the plane park on the left, and get Megan to keep a close watch on that side. It could be a smouldering fire from yesterday, and now they're gone."

Gustav made short work of the gates. They refastened them after going through and drove to the left, cruising in front of an open hangar where two RAF jets waited to be scrambled. Like Hawarden Airfield, the evidence of looters littered the area. Not slowing, they passed more fighter jets and an air-sea rescue helicopter before reaching three large aircraft: two Airbus 300YC cargo planes and a Boeing 757 cargo plane. All three were in RAF grey paint, just a few passenger windows near the front, and all appeared to be in good condition.

"Gustav, just look at this Airbus," Ryder said. "Looks brand new, apart from the leaf and grime that's settled on them in seven months. One has mobile steps to an open door. Shall we?"

"Yeah, but it means it's been ransacked," Abdul said. He was right, the cockpit had been vandalised with spray paint everywhere. Ryder looked in disbelief until Teresa interpreted.

"People, really frustrated, assume their problems are caused by science so take it out on modern examples like this."

"To be honest," Jena said, "Abdul and I have our aviation experience in American aircraft. I've clocked about a thousand hours flying Boeings and none with your European Airbus. Not a hell of a difference but..."

"You're right," Ryder said, "let's move the ladder over and see if we can get in the Boeing."

They couldn't get in the passenger, cargo bay, or pilot's locked exterior cabin doors and didn't want to use a crowbar.

"Two options," Gustav said. "Either find the keys, or force the cargo bay door. The cargo bay would be pressurized differently to the forward crew area and we'd get away with a jerry-rigged door."

Ryder put Megan on watch for the smoke, which drifted up and over to the north side of the runway. He and Jena went to look for the plane's keys in nearby buildings while Teresa and Gustav looked for a laden fuel truck and start-generator vehicle. Abdul made a closer inspection of the aircraft. He hosed muck off the windscreen, examined flaps, tyres and did other external pre-flight checks before looking for a place the engineer might have hidden a key. An aircraft sitting idle accumulates dust and grime on the wings, so he found a higher-pressure hose and gave the whole plane a blast, especially the airfoils and tailfin. Luckily, the jet intakes had been capped.

Ryder and Jena found an engineers' office that was the best candidate for holding the keys, but it had been hit by multiple earthquakes of the human variety. Jena knew what the key should look like, a metallic-plastic card.

"I wonder if they armed it from here," Ryder said, looking at a console after sweeping the furry debris of someone's lunch from the nearby raided snack machine.

"Good point," Jena said. "We did at Houston. Remotely locked and alarmed the military aircraft from a place like this. Well done, Ryder."

Ryder used his phone to get onto Gustav, and within twenty minutes, the generator he and Teresa found vibrated with a worrying loud noise. But it lit up the console. It took another twenty minutes to find the necessary buttons and codes to unlock the plane. It was seven in the morning before they had refuelled, loaded, and re-pressurised the tyres.

"I couldn't find Megan when I went for her," said Jena.

"Wasn't she on lookout?"

"Not when I searched for her. She said she needed the bathroom, but I thought you ought to know that when I looked for her, I thought I saw someone near the smoke, and we have to take off near them."

Ryder noticed Megan opening the passenger cabin door from the cargo area. He would have liked to have had a go at her, but other matters were more pressing.

"I think we should go," Jena said. "Now."

"Do it quickly then," Ryder said, looking out of the cockpit window. Jena acted as pilot, Abdul as co-pilot. Apart from Ryder, sitting in the cockpit, the others were belting up in the small passenger lounge behind the flight cabin.

"There!" shouted Abdul. "Over to our left, three, no four people, men, walking towards us. They look as if they might have weapons, oh, and a military vehicle is on its way."

Jena needed to manoeuvre the plane to the start of the longest runway, which meant heading towards their would-be attackers and then a 90-degree right turn to take off.

The military vehicle was an armoured scout car with a heavy-machine gun.

"Forget protocol," Ryder said. "We've a light load and should take off without having to use the whole of the tarmac. Just head 45 degrees away from that lot."

"Yes, sir," Jena said.

"We'd already decided that," Abdul said, as the engines made a satisfying roar, accelerating them away from the surprised airfield occupiers. "I don't know why they're upset. We've exchanged two good vehicles for one they don't know how to use."

Grateful for the relief from tension, Ryder and Jena laughed. Fingers crossed, they'd lift off before hitting the perimeter fence and before any bullets overtook them.

CHAPTER 39

Saturday 10 October 2015. 10:00 hours GMT:
Mid-Atlantic. Most people will have lost up to twenty-six years of
their memory.

THE NAVIGATION COMPUTER ON THE BOEING CARGO AIRLINER plotted the most efficient route to Rarotonga. A Great Circle route took them within a hundred miles of Banff, in the Canadian Rocky Mountains. Lit by the morning sun, Ryder watched the cyan-blue Atlantic shimmering six miles below. At that height, he would have been able to see ships, evidenced by their wake, but none sailed. He knew Jena had no worries about collisions with other aircraft although she kept the intercept-prediction and proximity-alert warning switched on.

"What if you can't raise Manuel?" Jena said to Ryder.

"Then we circle the airfield to check no one has parked a bus on the runway, land, and deal with the refuelling ourselves. I'd like to know how Manuel is."

"Yes, Teresa told me the same thing."

"Her interest in Manuel is as a biological specimen. He was one of the first to get ARIA."

"Is that your NoteCom beeping its low battery warning?"

"Plug it into the navigation console for recharging, Ryder," Abdul said.

As soon as he did, the NoteCom bleeped a different tune. "It's from Manuel, but it's just a message to say he's found his NoteCom, found my contact details, and is going to read the rest before getting back."

Abdul grinned. "That's promising."

"Depends when it was sent," Jena said.

"Yesterday morning, over twenty-four hours ago. Damn, I hope he hasn't lost it again."

Jena thought a moment. "Buzz it."

"What do you think I'm doing?" Ryder's frustration simmered.

"At the risk of being sulked at," Jena said, "I suggest you put it on an automatic buzz every five minutes."

"I wouldn't," Abdul said. "He might think it's just a repetitive noise from a faulty gadget."

"I can set it to buzz randomly with a maximum interval of five minutes," Ryder said. A memory flash hit him...angry at a computer pop-up message getting in the way of his watching a live image of an asteroid intercept with an unmanned lander. He pushed his clawed fingers through his hair.

"Hey, who wants coffee? Two, is that all?"

Ryder returned with the drinks. Megan, silent headphones acting as a hair band, followed him in.

"Megan, how you doing?" said Abdul. "I thought all our passengers were catching up with their sleep. How's Bronwyn?"

"She's fine, asleep. Can't I come up here? Or is this a private club?"

"Course not," Jena said. "You're always welcome. Wanna drive?"

"Yeah, as if." Megan chewed gum and leant back against the aluminium wall.

"Look, Megan, you can see the sea," Abdul said.

"Big deal, seen it before."

"Can you see the different hues of turquoise and blues?"

She stepped closer, put a hand on Abdul's shoulder. "Has the sea lost its memory as well?"

Jena said, "Hey, that's pretty deep, isn't it?"

"What, the sea?" Abdul said, then winked.

Megan's eyebrows raised in puzzlement at the others as if they didn't know the sea had memory. "How does it know where to send its currents, or how cold to be?"

Jena looked at Ryder, then at Megan. "I mean, Megan, you are a deeper thinker than I gave you credit for."

"Whatever. Hey, I need to go back into the cargo area. Is it safe? Pressure and all?"

"It'll be quite chilly, but there's enough pressure to breathe. I'd rather you didn't," Ryder said.

"I'm bored and my player's in there. I'm going to get it. Right?"

Jena shook her head at Ryder to shut him up. "Don't be long and shut the door properly when you get back. Okay?"

Megan left.

Jena said, "She's a teen, right? Didn't she have her player with her?"

Ryder's NoteCom tinkled the *Where are you now?* tune he'd selected for incoming calls. With an accelerated heart thumping, he grabbed it and plugged in the external microphone and speakers.

"Is that you, Ryder?" said Manuel. "Oh, I see your face now. Hey, you look older than I remember."

"I'm not surprised. Just a minute...you can't remember what I look like at all."

"I know, just kidding. But my notes tell me we went back to when you worked with me on several NASA projects."

"You still have your trademark sense of humour, Manuel. I need to ask you a gigantic favour, and it has to be done today."

"Sounds intriguing, Ryder. Every day is a new day to me, though here in the cabin, I expect I do pretty much the same thing every damn day. How can a feeble-minded duffer whose only skill is chopping wood, help you?"

"Do you have transport?"

"Probably. There's supposed to be a pickup with the keys under the mudguard down in the lane. I haven't looked today, though I might have done yesterday and found it had changed into a Cadillac."

"Manuel, I am with a small group of friends in an airplane over the Atlantic."

"Good for you. I could do with a trip to a warm country. Are the trolley dollies pretty?"

Ryder looked at Jena and Abdul. Manuel's brain assumed flights were a normal event. "Do you know about ARIA?"

"I've just been told about it by my cabin-mate. Oh, I get you. There haven't been international flights for several months, have there? Where are you flying to?"

"Our destination, Manuel, is one of the Cook Islands in the South Pacific, but we need a refuelling stop halfway. Guess who lives under our flight path?"

"Not me?"

"There's an airfield near you at Banff. We'll reach it at eleven a.m. your time."

"Good God, man. Are you crazy? According to our notes, we're lucky to have got out of Banff alive on at least two occasions."

Ryder fell silent. The roar of the engines occupied his head for a while. He had made the assumption that his friend would be willing and eager to help. He had not taken into account the alarming effects of losing memory combined with the trashing of everyone's life. How could he expect anyone, even a warm-hearted guy like Manuel, to leave a sanctuary from the madness to help forgotten acquaintances.

He tried a bargaining tool. "Manuel, we have something that might stop you losing any more memory."

"Just a minute," Jena said. "We know nothing for sure about what the second case will do."

"I know that," Ryder said. "That's why I said 'might.'"

"Ingenuous, aren't you?" Abdul said. "But on the other hand, we've exposed people in Conwy, same logic applies."

"Can you explain what you are saying to my friend?" Manuel said, over the debate and engine noise.

"Okay, Manuel," Ryder said, and waited a moment before a woman appeared on the screen. Ryder staggered back, recovered, and then leant forward to study the woman. "Julia?"

The redhead tilted her head. "Do we know each other—er, Ryder?"

"Yes, we do. You are Julia Tyndall who worked at NASA's Goddard Institute of Nutritional Science."

"Hey, you're better than my diary. Did we have a thing going, Ryder?"

"What? No, no, Julia. Is Karen with you? No, of course she isn't. And you won't remember her, let alone know where she is."

"Manuel says you have some news about ARIA?"

"A second case was found in orbit. It might stop memory loss getting worse and you can remember new things after exposure to it. But we have a biologist here, Teresa Stanwick? She has all your old computer-notes about ARIA and the new virus. In the meantime, I need Manuel to go to Banff and ensure the runway is clear for us to land in seven hours."

"Just a minute," Abdul said. "I've been checking the flight computer. It says Banff airport was decommissioned years ago. We might be able to land if they haven't built on it, but there won't be any fuel."

"Shit. Where's the nearest airport?" Ryder said.

"Calgary," said Abdul. "Sixty miles from Manuel."

Julia came back on. "I corroborate that Calgary is the nearest international airport according to our maps. We'll leave soon. I'll make sure of it. How do we talk to you and Teresa en route?"

"Take your NoteCom with you. Do you realize, Julia, that you should be famous?"

"Why? Have I invented a man with brains?"

"You discovered the alien virus that causes ARIA."

"But if people have lost their memory, they won't remember me, and if they hadn't lost their memory, there would have been nothing special about it for me to become famous over."

"I hadn't thought of that," Ryder said. "It's a kind of Catch-22 paradox."

"What's a Catch-22?" she said.

FIGHTING THE TEMPTATION TO CALL MANUEL, Ryder waited until the airplane was an hour away from Calgary. The landscape glided past close enough to see individual trees on the mountain slopes, buildings in previously well-ordered towns, mighty rivers flowing into mirrors of lakes carrying their unseen reflection.

A bizarre thought hit Ryder. If he looked out of a log-cabin window and saw an airplane flying overhead, having not seen one for months, he might have rushed out to gawp in wonder at the novelty. But to an ARIA victim, born seeing airplanes, it meant nothing unusual.

"We're there." Manuel's voice interrupted Ryder's musings. "I'd like to tell you of the nightmare journey. Mostly plain sailing but with some scary shocks. Passed through a township on fire. Groups of idiots running around demented. They threw empty bottles at us. No doubt you can imagine."

"Only too well, Manuel," Ryder said. "Is the runway clear?"

"Not bad, but the main east-to-west runway will be clear for you by the time you get here. We'll get busy now. By the way, do any of you guys know how to get rid of a pesky woodpecker? Woke me up this morning."

"Is it called Woody?" called Abdul.

"Now you're back in my memory zone," Manuel said and laughed. "Yeah, the only way to stop Woody Woodpecker was to chop down his tree. More firewood for next week. See ya."

"How are we going to organise this?" Jena said. "We can't invite Manuel on board."

"Teresa's been comparing notes with Julia for the last hour, I'll get her to come up here."

"And I thought she was busy making big holes in my parachute."

Teresa wore the face she reserved for encountering a putrid tramp on her doorstep.

"We lower the sealed case onto the ground and re-close the door while they open the case for five minutes, seal it, and leave to a safe distance. We refuel using a tanker they've checked out and have ready. They have some questions though."

"I've a few hundred," Ryder said.

"They want to know if they could keep one of the blocks in the case."

"No. Next question."

"Hey, come on," Abdul said. "Is it greedy for us to keep six?"

"It's possible," Jena said, "that the six work together. We might find subtle differences between them once they are examined in the labs on Rarotonga."

Teresa tapped her NoteCom, making Ryder think she'd already worked that one out. "What's the chances of them coming with us?"

"No way," Jena said. "We can't hang around for a few days for the effects of the second case to work. We could get ARIA—or worse. As non-ARIA, then exposed to ARIA-2 people, we could end up like Antonio."

"That's what I told them," Teresa said.

"How did they take it?" Ryder said.

"They expected it. They didn't mind. I think they enjoy their life in the cabin. Then they asked if we had any Huperzine we could spare. It's an enzyme preparation that affects memory. They find it helps them to learn quicker each day and maybe slows the rate of amnesia. I told them we didn't have any but they were welcome to all our ginkgo biloba."

"Hopefully, they won't need the Huperzine once exposed to the second case," Jena said.

"There is evidence we might not get ARIA even if we did get near Manuel and Julia," Ryder said.

"Dogs," Teresa said.

"You thought it through?" Ryder said.

"According to your own harsh rules," Teresa said, "we should have shot you, along with the dogs in that tunnel."

"Now that would have been a shame," said Abdul. "So we might all have some resistance to ARIA, from our contact with Antonio."

"Only if we assume those dogs were infected," Ryder said.

Jena said, "Anyway, the GPS navigation tells me it's time for auxiliary pumps to go on and passengers to get belted up."

FIVE MINUTES LATER, THEY APPROACHED THE AIRFIELD.

Jena said to Ryder, "We are coming in from the north into the wind. The main runway is north to south so we'll land on our first approach."

"I'd rather we had a fly-past to spot potential trouble."

"So would I, but the airport is on the northeast of the city and I don't fancy showing ourselves to all and sundry who might be curious enough to come along."

"Their loss of memory would make a flight into an international airport appear normal."

"Even so, I'd rather minimise our risks, and I'm the captain of this plane, Ryder. Or do *you* want to land it? Thought not. We've asked Manuel to keep the fuel truck at the main buildings while he and Julia hang out at the end of the runway. We drop off the case with them so they can open it and breathe in its heavenly aroma while we taxi back to the fuel truck. By the time we finish, they should have resealed the case and brought it to the plane for us to take it on with the rope and net we lowered it with."

"Why don't we taxi back to them and take off north, away from the city?" Ryder was thinking of attracting unwanted attention to the two on the ground if they flew over the city.

"We need to head into the wind to take off," Abdul said. "But suppose they don't give back the case?"

"I've told them we have to take it on to the scientists at Rarotonga. We'd have to suit up and chase them, shoot them if necessary," Ryder said. "I'd hate that to happen."

"It's another reason for having them at the isolated southern end of the runway," Jena said.

The Rocky Mountains jutted up into the sky to the west as the plane dropped towards the airport. Ryder counted two parallel runways at an oblique angle to the main one, north to south. Vehicles and assorted debris littered the airport just like in Britain. The detail grew clearer each second.

Ryder's worry cell came up with another thought. "I know it's a fine time to ask, Jena, but have you landed one of these without ground navigational aids?"

Abdul and Jena glanced at each other. In Ryder's opinion, they looked scared. He decided he shouldn't bother them anymore.

"What about airbrakes?" he said, breaking his own silence rule. They ignored him. He sat back, double-checked his seat belt, and waited. He could hear the two pilots utter warnings and give sharp replies, but he couldn't tell what they were saying. Doubtless in pilot-speak.

Their exchanges turned to sharp intakes of breath then a loud bang. Ryder thought there had been an explosion rather than just a heavy landing. His stomach lurched as the plane jumped back into the air. Then another bang as the wheels once more hit the runway, skewed off to the right and the engines screamed as they went into reverse-thrust. Ryder heard swearing and shouting from the passengers behind, but the pilots stayed silent, focussing all their energy into stopping the plane. Another minute and it had.

Ryder unbuckled and stood to look for Manuel. "Have we hopped runways? I can't see him."

"A 'well done, pilots' would have gone down well," Abdul said. "We are still in one piece, after all."

"Sorry, yes, a bit scary, but people pay for that at a funfair. Are we on the agreed runway?"

"We've left the runway, but there's no vehicle at this end of the airport. You'd better call him," Jena said, as she and Abdul went through post-landing checks and prepared to taxi back to the other end of the main runway.

"There you are, Manuel," Ryder said, getting through after three attempts. "In fact, where are you, Manuel?"

"Sorry, Ryder. We're not used to being punctual. There's no TV or radio programs, or work schedules. Moreover, although we don't remember what we do day-to-day, our bodies get into, or out of, habits. We don't even wear watches."

"Manuel, where the fuck are you?"

"Well, we had a bit of trouble with dogs here at the airport. But I brought an electronic bear-scarer I found at the cabin. Worked a treat."

"So are you both on your way to us, now? At the other end of the runway?"

"As soon as Julia's finished shopping."

"What?" Ryder couldn't believe his ears.

"We found the airport store intact. Marvellous range of whiskies, and Julia found a whole rack of gowns in her size. Here she is..."

Jena said, "You know, I thought people losing their memory would also lose the rest of their marbles. The glue holding their lives together comes apart along with their grip on reality. Tell your friends to haul ass out of the store and meet us halfway down the runway."

Manuel assured them they were heading for their pickup to meet them. Gustav and Teresa put the case in a cargo net and made ready to lower it out of a door.

Two minutes later, Gustav, suited up, let an orange nylon rope go hand over hand down with the second case in a net. Manuel caught it, carried it a few metres away and placed it on the ground. He waved to Gustav, who waved back from the cargo door before closing it, as an extra precaution. Jena taxied to a fuel tanker.

Risking not wearing suits but with antiseptic facemasks, Jena and Abdul prepared the fuel intake at the plane while Gustav and Ryder ran to the fuel truck and drove it back.

Ryder was relieved their journey had gone well, so far. At least in that they were still alive, intact, and running hard to reach their destination. He had to admire how Abdul and Jena examined unseen machinery, such as the refuelling nozzle assembly, and its electronic control panel, and sorted it within moments. Nevertheless, the constant threat of discovery or schedule hitches kept his pulse racing merrily along. He groaned when he spotted Megan coming down the stairs from the plane.

"I'm going to the shop," she said.

"Bloody hell, Megan, things are frantic enough as it is, don't give us more hassle. See if Bronwyn needs anything."

She stomped back up the staircase.

Jena and Abdul completed the refuel and exterior plane inspection while Ryder, Teresa and Gustav prepared to retrieve the case. They looked up the runway and saw Manuel's pickup driving towards them.

Jena raised her hand as if to stop them. "Damn, they're either coming for a chat or running off with the case. We'll have to shoot them if you don't stop them, Ryder."

"Manuel, stop there," Ryder said into his phone. "You need to wait until we tell you to bring the case to us."

"Oops, sorry, Ryder."

"We've every reason to believe you'll remember better from now on, but I'd head back to your cabin for your own safety."

"We intend to, thanks a bunch. Julia says, first, we're going to load the pickup with shopping so it'll hardly move. We'll keep in touch, don't you worry. Have a good flight."

"Cheers, Manuel. Our doors are shut now, so bring the case here. Leave it on the tarmac and go off to do your shopping."

A few minutes later, they were ready to take off.

"Ryder, you know how we took the case to start a recovery diffusion in the UK?" Abdul said.

"Are you suggesting we hang around here to do the same?"

"Well, Manuel and Julia are going to drive back to their cabin without contacting anyone. They are going out of their way to avoid people—and I don't blame them. A shame not to let others have a whiff of the second case."

"Like dangling it out of the door while we fly over Calgary, for instance?" Jena said.

"That would be too tricky, wouldn't it?" said Ryder. "We would be accelerating and climbing. We could lose it. And it'd be too high up for the contents to be any use. It would make more sense to grab someone around here—"

"I was floating the idea, Ryder," said Abdul. "But you could ask Manuel to breathe on at least one friendly or sleeping person during the next few days."

CHAPTER 40

Saturday 10 October 2015:
In the air over the Rockies.

FORTY MINUTES LATER, Ryder admired the snowy peaks of the Rockies beneath him. They had the look of the immutable for millions of years, give or take glacial erosion and the occasional earth movement. ARIA took Man away and allowed Mother Nature to start recovering.

"We've been in touch with Rarotonga," Jena said. "They've set up a ground signal our navigation computer will pick up once in range. It will guide and land our plane on automatic."

"Thank God. No more kangaroo impressions."

"That was my fault," Abdul said. "I've re-calibrated the near-ground altimeter."

"Abdul, you're a loyal and well-trained co-pilot, taking all the blame for all that seatbelt testing and rivet popping."

Jena said, "You're a stirrer, and isn't that your NoteCom beeping?"

Ryder, worried that Manuel had run into trouble, glanced at the clock and realized they had yet to load the pickup to axle-breaking point from the airport shop.

"Hi, Manuel, okay?"

"No, problems, Ryder, but you could have said you were leaving us with one of your passengers. And what an individual!"

"What? Just hang on, Manuel, I need to check on something in a hurry." A shiver ran up his spine. He turned and opened the door between the cockpit and passenger area.

"Where's Megan?"

Bronwyn, sucking a pencil, looked up from a word puzzle and shook her head.

Teresa and Gustav had their heads together at a laptop.

Gustav looked up. "She is a teenager. As such, she likes her privacy and there are a surprisingly large number of hiding places on this plane."

"She got off at Calgary," Ryder said, expecting them all to be shocked.

Teresa hadn't looked up from her screen. "Once she heard there was a shop, she wanted to raid the DVDs, cosmetics, and magazines. It obviously hasn't sunk in, Megan is a teenager with her own specific needs."

Ryder looked as if he was holding a set of invisible books with his hands as bookends. Then shook them up and down to emphasise the urgency of his concern. "Listen up. I think Megan might have got off in Calgary and didn't come back on the plane. She's still there!"

"Oh, Lordy," Bronwyn said.

Finally, with worry lines, Teresa said, "We'll have to go back."

Gustav raised his eyebrows. "How do you know?"

"Manuel just phoned."

Teresa said, "You have to hand it to that girl. She has guts. Not only does she disobey our fine leader's orders but—"

"Hang on, Teresa, I told her not to leave the plane."

"One word from you and she does as she likes."

Ryder dropped his hands. "I suppose I'd better tell Jena to about turn."

"Why, did you forget to pay the bill?" said Megan, having just come through the door from the cargo store. The others looked accusations at Ryder, who, reddened, went back into the cockpit and back on the phone.

"Manuel, what are you on about? Megan is here."

"Oh, you're back, are you? Before I could thank you properly."

"I assumed you meant our Megan had got off the plane and joined you in Calgary. I know it's laughable, now."

"Yeah, but your friend, Antonio, is a real card."

"He was, but I didn't realize you'd remember him."

"You are amusing, Ryder. He's sitting right here, having a warm Coke. He's been reminding us about ourselves. He knew both of us quite well, you know."

Ryder's neck hairs bristled. "Just a minute, Manuel, there must be some mistake. Maybe to do with your second-case exposure. You can't possibly be talking to Dr Antonio Menzies." Looking at the screen, Ryder saw Manuel smiling then the image rotated, bringing in Julia, who winked. The image continued to an old magazine with a photograph of Saturn. The magazine dropped.

"*Ciao*, Ryder," Antonio said. "My wounds are healing nicely, thank you. Give my regards to Rarotonga, won't you?"

Ryder couldn't speak. His left hand lashed out, hurting it on a wall strut.

"He's come back to life?" Abdul said.

"Is that Abdul I can hear?" Antonio said. "Was it you or Jena I have to thank for the bumps-a-daisy landing?"

"If I'd known you were a stowaway," Jena said, "I would have banged it down a lot harder. You must have been in the back of the pickup when we left Anafon. Not bad for a corpse."

"You always jump to the wrong conclusions, Jena."

Ryder tasted bile. He'd been responsible for putting a psychopath together with his old friend Manuel and another innocent. Not just any plain psychopathic killer, but one infected with an alien virus giving him God-knows-what extra powers.

"I know what you are thinking," Antonio said. "But don't worry, the bloodletting has steadied me. I'll look after your friends. After all, I'm a doctor, right?"

"I'm glad to hear it." He perspired trying hard to think of mollifying arguments. "An example of physician, heal thyself?"

"Very apt, but I had a little help."

"You said I could go with you," Megan said from the doorway. She stood with her arms folded.

"You are with me in spirit, young Megan. You helped me more than you know. Hey, you others, don't blame her. You could say I had her under my spell. Hah!"

"Do you have my friends under your spell?"

"He sure does," Manuel said. "A charming man. He's coming with us to the cabin to recuperate from his accident injuries."

"That's good," Ryder said. His real terror was shown to the others by his perspiration, and waving them back in case they said something inflammatory.

"We'd better be on our way now, Ryder," Manuel said. "Just in case people hearing the plane come to investigate, and I want to reach the cabin before it gets dark. Have a good journey and keep in touch."

"Will do, Manuel. Take care, all of you," Ryder said, shaking as he signed off.

Apart from Megan, who grumbled until her headphones turned her to humming and swaying, everyone took five minutes to settle their mental contortions.

Teresa said, "I'll send Julia a message via her NoteCom. It's not switched on at the moment, but I expect it will be when they reach the cabin."

"You'd have to be careful what you say," Ryder said.

"Naturally, I can't just say what we know. I have to assume Antonio might get it first. And I can't use technospeak because he's a doctor."

"He's not a virologist though," Gustav said. "I'm sure we could come up with something that sounds harmless but which indicates there is a serious problem with Antonio's particular pathology."

"Go for that," Ryder said.

"There is another angle," Jena said. "Antonio might be right. He could be going through metabolic changes, and the crazed part might have been a one-off."

"That's wishful thinking coming from the Queen of the Hard Nuts," Teresa said.

"He didn't harm Megan," Abdul said. "Maybe he considered us a threat while his brain was changing. While there's life, there's hope."

"You're right, Abdul," Ryder said. "Your glass is always half full, even when it's really empty." They all laughed at the accurate observation. "We still don't know the aliens' intentions. For all we know, they've gone for good, thinking they've done us some kind of favour."

"Or they might be back thinking there's just a few special humans left to either greet as fellow beings or as slaves for the taking," Jena said.

Gustav leaned back in his chair. "You are such a source of comfort."

"That is so true," Ryder said, making Jena laugh softly in agreement.

BRONWYN STAGGERED INTO THE COCKPIT. She held out an airline plastic tray with plastic cups filled with twenty-year-old whiskey.

"It is good to see you on your feet again, Bronwyn," Abdul said.

"I would like us all to toast your thought of a minute ago. Where there's life, there's hope."

They all repeated "Hope" and allowed the warming amber liquid to give them a well-deserved glow.

THE WARMTH TRAVELLED THROUGH RYDER, settling fears and building optimism. Through him, his fellow travellers, through the aircraft, and out through its jet exhausts as it left the American continent. There, at five miles high above the Pacific Ocean, the plane carrying a miracle case and seven bold optimists flew with expectation to tomorrow.

The euphoria lasted twenty minutes. After that, Ryder's attempts to snooze were snagged by stabs, flashes of Antonio's flashing teeth and taunts. What was the egomaniac going to do in Canada, and to Manuel and Julia? Who and what were the aliens up to? Hopefully, they'd leave Ryder's group alone on a tiny South Pacific island, but he somehow knew this was only the beginning of the endgame.

Need more luggage?

Read

ARIA: Returning Left Luggage

Never has Earth faced such problems. Survivors are either in hiding or slaves to aliens. How does Ryder's group prevent ARIA-infected boat people invading their island? Something alien stirs in France where free students live off their wits. A sliver of hope in America but the mad doctor could ruin everything. Is a girl in Australia, Earth's salvation? Never a dull moment as ARIA and Zadokians change Earth forever.

About the Author

Geoff Nelder has a wife, two grown-up kids, an increasing number of grandkids, and lives in rural England within an easy cycle ride of the Welsh mountains. He taught Geography and Information Technology for years until writing took over his life. Geoff's an occasional competition short-fiction judge, and is a freelance editor.

Publications include several non-fiction books on climate reflecting his other persona as a Fellow of the Royal Meteorological Society; over 50 published short stories in various magazines and anthologies; thriller, humour, science fiction, and fantasy novels. Recent publications include:

2005: *Escaping Reality* - a humorous thriller.

2008: *Exit, Pursued by a Bee* – an award-winning science fiction mystery with a hot-blooded heroine.

2010: *Hot Air* - another thriller that received an Award d'Or from an Arts Academy in the Netherlands. It's third edition will be published in 2012.

An urban and historical magic realism fantasy, *Xaghra's Revenge*, is in the hands of a literary agency.

Visit Geoff's website: geoffnelder.com
http://facebook.com/geoffnelder
http://www.twitter.com/geoffnelder

About the Publisher

"...taking the reader down a different path."

Established in 2008, **LL-Publications** is based in Scotland, UK and produces fiction and nonfiction both in paperback and in multiple ebook formats. Our talented authors represent both sides of the Atlantic.

We are proud to be a small, independent press providing **quality** over **quantity**. Our motto is "taking the reader down a different path" because the titles we publish are not recycled, formulaic plots with predictable characters in uninspired settings. We publish books that readers will remember.

We do not follow trends.

With that in mind, we invite you to take a short Reader Experience Survey to get your feedback on this book and your reading experience. Please go to the following web page:

www.ll-publications.com/33243.html

Your opinion is truly appreciated!

Best wishes,

LL-Publications
www.ll-publications.com

Other books by LL-Publications

Oops!
By Darrell Bain
ISBN: 978-1-905091-72-0 (print) / 978-1-905091-73-7 (ebook)

Oops! is the third collection of stories by Darrell Bain. When Cupid and a Gremlin bump heads, the sparks fly in a rare fantasy story by the author. Other stories in the collection include *A Simple Idea,* an almost ludicrously simple method of eliminating corruption and idiocy from the political process, one that has been around for centuries but gone unrecognized. *Cure for an Ailing Alien* finds a nurse who must come up with a cure for an alien, one whose bodily processes are completely unknown. You'll be amazed at her cure! *Retribution* is the story of unexpected consequences when alien meets human. *Robyn's Rock* is partially based on a happening in the author's life during a walk with his granddaughter.

There are many more stories in this collection, all written in the individual style that has kept Bain's readers coming back for more for the past twenty years. This a book to add to your collection, stories by a notable, multi-award winning author.

Bark!
By Darrell Bain
ISBN: 978-1-905091-15-7 (print)

Find out what happens when Tonto, a little, ADHD affected, one-testicled weenie dog, turns out to be the only thing standing between the Earth and accidental alien invasion!

Pure comic genius from multiple award-winning author Darrell Bain. Also includes the autobiography of the real Tonto, the little dog who inspired the story!

www.ingramcontent.com/pod-product-compliance
Lightning Source LLC
Chambersburg PA
CBHW020735250626
47155CB00003B/760